HOUSE OF PAIN

Also by Keith C. Blackmore

Mountain Man

Mountain Man
Safari
Hellifax
Well Fed
Make Me King
Mindless
Skull Road
Mountain Man Prequel
Mountain Man 2nd Prequel: Them Early Days
The Hospital: A Mountain Man Story
Mountain Man Omnibus: Books 1–3

131 Days

131 Days
House of Pain
Spikes and Edges
About the Blood
To Thunderous Applause
131 Days Omnibus: Books 1–3

Breeds

Breeds
Breeds 2
Breeds 3
Breeds: The Complete Trilogy

Isosceles Moon

Isosceles Moon
Isosceles Moon 2

The Bear That Fell from the Stars
Bones and Needles
Cauldron Gristle
Flight of the Cookie Dough Mansion
The Majestic 311
The Missing Boatman
Private Property
The Troll Hunter
White Sands, Red Steel

131 DAYS

BOOK 2

HOUSE OF PAIN

KEITH C. BLACKMORE

A special thanks to Mark E. Crouse, Sean Meadows, and Miguel Tonnies.

All rights reserved. No part of this publication may be reproduced, stored in a retrieval system, or transmitted in any form or by any means electronic, mechanical, photocopying, recording, or otherwise without prior written permission from Podium Publishing.

This is a work of fiction. Names, characters, places, and incidents are either products of the author's imagination or used fictitiously. Any resemblance to actual events, locales, or persons, living, dead, or undead, is entirely coincidental.

Copyright © 2013 by Keith C. Blackmore

Cover design by Karri Klawiter

ISBN: 978-1-0394-8351-4

Published in 2024 by Podium Publishing
www.podiumaudio.com

HOUSE OF PAIN

1

Blackness faced them, warm and moist as the halls of Sunja's public bathhouses.

Fire pits burned thirty paces behind a knot of Sujin sentries, but the three didn't dare turn around to look. To do so would ruin their night vision and perhaps invite the Jackals to creep up on them in the tall grass and cut their throats, right under the nose of the slumbering beast that was the Third Klaw.

If the Jackals were out there.

That thought made Marrok smirk as he stared off into the black pitch, where he could just make out the grass, rippling in the barest of night breezes, like sea weeds caught in a lazy current. The Jackals were *always* out there, watching, waiting, hoping for the men of the Third Klaw to relax their guard. Marrok smirked again, baring a half-rack of bad teeth and scrunching a scar on his left cheek. After the destruction of the First and Fourth Klaws, the Koors vowed bloody punishment on any Sujin dropping his guard while on the front. The lessons taught by the loss of those army groups were hard learned. A Klaw numbered around five thousand fighting men, not considering the hundreds of support staff required to keep such a force functioning. No one wanted another Field of Skulls on his watch, and Marrok and his fellow soldiers had to stand watch only until midnight, when they would be rotated in and three others would take their place.

He felt distinctly vulnerable despite the iron helm, the chainmail vest, and the shield he held across his chest like a great, black, rectangular bull's-eye. The heat of the night was only a few degrees less than the day, and the cloth padding underneath his armor clung to him like saturated rags, reminding him again of the bathhouses in Sunja.

Heavy clouds rendered the night darker than pitch, and distant thunder rumbled at times to the south, like frightening behemoths wrestling under the hills. Making war in early summer had been hot, and Marrok hated to think of the long marches they would yet endure. Hellish, miserable days—sweating, stinking, cooling off in the evening but rarely having the opportunity to bathe, insects that forewent a painless suckle and all but ripped blood from the veins—all foul additions to having to fight at any given instant. Men guarding Sunja's walls two weeks away could probably pick up the raw stench of the entire Klaw when the wind blew southeast. And the real summer hadn't even started yet.

The dull chirping of crickets sawed through the night air, filling the dark. Marrok sighed and stared straight ahead, focusing on one point as were the men flanking him almost shoulder to shoulder. Forward sentries ran the highest risk of being killed but were essential to the protection of the Klaw behind them. Another three men stood around the fire thirty paces back, no doubt thanking Seddon above for the time being. They would get their chance to stand guard at the tip of the tongue, daring the bastard Jackals to take a swipe at them. Marrok's group wasn't the only knot, for the protective formations surrounded the Klaw every night and, upon a Koor's command, would be rotated from the farthest point inward on a regular schedule, to the relative safety of the army.

The Koor measured time in rounds, meaning the time it took for two officers walking in opposite directions to circle the encampment once, from the onset of the first torches until dawn. In one sense, luck was with Marrok that night. He'd gotten the earliest watch and would have an uninterrupted sleep once relieved of duty. Simply glorious.

"See anything?" Vine asked quietly on his right. *Quietly* had they been within the breast of the Klaw, but since they were on point in the deep, ravenous dark, practically *daring* the enemy to leap upon them, the whisper sounded like a horn blast. Marrok didn't answer.

Silence ensued for long moments, then, "I said, 'You see anything?'"

Marrok closed his eyes in irritation.

"Did you—"

"He heard you, idiot," hissed Kreon on the left. "Now shut. Up."

Stillness, but Marrok felt the shrug and heated sigh from the mouthy Vine. The man prattled incessantly, and both Marrok and Kreon had balked at having to stand watch with his long tongue. He'd managed to stay quiet for almost half their shift, but Marrok knew—just *knew*—Vine was *bursting* at the seams to say something. *Any*thing.

Marrok blamed the Koor for pooling the talkative ass licker with Kreon and himself. Kreon wasn't a problem. He had ice filling his veins and snow lacing his balls.

"Them crickets grow as long as a thumb."

Marrok winced and closed his eyes. It was bad enough to speak, but he couldn't dare move lest a Jackal detect the movement in the dark.

"They'll eat anything too. Wager y'didn't know that."

Neither man rose to the bait. That didn't deter Vine.

"Heard that there are crickets in the Harudin that fancy warm flesh, and once every generation, a swarm blows in from the desert and will eat whole villages down to the bone. Livestock and all. Heard even once that a farmer, seeing one of these swarms rise up, opened his mouth to give warning, and before the sound passed his lips, the crickets had already devoured his tongue."

"Vine," Kreon warned. "Shut *up* afore I shut you *up*."

A pause. "Bored is all."

That was enough for Marrok. "How can you be bored while on point? Are you unfit?"

"I'm bored is all I'm saying."

"My blade up your hole will make things interesting enough," Kreon muttered.

"No need for that," Vine said. "I'm not screaming here. Only whispering. No harm in that."

"Saimon's shite trough," Kreon remarked softly. "I'll take latrine duty for the rest of the campaign before I get assigned with you again."

"Games start next month," Vine said, changing the subject.

"Eh?"

Marrok groaned mentally. Vine knew Kreon was a gambler. Say one thing for Vine: if you weren't interested in what he was talking about, he'd change subjects until one interested you. The man should have been a merchant instead of a Sujin.

"Nowhere near the start of the games," Kreon hissed back.

"Oho, I'd say they're at least four weeks out. Maybe even three. Would you say so, Mar?"

Marrok sighed. "Aye that. At least."

"Truly?" Kreon asked without any worry of noise now.

"Aye, I imagine so."

"Seddon above," Kreon swore. "What I wouldn't pay to see the opening day. Make a few coins on the side. I can pick the victors; tell you that for nothing."

"Only the Free Trained fight early on, don't they?" Vine asked.

"No, not at all, you'll see the scattered house fighter as well. Them brutes eat the Free babes though. Punish them. Butchery, really. But good for a show. Most early fights are the Free Trained, just to whet the appetites, but a handful of house fighters make the appearance as well."

"You wager on fights between Free Trained and house fighters?"

"No, no. No one wagers—well, *some* wager on those fights, but it's almost always a done thing. I'm talking about the house gladiators fighting other houses. Those are the ones you have to watch and put coin on. I had a system."

"A system?" Marrok asked, joining the conversation. "What system? The games were nothing more than arranged meetings and nothing more. Until the end, anyway."

"Arranged meetings? You saying the matches are fixed?"

"I've heard."

"Them games aren't fixed." Kreon scoffed. "I've seen my share before I became a Sujin. My father and I would watch the games every season. He was an old hand at picking winning fighters."

"It's all theatre."

"It's an art, I give you that," Kreon granted. "But nothing's decided beforehand."

"I'm telling you, I've heard stories about coin changing hands before a fight," Vine said. "And whispers of talks between houses."

"Oh, they talk," Kreon allowed. "Course they talk. Seeking information on individuals. Sometimes men will pay for valuable information, especially in the later rounds. If a gladiator's broken a finger or a rib, or perhaps is still suffering from the last fight, well, that's gold to some if they know about it. Anything that an opponent can use to their advantage. There's coin to be made knowing things, and nothing wrong with that."

Marrok shook his head, still staring into the early summer night. "That's only half of it. The real coin comes from bribes."

"There's no bribery in the games," Kreon said in a low voice, surprising Marrok with his naiveté.

"Certainly there is," he persisted. "Might not happen all the time, but the Chamber allows it. Probably has a hand in it themselves. The games are nothing more than blood, sand, and gold—*especially* gold. You don't believe they actually stay in that hell because of whatever code of honor they spout? It's a business, like any other."

"Ahhh," Kreon dismissed him with a throaty growl. "Believe what you want, and I'll believe what I want."

Marrok smirked in the dark. "They say there's the

games on the sands... and then there are the *real* games beyond the sands. How do you think the House of Curge has remained so dominant over the years?"

"Skill at arms," Kreon answered at once. "Curge is a right vengeful bastard, he is."

"I've heard it so," Vine threw in.

"Well, he is," Marrok whispered agreement, his head turning just a fraction in the direction of where Kreon stood.

"If you think Curge could be bribed, you're unfit in the head," Kreon put forth.

"Well, maybe not," Marrok said. "But you don't think he'd bribe someone *else* to lose? Or some other ploy? Threaten them, even? He has the clout. And the personality, I daresay."

"Daresay," Vine added with a hint of wary awe, perhaps recalling stories about Dark Curge from conversations past.

"I've heard it said that there's more coin collected off the wagers than..." Kreon trailed off, struggling for a suitable simile.

"What?" Marrok asked.

Then the cries went up.

The three outer sentries turned around, looking toward the encampment. Torch bearers and fire pits illuminated walls of canvas tents. Armed Sujins hurried between, through fluttering corridors. More shouts of warning and pain cut the night air, each one spiking Marrok's attention as he strove to find the source.

Then he looked up.

Comets blazed across the inky blackness, thick and bright enough to momentarily blot out the stars. Their angry hiss sizzled across the heavens, burning Marrok's ears and leaving him very, very vulnerable standing where he was. His mouth dropped open as he realized what was happening.

Fire arrows.

The sizzling missiles rained down, sinking deep into the heart of the waking Klaw. More shouts shattered the night's stillness. Some men screamed in pain.

"Stand firm," Kreon said, no longer whispering, and Marrok gripped the hilt of his shortsword behind his shield. On his right, Vine closed the gap and bumped his shoulder.

"Stand firm," Kreon repeated.

"Stand firm!" a Koor roared, pointing his sword at the clump of Sujins gathered at the nearest fire pit.

"Eyes sharp out there!" The same officer barked at Marrok and his companions. All around the camp, the defensive points crouched low and scanned the night for archers.

Some of the tents caught fire at once, and men soon teemed amongst the burning material, striking at the flames with blankets while other frantically shovelled turf at the fiery ribbons, momentarily dousing them. One Sujin fell hard, a smoking arrow protruding from his face. Another soldier, confused at being so roused from sleep, stood only to have a descending missile nail him through his unprotected head with a distinct *clop* and drive him to his knees. The shining figure of a Cavalier strode through the burning tents, heedless of the danger, directing Sujins as he went.

Marrok scanned the darkness ahead, the grass colored a fiery hue. The shadows of the three Sujins stretched over the sward in long, forbidding peaks while the sounds of crackling flames, working bodies, and shouting behind made Marrok's back stiffen. He gripped his sword and felt the energy building in his limbs, urging him to do something. *Anything.* But he didn't. His orders were to stand firm, to not budge from his position. And he didn't have to look to know the minds of Kreon and Vine. On his flanks he felt them, solid as bedrock.

Then another cry pierced the night, hooking his attention and making him glance up again. To his horror and ire, another bright wave of fire arrows trailed smoke across the night sky before crashing downward into the meat of the Klaw. More cries of pain rose over a murderous patter.

The first gauzy tendrils of smoke slipped around Marrok and his companions, but they didn't turn. Their attention focused on scanning the dark for the enemy.

Commanding voices cut through the clamor behind, giving directions. Water splashed. Men swore. Horses neighed somewhere deep within the folds of the Klaw. The acrid smell of smoke thickened. Marrok resisted the urge to look over his shoulder and grimly stared into the night.

A roar of voices burst from the distant right, growing, rising above the crackles of the burning encampment, climaxing with a raucous clatter of swords against swords.

Marrok looked, taking his attention off the dark, toward the deepening, fiery glow consuming the encampment.

And at the exact moment he turned, a wall of black specters rose up from the tall grass, detaching themselves from the night's embankment, startlingly closer than suspected. Their booted feet crushed the blades of vegetation. Their arms thrust forward, elongating into ungodly spears of pointed darkness. Steel blades flashed.

Kreon shouted a warning just as those terrible shafts struck shields and flesh. One took Marrok over the lip of his shield and through his face. As he collapsed, a fourth spear streaked by and shredded into the meat of Kreon's sword arm, bypassing chainmail links with a *pop* and piercing his heart. A stunned Vine died an instant later, a spear stabbing his lower leg while a sword hacked a grisly V between his neck and shoulder.

Black-armored Jackals, their features masked and grim, flowed over the dead men and swept toward the next flimsy line of shouting sentries, adding yet another chorus to the death knell of the burning Klaw.

2

The outer doors, great slabs of oak fitting together so well their seams appeared almost invisible, closed behind the founding members of the House of Ten. A row of Skarrs remained as motionless and impassive as the etched scenes carved into the walls of the Gladiatorial Chamber. Goll limped as he turned halfway around, favouring his healing toes smashed by the now dead once-champion known as Baylus the Butcher. The Balgothan gladiator had left Goll with a number of gruesome memories of their battle in the pit, all of which were slowly healing. The swelling in his face was receding, returning his ordinary looks under a head of short sandy hair. Bandages, however, still covered the mending cuts along his arms, ribs, and the stab wound in his right shoulder. Halm once commented that the wounds were really trophies, and that they gave the Kree character.

Goll wanted to bestow a little character upon the Zhiberian at times.

The Kree ignored his companions and glanced back at the guards. He imagined if he drew a blade they would come to life quickly enough. Giving them no more thought, he swung himself ahead on his crutches, already accustomed to the burn in his armpits where the meager padding pained him. Bald-headed, black-bearded Tumber walked with him on one side. The muscular Sapo trudged along on the other. Both men carried weapons, wore leather vests, and carried themselves with a pensive air of alertness. If forces had attacked Muluk for their collected gold once, the march to the Chamber would have been the final opportunity to strike. To the Kree's relief, no one had interrupted their procession to the Chamber's doors.

Six giant columns of white marble rose up from street level to the huge overhang of the Chamber, and the evening sun, not yet departed from the sky, blazed between them. Goll squinted against its light. The rays grazed the slanted gray slate tiles of nearby houses and made their dreary shells shine like gold.

"I'm off then," Halm announced from one side and handed the considerably lighter cloth sack to the man called Sapo. Having done that, the bulbous Zhiberian, shirtless and sweating from his breeches up, started marching back to the Pit. The man's constant oozing from the pores sogged the bandages wrapped about his gut, reminding Goll of a black-haired babe constantly pissing itself.

"Where are you going?" Goll stopped and asked.

"Where?" Halm sneered puzzlement. "Guess."

"You can't go back there yet."

"Why not?"

Goll didn't like the aggressive heat coming off the burly Zhiberian. The realization of what the Kree had done, gambling with Pig Knot's life to birth the House of Ten, had finally sunk into Halm's head. Perhaps it happened while they were all in the presence of the Chamber members. Goll had already mentally prepared for this eventuality, knowing he'd have to defuse it.

"I need you to come with me back to the healer's house," he stated simply. "Just in case someone attempts to rob us."

"What? What gurry is that? You have that pair of bears behind you, *weapon master*," Halm snarled, flashing black-and-yellow teeth while waving an open palm. His other hand gripped the hilt of the Mademian sword scabbarded at his waist, the belt it hung from obscured by his great, hairy gut and the stained bandages partially covering it. He took a moment to quickly scratch his belly fat.

"Come with me back to the healer's house, Halm," Goll persisted. "We have things to discuss."

"Let's discuss them here," Halm snapped and spread his arms wide, indicating the open space before the magnificence of the Gladiatorial Chamber and giving the three men an even better look at the Zhiberian's collection of wounds.

"No, it's…" Goll bit back his pleading, controlling his own anger. "Look. Walk with me. We'll talk, and I'll release you once we check on Muluk. You do remember him, don't you?"

"Oh, I remember him. I'm surprised you do, actually. Or maybe you have plans for him, too, hm? As you did Pig Knot?"

"Nothing of the sort."

"Be wary, lads," Halm remarked, waving a finger at the silent Tumber and Sapo. "Be very wary around this one. I'll warn you once for nothing."

Both warriors exchanged suspicious looks before centering on Goll. The Kree dismissed their glares with a roll of his eyes and focused on Halm.

"Halm. Please. Walk with me."

"What did you just say?"

"You heard me."

"I don't believe I did."

"You heard what I said."

"I did not."

"Halm!"

The Zhiberian crossed his arms defiantly, bracing for a storm.

Goll scowled hot enough to shatter rock. The master of the newly formed house took a moment to compose himself. He bit his lips before finally shaping his mouth into a contrary line.

Halm waited, enjoying seeing the other man squirm.

"I said it once, and if that's not enough, then damn you to Saimon's hell," the Kree said at last and spat.

Halm shrugged and got three strides away before hearing, *"Halm!"* But he kept walking.

"All right, *please!*" Goll grated, that last word laced with poison.

The Zhiberian turned about and pointed toward the arena's infirmary.

"I don't understand you, Kree. Pig Knot is only over *there*, the other side of the great Chamber. What time would it take?"

"You'll understand soon enough," Goll said, his eyes betraying fear. Then, apparently having had enough of the exchange, he turned away at his best speed and limped away. Tumber and Sapo followed.

Shaking his head, Halm shadowed the three men. After

a few paces, he drew alongside Sapo and patted the man's arm, getting his attention. The brute screwed up his face at the Zhiberian, who returned the disdainful expression before taking back the sack containing their remaining gold pieces. Throwing the cloth over his shoulder, he stepped up to Goll.

"Entrusting these with whatever coin we have left," he muttered. "Where's your mind at? Tell me that much."

"Where's your mind, since they're only just behind us?"

"So?"

"*So* you're calling them thieves, practically."

Halm regarded the pair behind him with an apologetic grimace and a shake of his head. Having done that, his features hardened once more upon speaking to Goll.

"This had best be good," Halm warned.

"Are you not one of the founders of the House of Ten?" Goll asked him. "Do you not *wish* to be a part of the decision process?"

Halm mulled that over. "Suppose so."

"What do you mean you 'suppose so'? We've listed ten names this day, and it was *your* blood that made it happen, along with Muluk's and Pig Knot's. There's a lot of work ahead of us, and we must further establish and focus upon our goals. Pig Knot can wait. *Muluk* can wait. As harsh as that sounds, fretting over them like some sobbing mother isn't going to help them."

Halm's face reddened at the lecture, and he refused to meet the Kree's eyes. Nor did either man say another word all the way back to Shan's house of healing. The wooden shutters hung open while a thin mesh of cotton draped the openings, reducing airflow inside but also restricting unwanted mosquitos and other pests from entering. Upon reaching the front door, Goll stopped and regarded

Tumber and Sapo with an approving eye. He measured them up for what seemed to be the first time.

"My thanks," he finally said. "You've barely made a sound during all of this, and for that you're to be commended."

The huge muscular mass that was Sapo didn't reply or show any indication that he'd heard. Black-bearded Tumber stood in the Sunjan's shadow and shrugged indifferently, though the corners of his dark eyes crinkled as if smiling at the scant praise.

"You'll address me as Master Goll while training and living under the roof of the House of Ten. Understood?"

Both men nodded. Goll caught the stiffening of Halm's neck.

"You'll address Halm, Pig Knot, and Muluk as *master* as well. Without them, there wouldn't *be* a house training, feeding, or sheltering you. Understood?"

"Aye that," Sapo muttered softly. "Muluk's the one inside?"

"He is."

Tumber peered through a window. "Seems to be a few lads in there."

Goll peeked and frowned. "Stand guard out here. Unless they're bleeding or near death, keep all others away. Understood?"

Both men muttered, "Aye that."

"Shall we, then?" Goll asked his Zhiberian companion and didn't wait for an answer. He threw open the door and swung his way inside.

Halm paused before entering and sheepishly regarded the two men. "No need to call me *master*," he said, studying them both under the barest self-conscious dip of his brow. "Just my name. That is enough."

HOUSE OF PAIN

Tumber's dark eyes softened with surprise just as Halm entered the building.

Inside, Goll frowned as he'd just caught his companion's words, not liking them in the least. In his mind, there had to be a division between the masters and the recruits.

Halm saw his disapproval and stared back without blinking, letting his own feelings on the matter be known. Goll shrugged, partly in frustration and partly to relieve physical strain. Their attention then focused on the men quietly gathered in the cramped area of the healer's house. Four of them sat at a table, including the healer, Shan. When Goll directed his gaze upon them, they struggled to their feet.

"This place smells like a dog's sleeping mat." Halm grimaced, pulling an expression of surprise from the healer, who sniffed and frowned in disagreement.

"Are you at odds again, fat man?" Borchus asked from a corner.

Halm lifted his chin in reproach. "You," he breathed, features pinching as if suckling a raw lemon. "Where'd you run off to back in the infirmary? You're like hot piss in a river."

"I had coin to collect," Borchus explained, unconcerned by the jab. "And I dislike doing business in infirmaries."

"Where do you think you are now, then?" Halm countered. "Or are your wits as short as your legs?"

"Perhaps your master and I should do business alone, then?" Borchus smiled diplomatically, turning his attention to Goll.

"Master?" Halm asked with an evil chuckle. "This is worth it. *I'm* a master in this house."

Borchus met the eyes of the Kree. "Really?" he inquired skeptically.

"I'm the head, however," Goll stated, setting his jaw as he regarded Halm. "You've already allowed me that. Back at Clavellus's villa."

For a moment, the two men stared at each other, daring a retort. The silence swelled uncomfortably as Halm took a moment to remember. Then his breath loosed in a low, conceding hiss. "So we did. You're the head of the house. Apologies."

"None needed. Think of yourself as a captain, Halm."

"Captain. Hm."

But Goll wasn't sure if the big man was being moody or not. "Are you fine with this? I ask this one final time before these men as our witnesses. I don't want any arguments on this matter in the future, especially if we're before noble company. Clearly, you hold rank over our fighters as a founder, but I wield the power of last word and which direction the house takes. Present your arguments or concerns now or in the future if you must, and I'll listen, but command is mine."

"What direction?" Halm's voice grated. "We're still talking about fighting, are we not?"

"We are. But my word in any matter pertaining to the house is final. Agreed?"

Storm clouds brewed on the unattractive features of the heavyset Zhiberian. His jaw rolled this way and that, chewing on thoughts and weighing the choice of whether to voice them. In the end, he sighed, and his great hairy shoulders slumped.

"Do what you like." He surrendered with a dismissive wave. "You've done it your way thus far. Seddon help you if Pig Knot dies, however."

The warning tone riled Goll, but he decided to hold his silence... *that* time. He faced Borchus, who watched the exchange with mild amusement.

"All done?" The agent smirked slyly.

"What's he for anyway?" Halm asked of Goll.

"Wheels within wheels," Borchus answered cryptically, his deep voice as hard as cooling iron. "Fighting is only half the battle in the Pit."

"I didn't ask *you*," Halm warned.

"What he says is true," Goll stated. "We have need of... an agent."

"A what?"

"An agent, you punce. An agent." Borchus growled, not impressed in the least with Halm's limited knowledge of his profession. He squared his shoulders and locked gazes. "*Me.*"

"What in Saimon's hell does an agent do?"

The question drew an indignant look from the smaller man. "I'll simplify the answer so you might better understand it. An agent does that which you cannot. You're all grown up now. You're a house. Now the lions will take notice of you, and like it or not, you'll need an able man out there, in the streets, to ferret out information you and your fighters must have—information that could mean victory upon the sands of the arena."

"You're right about one thing."

Borchus scowled. "No doubt you'll clarify what."

"I'm all grown up." Halm continued on, cautioning, "And I've a man-sized boot I'll smash your fruits with if you push me far enough."

"All right," Goll nearly barked. "That's enough from both of you. As it is, Borchus is correct. If we are to stand a chance in the arena, we'll need eyes and ears beyond the

Pit's walls—someone to glean information from the other houses and their fighters, their strengths and weaknesses. As a house, we cannot afford to be *without* an agent and a network of spies as our adversaries employ their own. Halm, you can be certain that there are people this very moment reporting upon the newly formed house and who is fighting under its banners. I expect word to have spread throughout most if not all of the existing houses by morning, and from there on, whatever is to be known about our lads will be eventually discovered. *They'll* find it. And if they can, they'll exploit it."

"You're serious about this?" Halm demanded.

"Of course I'm serious."

The Zhiberian became pensive for a span of heartbeats before jabbing a thumb at the agent. "Surely we can do better than *him*."

"I could ask the same of you, good Goll," Borchus said through a tight line of a mouth, "with regards to who fights in the arena from this day forward."

"What's that supposed to mean?" Halm wanted to know.

"Don't you have something to... *eat* somewhere?"

"Enough!" Goll snapped and glared, silencing the bickering. "Halm, we need Borchus's services. I've already talked with Clavellus, and he's vouched for the man's competence. We cannot go forward without a tried and reliable agent working for us. We don't have the time to find another of his mettle."

"*His* mettle?" Halm snorted with doubt.

"My work is every bit as hazardous as yours, large one," Borchus stated.

"Forgive me, I thought you said something about wheels before? I don't remember seeing any wheels while I was out there smashing in skulls."

"That was figuratively."

"Figure what?"

Borchus rolled his eyes.

Goll leaned in. "He's with us. Or I hope he still is, though I don't blame him if he chooses otherwise and does not work on our behalf."

Halm scowled. "I don't see where his *work* is. It's not on the sands."

At this, Borchus shook his head, even more exasperated with the Zhiberian.

"What exactly is he going to do for us?" Halm asked Goll.

"I can answer that," Borchus replied. "Think, if you can, about a match you might have. And knowing beforehand if, say, the man has the tendency to feint once before striking? Or perhaps the lad injured himself a day or two before your match and guards that secret for fear of his opponent learning of it, thus lessening his chances for victory. And it isn't always about finding such secrets. Even letting slip false information amongst the right ears can benefit us, so that a future foe might later attempt to capitalize upon it, and woe if he does."

"You mean lying."

"I mean lying."

Halm didn't appear impressed. "Dishonest."

"Yes, well, I'd allow you to go on thinking that, but unfortunately, since I'm in the House of Ten's employ, I won't. Your days of being an ignorant, bare-assed whelp with his paunch hanging out are over, oh pear-shaped one, and to be successful amongst the houses, you'll need me. And others. Which brings me to my next question: how many spies may I have?"

"Spies?" Halm asked.

"Not many. Our coin is limited, I'll have you know," Goll answered.

"Fair enough," Borchus conceded. "I'll try to make do. But the more men I have… the better."

"Whores say the same thing, I believe," Halm pointed out with a smirk.

"Oh, you are a *sharp* one." Borchus smiled with feigned endearment, regarding the half-naked man. "Oh, so very, very sharp. It's been a while since I've had to be on guard, but I will from now while in your company. Now, if play is done with—what are the names of your new lads?"

Goll told him, drawing the agent's attention away from Halm. Borchus recited each name until he remembered them, taking only two tries, and nodded with satisfaction. "Excellent. Well, then, my business is done. I'll be on my way."

"Where are you going?"

He blinked at Goll. "To get word back to Clavellus. He'll appreciate being kept abreast of matters. And I have to deliver the coin he won. After that, I'm all yours. Have no fear. I'll be in touch, Master Goll."

With that, the stocky man dipped his head in salute and turned his attention upon Halm. He kept his tongue, however, and departed the healer's house with an all-too-comfortable smile.

Halm didn't wait for the swinging door to be closed. "I don't like him at all."

"I doubt he cares much for you either," Goll muttered and then faced the other men present, nodding at Shan when the healer gestured toward a trio of faces he didn't know. They were older, perhaps in their late thirties or early forties, in shape, wearing cheap leather vests and bearing scabbarded shortswords at their waists. Gray flecked their heavy beards and gave the Kree a moment's pause.

The third man was a hard-looking individual who appeared to have just come out of a small war. He was barely average height, built solidly and wearing a plain white shirt and black trousers that seemed very well tailored despite shoddy fabric. The face under a mop of dark hair told another story, a recent, more violent one. A light beard was kept neat, but his cheeks were battered and hued a sickly yellow from fading bruises. His left cheek had at least ten stitches in it, while a large scab covered his right. Fresh ointment had been smeared over the wounds, making them gleam wetly. The smell of ripe onions hung around him.

"Who are these, then?" Goll asked, feeling pressed for time.

"These are the guards you asked about," Shan replied, pursing his lips. "The best I could do on short notice, but you were in luck."

"More than luck," the battered man said eagerly and smiled, baring healthy teeth.

Goll's expression made it clear he wouldn't be so quick to agree.

"This is Clades," Shan said, filling the awkward silence. "While this is Pratos, and Valka."

"Bit old, aren't you?" Goll asked, screwing up his mouth.

"I can vouch for them both, Master Goll," Clades spoke up. "Shan contacted me first, and I contacted both Pratos and Valka. They're Sujin, Lord."

Still unimpressed, Goll considered them once more. "Shouldn't they be on a front somewhere, then?"

"They've been retired by their Klaws, Master Goll," Clades reported. "As myself. Ah, war wounds and all. Though, if necessary, they will be called to return to duty if the city is ever threatened."

"So what good are you to me?"

Clades blinked, not expecting the question. Then he cleared his throat. "They're a bit older, sar, granted. And it's plain to see I've been cut. But make no mistake, I know the work. I'm no slouch with a length of steel. I know these men, and if you take me, you should know I feel best having them at my back."

"There aren't many reputable swords for hire in the city," Shan spoke up. "There *is* a war on, after all. To find three once Sujins—"

"You'll do, then," Goll declared, cutting the healer short. Relief flowed over the three faces before him. "Your first order of business will be providing night-and-day protection to the man upstairs. Which begs me to ask how he's doing."

"Still alive," Shan reported.

"Still alive," Goll repeated with a hiss and huffed with displeasure. The mental stress of the day flooded his skull all at once, and he felt the need for something strong to drink. Two men beaten within a finger of their lives, their winnings of gold, the establishment of the house, the confrontation with Halm in the street, and to make matters even more interesting, Goll figured it was probably just the beginning. He felt his armpits ache from walking and leaning on his crutches. The longing to lie down made his weariness all the more heavy.

"May I retire for the night?"

Shan nodded. "Muluk is upstairs. I gave him a sedative to help him sleep, so the only thing you'll hear are snores, but otherwise, go ahead."

"Thank you, good Shan."

The healer dismissed the comment with a look and retreated toward the back of the house, ambling toward an inner door leading to his private chambers.

"I'm for upstairs then," Goll said and reached for the nearby railing. On impulse, he left his crutches by the wall and hobbled his way up the steps at best speed. Halm followed, leery of the Kree leaving the wooden supports so early. Shadows grew and clung to the exposed support beams of the upper level, and the smell of an unknown medicinal concoction grew heavy in the air. On the top floor, six neat cots filled with straw and covered with gray blankets waited. Muluk lay sprawled on one, heavily bandaged and snoring peacefully. Goll hop-walked to his side, mindful of a wooden piss bucket with a flat cover over the top to trap odor. Clean white dressings covered the man's extensive wounds, reaffirming the belief that Shan was well worth the few gold coins tossed his way.

Behind him, Halm laid the sack of gold on the floor with a soft crinkle. "Is he all right?"

"He looks it," Goll replied out of the corner of his mouth. He glanced about the darkening floor, spotting a cot before the only open window in the place. Orange evening light shone through, casting a calming shine across the blankets and floorboards.

"This place is hot, though. Even with that window opened. Still…"

Using the posts for support, Goll made his way to his choice and nearly collapsed on it. Once stationary, he rubbed at his eyes and exhaled mightily, noting the lack of dust in the air.

"Dare I say it," he said in a low voice. "I didn't think

we'd do it."

"Hm," Halm replied softly, his face darkened by shadows. "Nor did I. Truth be known."

"Return to Pig Knot if you must. Just watch yourself out there. That one called Skulljigger is about, and he might not wait for a chance at you in the Pit."

"I might not wait for him," Halm returned, the coldness in his voice earning a warning look from the Kree. After a moment, he faced the open window, watching a red sun sinking beneath an irregular shadowed line of pointed rooftops and arched gables. Drooping lengths of Sunjan streamers hung off rafters, fluttering now and again in subtle evening breezes. Taller buildings loomed in the distance, their shapes slowly devoured in the creeping dusk.

"On your way out," Goll started, the weariness unmistakable in his voice, "count out six of the gold, divide equally, and pay the new guards below."

"They looked hard."

"As long as they're capable."

"Hm. Aye that."

Halm's lack of fight in the presence of Muluk's slumbering form might've touched anyone else, but not Goll. They stopped talking for a moment then and listened only to the soft rush of noise made by passersby on the street below the window. Goll rubbed his stomach, not hungry in the least, but that would change come morning. *Morning.* He sighed mentally, replaying what he'd witnessed *that* morning.

"You still here?" Goll asked quietly, well aware Halm hadn't moved, let alone departed. When the big man didn't answer, the Kree regarded his sole Zhiberian companion. Halm sat himself on a nearby cot and stared thoughtfully at the setting sun. Goll stared at the evening as well, and for a moment, neither of them said anything. The shock and wonder of the day's events washed over them as gloriously as the dying light.

"We're a house," Halm whispered, the awe just barely suppressed in his voice. "Saimon's black hanging fruit, we're a *house*."

"Surprised?"

Halm's bright, scary eyes regarded him. For a heartbeat, Goll thought he might swear at him. But then the overweight man sighed and smiled, exposing those rotten shards still passing for teeth.

"I suppose, for all of my hope, I never truly thought… we could do it."

"Well, we did."

"That we did."

"And we'll do more."

"We will?"

"Guaranteed. Master Halm."

Halm's brow arched at the title. His expression softened to pleasant surprise. He scratched at the stiff brush that was his hair and straightened.

"Never thought…" he trailed off and left it hanging. Then, having said what needed saying, he got to his feet and stood, running a hand over the bandages around his waist. He counted out coins from the sack, even taking an extra handful and making a show of doing so.

"Buy us something to eat with that," Goll said, with a wary eye.

"Hm," Halm grunted without commitment and smiled again, leaving Goll wondering whether he would follow orders or not. The big fighter then walked over to stand beside Muluk's snoring form. "He smells terrible."

"That's a master you're standing over."

That made Halm smirk. He placed a hand on his sleeping friend's head and kept it there for a brief moment. Then, before descending to the lower floor, he turned back, a tall shadow at the head of the stairs.

"Though part of me is still… angered at what you've done—what you commanded Pig Knot to do and the obvious, heavy cost—and even though the future is just as dangerous, I thank you, good Goll. If anything, you should be commended for doing what you set out to do. And for bringing me—us—along with you."

Halm paused and studied the floor for a moment, allowing the silence to thicken.

"But don't… command another one of our warriors to lose," he warned, raising his head. Not even the shadows could conceal his threatening expression. "Don't even consider it. Not ever again."

His dire message delivered, the Zhiberian turned and took his time descending the steps, failing to step lightly. The soft clatter, however, didn't seem to disturb Muluk's snoring carcass in the least. Goll watched Halm's shape sink into the floor in chunks before disappearing entirely. He rubbed his forehead and sighed wearily, feeling unwanted heat from Halm's quiet reprimand. He didn't want to think about it anymore. Or what lay ahead. What had been done *needed* to be done. Pig Knot had to lose for the house to exist. It was the only sure road. Goll recognized the opportunity and what it was worth when it happened, even though his actions might reach the new recruits. If it did, it might possibly become a source of dissension amongst the ranks.

If so, he'd deal with it.

He'd deal with it all.

The House of Ten was a reality, but he understood the path ahead. Now the work truly began. And every soul living under the house's banner would have to be watchful.

His thoughts then turned to Halm. Did he suspect what he'd discover back at the infirmary? Could he know? Goll wasn't certain. What the Kree knew was better left in the hands of the healers there—part of the reason he wanted to delay the Zhiberian as much as possible, to spare him, once again, from what needed to be done by the Pit's healers.

"You'll understand soon enough," Goll whispered and permitted himself to gaze upon the evening light beyond the window, hoping perhaps that he was mistaken.

A touch of sadness soured his features.

3

Night descended upon the city streets, flooding the alleyways as Halm hurried to the arena's infirmary. The thought of having Borchus work for him was not sitting well in his head or gut, and he dreaded to anticipate what manner of information the little weasel might pass on to him. To *any* of them, for that matter. Then there was Goll. Halm fumed over the Kree commanding Pig Knot to lose his fight, even though a part of him grudgingly wrestled with the reasoning behind the play. He struggled to convince himself the order was given for the birth of the house and not because of any ill feelings Goll might have toward the man. The result was still too costly, too dear. Pig Knot was perhaps the closest thing to a friend he'd had these past few seasons, and Halm *had* thought that Goll was becoming one as well. Presently, he wasn't so certain. Though he didn't want to admit it, as a founder of the House of Ten, he'd have to keep a close eye on the Kree.

HOUSE OF PAIN

When he reached the outer square of the arena, he quickly bypassed the patrolling Street Watch and entered the Pit through an open set of gates. Flickering torches leaned from bronze sconces, coloring the fitted stone of the corridor. His shadow flittered as he ignored the curious looks of two attendants lighting wicks as he passed by. The closer he came to the infirmary, the greater his urge to be there that very instant. He knew the way, having been there enough that season and in games long past.

In the subterranean air clung a curious, perplexing smell, one he couldn't place. Breathing hard, Halm rounded a corner and hurried to an open archway with a set of bright lanterns hanging on either side. The nagging smell became stronger. A shadow moved within the darkness just on the other side of the far lantern. Light reflected off steel.

A dagger.

A second weapon—a sword—came into view, its hilt grasped in a meaty fist. A towering wraith faced Halm, stopping him in his tracks. He gawked at the menacing hellion lurking outside the infirmary, a shot of uncertainty forcing him to feel for his Mademian blade. Then the shadow leaned into the light, and relief surged through the beefy gladiator. He recognized the man as one of the newer recruits but failed to remember his name. The giant's moustache drooped at the ends like thick spikes, well past his chin.

"All well?" Halm asked the lanky pit fighter, having difficulty locating the man's eyes.

"As expected," the other replied in a clear voice. "Been here for a while."

"Apologies for that." Halm winced and entered the infirmary. That haunting smell originated from within the chamber, teasing him with its mystery. Miserable moans dragged through the air as he beheld a long hall illuminated by a few lamps and torches mounted in iron brackets on the walls. Men lay sprawled on cots as if dropped from great heights, their bandaged forms either motionless or writhing. Someone coughed. A voice called out for missing companions. Steadying himself, Halm pushed through the many beds of the wounded and dying.

One unfortunate lad grabbed his wrist.

"See the sea," the patient hissed, wild eyes imploring before finally relaxing. Bandages covered his midsection, but a menacing blot of darkness seeped through at the center. Halm worked himself free of the delirious man's grip.

A half-naked specter draped in firelight and shade crept between the wounded, inspecting each one as if he were grim Death itself attending a grisly harvest. Detecting movement, the figure paused and straightened with the elegance of an old serpent, watching the newcomers with an unspoken question.

"You there, Zhiberian," a voice called and made Halm turn around. There, posted just inside the infirmary's entrance, were the two other fighters Goll had assigned to protect Pig Knot. Halm had completely missed them in his urgency. One fellow sat on a stool, but the other pushed himself away from the wall and threaded his way amongst the many islands of pain.

Halm warded him off with a hand and resumed searching amongst the wounded. As he went, pitiful whimpers rose up, distasteful as thick dust. Pungent ointments glazed the underlining reek of fresh and dried blood. One man lay on a cot, seized by delirium, his milky eyes glassy and haunting in the dim light. He waved a stained stump where a right hand should have been. Another unfortunate soul rested on his back, his foot heavily wrapped in cloth.

Halm felt pity for them all but continued looking for Pig Knot.

"Who are you looking for?" Death croaked with surprising clarity, his question silencing his crippled charges. The half-naked man had approached with nary a sound, a cot hiding his lower half. Halm thought he was staring at a skull, but then his nerves relaxed. It was the old healer.

"Pig Knot," he answered. "The man with the ruined legs."

For a moment, the healer didn't reply, then he gestured to a corner without any light at all. Smoky tendrils drifted from the nearby remnants of a spent torch.

"My thanks," Halm muttered and walked toward it, noting the empty cots crowding the foreboding section of the infirmary. Another smell lingered here, and Halm recognized it grimly, the same odor he'd caught a subtle whiff of earlier. A tangle of a man rested upon a cot bathed in gloom. A knot of horror clenched Halm's sternum, pushing against his ribs. He couldn't say Pig Knot's name.

He doubted the man could hear him.

Pig Knot's face had been wrapped in bandages dulled with dried blood. Only the eyes and mouth remained uncovered. His chest rose and fell in a slow, torpid rhythm. More blood-soaked wraps covered his shoulders, as if the thick dressings were the only things keeping him together. A fresh reek of herbal salves hung over the entire scene, drawing attention to Pig Knot's lower parts…

Where once he had possessed legs.

A stunned Halm stood in dreadful awe of the destruction crippling his friend. He knew the leg wounds had been *bad*, knew that even as attendants rushed Pig Knot to the infirmary, but he never imagined…

That thought drifted off as his own legs betrayed him. Halm sat on a cot across from Pig Knot's unmoving form. The Sunjan's shape appeared altogether much too short. Thick cloth bandages covered the meaty stumps although gruesome stains blotted the ends. *Seepage*, Halm realized in horror. From the cutting and the fire being applied. And sweat. No doubt plenty of sweat.

Halm sensed movement draw up beside him.

"It was…" the healer spoke, "it was a very near thing. Too much had been done to him, I feared. Too much *ruined*." Death hissed the word with hatred. "Bones were sliced. Both limbs were hanging off by strings of meat. There was no hope, ever, of that healing whole. So I did what had to be done to save the lad's life. I cut off those wretched ends and cooked what remained. To stop the bleeding, you understand. Did it just after you and them others left. The pain was… terrible for him, but mercifully, he passed out quickly. In truth, I thought he'd perished, but he didn't. Not much to look upon, but it's better than being stiff in a grave."

Those last few words sounded as if pronounced through a smile. Halm turned and glared at the older man, whose expression slackened at the unspoken promise of violence.

"No disrespect meant," the healer said gently. "He'll live, is what I meant. He was cut up badly, but he's strong. He'll live. I'd wager on it."

The intensity on Halm's face did not lessen.

"You're welcome to stay right there as long as you

like," the healer whispered and dipped his head in sympathy. "If you can stand the smell."

"Where did you put them?"

"The legs?"

Halm nodded.

"My apologies. I placed them just over there, where the stink hangs the strongest. You probably smelled the worst of it on your way in. No need to look. An attendant took the remains away. For disposal."

Disposal. The word horrified the Zhiberian. He didn't want to dwell on how the legs would be disposed of.

Sensing the pit fighter's unease, the healer retreated to another area of the infirmary.

Halm stared at the mess that was his friend until yet another presence intruded on his grieving.

"You there," a gravelly voice asked in a none-too-friendly tone. His words marked him as a born Sunjan. "I've been here for far too long. All of us have. We'll be leaving now since you're here."

Halm faced the speaker: another of Goll's new recruits whose name escaped him. "Do what you want."

The other hesitated. "You can't do anything for him."

"I said… do… what you want."

"Man's lucky to be alive," the other remarked callously. "I was the one who carried away his lower legs, you know. 'Twas no attendant. None too pleasant business. I hope to be compensated for that."

A look of dangerous disdain slipped over Halm's face. "What's your name?"

The other straightened. "Torello."

"Here, then," he muttered and tossed a gold coin at the man.

Perhaps it was the tone of Halm's voice or the strain

on his face, but whatever the reason, it rendered Torello speechless. Then, apparently satisfied, he nodded, put the coin away, and left. Halm watched him walk back to the others waiting at the doorway. The one with the necklace of crow heads joined the whispered discussion there. When their talk finished, Torello left with another behind him while the towering fright remained with a bare-chested man. Halm couldn't remember seeing him at all, but he nodded at the Zhiberian before stretching out on a nearby cot.

The tall reaver with the complexion as dark as pitch withdrew outside. As far as Halm could tell, at least one of them had decided to stay, a small gesture that he appreciated. He took in the motionless form of Pig Knot and, taking a deep reflective breath, settled in for the night.

The pair of men leaving the infirmary only got halfway into the corridor when Torello stopped and swore.

"What?" asked Kolo, staring at the other's scowling face, almost entirely consumed by the dark. Torello wasn't pleasant to look upon at the best of times, and in the poorly lit stone passage, he appeared capable of cutting the throats of children.

"There's no point in going anywhere else," Torello grated, considering both directions of the corridor. "I'd rather sleep here and see what happens tomorrow than go back to general quarters. At least the damn infirmary doesn't smell like piss and shite."

"Smells like blood though," Kolo pointed out. He was almost the same height as Torello and roughly the same heavy, muscular build, though not as harsh about the face.

"And that slop they smear on your cuts and such."

"It smells everywhere near the Pit. Don't you know that?"

"Now I do."

"This day was bloodier than most," Torello seethed and stared off. "I tell you. I'm not altogether certain about throwing in with this lot. We might've joined up too soon."

"We can always leave."

"I'll do the thinking," Torello informed him with a frown. "You just do… whatever it is you do. And right now, I think it's best to head back and claim one of them empty cots for the night. One night anyway. We'll see what comes of it all in the morning. If anything, we can always leave."

What Torello said wasn't lost on Kolo, but he kept his tongue all the same. He knew his friend could be difficult at most times and simply intolerable the rest.

"Come on, then," Torello hissed and started back toward the infirmary. Kolo followed.

Once the pair were out of sight, a shadow detached itself from a pocket of blackness nestled between fluttering torches. He considered the passageway as a snake might before striking. Then he backed away and stealthily exited the bowels of the Pit. Once through the Gate of the Moon he stood in the shade of the arena and breathed the warm night air, casually eyeing passersby. After the stink of the sublevels of the arena, the humid air tasted sweet.

He wore a vest of leather, complete with tight black leggings and soft padded boots. A scabbarded shortsword of Sujin design hung off his waist. When he felt ready, he struck for a nearby street and followed its fitted stones until he reached a familiar alley. From there, he slipped into the shadows and wove through the city's formidable maze until he arrived at an oak door to one side of a dead end. Being followed was not a concern, so he rapped on the surface three times.

When the door opened, he ducked inside.

A gathering of six men paused in their preparations. A bare lamp burned on a high shelf on the north wall, at times partially blotted by threatening figures. Leather armor appeared like knobby hides. Half-sheathed shortswords and daggers gleamed with menace. The smell of ale and spicy meats lingered on the air. A seventh warrior locked the door with a thick timber and placed his back against its girth.

"Well?" Toffer asked the visitor, half of his face twisted in a sneer.

"He's still there," the spy reported. "But now the fat one's back. The Zhiberian. He's there. And the ones we thought might leave didn't. All told, there are five men around him now."

Toffer caught the sly eye of nearby Klytus, his thumb frozen on a blade's edge. "We'll wait another hour, then. Wait until they're good and sleepy. Then we strike. And gut the lot of them."

"It *is* an infirmary," one of the other killers pointed out as he buckled a belt that held three daggers around his waist. "There will be others."

"I don't care if Juhn's royal ass is in there," Toffer spat. "Pig Knot's disappointed me twice now. The worst thing about him surviving Skulljigger was *surviving* Skulljigger. I'll cut his bells off and sling them from Sunja's walls *after* I've made him understand no one disappoints me."

The others remained silent, not daring to voice their

minds. As veteran Sujins, they recognized the need for and strength in maintaining discipline, and in the light of a mysterious attack on a storehouse in their possession—an attack which claimed the lives of four of their brotherhood—Toffer's promise of violence wasn't an entirely bad thing. The storehouse destroyed had contained a valuable amount of stolen goods, wares that had taken time to procure, and an example had to be made somewhere. No one simply burned their property to the ground.

But the gathered soldiers knew the *real* reason why Toffer was on edge, and it wasn't because of Pig Knot's defeat in the Pit.

It was because no one had a clue as to who had murdered the four Sujins guarding that bit of valuable property and then proceeded to put a torch to it all.

Pig Knot was merely the nearest target about to experience Toffer's pent-up frustration at the totality of the day's events.

"They're all pit fighters," the spy quietly pointed out.

Toffer's face went white with suppressed fury, near choking the hilt of his blade.

Then three hard knocks sounded at the door, silencing all within the room. The warrior at the door peeked through a hidden hole, and his grimace slackened.

"It's Rusk," the Sujin said, already pulling at the timber.

The murderous feeling permeating the room magically contorted into nervous energy. Even the monstrous Klytus drew himself up to his full height and appeared uncertain. At that one name, they all stopped and studied each other like sewer rats, even Toffer—who was but a cog in a greater wheel, a wheel that rolled upon the command of the man called Two Knife.

"Open it," Toffer urged, rubbing his mouth and glancing nervously at the door.

The Sujin did just that, and a man strutted into their den of knives, oozing enough authority and deadly intent to bring the lot of them to heel. Of the entire pack, he was the shortest but possessed great meaty shoulders and arms that could punch both of the shortswords secured at his waist through an armored man. Blond hair was shorn close to his scalp. A scowl contorted his face as frightening blue eyes located each killer in turn.

A fearful silence smothered the room as if the men knew their very lives depended on maintaining it. Rusk the Two Knife strode to the middle of the floor without challenge and spread his hands.

"Well?" he demanded, addressing them all but focusing on Toffer. "Where in Saimon's blue hell are you maggots going?"

In the light, Two Knife's closely cut head of hair appeared as a mat of nails. "Hm? Someone speak. Please. Pull them tongues out of your dog blossoms. What's all this? Looks to me as if you're going on a killing. You found the one responsible for cooking our lads, did you?"

Toffer cleared his throat. "No, we—"

Two Knife's eyes narrowed into slits, and Toffer's voice uncharacteristically took on a pleading quiver. "I was taking them over to the Pit's infirmary, to kill a man who disobeyed my orders to kill a pit fighter."

Toffer blurted all this as if about to choke on the words.

Two Knife wasn't impressed. "Someone's out there burning our lads and our property to the foundations and you're... doing... *what*?"

"Teaching a lesson," Toffer sputtered.

"Teaching a lesson? To a pit fighter? This man lose your coin?"

"He did. He did."

"He lost *your* coin?" Two Knife demanded clarification, raising a finger to Toffer's face. "Not mine. Correct?"

"Aye that."

"Well," Rusk softened his tone immediately, "don't worry about it, then."

"What?" Toffer swallowed fearfully, his throat bobbing.

"I said don't worry about it. All of you. There'll be no killing of any kind this night."

"But Rusk…" Toffer pleaded. "There's—"

Two Knife cut him off. "Are you questioning me, Toffer? Because if so, I'll gut you here and coat the floor with what you are."

"No." Toffer straightened his back. "I'm not. Never."

"Good. Then listen, all of you." Two Knife studied the lot of them. "Get a solid night's sleep. All of you. Before dawn, I want you to rise and report for duty at the Fifth's barracks. That's the Fifth, you miserable he-bitches. *Remember* it, else I'll paddle your collective bells and sing while doing it. Report to the barracks. While there, you'll act as a proper Sujin should, and if anyone asks, say it's on my orders. Nothing more or less. If you get a righteous Koor who gives you gurry for nothing, you remember his name or at least his face and inform *me, but you act the proper soldier,* understood? If I hear otherwise, I'll cut the tongue from your head, dry it, and use it later as an ass scrub. Understood? Good. That's right and proper good. Now listen. In two days, we're heading to Marrn."

"Marrn?" Toffer's mouth dropped open.

"*Marrn*," Two Knife growled, silencing the man.

"Seems there's a mission being quietly carried out, and that dog blossom Bloor has placed me in charge of handpicking four hundred stout Sujins to guard a koch heading north." Two Knife's face brightened for a moment, revealing an oddly disbelieving smile at this stroke of fortune. It appeared for only an instant before the scowl returned and blotted it out. "You, Toffer, have no time for killing sick dogs in infirmaries as I'm about to give you part of a much larger task to complete. And you have to get to work on this *now*."

Toffer blinked, clearly confused.

"*Listen* to me, you brazen stain of salted shite. Don't think, just listen. That's all you have to do. Gather up every man we know and any extra killer who can handle a blade. Gather up anyone who ever breathed a word of sedition in the past. You do that, and I promise you—I *promise* you all with every stinking black fiber of my being—very, very soon, we'll *all* be as rich as kings. Now then…"

Despite what might have been planned for Pig Knot this night, Two Knife's rousing little speech poked the embers of greed inside Toffer's heart, causing him to pay very close heed to what was said next.

As Rusk the Two Knife spoke, an executioner's smile seeped across Toffer's face, and all thoughts of punishing Pig Knot were forgotten.

4

As the evening sky faded to black, Gastillo stood on his balcony and pensively watched servants light the torches of the training yard. The fires turned the sands orange, making Gastillo think of warmer climes, of beaches and salty surf, and of women. He stood at the wooden railing with his palms resting on the hard grain and eyed the two men as they finished. Gastillo's mouth tried to make a line, but the task was too much for his savaged lips. Even then, he could feel the drool from the evening's meal bead up on his lower lip, soon to spill over if he allowed it. He nudged his mask out of the way as he dabbed a cloth at the building flood. It was either that or let his water spill onto his clothing, and the last thing he needed was to look the part of a man well into his years. Gastillo wasn't. In his honest opinion, he felt perhaps just past his prime but still more than able to wield a blade if he had to. If he must.

He didn't care to ever again, however.

"All taken care of, Master Gastillo," Danshon called to

him.

"Fine dinner this evening, Danshon," Gastillo complimented his servant. "The fish was agreeable."

"I thought you might think so, Master Gastillo. I was a bit tired of chicken and beef myself, though we should be thankful for anything on our plates."

Gastillo managed a smirk behind his golden mask. It was just like Danshon to say something and then garnish his words with a melancholy afterthought. He had initially found it annoying, but he found the old man's words oddly touching and even endearing, though he hated to admit it. He didn't know what he was going to do when Danshon was finally gone, and he dreaded to think of it.

"Good evening to you, Danshon," he said cordially.

"And to you, Master Gastillo."

With that, the old man met another servant, and both disappeared through an archway. Gastillo listened to the distant voices beyond the walls of his compound, too distant for him to identify what was being said. The occasional yell punctuated the night, belonging to someone taking to drink far too early for his taste. It was one of the disadvantages of having one's house located within the city, but he'd bought it with the riches he'd won when he became champion of the games. He knew then that he didn't want another season of fighting on the sands, yet he wasn't ready to separate himself from the terrible excitement of the sport. Owning his own house and training pit fighters seemed an agreeable fit.

At least, back then.

Lately, every season weighed upon his shoulders like the logs the taskmasters commanded the men to lift to put muscle on their legs and shoulders. He no longer enjoyed the company of the fighters, sensing an odorless poison clinging to them all in the ultimate tragedy of the games. One wrong move in the Pit could claim the life of any one of them at any moment, and he'd learned that the pain of losing a friend was just as cutting as steel. Faces crowded his memory, a ghostly parade of warriors and their smiling, joking personalities—ironic, given the grim trade they plied—dead or crippled and replaced with new faces, time and time again. Even the daily providing for the men grated on his conscience. The cost of the food for them all kept rising, as well as the price of weapons and armor. Then there was the issue of individual personalities clashing within the ranks—who was the best, the strongest, the fastest, who had the best odds of winning it all… such gurry no longer interested him and secretly taxed his patience. It was all an arduous chore that needed constant managing. The mental toll of handling a group of pit fighters had never occurred to him until he actually had to do it, and by the third year of operation, Gastillo knew he'd had his fill.

He needed to move on to other things.

The question was… what?

He maintained the business aspect of the house with an air of detachment. Mistakes had been made, but he managed to learn from them. He remained frugal with his expenses, repairing weapons and armor where he could instead of forging or purchasing new. If he ever wagered, he did so only on fights with the surest outcome.

With all of that, he'd kept himself out of debt despite the deepening costs associated with ownership. Though he currently believed himself financially sound, it would not take much to cripple his accounts. One bad string of losses, including deaths and lost wagers, would topple the House of Gastillo. And that was merely the foreseeable, for the unknown added further fear and weight to his shoulders. The constant stress made him long to be free of the games.

He needed to get out.

To find something else while he still had time.

While he was still sane.

The metal covering his ruined face felt cold, but he was grateful for the protection it granted. His golden mask hid his growing contempt for the Pit, all within it, and everything associated with it. Some owners eventually eased their mental anguish with wine or firewater or some other alcohol, and it was a wonder Gastillo hadn't taken to drink to alleviate some of that loathing, but he feared the spirits—feared the false confidence the grape gave a man. Furthermore, drinking to excess might release some inner hellion he might be unable to control, one bent on the house's destruction.

As much as he now despised the business, he couldn't allow that.

Control. Willpower. That was his strength now. His mask of gold was a shield, and soon, very soon, Gastillo would escape this hell. He believed he'd figured out a way.

Strangely enough, Nexus might be a part of it.

The notion of considering him as a house owner, an *equal* in the games, was one Gastillo had to force himself to not ridicule. Curge did enough of that himself. Curge was a relic of a much brighter—or darker, depending on whom one spoke to—age of the games, and Gastillo found the man to be a pretentious brute. Nexus, however, was perhaps even more pretentious in believing he could apply his mercantile experience to the Pit, a somewhat different commodity than wine, and bend it to his will. Gastillo's own dismay at the man's audacity was balanced by the fiery exchanges between the two men that shared the viewing box. Curge didn't think Nexus was altogether fit in the head to believe he could master the intricacies of the games from the very beginning. Personal experience was something coin could not buy, despite Nexus's boasting about employing seasoned taskmasters, trainers, and indubitably agents as well.

The fact galling both Gastillo and Curge was that Nexus wasn't doing as badly as either man had hoped. In fact, despite a few initial setbacks, the man wasn't doing too badly at all.

And he was a quick learner.

It all rubbed Gastillo's nerves a little rawer to see a pup in the ways of the games actually make a go of it while he was secretly hoping to escape with a few coins to rub together. Still, Nexus's experience in business matters interested him. Perhaps there was an opportunity afoot that might grant him the freedom he desired. Gastillo stroked his golden chin and mulled. The mask was only a feint, to mislead his opponents into thinking he was a prideful man with extravagant tastes and high expectations—perhaps even an expensive sense of worth.

So far from the truth.

Pride had long deserted him.

All that remained was the desire to get out. Such a longing had to be concealed until the time to leave the games behind—to leave it *all* behind.

And Nexus could very well be the key to his plans.

On the glowing sands below, a figure appeared and meandered toward the main gates. Gastillo recognized the arrogant way about him, how he didn't even bother to keep to the shadows, and mentally sighed. *Prajus*, whose head of white hair came from his first match in the Pit—or so some said—when a near brush with death leached all the color from his face and locks. Gastillo didn't know if the story was true or not, as Prajus had entered his house in its fifth year of existence and proved himself by defeating one of the older war dogs on the very ground below. Even then, the way in which he carried himself and the constant smiling all hinted at his true character, all misread and dismissed by Gastillo's own lying judgment. At the time, he thought the hellpup would bring riches to the house—thought the man could even be champion one day.

If time could be reversed, if moments could be relived, Gastillo would have never taken the proud bastard into the fold.

The pit fighter stopped and looked about, sensing him. He turned around and soon straightened.

"Ah, I saw the torchlight reflect off your mask, there." Prajus held his hips and regarded Gastillo high above. "You're a quiet one, I'll give you that."

"My thanks," Gastillo returned, bristling at the insult in the lout's failure to address him as *master*. "Now, get back to your quarters. Unless you're thinking about stealing away to some tavern the moment I'm out of sight. And getting into another worthless fight with the locals."

"The thought had crossed my mind, Gastillo."

"*Master* Gastillo, you discourteous dog blossom."

"Ah yes, Master Gastillo." But the owner could sense the curl of a smirk on the man's features. "Deepest apologies, as always."

"If you kept it in mind the first time, you wouldn't have to be so apologetic."

"Ah, yes, I'll do that. Keep it in mind, that is," Prajus said in a frivolous tone that suggested he would do no such thing.

The man kept getting under Gastillo's skin.

"Really, Prajus. Are you truly willing to chance coming back battered and bruised like last time? Just for a night of carousing in the alehouses and taverns and back alleys? Perhaps even risking the whole season?"

Standing on the training sands, Prajus shrugged. "I was, actually."

Gastillo felt the heat rise to his voice, but he clamped down on it. He'd already reprimanded Prajus and his youthful gang the morning they'd lined up for drills. His trainer Pius had first discovered the dull, angry blooms on their face from the night's battle. Just the memory of that heated exchange set the owner on edge. Prajus had set himself apart from his pack as he was the only one that actually had the plums to face Gastillo with the barest smile. Neither he nor any of his three followers had given any apology for their actions, electing to take their punishment in hard training and sweat.

Insolent *bastards*.

Gastillo knew he was to blame. If he had properly disciplined the four right there and then, perhaps he might have restored some measure of respect. The problem was he didn't want to risk harming his best investment. Worse still, instead of making amends, Prajus *continued* testing Gastillo's authority, edging so very close to a very deadly line.

"Go back to your quarters lest you tempt me to double the guard."

"That *might* keep me in."

Gastillo took a steadying breath. Though his mask held the same fixed expression, underneath that golden face, his mangled lips twisted with anger.

"Don't challenge me," he warned. "Else I'll inform Pius to make your exercise hellish in the morning."

"Well, I'd better get out of sight then. I wouldn't want to trouble the taskmaster with that. Or any of the trainers for that matter. Not after the first bout of hellish exercise. The effort might kill them, and where would we be then?"

Another jab, and though drool slid over his chin, Gastillo had to admit the threat wasn't very threatening in the least. Prajus simply knew his worth, and any punishment ran a risk to the owner. Even imprisonment struck Gastillo as useless, as he needed the pit fighter sharp. A day or two confined in a cell struck him as a joke, and anything longer would dull the pit fighter's skills. The realization made the owner's blood boil.

"Get back to your barracks," Gastillo ordered dismissively.

Yet Prajus didn't move.

"Well?"

"Well what?" the pit fighter asked.

"Get out of my sight!" Gastillo barked.

A knowing grin crept into Prajus's face, brightening the shadows. "Calm yourself, Gastillo. Calm yourself. Any louder and you'll rouse everyone to the training area. Not that I mind. Or care."

"You'll care if I cast you out," Gastillo said and hated himself the instant the words became sound.

Below, a smiling Prajus regarded him, unconcerned, not worried in the least. Gastillo realized then that the man was actually baiting him to say something more. *Anything.*

"Oh, you might," Prajus finally said. "And I wouldn't blame you in the least, *Master* Gastillo. But you might wait until the season is over before doing anything of the sort. Or at least until I'm eliminated from competition. I…

don't think you'll do anything, truth be known. I'm worth too much for you to lose."

There it was. Gastillo fumed. "You value yourself too highly."

"Do I?"

"Get moving, he-bitch."

But the young pit fighter didn't.

"Prajus, by Dying Seddon above, get moving, else in the morning you find yourself in chains."

"Chains?"

"Yes, chains."

"Chains." Prajus reflected on the words, his smile fading, though not in fear but rather feigned contemplation. "Well, then. That *is* a threat."

The pit fighter made a show of realizing what he'd done, chastised himself with a slap to the forehead, and marched back to the general quarters where the other twenty-nine fighters slept. Poisoned with anger, Gastillo watched him go. He was far too reluctant to follow through on any of his threats. Only when Prajus was finally gone from sight did Gastillo feel for a hand cloth to dab at his skin.

Insolent prick, the owner cursed and rued the day he had admitted the man into his house. Curge would have handled it differently, beating Prajus within a finger of his life and throwing him out anyway as an example to all others. It wasn't Gastillo's way to do such a thing, and in that admission, he realized another reason to leave the games behind.

He no longer had the stomach to instill fear where needed. He no longer wished to instill fear.

Prajus *needed* to be fearful. He'd *have* to be brought into line. But even as Gastillo thought it, he felt powerless to impart any severe punishment.

Weak—he'd become weak.

Having had enough of the night air, Gastillo turned about and went inside his private house, pulling off his mask and allowing the air to cool his disfigured face. The need for strong drink drove him to seek out a bottle of wine from the kitchen's cellar. All the while, he replayed the night's confrontation with the younger gladiator and burned for a different outcome.

He retrieved two bottles from the cellar and didn't bother with a cup. On his walk back to his private chambers, a figure stood waiting in the main foyer. A pair of flickering torches revealed the visitor to be of medium height, a few years older, and dressed reasonably well in expensive robes made of fine, flowing material that swished off the fitted stones when he walked. Gastillo knew the man enjoyed that sound very much.

"Master Gastillo."

"Varno," Gastillo returned, appreciating the use of his title. He didn't worry if the older agent saw him without his mask. Varno had been a pit fighter alongside Gastillo in their respective careers on the sands and remained one of the few people he considered friends. Despite having fought in the Pit for an amount of time rivaling Gastillo's, Varno had managed to keep an almost perfect set of teeth in his head, a feat which he was quite proud of.

"How are you this evening?" Varno inquired.

"Well, thank you." Gastillo released a heavy sigh and raised one bottle. "Care to have a bit?"

Varno considered it. "I would, thank you."

"I'll fetch another cup."

Gastillo went back into the kitchen and did just that. When he came back, his old friend hadn't moved. Handing over one of the bottles, Gastillo took a torch from its bracket and gestured for the agent to follow him though a darkened doorway. Inside, the unmasked owner lit two fat candles on his desk. Varno took the torch from him and returned it to the foyer. He reappeared a moment later and sat in a wicker chair opposite his employer. The agent gratefully accepted the offered drink.

"Your health," Varno toasted and drank. Gastillo drained his own and refilled his cup.

"I have some news this night," Varno said, smacking his lips.

"Really? What?"

"There's a new house formed."

"Oh, really?"

"Of Free Trained fighters."

That made Gastillo scowl with disbelief.

"The one called Halm of Zhiberia is a part of it," Varno continued. "Seems that while he wasn't so enthused with our offer, he was more than willing to throw in with the new house."

Gastillo shook his head. "He can do whatever he likes, for all I care. If it was Curge he'd refused, he'd have been sliced up and left in a shite trough."

"You are far too lenient at times."

"Don't start on that, Varno. I do what I do to sleep at night. If that Zhiberian thinks he has a better chance at success in the Pit by siding with more of his own kind, so be it. I've not lost sight of the fact it's still only sport."

"Not all share those sentiments."

Exasperated, Gastillo fluttered a hand to move the conversation to another topic.

"The head of the house is Goll of Kree. He was the one who slew Baylus the Butcher on the first day of the season."

That information arched Gastillo's brow. "Ambitious, isn't he? What's the name of the house?"

"They call themselves the House of Ten."

Gastillo poured more wine into himself and dabbed a cloth at his lips before any spilled. "Why's that now? Only ten of them?"

"You are correct."

"Well." The chair's fibers creaked as Gastillo leaned back. "A new house. I imagine that's the talk of the city this evening."

"It is." Varno took another sip and savored it. "Your instructions?"

"You have the names of their fighters?"

"Not yet, but I will."

"Then do that. Keep me informed of their doings. You can use that information to barter with others. Otherwise…" Prajus's smirk suddenly appeared in his mind. Gastillo sighed at the memory.

"My thanks."

5

Nordish Front

Wrinkled columns of trees thus far untouched by an axe held up a latticed roof of leaves, issuing rays of dawning light across panes of shadow. Dead forest debris littered the path, the air redolent with its subtle spice. Bare rock poked through the rotting vegetation like the hard noses of subterranean beasts. The terrain was a series of rolling hills, though the path in that part of the forest was flat and easy to run upon. Thin streams grooved the land in places, made dark from the slow shoving match of sun and shade.

These features made it an ideal escape route.

"Run, you bastards, run," hissed First Basten Kra in the Nordish tongue, urging his Jackals to move faster as they pounded over the earth. They had struck the Sunjan Third Klaw just before dawn, ripped its nose from its face, and quickly retreated in the ensuing chaos of burning tents, screaming horses, and dying men. This particular party had only lost six of the original fifty they started out with, acceptable losses given the destruction they'd wrought. Their mission was only to terrorize the Klaw, unhinge it, and if the enemy took the bait, lead them back to the waiting Grinders.

It was just their unfortunate luck that last night's work had taken them far beyond their accompanying Nordish heavy soldiers.

Once the Sunjans had recovered from the attack, they sent their lancers to hunt down the enemy.

And the horsemen had discovered the Jackals' trail faster than expected.

"*Skolla!*" Kra cursed as his soft-soled boots thumped over the terrain, rattling his knees and lower back. Like the men he commanded, he wore a light cuirass cut from leather and stitched to an undershirt of padded cloth. Bracers and greaves of more hardened leather protected their limbs, and metal rings scaled every piece of armor. Nordish armorers prided themselves on their work, producing a hide both tough and quiet. Kra wore no helm, but a black cloth mask covered his entire head, with only a narrow cut for the eyes. Sweat ran down his face, soaking the material and making it stick to his flesh. His scabbarded shortsword slapped against his thigh while he swung his rounded buckler. He'd left his spear in the chest of a Sujin ball licker. Those under his command wielded various weapons—swords, maces, axes—all chosen by the individual rather than standard issue. The Jackals, the *true* Jackals, weren't frontline warriors.

They were terrorizers.

And in their eyes, they were the sharpest and most feared blade in the night-borne army of the Ivus, their Nordish ruler.

HOUSE OF PAIN

This time, however, the hunters had their scent.

First Basten Kra held up his hand just before exhaustion claimed him, bringing the whole pack to a halt. He stopped and gripped his knees for breath. Around him, his men stopped running and dropped to drink at a brook running nearby. Their retreat had been a steady run through Sunjan timberland with the heat steaming the energy from their lean forms. Kra rolled up his black mask, knelt, and drank as well, careful not to overfill his stomach. He'd do that behind friendly lines. Once finished, the officer stood up with water dripping from his chin and surveyed his remaining Jackals—dull leather backs crossed with scabbards and weapons colored to disappear in the dark. Menace emanated from the lot.

Some of the masked men looked at him, but he paid them no heed, concentrating on listening.

Nothing.

Not a single note of pursuit.

The lancers hunted them still, however; of that he was certain. He'd seen their line from a hilltop, snaking their way through the ageless halls of the forest and appearing like a lengthy dragon unleashed. He wasn't afraid of the lancers. Kra wasn't afraid of *anything* in the Sunjan's armies. But he had to admit being captured after a hard strike at night would not be healthy.

All around, his men rose from the banks of the stream, listening, waiting, regaining their strength like a sinister cadre of ghosts. No one uttered a word. He recognized the wet beard of Arrus, his mask partially rolled up so he could drink. Next to him was Dogslaw, already pulling his mask down. Kestmir tucked away his thick beard soaked with water and sweat, paying heed to the silence and rising to his feet.

Then Kra heard it, like catching the barest scent on a breeze, distant but distinct.

A horn.

"We go," he commanded and broke into a jog, not needing to tell his men to pace themselves. Like a gathering of wolves, they bolted.

The haunting wail of a hunting horn lacerated the early-morning sleepiness of the forest. Nordish shadows bounded past thick trunks of wood and leapt over mossy rocks, their movements made less magical by the growing strength of the sun. The higher it rose, the greater was the Nordish Jackals' unease about being seen. Though they feared little, they felt most powerful in the deepest night. Kra glanced over his shoulder at times, scanning the country for pursuers. Every bellowing blast of the horn made him cringe, and he struggled to pace himself. Trees sped by. Sunlight flickered and flashed. The subtle rattling of weapons and rush of men on the run filled his ears. A hill rose ahead, and they clambered up its forested slope. At its highest point, Kra paused amongst boughs and gazed back while urging his men to scramble by without him.

There. Sunlight bounced off metal, nearly concealed by the brush. A serpentine line of lancers pushed into view, winding its way over the terrain, sniffing through the forest growth and sensing their quarry close. Kra clenched his jaw. They were far more numerous than his company. The hunting horn yowled yet again, this time sounding frighteningly clear.

Before that carrying note died, Kra turned and disappeared into the trees. Another telling blast of the horn stabbed the air, followed immediately by more, raising Kra's hackles and urging him to move faster. The

Sunjans had found their scent and, worse, actually spotted them. The Nordish officer caught up to the rear of his pack and passed them, slipping in and around trees with a ghost's grace. No one had pulled steel yet, which gave Kra a grim sense of pride. Panic hadn't touched his lads yet.

Shouts in the Sunjan tongue rolled up the slopes behind them, the undisguised eagerness in their voices easily understood. One bawled out over the others; Kra believed it was the lancer commander. The man probably thought victory was his just by spotting the retreating Jackals. Kra didn't know where the Sunjans purchased their arrogance, but the Nordish knew their enemies spent heavy coin on a cheap commodity.

But where were the Grinders? The question flashed in the officer's mind, and he anxiously scanned the woods ahead for the grim, heavier-armored soldiers of the Nordish Ikull. They would deal with the lancers eagerly.

The Jackals peaked the hill, raced across a flat stretch of woodland, and splashed through another stream until… there! Kra's spirits leaped as the ominous line of Grinders came into view, their conical helms peeking above door-sized, rectangular shields. They had positioned themselves on an uneven slope, between barrel-thick tree trunks, but caught sight of the approaching Jackals. Shouts cut the air, and the Grinders shifted, opening slots in their defensive formation, allowing the retreating Jackals to slip through. More shouts and a slight trembling in the earth as the lancers behind them struggled up the last incline. Kra followed his men up the short slope and into the porous line. Once the Jackals were through, a single command closed the gaps as stoutly as heavy doors being slammed shut.

Then, the Grinders waited with deadly patience.

Kra turned around and peered over the menacing armored plates and spiked shoulders of the heavy Nordish warriors, straining to see the pursuing enemy. The Grinders were selected not on skill but rather on size, and all were fingers taller than the Jackal first basten. Through the trees and at the far end of the wooded area, horses prepared for war trotted to an impatient stop. Their riders milled about and mulled, seeing their enemy's prickly position. The slope rendered a charge ineffective, and the lancer commander seemed hesitant to engage a foe whose numbers commanded high ground.

Even worse, the numbers had unexpectedly doubled.

"That's right, you stupid shite-swilling bastards." A Grinder hissed, his voice made metallic by his helm's grinning visor. "That's right. The run stops here."

"Come on, then," growled another and rolled the spiked pauldrons protecting his shoulders. "Show some balls and have them handed back."

"Them bastards have been chasing us for most of the morning," Kra said to no one in particular.

"And now they've caught us," said one of the Grinders. "Bled the fight right out of them. Look at them prance. No idea what to do now. Typical. How haven't we won this thing sooner?"

"Been years, certainly," muttered another.

"Shaddup," one Grinder lashed out, silencing the wall as he appeared around a tree and walked down the battle line. The basten warily glanced at Kra before dividing his attention between his own men and the lancers beyond. The Grinder officer carried no shield, but a huge mailed fist choked the grip of a bared broadsword gleaming in the forest light.

"Where's your first basten?" the Grinder officer

demanded of the nearest Jackals. Kra stepped forward.

"You were a bit late this time around."

"You moved your men back," Kra countered.

"Had to. Wasn't comfortable on the lowlands, so I found a place where bastards like them wouldn't dare charge. Found this ridge. Wasn't hard to find us, was it?"

"Not hard, but I'd be lying if I said my blossom didn't pucker when I heard those hunting horns."

The Grinder basten directed his attention to the lancers, still mulling about in the distance. Then, perhaps coming to the conclusion it was better to face the wrath of their superiors, the enemy reined in and sullenly retreated, showing the Nordish their backs before disappearing into the murky woods.

"Smart," the Grinder basten commented. "It's good fortune to kill smart officers. How went things?"

"Good," Kra replied. "Very good."

"Excellent."

"We should get moving."

The Grinder studied the Jackal for a moment. "Who says you Jackals are only good at stabbing things in the dark?"

"The dead," Kra answered.

The Grinder did not argue.

In two columns, the combined groups of almost a hundred men marched back through the forested lowlands, stretching the distance between themselves and the Sunjan encampment. They pressed on for a day until they reached a meeting point amongst wooded hills. There they connected with two more ambush parties composed of both Jackals and Grinders. The Jackals of those groups had rained down a firestorm of arrows on the Sunjan Klaw from another direction, distracting the Sujins long enough for Kra's and another basten's company to drive into their enemies' flanks, leave steel in the Sunjans' bones, and quickly withdraw and scatter before a counter could be organized.

As a first basten and commanding officer, Kra consulted with his Grinder equivalent, and both men gathered their junior officers, peeling off helmets and masks that rendered one man indistinguishable from the next. Part of the malefic aura surrounding the Jackals was the covering of their faces, be it in black cloth or metal—a shedding of their humanity and a becoming of something more. Over the years, the Jackals had earned a fearsome, almost ghoulish reputation for their deeds done at night. Masks off, they were men like any other. Masks on, they became Jackals, exuding monstrous unease and capacity for violence.

Kra had to admit, when he wore his own mask, he felt more like a hellion than a man.

Listening to reports, the first basten learned that his company had been the fortunate ones as the other group of attacking Jackals, the ones targeting the right flank, had encountered a handful of Sunjan Cavaliers. Those highly skilled warriors possessed their own bloody reputation amongst the Nordish, and Cavaliers, *experienced* Cavaliers, were viewed as prized trophies. Kra couldn't think of anyone who wouldn't rise to challenge one of those formidable swordsmen, for their scalps were treasured as much as gold. He knew several Nordish who had sought them out on a battlefield. Most of those same men had perished in the encounter. The only reason Sunja hadn't turned the tides in this aging war was because they didn't have more of those reavers.

The Cavaliers were Sunja's best and were rarely found lacking. As good as they were, however, their numbers were dwindling. One by one.

The first bastens stoically accepted that one pack of Jackals, the group of fifty attacking the Klaw's right flank, had been decimated to seven. Their commanding officer wasn't amongst the survivors.

"Well," grunted Vilak, a towering hulk of a man. He regarded Kra. "Looks like the right flank goes untouched next time."

"Next time, my men and I will do the stabbing," said Jalmar, a lower basten whose Jackals had unleashed fire arrows upon the Sunjan Klaw. He focused on Kra as he put forth the request. "As you promised."

Vilak scowled at the officer's impudence. Kra knew what bothered the Grinder. Vilak had previously made his thoughts known in confidence that he believed Kra was too accommodating with his underlings, something the Jackal commander never suspected until it was pointed out to him. Kra actually respected the menacing Vilak, whose brick of a skull contained not only a brain but a sharp wit as well, unlike some other officers. The Grinder had repeatedly proved his worth on the field.

"No," Kra said firmly, remembering the conversation with the Jackal basten. "You lads punished the enemy the other night. You'll do so again."

Jalmar's jawline clenched in disappointment.

"We'll rest tonight," Kra announced, "but in the morning we'll circle about and see if we can't find this Klaw again. And we'll stab its right flank once more. They'll probably be thinking we won't go at either flank, but we will. I'll take those seven survivors with me. Jalmar and his dogs will light up the night sky with arrows as before, just before we strike. First Basten," he directed at Vilak. "Would you be so good as to follow along, set up a line at a mutually-decided-upon point and then, perhaps, *stay* there? We'd all feel better about it."

Vilak smirked, his eyes flashing a warning. "You whine, Jackal. I'll see what I can do."

"Very much appreciated."

"If you don't come back, we'll come looking."

Kra knew the Grinder would do just that.

"Anything else?" he asked the gathered officers. No one spoke, not even Vilak.

"Good. Then rest. Tomorrow, we go back into hell."

With that, the men dispersed. Kra expected Jalmar to protest his role in the next engagement, but the man kept his tongue and moved off. That pleased the Jackal commander, and he meandered through the woods where they had established camp. Nordun's Ikull—the main army—remained weeks away from the Klaws, but it was their task, as a smaller striking force, to inflict as much damage as possible on the enemy before rejoining the advancing Nords. Losses would be high. In fact, his commanders had informed him it could very well be a death march, but he accepted the mission regardless. In his mind, only the careless or unlucky got killed. He wasn't careless, and as of this day, he wasn't unlucky either.

The majority of the Grinders had stripped off their heavy armor and laid aside their smiling helms. The Ikull's heavy infantry stayed with their own, rumbling at each other in low, guarded voices, like heavyset bears huddling around a corpse. The smaller, leaner Jackals kept their own company, though all remained in their leather vests and bracers. Kra nodded at those he recognized, and when a small circle beckoned, he joined them.

"First Basten," Kestimir greeted cordially. "Something to eat?"

"Bit of rabbit?" Kra asked, inspecting the pot in the middle.

"Grinders caught them," Lokan smiled, sporting an ugly scar that ran uninterrupted across his face. His eyes glittered at his companions. "Nice to know they were minding the kitchen."

Kra declined with a shake of his head. "I'll eat later."

"I hear we head out again at dawn? Is that right?" asked a man with a beard so thick it appeared as if his mouth barely moved.

"At dawn. Back into the chop."

"Heard there were losses on the right," another commented.

"There were losses," Kra admitted. "Met Cavaliers. Nothing's certain with them."

"Nothing," Kestimir agreed thoughtfully and considered the leg of rabbit he held.

"We'll take the survivors, make up for the few we lost."

"And tomorrow?" Lokan asked.

"Tomorrow, we hunt the same Klaw. And this time, when we bite, we shake it until a chunk rips free, just to remind the Sunjan *poltues* who owns them in the night."

Grim faces nodded at Kra's words, igniting a rush of deadly pride within his chest. The Nordish weren't overly talkative when at war. They'd learned long ago the best talking was left behind in the smoke and ashes of the conquered. Kra wasn't sure if the years had done that to them or if they were just naturally vicious as a people. He got confused at times. He'd been at war for so long, he sometimes had to sit and think about what he'd left behind in his homeland. On the front, conversations were curt and spiced with cruel humor. He'd perhaps said more in the last little while than he had in the past week, and he felt strangely unused to ordinary conversation. When Nordish spoke, points were made quickly, and people listened.

"They took near fifty of ours… but we'll take thrice of theirs," Kra said, staring into the boiling pot, his Jackals leaning in and absorbing every word.

"And leave the rest pissing ice."

6

The dawn sky blazed a golden hue over the city's dusty battlements. Peddlers and merchants roused themselves and prepared their wares for another day while early risers trickled from doorways into the larger streets. The sun burned away the shadows, scouring the side streets and back alleys, and touched the planks of a cellar door. Boot steps sounded from underneath, stopping just below. Fingers scrabbled upon the wood, and the slab lifted just a crack. The presence beneath considered the empty alley and approved. Borchus pushed the door up with his shoulders, freeing himself from the earthy-smelling cellar. It wasn't the most comfortable of places to rest for the night, but it was safe, and in his business, one took precautions.

The sun warming his bare, muscular arms, the agent closed the cellar door and inspected his clothing for a moment—brown vest over a sleeveless white tunic, freshly cleaned, and gray trousers. He eyed his leather boots, decided he might have to replace them soon, and bent over to give a quick brushing to the toes. The owners of the house, whose cellar he'd paid coin to sleep in, were cobblers and dealt in leather boots and sandals. The quality wasn't the best, but then, Borchus didn't need the best, didn't want the attention that came with wearing finery of any sort. He felt his long sideburns and then the stubble of his chin. He wasn't sure if he'd allow his beard to grow back. It had been a time since he'd had one, and the weather was particularly hot that year.

The extra growth would be helpful in concealing his face, though not from the more astute watchers. And not the ones with long memories.

Borchus sighed contentedly. Though there were elements in the city that harbored grudges against him, it still felt good doing what he did best—gathering information.

The dull heat made him glance at the cloudless morning sky, and he caught the blinding edge of the rising sun. There was much to be done—spies to contact, networks to be arranged—and the very thought of it split his face with a wry smile. Some would be interested in seeing him alive while others would not, and others still would take every opportunity to even old scores in the most painful manner available. The thought of sidestepping and evading those particular efforts thrilled him. Borchus lived for his work, his true talent, and the dangers attached were only stony avenues to be mindful of and avoided where possible. The idea of arranging protection struck him, at least for the duration of the season. And a month beyond. Just in case.

He walked near soundlessly over the cut stones of the alley before connecting with the larger street. A short stop at a cook's open stall and fire pit provided him with a small breakfast of warm bread with honey butter and a fistful of hard-boiled eggs. He ate the bread and the eggs while standing in the street, facing the old cook while studying passersby in his side vision. Once finished, he bought more food and got on his way, merging with a thickening stream of people. A sense of secrecy filled him. Just the day before, he had been one of them, but as of that day, he was something more, and no one suspected a thing. He thought of the first man he had to see and altered his course toward the west end of Sunja, toward the arena and some of the lesser gladiator houses.

It took him half the morning to find the man, but he eventually spotted him sitting in the shade of a thin alley, miserably squinting at the passersby and holding out his shaking hand—an old ghost who haunted an avoided corner. Silver laced his shabby beard and a frightening mess of hair, but it drew attention away from the stained rags that passed as clothing. His face appeared harsher than it had the last time Borchus spoke to him. Someone tossed the beggar a coin, and he bared a horrible grimace of teeth.

Borchus rubbed his face, questioning himself if he should actually talk with his old acquaintance. The years hadn't been kind to him at all. Then again, the years hadn't been kind to Borchus either.

Gathering himself, the blocky agent meandered over to the man begging on the street. Borchus came within three strides of him before the smell of dried sweat, urine, and another unspeakable fragrance stopped him cold in his tracks. He suspected stomach juice. Holding his nose briefly, Borchus edged closer to the unfortunate soul, who was reaching in another direction.

"Greetings, Garl."

Garl's filthy face jerked around and looked up, sunlight causing his face to snarl for a heartbeat before slackening with recognition.

"Borchus?"

"Aye."

"You... shaved."

"Just a bit," Borchus smirked in good humor. "I'm in disguise."

Garl blinked and studied him from head to toe. Borchus kept his own eyes on the beggar's face and not the place where half the man's right leg should have been.

"Borchus." Garl exhaled, his features shaking ever so slightly in wonder. "I wouldn't have recognized you except... for your voice. And that's changed a bit as well. Haven't seen or heard tell of you in years."

"Not since I gave the business up."

Garl cocked his head with horrific realization. "Is that what you tell yourself?"

"I do."

"Well, doesn't look to have hurt you any."

"May I?"

Garl remembered his manners despite conversing in an alleyway and gestured for Borchus to sit, which he did, placing his back against the opposite building. The agent shifted for a bit until comfortable, mindful of the dust-caked rags masking the stump of the beggar's hacked-off limb.

Dark circles ringed the flesh underneath Garl's ogling eyes, and he scratched at his nose with a hand missing the last two fingers.

When Borchus settled down, a frown stole over his features. "You don't look so well."

Garl inspected himself, shrugging as if realizing for the first time how deplorable he appeared. "Been a hard few years. Seems like… only a couple of weeks. Really."

"But you managed to stay alive."

Another shrug. "Always managed to do that. Haven't decided if it's a blessing or a curse yet. The city keeps me alive, mostly. Her people. Their scraps."

Garl gestured to the thickening throngs passing before them at not quite an arm's length. Borchus diverted his attention to the people before the smell emanating from the beggar finally overcame him. He covered his mouth and nose with a hand.

"Apologies," Garl muttered sincerely and scratched at himself. "Haven't bathed just today."

"This year, I wager."

The bearded features drooped in embarrassment, and Borchus scolded himself for the jab. He remembered this man was far more sensitive than any other person he knew.

"Garl, I'm going to gather a new network."

"What?" His eyes, haunting and gray, suddenly became attentive. Borchus wondered how unfit the man's mind might have become after all the years living as a parasite.

"I'm going to start another network. I need men I can trust. That's why I came here this day."

"Why didn't you see me any other day?"

"I've been… busy," Borchus lied. Truth be known, survival was singular, and he had been doing the same, in other parts of the country or its neighbors. Regardless, in the end, he still remembered his henchman, which should have counted for something.

"Busy?"

Borchus nodded, trying hard not to comment on how

aggressively Garl clawed at his chest, his beard, or his armpits. The agent hoped Garl didn't scratch at his kog and bells with such force.

Garl's eyes flickered to the street then back to Borchus, like a wild animal debating if it should flee or not.

"You want me to watch and listen again?"

"Aye."

"I don't… understand, Borchus. Look here." With that he slapped at the empty space where his leg would've been. "And this." The hand with the missing fingers flashed up as if about to summon rain. "I didn't do this to myself."

Borchus set his jaw. "But I wasn't responsible for any of that."

"I was working for you when they took my fingers."

"You were, but I didn't take your leg. The arena took that. Nor did I take your fingers."

"Or break my ribs? Or my jaw? For a month, I was breathing shards of bone. Every meal was a taste of Saimon's hell. And one bad twist in the night, and I could've speared my own heart with a splintered end. I had to… I had to pinch my *food* into a pulp and swallow it down without chewing. I had to—"

"I didn't do any of that."

"But I was working for *you* when they did it."

"You were."

"They were *looking* for you. And I told them nothing."

So you said, Borchus thought but murmured, "I know."

"And you still came back. Here."

"I didn't forget you, Garl. I… knew you'd be needing help. Needing work. If you're agreeable, if you think you can manage the old job."

"Oh, aye that, I can do it," he quipped. "Who would

suspect me in this condition?"

"No one, really. Which is why you're perfect."

Garl shook his head in disbelief. "You're serious? After this? And after all these years?"

Borchus found himself at a loss for what to say. While he was most adept at scorching bridges to their moorings, he discovered mending them was a chore altogether different. He simply wasn't used to it.

"Here," Borchus fumbled in his pocket and held out a fist.

"What's that?" Garl asked guardedly, scratching at his throat.

"It's coin."

"I can't take that."

"Certainly you can."

"No, I can't. I'm not here asking for coin; I'm asking for table scraps: peels of fruit, bread crusts, half-eaten slivers of meat. Sometimes I'll get a coin or two of silver, but I don't keep them. If the others see it, they'll beat it from me."

"What others?"

Garl regarded him as if he were a dead man talking. Then the beggar leaned in close, making Borchus flinch away just a finger's width before he could recover.

"The streets are a merciless place, Borchus," Garl hissed. "You know that. But it's only when you have your ass cheeks dragging on the stone when you *really* see how merciless."

"What are you talking about? Thieves?"

Garl nodded, his eyes darting furtively left and right.

Borchus's fist trembled for a moment before he withdrew it, following the beggar's gaze and suddenly feeling watched. "You show me these men, and I'll make sure they won't do it again."

"You can't do that, you idiot."

"Why not?"

Garl's eyes almost bulged out of his hairy skull. "You're going to sit about with me while I find things out? Hm? I don't think so. The moment you're gone, they'll be on me. Either today or tomorrow, or the very instant you're out of sight."

"Garl, if you agree to this, I'll see to it no one hurts you ever again."

"And if they do?"

"If they do, just give me a name. Or point out a face. I'll make certain they suffer for it."

The great rotten beard festering about the beggar's throat trembled, and the man's eyes watered. "You... you don't know..."

"You're right, I don't know, *but*," Borchus paused to steady himself, "but if you come back, I'll... look after you. Until things are better, at least."

Garl's big gray eyes blinked as he mulled it over. "Your word?"

"My word—and Seddon above, I can't talk anymore without tasting that stink coming off you."

The words came out faster and with more poison than Borchus had intended, and they struck the beggar hard. The light in Garl's eyes went out, and he sat dejectedly and scratched at his belly, not meeting the other's gaze.

"Apologies," the man whispered.

That one word almost made Borchus get up and march off. He didn't need to feel guilty over Garl. He wasn't the pit fighter who took the man's leg, and he wasn't the brutes who tortured him for information on his whereabouts years ago. And he *certainly* didn't need the memories of some very dark years in his own life, when he'd been a different person. Studying the broken wretch before him, he couldn't help but notice the scalding, disapproving expressions of passersby or, even worse, the quick glances away, as if they didn't exist in the first place. Those looks shifted emotions around inside Borchus like broken bones being reset. Painful memories surfaced, of things done and left undone, and part of the agent wondered if perhaps he *was* responsible for some of what happened to Garl, just from association alone. The thought provided him with more than he wanted to remember and more than he wanted to admit.

Borchus climbed to his feet and dusted himself off. "Let's talk some more about this. In a bathhouse."

"A what?"

"A bathhouse."

"The public ones?"

"Are there others?" Borchus stood with his hands on his hips.

"I can't go there!"

"What gurry is that?"

"Look at me."

"Oh, I've been looking."

"They'll never let me in."

"They will with me about."

"What?"

"How do you get around?"

With some uncertainty and a little indignity, Garl reached behind himself and pulled out a pair of crude crutches, each made of two pieces of wood nailed together to create a T. Borchus remembered Goll's walking aid but these, it occurred to him, seemed more like weapons. *The streets are a merciless place.* Garl struggled to his feet, using one length of wood and the wall behind him. Borchus made no move to help, and Garl didn't ask for any, which pleased the agent. Finally standing, though leaning on the crutches, the beggar was still several fingers taller than the shorter man.

"A bit rough, but it serves the purpose," the beggar said of his walking aids.

"I'll walk slowly," Borchus commented.

"You still think you're going to get me into a bathhouse?"

"I'm past thinking. You want to stay like this?"

A pause, then a weak, almost ashamed, "No."

"Then have some push and follow me. I'll show you some magic."

He started walking. When he glanced over his shoulder, he saw that Garl wasn't there. The ratty beggar lingered in the mouth of the alley, flies buzzing around his frame, his eyes wide, as if expecting to be struck down the moment he left the safety of the narrow passage.

Borchus returned. "What's wrong?"

"I'd rather…"

"Rather what?"

"Rather we take the alleys."

"The alleys? Why?"

Garl scalded him with a look. "The alleys, or I'm staying here."

The request wasn't an outrageous one, for whatever reason it was put forth, so Borchus agreed while screwing up his face at the stink radiating from the once-spy.

"You know the way through that maze?"

"Have you forgotten?"

"No, but I haven't travelled them recently."

Without saying another word, Garl backed up into the

alley, turned himself around, and skipped away in a practiced gait. Borchus had to hurry to keep up.

They entered a maze of houses and buildings constructed of white and red stone and heavy timbers and wired together overhead by lines of hanging laundry. At times, smells of baking bread or scrub water either tantalized them or wrinkled their noses. Children playing in the narrow alleys stopped and watch them pass with guarded eyes, only to brighten when the strangers had passed. Their journey took them through old husks of deserted houses; one in particular had a collapsed roof, and both men had to crawl under wooden beams to carry on to the other side. A little later in the morning, they emerged from the puzzle of paths and arrived at the brick bulk of Sunja's public bathhouse. It required crossing a main street to enter the place, and Borchus had to coax a clearly uncomfortable Garl to proceed to the entrance. The arched doorway, while closed, leaked curls of white snakes into the air. Windows opened just a crack vented thick coils of steam. Though the morning heat continued to rise, both men felt the tepid moisture radiating from the building.

They stopped at the arched door, and Borchus addressed Garl. "Stay here a moment."

"They won't let me in there. This is madness."

"They will after I talk with them."

"I look like the scorched underside of a cow kiss."

Borchus badly wanted to agree with that sentiment but held his tongue, knowing Garl would wither and bolt upon hearing it, and the agent had no desire to chase after a one-legged man swinging along on crutches and smelling of shite.

The agent opened the door and released a cloud into

the street. He stuck his head in and called out. Words were exchanged, and after a moment, Borchus leaned back out. A clean-shaven attendant of the baths appeared and balked in horror upon seeing the chore ahead of him.

"You're not serious, are you?" the middle-aged man asked.

A self-conscious Garl scratched at his beard and appeared desperately close to fleeing.

"What do you mean?" a vexed Borchus declared, sizing up his companion. "The man needs to be cleaned. You're in the business of cleaning people. I don't see the trouble. Think of it as a challenge."

"But he's—" The attendant never finished the thought as Borchus immediately glared at him.

"You'll pay for this," the attendant warned the agent, who rolled his eyes.

"Of course I will."

"We can't have him in here like that. Follow the wall and go around back. I'll meet you back there."

The man retreated inside, closing the door as he went and leaving the pair in the street.

"Come on, then," Borchus ordered Garl. They wound their way around the brown brick hide of the bathhouse, leaving the street and following the wall to a smaller, less striking door. It opened, and the attendant appeared with another younger man. The youth disappeared inside once more, and Borchus heard the grating of wood on stone floor.

"What's that?" the agent asked the attendant.

"*That's* the only way we'll allow him in. That is, if you pay now." The older man held up a hand and, in the doorway, a large wooden barrel almost too big to fit through came into sight. The youth's red face lifted above the rim at the rear, struggling with the awkwardness of the container.

"What are you going to do, then?" Borchus wanted to know.

"We'll clean him up before we clean him up."

That made the agent chuckle and rub at his sideburns. "Here." He handed a single gold coin to the attendant, who made it disappear before giving the youth a nod. The younger man rolled the barrel into the alley and, once finished, darted back inside. Two more men came out carrying buckets of water. Steam misted the air as they filled the barrel.

"Step up, then," Borchus said to Garl. The first youth returned with an armful of towels. A yellow cake of soap, a pair of scissors, and a razor lay on top.

Garl suddenly appeared apprehensive. "What's he going to do?"

"I daresay he's going to shave you."

"Don't want to be shaved."

"Oh, but it's entirely necessary," the attendant declared. "Once you've washed and while you're still in the barrel, I'll send for some delousing powder."

Garl scratched in silence, eyeing the men with distrust as they continued filling the bath. One brought out a short ladder and placed it against the wooden ribs.

"Has to be done, I suppose," Borchus muttered.

"Yes, indeed. Very much so," the attendant declared with a concerned expression. "Also, that gold piece only affords you *this* bath. If he wants to go inside, that'll be another coin."

Borchus frowned at that revelation. Generosity, even pity, could be short commodities in Sunja at times. He sized up Garl once more and decided he probably should be thankful. This wasn't going to be a quick dip and scrub.

"And I suggest finding him some new clothes," the attendant observed. "The rags he has on can be dumped on the ground, and I'll dispose of them later."

"There's silver for one of your lads here if he does just that. Two new changes of clothes."

"I'll see to it," the attendant said and peered into the barrel. "You may climb in now," he instructed Garl.

The beggar regarded the raw bath as if it were a hot roast of beef. He swung himself to the ladder and dropped his crutches. He stripped, exposing dirty skin stretched a little too tight over a set of ribs. The points of elbows jutted. His flesh was mottled brown and fish-belly white from where the rags protected him from the sun, blotched with the red bites of countless unseen lice or vermin. Borchus cringed inwardly when Garl dropped his breeches and hop-climbed the ladder. He made a mental note to get some food into his first and oldest spy. *I'm asking for table scraps*, echoed a voice.

Garl didn't need assistance lowering himself into the barrel. His arms and shoulders, while horribly thin, were deceptively strong. He gasped when his lower bits touched the water, his face a grimace pointed heavenward.

"Feels good?" Borchus asked.

"Wonderful," Garl gasped, face alternating between a smile and an uncomfortable rictus, and offered his head for one of the water men to dump a bucket over it.

"Not yet," the attendant said and snipped scissors before offering them. "I suggest you lean over the side while cutting off your beard. Once you've cropped it, one of the lads will assist in shaving the rest."

A suddenly nervous Garl glanced at Borchus. "You'll be about?"

HOUSE OF PAIN

The agent put on a pleasant face despite knowing he should be off. He really *didn't* have time to nursemaid the spy, but one look at Garl informed him that the tortured soul wasn't quite ready to be left alone. Borchus mulled and agreed to stay—because of their shared past and Garl's current condition—though he hated to think word of the morning's activities might spread.

"I'll be right here. Until it's all done."

That pleased the new spy, and he relaxed visibly. Garl leaned back against the lip of the barrel, naked shoulders slumping, and squinted at the glare of the rising sun. The curls of his beard failed to conceal the smile underneath.

7

The morning had been pleasant enough for Goll, despite having to hobble about as if someone had stomped on his foot, but the Kree preferred that to crutches. Concerned about the sounds of people outside the healer's house, he checked on Muluk, but he was still sleeping under the power of Shan's sedative. Seeing the bandaged man's chest rise and fall with regularity, Goll eased his way downstairs and nodded at the others gathered below. He sent Tumber and Sapo off to buy breakfast for the rest of them. With a quick word, he dismissed the three watchmen he hired the night before, informing them to return in the evening. Shan entered through his private door and made his way up to the steps to check on Muluk while Goll sat and waited for the return of the healer and his new pit fighters. Halm was absent, and the Kree surmised the Zhiberian had remained with Pig Knot.

Tumber and Sapo returned after a long while and brought in a feast of warm bread, hard boiled eggs, fruity

HOUSE OF PAIN

jam and butter, and cold slices of beef—well worth the wait. They'd only just finished eating when a hard rap at the door stole their attention, and in walked a snow-bearded Clavellus. The equally bushy eyeful of Machlann followed him, along with the muscular Koba and a handful of guards placing their backs to the door.

"What happened?" Clavellus demanded as he took in everyone crammed into the house's interior. A surprised Shan appeared on the first landing and looked on at the deeply tanned taskmaster and his company.

"Lower your voice," Goll said with a frown. "Muluk is sleeping upstairs."

The taskmaster's eyes, an unnaturally bright blue in contrast to his browned skin, flicked to the stairs and then the ceiling before settling on Goll once again. Clavellus's dark features clouded with a scowl as he strode toward the steps and climbed them with his trainers in tow. They barged past the sitting pit fighters, but Goll got to his feet and hobbled up the stairs after them.

"I know them," the Kree informed Shan before focusing on climbing the stairs.

A concerned Machlann and Clavellus stood on either side of Muluk's prone form, poised like dried-out vultures of war, while a stern Koba leaned against the frame of the open window and peered outside.

"Sweet Seddon," Clavellus breathed and faced the new master. "Who did this?"

"We don't know," Goll answered, as he reached the top of the stairs.

"Where's Borchus?"

"I don't know that either."

Clavellus blinked, and for a moment, Goll thought a great blast of thunder was about to erupt from the older man. The taskmaster remembered Muluk's resting form and defused himself with a sigh that sounded like hot steam escaping a pot. "What *do* you know?"

"I know I'm the head of a new house this day. I know that you're in my employ, and if you wish to remain so, you'll show me a greater degree of respect."

Clavellus's face darkened while Machlann stiffened with offense. At the window, even tall Koba turned around with a scowl of disbelief.

"Other than that," Goll continued on, "I know Muluk killed six men with nary a stitch on him and probably saved our pot of coin we'd kept."

"Who were these six men?"

"No idea."

"Have you set Borchus onto it?"

"I will."

"Borchus sent a runner. The man arrived at my residence last night, and I would've come then except for my wife and Machlann. Too much has gone on since I last saw you, and I grew impatient for you to return. I received news that your house was established, that six strangers butchered a handful of patrons at an alehouse, that Muluk killed the six murderers and damned near died in doing so."

"That's true."

"So you're now a house."

Goll deposited himself on a nearby cot. "I am. We are. The House of Ten. After the attack on the alehouse, it was time for Pig Knot to fight. You and I both know his mettle, so I ordered him to lose, and I wagered on his opponent winning. To ensure I'd get the funds needed to establish the house and any other necessary coin needed. For the short term, anyway. That part was successful, if at a cost of having Pig Knot mauled almost to death."

Clavellus's face did not brighten as Goll had expected. "What did you say? About Pig Knot? You… *ordered* him to lose?"

"I did. It was the surest way of getting the coin I needed."

The taskmaster regarded Goll with a suspicious air, rendering the Kree uneasy though he kept it concealed. Goll glanced from Machlann's drawn features to the taskmaster's. "What?"

Clavellus took a breath. "You didn't know this, as there was no need to know, really, but I'll tell you it now. You remember me warning you about my reputation amongst the houses here? Well, that goes back many, many years, when I was a taskmaster for the House of Curge. It was old Curge that cast me out, made a pariah of me to the games, as I spoke out against him for what he practiced."

He let the words hang in the air until Goll asked. "And?"

"Curge would command his fighters to lose and collect a huge sum in wagers. Wagers, lad, are the lifeblood of the games. You don't hear of it, but fortunes have been made and lost at these games. Make no mistake, coin rules *all*, and Curge made it a point to ensure he got his share of it. He was careful about it, not always setting his own men up to fall, and even going as far as paying off his lads' opponents as well. I didn't know how long he was manipulating the matches behind the curtains, but he let it slip one day while we were on his practice sands, and Machlann and I were training his lads. Neither one of us were pleased with the knowledge that what we were doing was being tossed aside in favor of methods that not only cheapens the sport, but demeans the blood and sweat paid in training sessions. We prepare our men to fight and *win*. We enhance their strengths and improve their weaknesses to that end… not to fall on an owner's whim so that he might profit."

Clavellus locked gazes with Goll. "I made the mistake of becoming angry and confronting Curge right there on his own sands. Thinking back, it's a wonder the old topper allowed me to live at all. But instead, he cast me out and warned all others not to risk employing my services. Back then, most of the houses feared Curge's wrath and rightly so, I suppose. Machlann left with me. Koba, well, I didn't know him then. Regardless, I'll tell you this now so there is no misunderstanding in the future, and since you'll be training upon my grounds, I *do* have a say in what happens on it. And my say is this—don't ever do that again. Your lads, *our* lads, train to *win*. Not to be told to lose a fight at the last possible instant, for the jingling of a few coins. The very thought turns my guts rancid. What would your masters back in Kree say about you for this? You have the bells to ask for respect? I'll give you a warning instead. If I learn of you doing anything like this again, I'll heave you and your lot out and clean my hands of you all. I'll not sully my name any further for a lot of untested but gold-empowered *Free Trained*. That's my promise. Understood?"

The heated lecture ended in a constant but soft drone of street activity from the open window. Only when Clavellus put the question to a chagrined Goll did the Kree realize the man had been close to yelling. Momentarily speechless, Goll cleared his throat and gathered his thoughts. First Halm and now Clavellus, but then he had known his decision at the time would not be popular even though it was the *right* one. Still, to be reprimanded in such a way… thoughts and feelings churned within him, leaving a sour taint of chagrin, but he knew, given the time of the season, he had nowhere else to go. Nor did he possess the experience Clavellus and his trainers possessed.

"Understood," Goll relented quietly, lowering his gaze in defeat.

The taskmaster huffed as if about to charge. "Where is Pig Knot?"

"In the arena's infirmary."

"Who's with him?"

"Halm is, as well as most of the new recruits."

"Seddon above, you have *recruits* with him?"

"There was no one else. But Halm is there."

"I'm off for the Pit then," Clavellus said to Machlann, who nodded sagely. The old trainer had been stoically inspecting Muluk's bandages. Koba lurched from the window and joined the taskmaster at the stairs. There, a pensive Clavellus paused. Goll thought he was about to give another stern warning. After a nervous heartbeat, the subsequent storm brewing upon the old taskmaster's face didn't lash into the new master. Instead, he thumped down the stairs with both trainers behind him.

Goll wrapped a hand around the back of his neck and squeezed gently, massaging the tension collected there. He noticed that Machlann lingered. The stern trainer inspected the still form of Muluk. Without a word, he studied the gravity of the man's wounds while Clavellus reached the ground floor with a clatter.

And then, ever so quietly and paying no heed to what Goll might think, the trainer placed a warm hand on the sleeping man's forehead, patting it softly.

A moment later, he left and lumbered down the stairs.

Six personal guards fell into line behind Clavellus and Koba as they left the healer's house. The taskmaster's blood burned with angered dismay. *Free Trained*, his mind chided him. *What did you expect?* Goll certainly displayed initiative and push, but the taskmaster feared the man lacked common sense. Clavellus didn't invest time, sweat, and blood in preparing a gladiator to fight to his fullest only to have him commanded to fall in a match. He wondered if Goll would try such a thing again, despite his warning. He hoped the Kree would not.

The taskmaster stopped in the middle of the street when he realized Machlann wasn't with him. Then the old trainer appeared, leaving the healer's house, looking as grim as ever. Clavellus waited for him before continuing on without a word. Neither Machlann nor Koba spoke during the walk to the arena. Clavellus knew what they were thinking, who they were looking for. The heat was terrible, and the press of bodies quickly tested the taskmaster's nerves, making him long for a drink. Sunjans crowded the street from one side to the other in all their colors, shapes, sizes, and smells. Some haggled with merchants over stringed baubles of Zuthenian copper and gold while others held up shimmering lengths of fine silk rippling in the sun. They quibbled and swore at times, which brought out Clavellus's scorn. There was a damn war going on, and people seemed everything but concerned. Some of his countrymen glanced curiously in his direction, enough to unleash tendrils of unease about his mind. Curge's warning echoed on reeking air currents, reminding Clavellus of the risk he had taken in coming to the city.

But the Pit beckoned with an ache so nagging the

taskmaster couldn't stay away. Not with events involving his lads happening in the city.

His lads. Already he considered them his own, Seddon damn him.

The small group pressed on through the masses, closing in on the stony magnificence of the arena. Bare wires and ribbons crossed the street heights, straining to contain the Pit as it reared up, like netting failing to contain a beast. The arena revealed itself in ominous fashion, looming over the rooftops of nearby houses, casting an imposing ambience that weakened the knees. Fear and joy surged through Clavellus upon sighting the towering outer shell of the ancient battleground, fondly recalling better times so very long ago. The thought occurred to him that, although he'd married Nala, the woman who'd stolen his heart, he'd secretly married another.

The Pit drew them into its shadowy archways and tunnels. They descended steps and traversed torchlit passages until they approached the infirmary. A giant of a man detached himself from the entrance with silent grace. The tunnel guardian prompted Koba to draw his sword and step in front of Clavellus.

Then the large brazen belly of the Zhiberian pushed through the door.

"Koba! A surprise to find you here. And is that Master Clavellus behind you? And the other one?"

Though Clavellus sensed a joke, he felt heat rising off Machlann.

"Where's the lad?" the taskmaster demanded.

Halm's joviality dropped. "In here. This is Brozz, one of the new men with us. Scary bastard, isn't he? Lad, this is our—and soon to be your—taskmaster and both trainers."

The swarthy man with the necklace of crow heads dipped his head in greeting. Stepping out of Koba's considerable shadow, Clavellus briefly studied the disturbing ornaments dangling from the warrior's neck. He then faced Halm.

"Lead on, then. You men stay here," he ordered his guards.

Halm guided the taskmaster and the trainers into the infirmary, past cots of fighters suffering from frightening cuts and stab wounds. "Didn't expect to find you here this morning."

"A good amount has happened since I saw you last," Clavellus said as the smell of strong onions accosted his nose. He recognized saywort, having been around it much longer than he cared to remember. "I heard you've become a house now."

"We have," Halm said with a smile, "and I'm one of the founding masters of it."

"You must be overjoyed."

But Halm said nothing to that. More cots lined the infirmary's walls, and men lay quietly or twisted in pain. Clavellus shook his head and scowled, hoping the poor bastards' wounds weren't too life crippling. He'd heard far too many unhappy stories in his time.

"Where's the healer?" he asked.

"Gone just now," Halm answered. "The new lads and I were about most of the night, watching in shifts."

"I can't believe Goll put them here in the first…" But his words faltered.

Halm stopped at one dark cot and swept a hand, introducing a mess of a man lying on his back. While Pig Knot's face and upper body were wrapped in clean bandages, his legs drew most of Clavellus's attention—

rather, his lack of legs.

"Dying Seddon," the taskmaster cursed.

The following trainers gathered around. Koba's dismayed hiss spoke volumes while Machlann kept his tongue.

"The bandages look clean," Clavellus said finally, feeling the awkwardness of the words but at a loss to say anything more.

"The healer changed them this morning. And applied more of that salve shite. Not the first time Pig Knot's been buttered, I wager, but probably by more attractive, ah, professionals."

"Muluk's wounds were done in the same fashion… but the healer's house had open windows for at least a breath of fresh air. Seddon above. Who did this?"

"A pit fighter. One I know the name of."

"You can't let this go, you know."

"I won't," Halm said with quiet lethality. "I know who did this. A dog called Skulljigger. I'll put him down. He's the reason why Goll placed the recruits on guard here and half the reason why I'm here."

"What's the other half?" Clavellus asked, his eyes still on the stumps.

Halm paused before his eyes fell on the unconscious Pig Knot. "He's my friend."

Clavellus faced the Zhiberian with a reflective silence filled with the moans of the suffering. Machlann broke the moment by moving in on the other side of the cot, a frown rendering his features truly unsettling in the low light.

"We should move him," the trainer said. "Get him back to the villa."

"I agree," Clavellus grunted, "but the move might be

too much for him."

"At least get him back to the healer's house. Alongside Muluk. Then we'd have them together. Easy to watch."

A wise thought, Clavellus conceded. "Where's this healer?"

"Gone, but he should be back shortly," Halm said.

"You have some gold on you?"

"A few coins."

"Good. Perhaps buy a stretcher from him if you can and do as Machlann's suggested. Bring Pig Knot back to the house. Have your recruits come along. They'll be returning to the house anyway, sooner or later."

"You've spoken to Goll, have you?"

"I have," Clavellus said with a frustrated expulsion of breath, enough to quell any further questions on the matter.

"I'll meet you back at the healer's house then."

"Where you are going?"

"To look for this Skulljigger," Halm said. "And to lay down the challenge for a blood match. Why so glum, good Machlann?"

Machlann glanced up from the prone shape of Pig Knot. "You just find this *Skull* bastard."

"I will. Ah. Meet the new lads, then." Halm directed the men's attention to four men coming into the infirmary.

"Who are these toppers?" Torello quipped, eyeing the pair of older men with disdain and stopping at Koba. "And this ugly bastard. What in Saimon's name took a lick of you?"

A scowling Koba squinted at Clavellus, who quickly shook his head.

"These are your *trainers*... and taskmaster." Halm cleared his throat. "And if you still wish to be a part of the house, I'd suggest you'd apologize right now."

This didn't seem to initially impress Torello, but his insolent posturing wilted just a little under Koba's menacing glare.

"My apologies, then," Torello mumbled. "Didn't mean anything by it."

"You keep that in mind then, boy," Machlann warned, "when, in a day or two's time, you feel my boot up your dog blossom."

The tightening of Torello's jaw and the brazen glare was all Clavellus needed to know. Torello's attitude didn't surprise him. There was always one troublesome he-bitch in every pack.

Halm formally introduced Torello, Junger, and Kolo and sent the one called Brozz off to find the healer. In short time, the man was located and a wooden stretcher purchased. The healer didn't care for the idea of carrying Pig Knot away but brightened somewhat when Halm gave him a pair of gold coins for his trouble. After that, the healer changed his mind, waved them off, and wished them well. Traversing the stony bowels of the Pit's underbelly, the group of them carefully transferred Pig Knot to the sunny surface.

Once in the blaze of the sun, Halm turned to Clavellus. "You know the way to the healer's house?"

"I do."

"Then we part ways here."

Machlann stopped him. "Perhaps Koba should accompany you?"

But Halm's gruesome smile made his thoughts clear on that matter. "No. I'll find him on my own. And I'll make the blood match known. I'll meet you all back at the healer's house. Later this day."

"We'll be leaving the city later this day."

"I'll meet you back at your residence then, Master Clavellus. One place or the other."

"One piece or the other," Machlann said with a hard expression.

The Zhiberian flashed an appreciative smile at the jab.

"Be careful, Zhiberian," Clavellus warned.

If Halm wasn't mistaken, he believed the taskmaster wanted to go with him. With a departing nod, Halm left and wound his way back into the tunnels, turning at junctions lit by flickering torches and following the smell of sour sweat and urine. At times, the darkness enveloped him, and burly shadows passed without word. As he drew closer to the general quarters, Halm felt anxious to get the next bit of business out of the way. Up ahead, a familiar dull chatter could be heard, hundreds of ghostly voices growing in strength as he marched through the corridors. Light and dark coalesced, blurring the lines of the passageways' fitted stone and rendering it seamless. Energy filled him, rising up through the floor, permeating his boots and lower legs, quickening the beat of his heart. He knew the feeling, the building rush of power and excitement before any confrontation. Ahead, shadows of men prepared themselves for battle, voicing their anxiousness to pull steel as clearly as dogs barking to be fed. The underguts of the Pit channeled the sounds, amplified them, and urged Halm to hurry.

He knew Skulljigger would be there.

And he meant to find the fighter who'd almost killed his friend—find Skulljigger, challenge him, and when the time was right, punch his Mademian steel through the man's black heart.

8

The teeming mess of general quarters seemed to stink more with each visit. Halm wrinkled his face at the unholy fragrance wafting about. He wondered if the games happened only once a year because the event took the remaining three seasons to clean the place. Breathing in the foul air, he studied the shadows and torch-lit forms as they shuffled past his eyes. Men regarded him in turn, some with a careful glance, others with undisguised annoyance. One bumped him and apologized while twice more he was nearly knocked off his feet. Those rough encounters left him sputtering oaths at armored backs as they melted into the mass of fighters. He felt the hilt of his sword and swore blood if he were hit one more time. The Madea shouted the names of the first combatants of the day, and Halm decided it best to ask questions of the arena official.

Along the way stood a man studying an open helm with fear on his face. Ill-kept leather armor covered the lad, no doubt taken from the dead and stitched together in poor fashion. A round shield decorated his arm while a shortsword hung off his waist, sheathed in a scabbard. Halm wouldn't have paid much attention to the youngster except for two things: the distress infecting his features and the war braid at the back of his black-haired head.

For a haunting moment, one that made him falter in his tracks, Halm believed he was looking at a youthful version of Pig Knot.

Feeling eyes upon him, the lad met his gaze and frowned.

"I'm not a daisy," the youth said.

The words slapped Halm out of his stare. "What?"

"You heard me, you fat ass licker. I'm not a daisy, so get that loving look out of your eye else I poke it out with this." He gripped the hilt of his sword, no longer fearful.

Halm broke into a smile. "Ah, apologies, I didn't mean any offence."

"None taken. Just stating facts is all."

"Yes, well, it's good to know them."

"You a fighter?"

"Me?" Halm put a pair of fingers to his chest. "Aye that."

"Don't look like one."

"What?"

"Too fat around the middle. Looks like someone already cut you up as well. Like a hairy ham. Cut you up and then slapped some wrapping on you for later."

Seddon above. The lad *sounded* like Pig Knot. Halm's smile widened. An elbow jostled him from behind, and he shot a withering glare at the owner. Then he put the face away and regarded the lad again.

"What's your name?"

"What?"

"What's your name?"

"Why? I don't want to know you."

"Fair enough. I probably wouldn't want to know me either."

"Aye that," he said with contempt.

The retort put a smirk on Halm's face.

"Now what?" the lad grated. "Can't you see I'm about to fight here? I don't want to talk. Off with you."

"How many fights you have?"

"What?"

"You say that a lot."

"And you speak funny. Where're you from?"

"Zhiberia. You?"

But the other man didn't answer right away. "You're the Zhiberian? The one that the House of Curge wants to cut up?"

Halm rolled his eyes. "Aye that. Well, probably so. I don't think there are many of us at the games. Or in Sunja for that matter."

"They even call you Ham."

"*Halm*," Halm grated.

"Apologies. But you know you're a dead man?"

"I'm probably a lot of things, but dead isn't one of them. Not yet."

"Well, to answer your question, I've had two fights before this."

"Ah. That's the reason."

"What? What do you mean?"

"You look as if you're about to let slip a cow kiss."

The youth appeared bothered by that. "I'm not, then."

"Well then, steady yourself. Relax for a moment. Take a breath. You've already fought twice before, so you know what to do. What to expect."

The other man didn't share Halm's confidence. "I was like this before the others as well."

"And you got through it and won."

The youth looked at his feet.

"You didn't win?" Halm asked in confusion.

"I won. But… the first one was so drunk he stumbled and fell, and I was on him. The second one wasn't much better. Another bastard just as nervous as myself, really. We must've goaded each other for damn near half the day before the first swing, and even then it wasn't anything to look at. I cut him down and got him to yield, but…"

"It wasn't anything to look at," Halm finished.

"Aye that. Not at all. Not really."

"Hm. What's your name?"

"Targus," he said without any hesitation that time.

"Targus. The first thing you do is get that look off your face. You look ready to piss yourself right now, understand? And I saw it while just walking along. In this terrible light, I might add. What do you suppose your opponent is going to think if he sees you like that? And he will. It's day out there."

"He'll kill me." Targus's face sagged with worry.

"Right and proper, too. So at least *look* as if you're not about to let loose with the scutters. There's no time for that now, anyway. Firm up and focus on pulling steel. Understand? Get rid of the lamb face. At least look the part of a pit fighter with two victories to his name."

Targus took a breath, seemingly bolstered by the talk. Unease still mired his features, but at least he no longer seemed in dire need of a shite trough.

"Anything else?" Targus asked.

"That's it."

"Do you fight this day?"

"Me? Seddon above, no. I'm... looking for someone."

"That one that killed your friend?"

Halm faced the younger man and didn't say anything for a moment. "How did you know about that?"

"Most all are talking about it."

"Well, aye then, I'm looking for him. He didn't kill my friend, though."

"From what I heard, he should have."

Halm was at a loss for words a second time. Targus had a way of doing that.

"Targus!" a voice called.

"That's it, then," the younger warrior said. "Thank you for the words."

With that, the younger version of Pig Knot hurried off toward his moment on the sands.

Halm watched him until the white tunnel swallowed him whole. *He should have*, still rang in his head like the ominous chimes of a temple. *He should have*. The stark reality of it all chilled his core. Pig Knot had no *legs*. What happened to gladiators who lost limbs in the pit? Halm didn't know what, and he didn't care to dwell on it, but he called Pig Knot a friend—one who would need plenty of support in the days to come.

He should have, came the grim echo once again.

Drawing a hand down over his face, Halm sniffed, cleared his head, and concentrated on the task at hand. A fence of armored Skarrs stood across the way, ever vigilant for the safety of the Madea. He spotted the arena official, mulling over his papers, set before him on an elevated wooden desk as big and scarred as a slab of cut granite. Lamplight made the large matchboard beyond the Madea glow with arcane luminescence, its surface marred by lines and unfathomable scribbles that made Halm's head ache. He pushed through the fighters in his way and stopped before the solemn official, who had his head down and offered a fine view of how he parted his thinning white hair down the middle. Two of the Skarrs turned their iron visors toward Halm, their hostile scrutiny palpable.

The Madea looked up from his papers, his old face pinched and stern. "What is it?"

"I want a blood match."

"Against who?"

"The one called Skulljigger."

"Hm." The Madea squinted at the papers on his desk and shook his head. "Will take some time to arrange. I'll have to find and notify this Skulljigger. See if he accepts. The tournament takes greater precedence these days. Not like in the beginning. What's your name?"

"Halm of Zhiberia."

"Right. I remembered the gut. Forgot the name. But…" The Madea's mouth puckered up as if about to deliver a sour kiss. "Aren't you already in a blood match? With the House of Curge?"

"I am. If they wish continuing it."

"I'm sure they will."

Halm supposed he was right.

"And theirs is first," the Madea continued, "priority since you've killed a couple of their lads now. You're a bloody one, aren't you?"

Rancid approval laced the last few words, and the Madea studied Halm until he felt uncharacteristically uneasy.

"I'll make note of the blood match. Keep an eye on the matchboard for it." With that, the official lowered his head and resumed his work.

HOUSE OF PAIN

Dismissed, Halm backed away from the desk and the watching Skarrs, wary of them all. It was the second to-the-death fight he'd issued, and while he was gladdened by knowing Vadrian the Fire was days dead, something about this recent challenge bothered him. Pit fighters eyed Halm shadily, and they didn't glance away when he confronted their gazes. Ignoring them, the Zhiberian meandered toward a wall made orange by flickering torches.

With a little luck, the man known as Skulljigger would appear shortly, and they'd have a talk about their bloody future together.

9

Sunlight poured heat into the open arena, scorching the combed sands until shimmers rose and distorted the air like rising hellions. Thousands of onlookers dressed in a deluge of colors ringed the Pit from top to bottom, with the thickest of them gathering at the stone lip overlooking the sands, where they flourished like animated grout. Curge regarded the terraced stands brimming with eager spectators and then squinted at the sun, hanging above the highest arches of the arena's stone structure. He recalled conversations and plans for erecting poles from those arches so canvas could be strung out to offer shade to the people below. The open boxes had their own tarps to block the sun, a welcomed benefit of being an owner, but nothing could completely stop the searing summer heat.

Thankful to escape the sun's scalding wrath, Curge ground his teeth as he plopped down in his seat and took an offered goblet of wine from a servant's tray. He took a drink, gulping rather than sipping, and frowned at the vintage before directing his distaste at the woman.

"Did someone piss in this before you poured it?"

"No, Master Curge," the woman replied.

Curge grunted and drained the rest of the wine in one swallow. He placed the goblet back on the tray heavily and turned his attention back to the Pit with a harsh snort and a swallow, dismissing the servant.

"Crack open another, then. Something that doesn't taste like a latrine."

"As you wish, Master Curge."

"Trouble, Curge?" Gastillo asked, his golden mask lending his voice a metallic quality.

Curge thought he'd heard the door open to the viewing box and shook his head in disdain. He'd hoped the whole area would be his alone that day. "The wine," he muttered without facing the owner. "Tastes like piss. Or what I imagine what piss would taste like if I had to drink it. Tell me if I'm right…"

Gastillo didn't reply, and Curge smirked. The gold-faced once-gladiator was a whelp when it came to exchanging jabs.

"You disappoint me, Gastillo. I thought for a moment that I might be up here alone for the day's fights."

"I hope most of your thoughts are equally mistaken."

"Harsh words… harsh." The words bubbled from Curge's throat. "Uncalled for."

Gastillo took a goblet from the servant and brought it to his metal lips. The mask drank, only to emit a grunt. "Seddon above, that is bad."

The owner immediately produced a hand cloth and slipped it under his mask.

"So what is it?" Curge asked, feeling sweat pop on his skin and wondering how the people managed with no shade at all. "Piss or just swill?"

"That one's certainly off." Gastillo motioned for the woman, and when she came, he returned the goblet. "Throw that whole bottle away."

"No," Curge interjected, scouring the ripening audience, "keep that one for the master of wines. Let him choke it down."

"But bring us another bottle. Separate bottles," Gastillo corrected.

"You don't wish to share wine with me?" Curge inquired innocently. "It is a precursor to information, you know."

"Information," Gastillo hissed, settling into his seat and surveying the audience. The orator's voice cut through the rabble of noise, introducing the first fights of the day.

"Aye, information."

"You can't be talking about the new house, can you?" Gastillo asked without turning his head.

"Ah, you know of it already?" Curge smirked. "Your agents are more effective than I thought."

"They manage," Gastillo let slip, which blunted the smile on Curge's face.

"Then out with it."

Gastillo rocked in his chair as if pleased with his hidden knowledge, displeasing Curge. He thumped the stump of his left arm against the stone wall of the box, the rounded flesh resembling a battering ram. "Did you hear me?"

"Did you say something?"

"You heard me. I swear, Gastillo, only now do I see the strategy behind always wearing that slab of tin on your face. And all this time, I thought it was only to cover your fright of a face. Now I see its true merit. Perhaps I should invest in my own mask to hide my thoughts and expressions."

"Well. Perhaps you should."

Curge turned back to the arena. Two men stood poised just outside the lowering portcullis, shifting on their feet. Both wore the fitted leather of the recently dead. Both held shortswords and round shields. To Curge, they appeared like mirror images, which elicited a sigh of bored annoyance. Free Trained shite. Still, he paid mind to all of them just in case one proved to be something more than their class suggested.

"Who are these punces?" Curge asked. "I didn't catch the names."

"The one with the war braid is called Targus while the other one is called Nadus. The new house has called itself the House of Ten."

"I heard that already. Did you hear anything else?"

"The one who gutted Baylus the Butcher is its head, it would seem. Perhaps he thinks overseeing a pack of pit fighters is more of a challenge. In any case, your friend the Zhiberian is with them. As well as a handful of others. All with winning records, those who are still in the tournament."

"Halm of Zhiberia." Curge spat the last word as if it were filth.

"You remember him, don't you?"

"Don't play with me, Gastillo, not about that fat pig-bastard."

"My apologies. The deaths of your men still sting, I see."

Curge directed a look of warning at Gastillo before the fight below drew their attention. The fighters thundered across the sands, bellowing all the way, and met in the middle. A flurry of wild strikes cutting nothing but air made the audience cry out in pleasure, but those cries quickly soured when the more astute spectators realized the two pit fighters were only flailing at each other. The one called Targus swung at his opponent's head as if he were attempting to cool the man off. Sucking on a tooth in contempt, Curge looked away from the match and focused on the dull gleam of Gastillo's mask. The woman brought them goblets of wine, which they lifted from her tray.

"Who's training the house's gladiators?" Curge asked, suddenly wary of revealing any emotion around Gastillo.

"I don't know."

Curge sighed and heaved his shoulders in frustration. He'd have to find out if Clavellus was with them.

"You've become quiet, Curge," Gastillo remarked, his mask pointed at the sloppy dance below. "Something bothers you?"

The clang of swords distracted Dark Curge for a moment. Such a resounding clash of metal might have signaled something interesting happening on the sands. Much to his disappointment, Curge saw the two men continuing to flail at each other. *Free Trained shite.*

"Nothing bothers me, good Gastillo," *you sunny tit,* he thought blackly. "But since you shared, allow me to reciprocate. I heard about this House of Ten this morning, and I know the Zhiberian is with them. My agents are in the process of finding out who these ten are and who trains them. I expect the answers soon enough, which I'll share with you. The taskmasters and trainers interest me greatly. Knowing who they are is just another piece of the puzzle needed for victory in the Pit."

"Agreed," Gastillo said and drank from his goblet.

Curge cautiously took a drink of his own and found it pleasing—not as sour as the previous wine.

"Much better." He smacked with approval.

On the sands, swords clattered once more and ended with a yelp. Nadus dropped to his knees, his weapon on the sand while he buckled over and cradled his guts. Generous dollops of blood blotted the sands. With a casualness Curge approved of, Targus walked around his fallen foe, stained blade in hand. He stopped behind Nadus's rocking form and pointed the tip of his weapon downward, much to the exultation of the crowd.

And he stabbed the man through the back of the neck.

Nadus toppled, to cheers and applause. Curge wasn't certain if that was in appreciation of a terrible match being finished or the death. Probably the death. A good one often made up for a poor showing.

Nexus sat down between the pair of owners without greetings. "First blood of the day, I see."

Curge regarded the merchant's pallid features and eyed the oily slick of his graying hair. Nexus strained to see what had just happened in the Pit, thrusting his almost nonexistent chin out and squinting at the marred arena floor.

"Decided to join us, Nexus?" Curge inquired.

Nexus took a goblet from the servant's tray without thanks and tipped it back before answering. That rude act alone made Curge want to bounce the old prick's head off the box's stone wall.

"I was attending to business," Nexus said after studying the wine with an appraising eye. "*Real* business. And not this spectacle. Not that it's any of your damn concern, your darkness."

Curge caught the slight dip of Gastillo's mask, as if that gold-plated cow kiss were smiling. He didn't appreciate that at all, and the urge to smack the old bastard next to him swelled dangerously.

"You've missed the news we were just discussing," Curge seethed, and in an admirable feat of self-control, turned back to the pit in time to see the victor walk off while the attendants labored with the carcass.

"Discovered a new way to gut someone?"

"Hardly."

"Then I'm doubtful it was anything of interest."

"You'd be surprised."

"What is it, then? Out with it. Tell me, since you're bursting to do so." Nexus signalled for more wine.

Curge wagged a finger at the servant. "Is that the wine we're drinking or the earlier vintage?"

"The earlier one, Master Curge," she replied.

"You're enjoying that slop?" Curge asked the wine merchant.

"This?" Nexus held up the filled vessel. "It's a damn sight better than the sweetened rat sluice I usually drink here. At least this has both flavor and sting."

"I thought it was piss."

"Yes, well, you're an uncivilized brute who somehow broke his chains and learned to speak language. One wouldn't expect a fellow of your nature to judge proper wine. Not even if it was pissed down your throat." Nexus inspected his drink and then the sands below while the jab slackened Curge's weathered jowls. Even Gastillo froze visibly.

"You go too far, Nexus," Curge said in a dangerously quiet tone, insult coloring his cheeks.

"Your trouble, Curge, is that I have no fear of you. Never did. Never will. You know what I like about dallying with you both? It's the lack of pretense I must otherwise force when negotiating with others of my ilk. It's refreshing. Speak candidly, please, I insist. And if it's a jab, I'll give as good as I get. *That* I guarantee. But have no grand misunderstanding. You're no friend or ally of mine. You're both my rivals. And as such, I've yet to see any reason why I should discuss any of my affairs pertaining to the arena with either of you. Is that understood?" Nexus finished as if admonishing a child. "It's not that I think you have nothing of interest for me… it's because I *learn* fast."

Curge's murderous visage might have struck dead an entire mob, five ranks deep. Instead, he set his jaw and sniffed at the air in another impressive display of self-control. Only Gastillo knew how close Nexus was to flying over the edge of their mutual box.

"I believe what Curge meant," Gastillo put in before disaster struck, "is that… despite our own differences, some knowledge is best shared for our mutual advantage. In this case, a new house has entered the games. A new and potential threat to us all."

"Hmm," Nexus grunted. "Interesting how your words aren't as *veiled* as Curge's—talking about the wine as a preamble to whatever scraps of information he might have. Shame on you, Curge. Get to the point next time. You, however, Gastillo… that gold you wear must be rubbing off on something."

"Just an attempt at keeping the peace. I only wish to watch the games and make some coin."

"Ahhh," Nexus said, waving a finger near his ear. "*That's* talk I can appreciate. In that case, yes, I've heard about this new house. House of Ten or something or other? Heard it was only a dozen or so Free Trained who came into some coin. Just enough to formally enter as a house. I also heard that one of their lads was involved in a morning street brawl that left five or six men dead, the same men responsible for butchering the patrons of an alehouse not two or three days ago. While the drunks lay sleeping, no less. Not how I want to leave this life, I tell you."

This information defused Curge, and the heat seeped from his face.

"That interests you?" Nexus asked him.

"It does."

"I suppose it would, since the Zhiberian is with them. Something, that. The man who's chopped down two of your lads now, suddenly part of a budding house. Unbelievable. Now he has pit fighters at his back, ready to avenge him if he falls. Am I correct in that? You kill him, and if they declare a blood match against you, *well*, things could become very interesting, couldn't it? Correct me if I'm mistaken. Ah, it's not near as amusing as butchering Free Trained without fear of reprisal, is it?"

The color returned to Curge's face. "Doesn't matter what house he pledges to, newly established or rotting in its foundations. I'll have my revenge. I always do."

Nexus eyed him. "What was that? Was that a subtle threat? Good *Curge*." The wine merchant tutted. "I don't doubt you're a vengeful man in the least. To do so would reflect badly upon my ability to navigate dangerous waters. Regardless, if I hear of anything more on this… House of Ten… I'll be sure to let you both know, in the spirit of sharing knowledge amongst our houses."

Curge didn't like this merchant of grape's patronizing tone, pretending to know the workings of the arena. Once again, however, he held his tongue.

"Well then," Nexus declared, gazing expectantly at the arena sands. "Let's see some blood."

10

Flickering torches held precariously onto existence as pit fighters strode through their orange radiuses. The shadowy underlight of the general quarters, brightest only around the station of the Madea, made the smile spreading across Grisholt's wizened face all the more sinister. He stopped in his tracks, halting the four men following at his heels without warning, and stroked the point of his beard with an air of undisguised wickedness. Brakuss nearly ran over his master while the accompanying house fighters, Hease and Seel, bumped into Brakuss from behind. The early morning rise and trip to the city had been a punishing one for the old stable owner, leaving Grisholt in foul spirits all the way to Sunja's south gates. But this... seeing the Zhiberian speaking to one of the Free Trained punces... *this* was opportunity.

With a slick sneer skewing his carefully groomed features, Grisholt watched the pair converse. Warriors walked by, momentarily blocking his field of vision. *Halm of Zhiberia,* his thoughts whispered, *an enemy your unfit mind has no doubt forgotten about is near, and you're sadly unaware.* Grisholt sensed Brakuss at his back and looked to see his bodyguard more than ready to walk over there and pummel the pit fighter.

With false nobility, Grisholt frowned, denying Brakuss that particular entertainment. This wasn't the place or the proper time. This was business. Revenge upon the Zhiberian would be something sweet for another day.

The name of *Targus* cut the air, shouted by the Madea, and the pit fighter speaking with Halm broke away to make his way to the white tunnel. *Targus.* Grisholt would instruct his agent Caro to investigate this warrior for anything deliciously useful—maybe even bring the true nature of the Zhiberian to Targus's attention. That idea put a smile on his face.

"Grisholt." A cheerful voice stole his attention, and he found himself blinking at Vorish, owner of the School of Vorish. A plump individual, younger by only a handful of years and not nearly as well dressed, he smelled of some mysterious, almost woodland scent that wasn't at all pleasant. Vorish was smiling at him, but Grisholt didn't bother returning it. The fourth fight of the day would have Hease battle Trako, one of Vorish's more brutal lads.

"Master Vorish. You look well."

"As do you," Vorish responded with a touch of frost. "How's your fortune on the sands this season?"

Grisholt disliked discussing such affairs with anyone. "Ah, the games arrived too slow this season. Too slow."

"I'm sorry to hear it." Vorish's fleshy features darkened for the barest of moments. "Anything I can assist you with?"

The offer made Grisholt hesitate because of the blatant

lie he knew it to be. For all of his pudgy joviality, Vorish was no ally of Grisholt's. He saw the overweight owner only during the games and rarely anywhere else, including the rare social functions the Gladiatorial Chamber might hold, and when Grisholt did lay eyes on the man, he'd just as soon not. Vorish was as two-faced as any of the rival owners. Grisholt loathed the deceitful camaraderie Vorish projected and wondered if the apple-shaped pisshead believed his poor act of commiseration actually fooled anyone.

Grisholt decided to put the man in his place. "Ah, no, I don't think… well, interestingly enough, perhaps there is something you might assist me with."

"What might that be?"

"My line of credit seems to be at an end in the city. Would you be able to perhaps manage a loan? Not a large one, mind you, but enough to see me through these difficult times."

"A loan?" Vorish's eyes nearly popped out onto his jowls. "I'm afraid I can't offer anything of the like. My own finances are stretched thin as it is. "

Undoubtedly, Grisholt thought.

"Matter of fact, the real reason I approached you was to ask if you wished to place a wager on today's contest between our two houses."

"A wager?" No surprise there. *Stretched finances indeed.*

"A small one—but enough to make things interesting."

"Good Vorish, I can't afford even that."

"No faith in your man at all, eh?"

That was the Vorish Grisholt knew. The abrupt change in tactics caught him unawares for a moment, inspecting the hunter's gleam in the round man's eyes.

"If I know you, you probably have coin on Trako

anyway," a sly, grinning Vorish accused brazenly and appraised the men behind Grisholt. "That's him there, isn't it? The sleepy one?"

"Your man will see him shortly," Grisholt said, his dislike burning in his chest. "I'll wager ten gold on Hease. That he beats your man down."

"Only ten?" Vorish brayed a laugh.

"As I said, times have—"

"But *ten*? That lavender water you stink of costs more than ten gold!"

"Ten," Grisholt snarled, becoming ruffled. "Take it or nothing."

"Oh, I'll take it," Vorish sneered and offered his fist. Setting his jaw, Grisholt shoved his own against it, and both owners pushed hard into each other.

"I'll come looking for you later," Vorish promised. "All ready for this day, *boy*?" the owner flung at Hease before walking away without waiting for a reply.

Grisholt had to admit he preferred Vorish as his usual bastard self than a good-natured punce. The fat man vanished amongst the crowds of fighters, and the need to get to his own private viewing chamber gripped Grisholt. He looked for the Zhiberian, but the lout had disappeared. Just as well. Grisholt wasn't yet prepared for him.

"This way," the owner said, leading his men through shadows and torchlight to the Madea. After checking with the arena official, the group then walked to Grisholt's private chamber, navigating the stone corridors while the ceiling thrummed with the voices of thousands. In short time, they were inside a clean-swept brick room with an arched window offering a view of the sands at ground level. Grisholt sat on an uncomfortable chair in self-absorbed silence, enduring the cold-oven feel of the chamber and feeling none too pleased about his encounter with Vorish.

He gestured for Brakuss and Seel to help Hease armor himself, which they did dutifully, taking their time transforming a man into a pit fighter. A tusked visor turned in Grisholt's direction as Brakuss fitted a round shield to the warrior's arm. The chainmail Hease wore gleamed.

"Shall I kill him?" Hease growled, meaning Trako. His hand reached for the pommel of his sheathed sword for dramatic effect.

"Trako?" Grisholt asked with indignation, not appreciating the theatrics. "No, you idiot, don't kill him. The last thing I need is a war with the School of Vorish. You just beat him into submission and leave it at that."

"What if he kills me?"

"What gurry is that? Vorish isn't going to risk war with us either. Neither of us can afford it. Not this day, anyway. Just pummel the ass licker and leave him battered and bleeding. But not bleeding *too* badly."

The wager with Vorish irked Grisholt. He'd been easily baited to take it. As it was, Caro and his spies had already delivered word about Trako. The man was a beast, prompting Grisholt to arrange a hefty wager on the School of Vorish's man, placed by Caro's spies. Grisholt saw no need to order Hease to lose as the poor bastard didn't stand a chance in the least. The shifty owner fumed. With a bad draw from the Madea, Hease's season was only moments away from being finished. Meeting Vorish and being forced to take a wager for appearances was just Seddon-damned luck.

But what really disturbed Grisholt was how that bouncing ball of slime Vorish had correctly guessed where his wager would be. Had Grisholt become that predictable?

Every house, school, and stable had their spies slinking about, all faces and ears, unobtrusively observing each other's business. Could one or more have detected a pattern to Grisholt's wagering? And could that observation have been shared with others? It was possible. He reluctantly admitted that, even though he believed he'd been careful with his gambles, there was every chance his pride in believing himself so cunning might have blinded him to the obvious. Even Dark Curge had shocked him with accusations of losing battles for rewarding wagers, had called him on it in their last encounter. Curge! A mindless brute if there ever was one. Vorish wasn't so mindless, which was exactly why he made the wager as public as possible, knowing Grisholt would have no choice but to accept it.

Only ten pieces of gold, but the *significance* of it all and the notion of how the other owners perceived him and his Stable—an easy victory—made it feel like a mountain.

"Sweet Seddon above," he moaned to himself. The revelation horrified him, bringing on an urge to scream at someone. If his thoughts and instincts were true, if his questionable wagering practices had become common knowledge amongst the other owners, then... the reputation of his stable had been unwittingly destroyed by his own hand, his own vaunted craftiness.

His long-dead father would curse him blind for plopping the stable's name into the shite troughs.

Grisholt studied Hease for a short moment and then tiredly waved at him to be on his way. Hease left the room with far too much enthusiasm for his manager to bear. Outside, the air and stands trembled from the sound of thousands, but Grisholt paid it very little attention.

Again the crowds roared, as startling as a heavy wave crashing upon a beach. Then came the tinkle of steel on steel as two fighters met.

Grisholt met the singular gaze of Brakuss's scrutinizing eye and shook his head. "Unfit," the owner said, all at once feeling very old.

Brakuss and Seel did not disturb him until Hease took to the sands. Grisholt didn't want to watch the fight, but he pulled himself to the window, feeling as defeated as the outcome. For an instant, he hoped that Hease would surprise them all and overthrow Trako, even though it meant losing his sizeable wager with the Domis.

But then he beheld Vorish's gladiator.

There was a monstrous quality to Trako that momentarily chilled Grisholt's bones. Shadowy leather armor fashioned into a god's physique draped his body while his shoulders sported two fearsome spikes. A simple yet sinister black iron helm covered his features and oozed a brutal coldness. Trako carried two weapons: a long-shafted mace and an offhand, single-bladed axe. Bristling, spiked cups protected his fists and gave destructive power to a punch. Just gazing upon those iron points made Grisholt set his jaw in defeat. The only thing missing from the picture was a broken chain leash. By Trako's hunched over yet bobbing posture, and knowing the mettle of his own man, Grisholt knew Hease would be lucky to survive the encounter.

Upon the last dying note from the Orator's introductions, the two gladiators waded toward each other.

Hease struck first, bringing his blade up and over his shoulder in a downward chop fit to split steel. It didn't connect, however, as Trako, surprisingly nimble, got out of the way of the weapon. Hease released a series of cuts Grisholt recognized his own trainers having taught: a flat blade sweep powered by arm and hips followed by another murderous, over-the-shoulder chop, then a punch delivered with the shield's edge—all delivered with practiced ease.

Trako dodged right, left, and jumped back, well away from the last blow.

"He's fast," Brakuss breathed.

"He is," Seel agreed nearby.

He is. Grisholt clenched his jaw.

Trako stepped to his left, and Hease slashed at his foe's body. Trako stopped the sword stroke decisively on the shaft of his axe and spun around, smashing the spiked cup of his mace across the armored cheek of Hease. The man staggered. The crowds squealed at the connection, and jeers and insults rained down on Grisholt's man. Hease struggled to right himself. Though his helm had saved his life, having one's chin abruptly torqued to one side was enough to summon stars.

Trako didn't press. Standing at guard, he allowed Hease to recover.

Grisholt sensed Vorish's orders behind the respite.

Trako then leaped to the attack, his weapons clanging off Hease's upraised shield. Four angry notes crashed out, each one forcing Grisholt's warrior back toward the looming arena wall. Hease scurried to his right, avoiding being pinned against the far stone, and circled back to the middle of the arena while Trako's black iron helm tracked him.

When Hease reached safe distance, his opponent pursued. Hease readied himself for the coming barrage—and then it came. Swift, heavy blows punished Grisholt just for watching. Hease parried what he could, hanging onto his shield for dear life. At one point, Trako stood off at an angle as if felling a tree and bashed the shield repeatedly, each connection dropping Hease's barrier just a little more. Hease tried to back away, but Trako matched him step for step until, finally, his opponent's shield fell far enough for a hand axe to lash across Hease's head.

Grisholt's man jerked to his left, escaping the axe but too tired to defend what happened next.

Trako landed two successive blows with all the weight of bouncing boulders, almost ripping the shield from his foe's numb arm, before closing and snapping a spiked fist into Hease's helmed cheek. The crowds cringed and shrieked with delight at the pop of metal piercing metal.

A sheet of blood ran down Hease's chest. His knees wobbled. His sword hung uselessly in his hand.

Another spiked fist crashed into his chin, splaying him onto his back.

Trako lifted both his weapons to the skies, and the audience cried out with him.

On the sands, Hease wasn't completely done and struggled to his knees. He used his sword to get himself almost standing.

The crowds betrayed his recovery.

Hearing their warning, Trako turned around and spotted his rising opponent. Mace in hand, the pit fighter took three steps and smashed the back of Hease's helmed head, dropping the warrior face down in a cloud of dust. He did not rise again.

"That's it, then," Seel muttered, just heard over the screaming approval of the people above.

Grisholt wanted to throttle him.

The owner eventually sighed and wagged a hand at

Brakuss. "See to it that he's looked after in the infirmary. Take care of the arrangements. With luck, he'll be able to travel back with us. Seel, I hope you'll do better in your match this day."

The man didn't reply, nor did Grisholt blame him for his silence. They both knew his chances in the Pit. Brakuss went to the door of the chamber and opened it, denying Vorish, who stood just outside, that very opportunity. The portly manager straightened up and smiled benignly at the one-eyed guard. Brakuss didn't return the gesture. Nor did he move.

"Ho there, Grisholt!" called an unfazed Vorish, leaning around the warrior.

"Vorish," Grisholt acknowledged, wondering if the man had his ass on fire for arriving at his door so soon after the match. "Brakuss, pay the man. Ten gold."

The guard did as he was told, reaching for the purse hanging from his waist.

"A pleasure, good Grisholt," Vorish said with his hand stretched out as a beggar might. "Are any of your lads fighting again this day?"

"One is," Grisholt said, speaking before his instinct could forbid him.

"Then I'll be watching. And wagering." Vorish smirked. "On the competition, of course."

"Brazen of you." Grisholt stood and faced the man. "My men fight with courage and skill in the Pit. I have nothing but praise for them."

Vorish chuckled and regarded him as if seeing through a lie. "Oh, I can see you have... nothing. I suppose there's some other reason for your floundering from season to season? Have no fear, good Grisholt. All the managers know how important it is to fight one of your lads. There's never been a surer wager in the whole city. Or a better joke."

"I think it's time for you to leave, Vorish. Your lack of respect is trying my patience."

"You have bigger problems than my lack of respect, Grisholt," Vorish remarked snidely. "And none of them are because of me. And respect? *Respect?* Really, Grisholt? That's almost a bigger laugh than what I just witnessed on the sands. Of all the houses in the games, I don't think there's a man, an *owner*, who commands so little respect as yourself. There are Free Trained who are looked upon as more of a challenge than you or any of the men in your stable. *You* consider *that*."

"I'm considering having Brakuss roll your fat dog blossom up the corridor." Grisholt near barked, taking two steps toward the threshold. "Close that door."

Brakuss slammed it in Vorish's face. Scalding laughter sank through the wood, wounding Grisholt's pride.

"My thanks," the owner huffed to his bodyguard. "Wait a moment, until he's gone."

A chagrined Grisholt wandered to the window and placed an elbow on its sandy ledge, leaning toward the outside and taking a steadying breath of hot air. He held that pose for a moment before turning upon his men. "What Vorish says… is it true? About there never being a surer wager in the games?"

Seel looked at Brakuss, who cleared his throat and said, "There's always talk."

"And?"

"And we aren't the most respected in circles."

Grisholt shook his head in disbelief. His ego had been shattered this day, and by one of his own kind. "Are we not feared?"

"*Feared* is not the word I would use."

"Stop prancing with words, Brakuss. What do you hear?"

"We've ranked last in previous years. There are many who don't place much stock in our worth. There are some who believe it's only a matter of time, perhaps even this season, when the Stable of Grisholt will cease to exist."

Those words made the old owner straighten up and face his men. Anger flared within him as he glanced from one face to the next. "Then perhaps it's time for us to start placing some fear into our adversaries."

11

"You still here?"

The question broke Halm's concentration and startled him a little. The voice belonged to Targus, who stopped before him, almost devoured by shadows.

"I suppose I am. Was I that easy to see?"

"No, not at all. I was walking this way and only just noticed you. Not many, ah, *shaped* like yourself."

Halm supposed that was true. "Did you win your fight?"

"Aye that." Targus broke into a smile. Halm noted the man's bottom teeth jutted just a bit over his top ones. "Killed him as well. Not that I'm worried. He's only a Free Trained."

"So you're off to spend some coin?"

"More or less. You haven't found the one who butchered your friend?"

Halm shifted uneasily. "Bit harsh. He's still alive."

"Hm. Well, his fighting days are finished. So you didn't

find the lad who cut him up?"

"Not yet."

"The day's fights are half over. He might not show up this day."

"That's a chance."

Targus shook his head and glanced about the torchlit general quarters. "Well, as you say, I've coin to spend."

"Be good to yourself, then."

Targus fixed Halm with a strange look. "Of course I will." He left, shaking his head.

The fighter's form melded with numerous other bodies walking about the chamber, and Halm couldn't quell that feeling he'd just had a conversation with a younger—if not coarser—version of Pig Knot. He adjusted his back against the wall, feeling the stone warmed by his body heat, and took a fresh interest in the men interacting with the Madea. Time stretched on. Fighters came and went. Attendants wheeled the meat cart bearing dead bodies to their final fiery fate. Victorious warriors bursting with excitement emerged from the white tunnel, catching his attention, but still no Skulljigger. At one point, he walked around in search of the nearest latrine, passing through the flickering hues of a fire pit. The latrine consisted of a disgusting trench made of overlapping tin, laid into the floor at one end of the quarters and separated by a low brick wall only strides from where some men sat and talked. The smell alone almost made Halm hurry to the surface and piss in the street. With a huff, he assumed the stance and relieved himself, taking note of how the flow disappeared into an ominous hole cut in the metal. Once finished, Halm tucked himself away, slapped his roll of belly fat covered in bandages and stepped back just as two men crowded around him to get to the latrine.

HOUSE OF PAIN

"Enough of this," he muttered, thinking he'd return to the healer's house. Skulljigger had failed to appear so far that day, and he realized he could stand the bowels of the Pit only for so long before the high ceilings stopped seeming so high.

A short time later, he stood on the surface and squinted against daylight's glare. Though the air was hot and moist, it was nectar compared to the lower chambers. The time it took for him to navigate the streets back to Shan's house helped him adapt once more to the surface.

Guards lined the front of the healer's home, and as he drew closer, he recognized them as the new recruits along with the three new guardsmen, though he couldn't recall their names.

"Lads," Halm greeted. "Having a talk out here?"

"They're having a talk in *there*," Torello muttered. "We'll be leaving shortly, they said. Back to Clavellus's estate."

"You got here just in time," the man called Junger said.

"Pig Knot is in there?"

"Aye, he is," Torello said. "But they're talking about taking him out of the city."

A frown etched the Zhiberian's face, and he parted the wall of men to reach the front door.

"Well, Master Halm," Goll hailed from behind a table as Halm entered. "Pleases me to see you've returned. And thank you for bringing us back something to eat."

Halm winced. "Apologies. I was taken up with other matters. Didn't even buy anything for myself, really. And now that you mention it…" His hand rested on his gut.

"I can see you're starving," Borchus observed drily as he handed a small leather purse to Clavellus, sitting next to Goll. Koba and Machlann leaned against walls, while Shan was nowhere to be seen.

"You're right on time." Goll stepped in before Halm could fling a jab at the agent. "We're returning to Clavellus's estate to begin training. Get out of the city and more importantly, out of Shan's house."

"I thought we were fine here," Halm said.

"We are, but there are more of us now. And I'd feel better out of Sunja before any more bad luck finds us. I've hired Shan to travel and stay with us at the villa until such a time as the lads are completely out of harm's way."

"No one fights right away," Borchus put forth, "and I've started recruiting eyes and ears for you. It isn't much right now, but I'll have people in place soon enough. That includes a rider who'll be sent out to you with any new information as it happens. Or is discovered."

"Not too many," Goll warned him. "Not until I have a greater understanding of our finances."

Borchus nodded solemnly and made no comment.

"Any luck with finding this Skulljigger?" Clavellus asked Halm.

"Not yet."

"Shame."

"I've called for a blood match, however," Halm reported. "So word will reach him. I'll remain in the city. Here even, if Shan won't mind. The fight might happen soon."

Goll didn't appear too pleased with the idea, and he stewed in his seat.

"What?" Halm asked.

"You should return with us. It would be safer, I think."

"I'll stay here, Master Goll," Halm replied. "As I've said, the challenge has been made."

"I'll be nearby," Borchus said out of the corner of his

mouth. "I can watch him."

Now it was Halm's turn to be none too pleased with the idea.

Just then, the door opened, and the warrior called Clades leaned in. "Your pardon, but the wagons are here."

"Well then," Clavellus exclaimed, getting to his feet. "Time to get out of here. With luck, we'll reach the villa just after nightfall."

"Are the lads awake?" Halm asked.

"They are, actually," Goll answered.

Halm went to the stairs and hurried to the second level. There, the bandaged forms of his remaining companions greeted him, still lying in their cots. Shan hovered over the shape of Muluk while Pig Knot grunted as the Zhiberian came into view.

"Pig Knot?"

"Aye." The legless man winced.

"I'm here as well," Muluk grated.

"Apologies, lad," Halm said. "No offence. It's just that you were already looked after by the healer here. While this one… we weren't so sure of."

"Still alive," Pig Knot grunted.

Halm walked over to him and felt suddenly awkward about what to say. "I've issued a blood challenge to this Skulljigger. He won't get away with doing this to one of ours."

Pig Knot took his time answering, clearly feeling the effects of some unknown curative concoction. "Don't die over it."

"I don't intend to."

"I can… can still feel my legs."

That admission robbed Halm of any reply.

"I've given them both herbal mixtures, to sedate them

while they travel," Shan informed the Zhiberian.

"So you're going with them as well?" Halm asked.

Shan shrugged, rolling tanned shoulders and dusting sandy hair from his eyes. "My wife will stay here for now. It's not that busy for us. And a bit of the country air will do me well, I believe. I'm not so worried about this one." He pointed at Muluk then gestured toward Pig Knot. "But him, I'd feel better watching for a few days."

"Good man," Pig Knot grumbled.

"Very good man," Muluk slurred, the medicine hitting both men hard now.

"Would it be acceptable if I slept here?" Halm asked. "While I'm in the city?"

Shan didn't hesitate. "Indeed it is acceptable. I'll let my wife know."

Koba and four of the new gladiators climbed the stairs, bearing stretchers. Shortly, they gathered up the serene Muluk and Pig Knot and carried them down the steps to the waiting horse-drawn wagons.

Outside, Goll watched how Muluk blinked in the open light, his eyes unaccustomed to it. The stricken man held out a fist as he passed by, and Goll dutifully pressed it with his own, but only at a fraction of his strength.

"Where's your push?" Muluk scolded in a medicated haze. "You're a *master* now. Need more push than that."

Goll waved the towering Brozz and Sapo past, and they bore the wounded man to a nearby wagon. Canvas covered the wooden vehicles, providing protection from the sun as well as privacy. A handful of guardsmen, most of them in Clavellus's employ, watched the streets like wary hounds. Clavellus sat atop one wagon's seat, next to a driver fiddling with the reins of the team of horses, while Machlann stood nearby, frowning at the procession. Koba rejoined them and spoke to them in low tones.

Kolo and Torello bore Pig Knot to the rear of a wagon, and Goll held out his fist as they passed.

The Sunjan glanced away with a drunken scowl.

The Kree stood there with his fist outstretched for a heartbeat before dropping it, chagrin creeping into his neck and face. He looked over his shoulder and met Halm's knowing smirk. Not needing that in the least, Goll turned his attention back to the wagons and spied Borchus whispering to Clavellus, who hefted a leather purse the agent had handed over, something that didn't go unnoticed by the Kree. The short, stocky agent then gave a curt nod to the taskmaster and trotted off down the street without a word to Goll.

And Goll didn't like it. "Borchus!"

The agent turned about, a mild question on his features.

"Where are you going?" Goll called out. Clavellus even turned his head for the response.

"Work calls, Master Goll," Borchus replied with a flourish of a hand. "Work calls. I'll be in contact."

With that, he disappeared down an alleyway, leaving a note of irritation in Goll's mind. He met Clavellus's gaze before the old taskmaster turned about in his seat. Goll didn't like that either and limped at best speed back to his own waiting wagon. The Kree swished open the canvas sheet covering the rear and hauled himself in with the others.

The wagon itself was a long-distance variety, a full seventeen feet long, with a stout wooden suspension underneath a worn body. Long benches ran along the sides, and the men travelling back to the villa squeezed in around Muluk's stretcher, mindful of their feet and leaning back against the bowed metal ribs that rose up on either side and supported the canvas shell. A faint smell of tar, used to seal the seams in the wagon's body, hit Goll's nose, and he cursed when his foot caught on a toolbox in the rear. Righting himself, he squeezed in beside the bottom part of Muluk's stretcher and yanked the white canvas sheet across, sealing the interior.

Halm pulled the canvas back open and regarded him with a darkly amused expression. "Something bothering you, Goll?"

"Nothing."

"Your face says otherwise."

Goll glared at him from the wagon's cool shade.

"Now it says something else," Halm noted.

The Kree's face soured even more, and he reached out and hauled the canvas closed once again.

Machlann hauled himself up into the rear of Clavellus's lead wagon and barked that all was ready for departure. He waved grimly at those behind. Another voice answered, reins snapped, and the wagons pulled away from the healer's house, rattling toward the crowded main street.

Halm was left standing alone in front of Shan's house.

"Wasn't being saucy that time," the big man muttered as he watched his companions roll away.

12

Nordish Front

Rain crashed through a canopy of tattered foliage and drizzled through outstretched tree limbs. Some droplets smashed their way through the leaves and plunked earthward, disappearing in the saturated gloom of the wet forest undergrowth. Down there, in the soggy shadows, the Jackals pressed forward in ruthless silence, their soft-booted feet soaked from the ground and clinging vegetation. The sound of pattering rain concealed the noise of every careful step. Growling thunderheads had brought miserable weather with the morning and unpacked it right over their heads. Most soldiers cursed the rain and the misery it bestowed. First Basten Vilak swore at it in the dismal predawn light, and a man would have to have both ears stabbed to miss the rumblings of his armor-bristling Grinders.

Since Kra and his Jackals reveled in inflicting misery

upon their enemy, the rain meant little to them. If anything, it meant a lowering of a sentry's alertness, and that, Kra informed his men, was a good thing. The commander secretly enjoyed the smell of a wet forest; the fresh air after a good dousing was a wonderful thing to inhale and savor.

Kra carefully stalked through the drenched wilderness, his mask soaked against his skull, the sound of his passing drowned out by the wet weather. A huge tree with a gnarly hide rose before him, and he placed his back against its solid mass. He waved his Jackals past, and they slunk through the dribbles and shadows on either side of him, a grim tide of leather and steel and murderous intent. Somehow—even Kra failed to fathom exactly why—the dreary showers seemed to energize his dogs while sapping the strength from the others. Far behind their advancing line, the Grinders followed yet were nowhere to be seen. It was standard practice. If the forward Jackals encountered any danger, they would quickly fall back to the heavy soldiers' line and make a stand if necessary. All told, Kra commanded nearly a hundred soldiers while Vilak still retained his full one hundred fifty Grinders—enough to give anyone second thoughts about engaging them.

One figure stopped beside Kra, and brown eyes just barely seen through the cloth slits of a drenched mask regarded the commander with a question. Kra rolled up his own mask, uncovering his lower jaw, and bared his teeth at the soldier in a snarl. He held it for only a moment before it melted into a sorry smile.

"Of the whole pack, you have to be the only one to *not* enjoy this weather," Kra said.

The Jackal leaned in closer and whispered, "I'm the only one sensible."

HOUSE OF PAIN

Arrus. Kra recognized his brother from his walk even before he heard his voice. "Embrace it. You'll feel better."

Arrus cocked his head as water ran from the edges of his mask and into his eyes, causing him to blink. "Oh, I'm embracing it. Truly. I'm convinced it's really warm sunshine soaking my feet. That it's massage oil running down my back into the crack of my ass. That any moment, I'll wake up, and the bare-tit wench rubbing me down will—"

"All right, leave the women out of this."

"What, and stop embracing *all* of *this*?"

Kra's face hitched into a scowl as he lowered his mask. "This is nothing. You forget your training."

"Ah yes, I forgot about that. Hard to remember it when your balls are soaked through. Much rather remember my oil massage."

Kra pointed a warning finger at his brother, a gesture he'd repeated many times. Arrus lowered his head and moved around the tree, having voiced his mind in a fashion typical for him. The first basten would keep an eye out for his younger brother to a point. If this mission went well and Arrus performed as a Jackal should, Kra had every intention of field promoting him to basten. There wasn't anyone more capable or, more importantly, reliable—no one else he wanted guarding his back. The only trouble with Arrus was his personality. Kra had to admit his brother… was a he-bitch—worse, a he-bitch begging to be slapped at times. A part of him wondered if he would have to do it again as he'd done when they were boys. He would if necessary, but he'd give his brother the courtesy of not doing it in front of the pack.

Adjusting the mask's hem at his throat, Kra left the tree and stealthily caught up to the glistening back of the nearest Jackal, a soldier carrying a shortsword and a spiked buckler. The commander moved past and pushed on, mindful of the others around him.

As Kra walked, the rain lessened and eventually stopped.

Arrus will be happy.

The line of leather-clad warriors crept on, water dripping upon them from hidden heights. Wet trees shrouded the land, which tilted into an easy slope. The forest's spice scented the air. The undergrowth became unsettled, and Kra and his men had to be mindful of where they stepped for fear of slipping or tripping. They knew the area, having come the way before, but the rain had left the ground soft and slick.

Kra instinctively glanced up before hearing a crack of twigs in the distance. The Jackals ahead froze in their tracks, scanning the brush. Kra held up an arm and peered into the dripping woods. An instant later, his startled breath caught in his throat.

At the top of the slope, within a cage of tree trunks, stood a single figure with a bare skull. His fearsome shortsword gleamed in the wet light, opposite a round shield poised over the man's thigh. The forest's breath clung to his dark frame, coating him in a fine, glistening mist. Kra realized the warrior wore leather armor, and the skull was in fact a helm.

One man was confronting a pack of almost a hundred Jackals bent on bloodletting.

Kra could only stare, for the gall of the lone warrior unnerved him more than he dared admit. A nearby Jackal whispered to him, a word that nailed Kra's attention to the single figure atop the slope, for no other could be so bold…

HOUSE OF PAIN

Cavalier.

A wave of dread coursed through Kra, and he hesitated. The Nordish commander couldn't believe the insolence of the unmoving gatekeeper before them, insulting his entire force by simply standing tall and *being*. It had to be a trap, a ploy the Jackals used themselves—bait a more powerful enemy with a smaller group, harry them, retreat, and lead whoever was eager enough to follow back to friendly lines, to their deaths.

The Jackals surrounding him remained motionless, wary of the very air they breathed. Rain hissed and began pattering off leaves. The Nords stared at the lone swordsman, seemingly bedazzled by his singular bravery. Then, somewhere along their ominous line, a branch snapped. That crack of fibers, loud as thunder in the forest stillness, broke the spell.

The Cavalier half turned then, almost dismissive of the force before him.

Kra gestured at a handful of Jackals who carried bows and pointed to the Sunjan on the hill. The masked men readied their weapons and took aim, but before they could release, the cavalier casually stepped behind one of the trees surrounding him.

The Cavalier barked a laugh, harsh and scalding. He spoke to the Jackals, chiding them in his foreign tongue. Though the language was incomprehensible, its meaning was clear.

Kra's countrymen tensed, eager to be released.

"He's only one," came a whisper.

"I can't hear anything else," muttered another.

"We could gut him in a heartbeat."

The voices did nothing for Kra's confidence in the matter. What manner of man dared venture into the wild to confront superior numbers? Trouble was afoot, lying in wait—perhaps not close by, but when the fight began, close enough to rush to the lone Sunjan's aid. Kra suspected Lancers.

The Cavalier appeared between the trees, exposing himself. The archers released their arrows, and a pointed mist flashed toward the single warrior, who darted out of sight. Arrows sped through the empty space, and some struck trunks with a rush of *whocks*. The brief echoes made Kra cringe.

But the Cavalier's chuckle, a sound creeping over the slope like rasping chains, angered him.

Insolent hellpup.

Kra pointed his sword in the Cavalier's direction.

From out of the shadows and the wet underbrush, the Jackals advanced. Swords, axes, and maces bared, their weapons gleamed in the dewy light. At the top, the Cavalier watched them ascend with interest, his own weapon poised and dripping rain. The pack stretched out in places and soon fragmented as men struggled with their footing. Dead vegetation slicked the hillside, rendering it slippery. More than one man dropped to a knee from an unseen dip or rabbit hole. Even Kra discovered how treacherous the hill was, and he grimaced with each uneven step, actually dropping to a knee and catching himself when his foot slipped into an unexpected hollow.

The foremost Jackals reached the Cavalier. The Sunjan stepped back to allow the first attacker to clamber atop the mound. The Nordish warrior righted himself and lashed out with a blade, the flashing steel a flat arc, seeking to split his foe to his backbone. The Cavalier stopped the slash and hacked through his attacker's right shoulder, parting meat and bone in plume of fine arterial spray. The

HOUSE OF PAIN

Jackal crumpled with a quiet grunt.

The Cavalier kicked the dead man off his blade and sent him tumbling back…

Just in time for another warrior to pass through the tall columns of wood atop the hill.

Clang! Schloop! The Cavalier parried his enemy's sword to the outside before whipping lightning across the Nord's face, cutting off a shriek. A second flash of steel drove the dying man to his knees. The Sunjan put a boot to him as well, toppling his dying victim.

A third Jackal rose and challenged the Cavalier. The Nordish warrior slashed, seeking a head. The Cavalier ducked and countered, and the Jackal crumpled, cradling his stomach before a shield's edge chopped the back of his neck.

Kra stopped halfway up the slope. *Who* is *this hellion?*

He hissed twice, two terse expulsions between teeth, and his men lurched up the hill. Kra doubled his own efforts to close the distance, cursing as wet ground crumbled underfoot in places. The Sunjan had chosen his battlefield well, Kra realized darkly, and terrain was everything in a battle.

At the top, the Cavalier greeted the Jackals one by one.

One man's head was half shorn away, his windpipe parting with a frightful hiss. A Jackal swung a mace and splintered the bark off a tree. The same man buckled from having his guts sliced to his backbone. Yet another Jackal crossed steel with the Cavalier, disengaged, and swung again, only to have his weapon hand sliced off at the wrist an instant before a horrific gash opened almost magically from his right shoulder to left hip. Blackness splashed onto the ground as he toppled.

Two more Jackals attacked as one. Both died in an

almost sorcerous display of swordsmanship, their bodies wilting around the Cavalier. The Sunjan stepped back and gestured brazenly for more.

And the Nordish terrorizers of the night pressed on in unnerving silence, like the blackest insects rising up to feast on fresh carrion, drawn to the inviting clatter of steel on steel. Their masks covered their faces, hiding their expressions, rendering all darkly stoic.

The Cavalier bashed his shield into one attacker's face, stopping the man in his tracks before spinning and catching another Jackal rising from the opposite quarter. That warrior dropped his weapons and staggered, clutching at the redness spouting from his neckline. The Cavalier spun again and slashed the legs of his shield-bashed victim. The Nord collapsed onto his back before being stabbed through the gut with authority, the Cavalier's sword nailing him to the moist earth with a soggy *chuff* of flesh and dirt.

The Sunjan paused then, his gleaming skull-like helm regarding the swarm clambering forward. He yanked his sword free, stood, and beckoned.

Kra looked on with a sense of awe and hatred. The Cavaliers were damned near legendary for their fighting skills. It was his misfortune that an *experienced* Cavalier faced them.

"Forward, from all sides!" Kra seethed, breaking silence and stumbling up the hill behind three of his men while his Jackals converged upon the top.

And almost impossibly, as the Nordish terrorizers reached the crest in ones and twos, the Cavalier put them down with a speed unimaginable. One Jackal floundered backward, clutching at his slashed and bleeding face. Another's arm was hacked off at the elbow before his skull was slammed by a shield. The Cavalier's sword stitched another Jackal through the torso and left the man dead on his feet. His shield crashed across a Jackal's jaw, and while the Nordish fell, the Sunjan killed two more in a heartbeat, his sword ripping their lives from their chests in splashing ruby arcs.

Those last two soldiers were ahead of Kra, and the commander shoved the third man out of the way in order to reach this Sunjan executioner. The Cavalier didn't pause, his sword snaking through the air in a grand flourish, marking his boundary. Kra lunged, crossed blades, locking their weapons in a tense struggle for supremacy. The Nordish officer tried to push, then twist, and discovered with horror the Cavalier was stronger. Connected as the two warriors were, Kra couldn't help looking into the Sunjan's flinty eyes.

The corners crinkled in a smile.

The Cavalier stomped on Kra's toes, crushing them into the soil and sending a jolt of agony shooting up the basten's entire frame. In that mind-freezing instant, the Sunjan grabbed the back of Kra's head and pulled him down onto his blade, impaling him through the heart.

There was a brisk twist of steel before the swordsman shoved him off, pulling the mask off as a dead Kra fell and crashed into the underbrush.

The Cavalier took a quick look at the Jackals converging upon him, more than even he could handle, and decided he'd held his ground long enough. Without warning, he turned and fled through the brush, leaving the Jackals clambering over a low wall of dead and dying.

Arrus reached the top of the slope and stopped in his tracks as the other Jackals bounded after the retreating Cavalier. He turned around, surveying the corpses at his feet, feeling dread the likes of which he'd never experienced before. The decision to hide their faces with black masks served several purposes, and only now did Arrus realize one of them with swelling alarm.

Kra lay amongst the dead, his white face unmasked.

Arrus gasped, seeing his brother's blood ooze into the dark earth.

"Kra," he whispered hoarsely as a Jackal ran past, leaving him behind. *"Kra."*

Arrus stepped over a corpse to reach his brother. Kra's eyes were closed, his mouth open as if drawing air, but Arrus spied the frothing slit in his brother's chest. Any other man might have raged and charged into the brush after his brother's killer, but the battle lust left Arrus in a gush. His knees buckled, and he fell to the corpse's side. Dropping his sword and shield, Arrus found and folded Kra's mask into a black pillow, which he tucked underneath his brother's face, keeping it from the dampness of the ground. A great shuddering breath took Arrus, and he was only faintly aware of screaming and the sounds of battle in the distance. Not that any of that mattered to him anymore. His brother was dead while he still drew breath, while he just sat and stared.

He had no more strength but to sit and mourn.

Cold with misery, his throat painfully constricted to the size of a reed, Arrus patted Kra's ashen features, hoping that maybe he'd crack open an eye and smile at him in that fond yet scathing way he had. Death wasn't unknown to Arrus, and he certainly had had friends perish in battle, but…

This is different. This is Kra. This is family.

Frame trembling, eyes and sinuses flooding with grief, he was oblivious to the echoes of a dying battle beyond.

HOUSE OF PAIN

Arrus stayed by his brother's side longer than he should have. He knew every passing moment endangered him, but he couldn't bear to leave.

And then, it didn't matter. Brush crackled. Arrus lifted his eyes to see warriors in dark chainmail rising above his line of sight; rectangular shields splashed with red; short swords poised to stab; the guarded whispers of an alien tongue he knew but couldn't speak.

Sunjans. Worse yet, they were *Sujins*, harsh slayers devoid of any emotion, the equivalent of Nordun's own Grinders. Arrus glanced around the forest, seeing the gaps between trunks fill in with bulky warriors cutting off any escape. Not that Arrus would have fought. The fight had long left him.

A handful of wary Sujins, their shields and breastplates dented and scratched, closed in and formed a ring around the slouched Jackal. One of the men spoke, a low, menacing gargle of words Arrus didn't understand in the least and didn't bother answering.

When he didn't respond, the Sujin's tone became even harder.

Sujins. Arrus shook his head. He'd been better off fighting. At least then there was the chance of being killed.

The Sujin talking stepped in close, imposing his presence. The warrior spoke again, curtly, stressing his point by hitting the Jackal's shoulder with his shield.

Arrus didn't care for that. Couldn't they see he was mourning? He knew Sunjans were an ignorant lot, but by the Nordish Ivus's grace, he hadn't realized they were *stupid*.

"*Vudosto*," Arrus swore, implying the soldier should ardently violate himself with the genitalia he'd been born with—the worst Nordish insult he knew.

The Sujin paused, seemingly pondering the meaning of the word, and for a short satisfying moment, Arrus believed the lout had actually understood him. His hand rested on Kra's unmoving brow, cool to the touch. A lock of his brother's hair brushed against the back of his fingers, and for a dreamlike moment, Arrus believed Kra really was only sleeping.

Then the Sujin's shield crashed into his head, and the world went black.

13

Borchus felt lighter after delivering Clavellus the sack of coin the old taskmaster had won on Pig Knot's fight. The original wager had been meant to be placed on Pig Knot, but Goll—Seddon bless him—informed the agent of his grand scheme for the Sunjan, thus averting the costly loss. Borchus had certainly appreciated it, but he suspected Clavellus wouldn't approve of Goll's ploys. Pride or something or other—Borchus wasn't completely sure which—blinded the taskmaster to the realities of the world and maintaining a full purse. Borchus had no such qualms, not when it came to the fighting season. Or so he told himself.

With Garl recovering from his bath and resting in relative safety, Borchus concentrated on recruiting the next set of eyes and ears for his network. He knew just the person. Unlike Garl, that particular spy was perhaps the best placed of any Borchus knew of, as well as being utterly unassuming and completely trusted by the locals.

The challenge—he never thought of it as a "problem"—would be convincing her to join his efforts.

The sun baked the stone slats covering the streets, rendering them as hot as coals and warning Borchus to replace his aging leather boots. He swung his muscular arms as he slunk through the back alleys, threading a path through a brick, mortar, and wood maze as surely as a sewer rat. At times, he scratched his long sideburns and his shorn mat of dark but graying hair, hoping his appearance was respectable. He headed north, toward King Juhn's palaces.

His destination, an alehouse, was located a bowshot from the inner walls of King Juhn's palace, and it serviced Sunja's more polished citizens, the flowers of the evenings, the upper-class revelers…

And the house gladiators of repute, good and bad.

As he bypassed the main streets and the throngs of people going about their afternoon business, Borchus remembered how Garl had recognized him by voice. By voice! He'd always firmly believed if anything were to give him away, it would be his height. His current disguise shielded him from second glances, and he knew the areas of the city to avoid—not even the underchambers of the Pit bothered him. Still, Garl had managed to guess him by his voice, of all things—even after all those years. Borchus cautioned himself. Others might very well do the same.

The thought disturbed the agent. Borchus knew he could be overconfident at times. Had he fooled himself? He hoped not. He couldn't possibly disguise himself any better unless he started wearing a sack over his head or moved to another country to ply his trade.

Those alternatives didn't sit well with the agent.

A few fellow alley lurkers passed him, their features

forgotten as soon as they were gone from sight. The armored backs of what appeared to be a full Street Watch stood at the mouth of a side lane, and Borchus walked on without worry. The city authorities didn't concern him. The law could be more than willing to provide useful information when offered coin.

The shadows between the buildings deepened when he arrived at the back entrance of a particularly sturdy-looking alehouse. Great slabs of timber, cracked and stained in places, rose up two stories and tapered into a high, tar-lathered roof. A crow watched him from its perch, a bare pole used for hanging wet clothing. Borchus thought the bird quite handsome, though he hated the voice of the creatures. He approached the rear door, mindful of the creature for fear it might defecate upon him. The smell of fresh baking bread wafting from a kitchen window perked his head up, and the thought of supper entered his mind.

The door swung open with a creak. A woman backed out, wearing a gray work dress with matching white shirt. She labored with a wooden tub of wash water, and her grunts punched the air as she turned the edge of the container around and tipped its lip. Gray suds spilled onto the alley floor with a hiss, flowing toward a grated drain.

"Excuse me," Borchus said softly, and the woman jumped. She grabbed at the fabric covering her neckline, glaring at him with a mixture of horror and surprise.

"My apologies," Borchus offered.

"You damn well should be sorry."

"I am."

"You frightened me right and proper," she declared, pulling on a strand of straight black hair.

Borchus nodded.

"You shouldn't be back here anyway. What are you

doing here? I don't know you."

"Ah, I was wondering if Sindra still works here?"

"Sindra?" The woman scrunched up her face unpleasantly, revealing yellow teeth. "What do you want with her?"

Borchus smiled. "Well, that would be my business, wouldn't it?"

"Besides frightening honest women like myself in back alleys?"

No, that's only a pastime, he thought, but what he said was, "My apologies again."

"Who are you, anyway?" she queried, her nose flaring as if smelling treachery.

"I'd rather keep that secret for now. As a surprise for Sindra. If she's within."

"Ohhh… surprises, eh?"

"Uh… yes."

"You look like a pit fighter. A bit short, but one nonetheless. Are you one?"

"I'm not." Borchus rattled his head in mild annoyance. Whoever she was, she'd gotten over her surprise quickly enough.

"Well, you look like one."

"Well… I'm *not.*"

"I love the gladiators, the games of the season. Love the fighting, the killing. Ah."

Borchus almost forgot to speak. "I can return tomorrow…"

"No, that's fine. Just a moment." The woman fluttered her fingers at him. "I'll see if I can find her. We have Gurga about, anyway. If you do anything bad, he'll squash you."

Borchus held up empty hands as the cleaning woman

withdrew inside. *Squash*. The word hung in his mind, and he sighed. Too many louts had thought he'd do that very thing but had died because of it. The faces of dead men clouded his memory.

But then a beast of a man came into view, rendering Borchus thoughtless and equally speechless. Black breeches covered the brute's legs while a beige shirt, untucked, lay open almost to the navel. An oily tangle of hair burst from the parting of cloth, and Borchus couldn't stop staring. Premature gray hair covered the head and face of the ogre, for that surely wasn't a man. The sweating giant stooped to clear the upper frame of the doorway and glared at him.

"You see him, Gurga?" the woman's voice asked from somewhere inside.

"The little fella?" Gurga rumbled in a voice that might shatter bedrock, hooking a thumb over a belt that could have stropped steel. A spiked club hung from that band of leather, intimidating enough for Borchus to deem it best not to react to the "little" comment. Gurga's mouth skewed up to one side in distaste, and the great rug that was his beard moved with it.

"Aye, that's him!"

Gurga sized Borchus up and down, unimpressed. "You want to look?" the big man growled out of a corner of his hairy maw.

"All right," another woman's voice answered, and Borchus faltered, recognizing it at once. Some things didn't change.

Sindra edged around Gurga's girth. Older, her hair tied back, also graying but only in sparse strands, and her face and throat a little more lined, she gazed upon Borchus with those enormous brown eyes of hers—which he believed were her best features—and stopped in her tracks. Puzzlement clouded her face, which despite the years, had aged well. She took no offence to him sizing up her modest white dress in return.

She slowly drew breath. "Oh, sweet Seddon above."

"Wha?" Gurga asked, his dense brow furrowing as he looked from Borchus to Sindra.

"Yes, what?" chirped the first woman from somewhere inside.

"Nothing, nothing," Sindra said, blinking. "Telda, get back to that roast. And mind what you're doing with the sauce."

"You want me to kill him?" Gurga asked, rubbing his chin.

Sindra shook her head.

"Smack him?"

That earned a scowl from her, and Borchus bit back a smirk. Many a time, he'd earned that very thunderstorm of a glare. Several times, lightning had accompanied it and scorched the air.

"None of that." She exhaled testily before she flashed those liquid pools of night at Borchus. "Well, not yet anyway. Stay here."

Gurga's glare reappeared, and he directed it at Borchus.

Sindra stepped outside and circled the agent, the hem of her long dress just grazing the alley's fitted stone. She studied him from top to toe before scrutinizing his face.

"You cut your hair. And beard."

Borchus shrugged. "You've gone all modest. You used to…" he cleared his throat, "expose more."

"I was younger then."

"Still young."

But the compliment didn't flatter Sindra as Borchus

hoped it would. He recalled then, this was *Sindra*, who used to confide in him her scornful amusement over any man and his attempts at sweet talking. That memory burned him—he'd just made a fool of himself in her eyes. She was a woman who traded barbs with the best of them and won—him included.

Trouble was, as pitiful as it sounded, he *meant* the compliment.

"How many years have you been gone?" she asked in a hushed, incredulous tone.

Borchus cleared his throat. "I don't remember."

And Sindra smiled, a cutting sickle of teeth carefully maintained, ready to let loose a scathing barb of a reply or a killing lance of sarcasm. He'd seen it before, *chuckled* at it before. Now he braced for it.

But she simply shook her head in slow dismay instead, sparing him.

"I can smack him," Gurga offered again from the doorway.

Sindra shushed him with a hand and a dirty look.

"He's eager to crack some heads," Borchus observed.

"Only yours."

That wasn't something he needed to hear.

"Gurga is our main enforcer, for reasons I'm sure you appreciate."

"He's a tall one."

Sindra shrugged. "Oh, he's a savage. Most times, he's only intimidating. When you're that big, you really only have to look unfit in the head to make the patrons behave. He's been with us now for almost ten years, and not one person has openly challenged him. Not one. Think on that when you consider who frequents here. And if I give the nod, he's quick to rub troublemakers into a cow kiss outside."

All the while, a suspicious Gurga considered Borchus, quietly chewing on something that didn't appear ready to go down his gullet. It was difficult to imagine the enforcer looking pleasant.

Sindra continued, "There hasn't been a—"

"Where's Hadree?" Borchus interrupted, wanting to change the subject.

"Dead."

That shocked the agent, and it showed on his face.

"Nine years now," Sindra informed him, unflinching. "We're not sure what happened there. He was old, though you couldn't tell him that. Near sixty-nine. He was tending the bar when he dropped a mug and collapsed right there. His heart simply stopped, or so the healer said. We buried him outside the city the next day. Underneath the shade of a tree."

The sounds of passersby from the main street rustled into the abrupt silence. The news of the man's death stunned Borchus.

"I'm sorry," he offered, meaning it in the most respectable manner possible while seeing the cantankerous old bastard in his head. Hadree had been a fair man and could discern the good from the bad.

"We've long gotten over it," Sindra stated stoically. "Though there are times I can still hear his voice. Or even expect him to come through the front door, swearing at someone from the common market. So, where have you been?"

Borchus hesitated before answering. The revelation of Hadree's passing softened his stance on keeping his past secret. Perhaps that was Sindra's plan. She was crafty that way. "I've been in and out of Sunja. The city and the country. I had to leave abruptly, for fear of bloody reprisal from an employer."

"What about?"

"Ah." Borchus smiled feebly. "Some information I was given wasn't entirely truthful. In fact, looking back, someone might have recognized who I worked for and used it to their own advantage while ensuring I appeared to have profited at the expense of my employer."

"Outsmarted? You?" Sindra asked, the barest twinge of amusement in her voice.

"Yes."

She chuckled, the bell-like quality surprising him. He'd missed it. "Wasn't funny at the time."

"And you up and left without word to anyone?" Sindra probed.

Not even you. "Yes."

"With no word for all these years. Until now."

Borchus nodded in defeat. "It wasn't that kind of departure, Sindra."

"What kind was it?"

"The kind where one ran as fast as one could. Without any goodbyes. And without looking back." *For fear of your safety.*

"I remember the business, Borchus. I remember the risks. It's just… surprising to discover that perhaps, under your cavalier demeanor and wit, the business caught up with you. I thought you were smarter than that. We were certain you'd been cut up and fed to the pigs somewhere."

"Always a possibility."

"What do you mean? You're still in danger?"

Borchus brushed his fingertips against his bare chin. "Thus my disguise."

Sindra folded her arms. "But you've returned to see

me. Now. Why? You could've gotten word to us that you were alive years earlier, but you didn't. No, you left and decided it was best to be forgotten, but you're here now. You want something. You want me to *do* something."

From the doorway, Gurga's grim but attentive face flicked from Sindra to Borchus with each exchange. He gripped the overhead frame and leaned out, squeezing his head and shoulders through the opening.

But Borchus barely noticed him. Sindra—lovely, *intelligent* Sindra—had sniffed him out. Foreboding gripped his guts.

"That's it," Sindra stated, sensing she was right. Her dark eyes bored into him, making him blink uncomfortably, and he cursed himself. "You want me to do something. What is it, though. I wonder…"

"Could we do this inside?"

Gurga growled and bared his teeth. Sindra warded him off with a hand. The enforcer snorted but heeled, touching the fearsome club hanging from his belt.

"No," Sindra said. "Here's fine. I didn't run back then, without a word to anyone. I just hoped you were alive somewhere and that perhaps you'd return with this grand story of why you'd left in the first place. Only you didn't return when I expected you to. Not a few days, not a month, and certainly not a year. Even Hadree wondered about you. Yes, he did. He might've been a rotten punce to you half of the time, but he thought well of you. *Highly* even, I daresay, though he didn't show it. He enjoyed your talks. And he died with that same puzzled expression you often left him with."

A pained scowl overtook Borchus's features. That was a deep cut. Even for Sindra.

"No," she finally declared with nonchalance. "I don't

care what it is you're about or want. I don't want to have anything to do with you. Things are simpler now. Without you."

"I'm organizing another network," Borchus said, almost pleadingly. "You're very important to those plans."

"Ah…" She arched her head back as if savoring something fragrant. "You want me to spy again. To pick up morsels of information from the gladiators."

"You were my best."

"And that's all?"

"What do you mean?"

"Nothing, I suppose. And the answer is still no. Years have passed, Borchus, and I'm but one thing that's changed in our fair city. I suggest you stay with the life you found beyond Sunja and forget the one you left behind. That one chased you from the city and most of the people who knew you. If you go back to it, escape might not be an easy thing a second time."

"Sindra…"

But she was done, already walking back to the door of the alehouse. Gurga moved into the alley to allow her entry. Borchus thought about pursuing the matter, but something in Sindra's tone stopped him. Gurga noted his hesitancy and blocked him from following her, glaring a warning. Borchus had no stomach for a fight so early in the afternoon. Not with that beast of a man.

So he left.

Retracing the path he'd followed, Borchus mulled over the encounter with Sindra and felt undone by her piercing manner and stabs of truth. After so long, she still knew him too well. In addition, the news of Hadree's passing had struck him hard, harder than he would admit to anyone. The old man had been a favorite of his as well, like an old, iron-willed uncle one continuously tried to impress, who dispensed nuggets of wisdom when most needed.

Stay with the life you found beyond Sunja, her voice resonated, haunting.

Borchus couldn't do that.

And Seddon above damn him for it.

With the day's heat breaking and a red evening setting in, Borchus returned to his cellar. The slab of wood serving as a door felt heavier than usual. Thoughts of Sindra occupied his mind all the way back, weakening him in ways he'd once believed impossible. He gripped the latch of the cellar door, pulled it too hard, and ripped a fingernail free for his effort. The wood slammed down.

Borchus stood in the alley, favoring the sting of his bleeding finger, and stared hard enough at the lid to scorch it. He glanced both ways before stooping and trying again. That time he lifted the cover and got under it, descending the stairs into a vat of darkness smelling of earth and wood.

Darkness.

"Garl?" Borchus whispered, sucked at his finger, and spat blood.

A length of wood lashed out and smashed across Borchus's unprotected shins. He tumbled the rest of the way down, the door slamming above and enveloping him in pitch blackness. His side crashed against the earthy floor, jamming his arm into his ribs. He rolled onto his back, and before he could recover, a weight fell upon him, flopping across his body and robbing him of any wind remaining in his lungs. Stricken, the agent groaned as if kneed in the balls.

"Borchus?"

He wheezed out a whimper.

"Borchus!"

Garl.

Hands patted him down as if he were ablaze. "Apologies, Borchus, apologies. I thought… I thought you were someone else."

"Who?" Borchus squeaked, the air beginning to return.

"Them," Garl blurted out. "The ones who… who I report to."

"What?" His voice gained strength.

"No one saw you come here?"

Borchus lifted himself up on his elbows and eventually rubbed at his tender shins. "What? No, of course not. Who is it you're so frightened of?"

The darkness seemed to pause, and for a moment, Borchus could just make out a shape against the light peeking in around the cellar door. Garl backed off and groped around in the darkness. He struck a flint and lit one of the few candles Borchus kept below. Beyond the orange light, Garl's shaven face loomed worriedly, regarding the cellar door.

"Shhh," he insisted.

Borchus listened and heard nothing. His attention moved from the candle and Garl's face to the closed entryway above the stairs.

"Can you hear them?"

"No," Borchus said and got to his feet. "And if someone was out there, they would've been in here already."

Garl blinked in the candlelight and looked toward the door once more. Borchus did the same, a sliver of paranoia sinking into his conscience.

Still, the cellar remained undisturbed.

"They could be outside," Garl whispered.

"There's no one outside."

"They might have followed you."

"*Who?* And this time answer me, or I'll twist your bells like a washrag."

For moments, Garl did not answer him, and Borchus had the sickening—and depressing—notion that his spy might be unfit in the head.

Garl gathered up his crutch and beckoned Borchus back into the recesses of the cellar, around a corner, where a single cot waited. There, the beggar placed the candle in a metal cradle and left it, his clean-shaven face just beyond its glowing hue.

"The streets of Sunja have become a dangerous place, Borchus. Very dangerous. There are killings that go unreported to the Skarrs, and even if the constables did respond, some say they wouldn't do a thing. I've seen men like me be stabbed and left bleeding in the dirt because they didn't have enough coin on them."

"What are you saying?"

Garl took a breath and leaned in. "The streets. Have you noticed there are more beggars around these days?"

"No."

"Well, there are. But some of them aren't beggars. Some of them only wear the clothes and oversee the others, the real ones who plead for coin."

"And table scraps?"

"That as well." Garl nodded. "They're always watching someone. The trouble is, you won't know *when* they're watching. If you had tossed me a coin and left, they would've been on me in moments for that very coin."

Impatience made Borchus sputter, "*Who*, by dying Seddon, *who?*"

"There is a pack of rats ruling the streets. The leader is a snake called Strach. He has a number of beggars working for him. I'm not sure how many, but there's *many*. Whatever they get—*we* get—we hand over to him or one of his brutes. If not, well, he'll break fingers… twist bells. He'll… he'll put a knife into your eye and—"

"They're thieves?"

Garl frantically shook his head, information gushing from him. "Not wholly thieves, though I'm certain it's not above them. Strach is only one man with a few lads… but to rule, one only has to be ruthless. They're one of many packs gnawing on Sunja's bones. The Skarrs are pressed too hard with other matters to concern themselves with gutter shite like us. Some even say Strach pays the Street Watch to mind their business. He takes everything we might get or already have. Well, except food, that is. But if you don't have coin when he comes around… he has men, and they… they *punish* you the first time. And you'll disappear if there's a next. I know of men who have vanished because they tried to hold coin back or even attempted to cross Strach and his lads. I know of others who've had their very eyes scooped from their heads. They're *animals*, Borchus. *Animals*. You don't know the pain these bastards inflict. They don't look upon us as men or women anymore. We're… we're…"

Garl's whisper cracked, and he held his tongue, lowering his eyes while he composed himself. Borchus allowed him that and glanced in the direction of the cellar door. A length of timber leaned against a wall, used to throw across iron hooks and bar the cellar door from the inside. Though he didn't say anything, Borchus knew he'd be using it this night.

"And now that you're with me?"

Garl's face became a contortion of fright, real enough to worry Borchus, and he wasn't one to unease easily.

"Why didn't anyone try and leave the city?"

"Some have, but they're never heard from again."

"Because they've left the city," Borchus pointed out, darkly amused.

"No, no, no, I've heard that Strach will send out lads. Men who'll track you down and butcher you. Do things that'll make children shiver at night. We've been warned. Leaving the city means a slow death."

"And staying is Saimon's hell," Borchus said, disliking Strach already.

"Worse," Garl breathed. "I knew of a boy, not yet nine if that—born on the streets and lived off them. Had fingers as light and sticky as a spider's. Strach got a hold of him, made the youngster work for him. I don't know exactly what happened or how the boy crossed Strach, but I know the lad disappeared. Stories have it that Strach and his killers mauled that child—spiked his little body to a wall and let him hang there, Borchus, like curing meat. A *boy*. They killed a *boy*. Over maybe a few coins, just as a lesson to the rest of us."

"You didn't mention this before." Borchus glanced once more in the direction of the cellar door and felt the need to secure it.

"I tried!" Garl whispered. "You said you'd protect me. I tried to tell you, but you offered me... you said you'd—"

"That was when I thought it was a few punces! Not a pack of street lice."

Garl struggled with his obvious fear. "You haven't changed. You're still you. I lost *these*"—he thrust his hand

and its uneven stumps into the light—"because of you."

Borchus had an urge to shout at the man, but fear gripped Garl. The beggar eventually sighed and slumped, clicking his teeth together while straightening out his thoughts.

"Look," Garl said, more softly. "You need spies. A lot of spies, yes?"

Against the churning of his guts, Borchus nodded that he did.

"If you can get rid of Strach, I can convince some of the others to work for you—provided you do this and treat them as you've treated me."

"You're asking a lot."

"If you throw me out…"

"Might we pay him off?"

"Strach? How much do you have?"

"Not much." Borchus could give Strach a few coins, but that might not mean anything to a dangerous street snake. He rubbed his face. He'd fled the city and his people once before; he didn't think he could again. Not after coming back. He sighed. He should never have returned. Should've just kept on running errands for Clavellus to the other towns and cities and stayed clear of Sunja.

"You know what he looks like?"

"Strach? Of course."

Borchus took a breath. "All right."

"All right what?"

"I'll… help you."

But in the candlelight, Borchus could see the distrust on Garl's face.

"Why exactly did you leave, Borchus?" he whispered. "I never really knew. No one did."

Borchus didn't want to remember that time, didn't want to talk about any of it, but surprisingly, the words came out easily enough. "Someone knew I was an agent working with the House of Tilo. Someone knew and used that information. Framed me. I overheard that a fighter from the Stable of Vorish had broken his ribs, but he was going to fight his match anyway. Such a morsel would have meant a quick victory on the sands, eh? So I told Tilo about it, whose man was going to face Vorish's lad. Tilo trained his fighter—I forget the name—to play upon that weakness. Trouble was... there was never any such injury. It was bait. And Vorish's man gutted Tilo's. Worse, I was living out of a rented room in an alehouse at the time. Tilo knew this and sent over a few of his pit fighters to talk to me, which they did. They caught me and also found a purse of gold under the bed. Under the *bed...*" Borchus smiled coldly at the memory. "As if *I* would place coin under a bed. Lords above. But try explaining that to Tilo. Or one of Tilo's cutthroats. I had to kill one to get away. I realized then the wisdom of getting out of Sunja for a while. So I did. At some point, they found you."

"They did that."

"So. There you have it. Told no one else, really. Travelled Marrn, Balgotha, and Pericia over the years. Even Vathia. Then I came back to Sunja. Never did find out who placed the gold under the bed or who let slip that a man's ribs had been broken. Not even sure it was Vorish, though I imagine him being capable. Someone, though. Someone looking for revenge. Perhaps for gathering information on one of their fighters that tipped the balance in a match. It could have been anyone or anything, really."

Garl remained silent.

"Well… tomorrow you go into the streets on behalf of the House of Ten," the agent informed his spy. "Stay to the shadows during the day; the night will be easier. Be alert. You've cleaned up considerably, and I suspect anyone would have a time recognizing the Garl of old. Do what you do, hang around the alehouses and such—anywhere people are talking about the fights. Anywhere gladiators might frequent. Come back here each night. I'll meet you, and we'll talk. That's a start."

"And what are you going to do?" Garl wanted to know.

Borchus looked him in the eye. "What has to be done."

14

Just after noon the following day, Halm returned to the crowded squalor of the Pit's general quarters. With Shan away from his house, he hadn't felt comfortable troubling his wife by staying there the night before, so he searched for an affordable alternative. And after sleeping in a clean bed in a rented room of an alehouse, the bloated stench of the underground chamber threatened to turn his stomach. However, he endured it, intent on confronting Skulljigger to see the man's face when he learned of the impending blood match. The wall Halm leaned against felt hot and sticky against his bare back, making him hope the pig bastard appeared soon. Wallowing in the sour air of hundreds of pit fighters did nothing for his patience, nor did watching the clamor of activity before the day's fights. Men stayed within the radius of overhead torchlight as the sounds of the Pit enveloped him—boisterous conversations ebbed and flowed, armor slapped and buckled onto muscle. His ears picked up the unsettling whisper and grind of blades being sharpened. Any other day, Halm would have had his own preparations, but not that day. Shadows hid his face while his guts insisted upon returning to the surface for fresh breath.

In the end, he gave in.

Torches cast their flickering light down from iron brackets, and he walked through arcs of orange hues and wells of darkness until a stairwell came into sight. He rose from the Pit's blackness two steps at a time and exited the Gate of the Sun in short order. The lines to the Domis caught his attention. The solid stone and timber booths peeked over the citizens waiting to place their wagers. A patrol of Skarrs walked by, drawing his attention, as did another intimidating group stationed with their backs against the outer shell of the Domis, their steely visors vigilant.

The hot sun punished people as they milled about the open area encompassing the arena, the heat stamping their faces, while a good many Sunjans crowded the shade offered by the arena's towering walls. Halm wasn't sure how many fights remained that day, but the number of people placing wagers seemed thicker than flies on dead meat. Perhaps they knew something he didn't. That etched an ugly smirk on his rough features.

The smell of grilled meat caught Halm's attention, and he spotted several wooden stalls selling both food and drink to spectators. Feeling the heat even in the shade, he backed up until he bumped against the stone wall of the arena. He spied a few women amongst the crowds, all of various sizes and attractiveness, all gleaming with sweat and some with perfume strong enough that he caught a whiff. *Women.* Halm ogled some of the fairer ones, envisioning their shapes without their robes, britches, or tunics. Some felt his lecherous gaze and glared back, and that only emboldened the Zhiberian even more. Eventually, he tired of the game and looked elsewhere.

Cheers reached a crescendo within the Pit, loud enough to make him look up for falling timbers or stones. Children raced by, and while he wasn't averse to them, he was secretly glad they didn't take notice of him. He found young children to be shameless. They had stopped and stared at him before, marveling at his hard looks and the size of his bare belly. He secretly cared little for such attention. He then realized he was doing the same with the women in the area, and that tiny pinch of understanding made him scold himself. He thumped his head against the Pit's hide in a slow, poisonous self-loathing.

And there he stood for the rest of the day, even when the arena fights finished and the crowds noisily leaked out from the Gate of the Sun. A few people stopped at the windows of the Domis and collected their winnings, while others lingered in the streets. The sounds of excitement diminished into murmurs, and the shadows lengthened across fitted stone. The sky ripened orange, and the heat abated just a little. For that alone, Halm's spirits improved, but he didn't see the man whom he wanted very badly to punish.

Only a few people walked along the Pit's constructed fairway, seemingly following their shadows while the city's evening sounds emerged. Huddling in food stalls, merchants roasted sticks of meat for one or two customers remaining here and there. Halm felt his need for revenge softened by the urges of his belly, yet he didn't want to stand and eat. Alehouses and nearby taverns called to him, so the decision to seek one out wasn't difficult. Another day had passed, and Skulljigger hadn't shown. Frowning more from tiredness than disappointment, he detached himself from the darkening wall and made his way down across the open area and down a street.

People drifted in and out of his way as he eyed open doors, signs, and the unnecessary ribbons and festive streamers the Sunjans seemed to favor. While Halm found the Sunjans friendly enough at times, he thought the year-round decorations off-putting and more than a little garish at times, especially while a war was being waged beyond their plains and forests—a war hungering for their young men.

Still, it wasn't *his* war, so he let them do what they liked. Halm pushed it from his mind.

An alehouse lured him toward its quiet open doors. He stuck his head inside, and the smell of some good cooking over an unseen fire pit pulled him toward a long counter. Oil lamps glowed from their perches high on rustic wooden pillars. Serving women in frumpy white dresses moved through a large interior sparsely filled with diners and drinkers. Some of the patrons sitting about their tables spared the Zhiberian only a glance before turning back to their business. Halm stopped and rapped his knuckles on the bar, inspecting the many barrels turned on their sides, containing all sorts of fermented goodness. A fence of clean-looking mugs and brass pitchers gleamed on a shelf just underneath them all, capturing the enticing flicker of the light just right.

"Yes?" asked a fair young woman dressed in a green shirt.

Halm nodded with approval. "What's good here?"

"We're roasting rabbits this day. Seasoned with garlic and onions."

"I'll have one of those. Right here. And two slices of

bread if you have any baked. What's there to drink?"

"Beer, Sunjan Gold, Sunjan Black, wine…"

"A pitcher of beer. And do you have rooms above?"

"We do. A gold coin for the night."

Cheap. "Then I'll have one of those as well," Halm ordered and rested his elbows on the counter while he studied the interior of the alehouse. The second floor wasn't visible from the first and had to be reached by stairs cut from heavy wood, unlike the place he and the lads had frequented before. The image of Muluk and Pig Knot cut to pieces darkened his mood, and he hoped he'd have more luck with his hunt for Skulljigger the next day. That night, he'd drink to his friend's health and spend some of the coin he'd taken from Goll's sack.

The beer arrived first, and Halm quaffed it. He ordered a pitcher afterward and took it to a table near a wall. This alehouse didn't have alcoves like the other one. That was probably for the best—no memories.

Then a recollection slunk into his head, like a dead thing brushing against skin. Pig Knot didn't have any *legs*. Lords above. The man was crippled in the worst way possible. How would he cope? What could he do? Halm had his doubts and took a long pull at the pitcher, drinking his beer straight from the clay lip. A gasp punctuated the air when he finished. Pig Knot. Lords above. He wondered what he would've done if it had been his own legs chopped off. The notion made him screw up his face. Death. He'd hope for death. For the life of him, he couldn't see what the Sunjan's future held.

"Drinking alone?"

Halm's mouth hung open when the cleaned-up pit fighter that reminded him of Pig Knot sat down at his table, opposite him. *Targus—that was his name.* He carried his own pitcher and filled a brass mug with wine that shone berry red.

"Targus," Halm greeted, forcing cheer into his voice. "You're actually easy to look upon when you aren't readying to gut someone."

The man had cleaned up quite respectfully. His dark hair hung in a braid and draped over his shoulder. A clean white tunic, sleeveless, showed off the thick musculature of his arms. Once again, Halm felt as if he were gazing upon a youthful version of Pig Knot, right down to the crazy-eyed look—and a lot fewer scars.

"You make me worried when you do that." Targus frowned as he sipped his wine and hissed at the tart taste.

"I've only done it twice." Halm looked into his own drink.

"Well, stop it."

"You really do look like him, though."

"Who?"

"My friend."

"Ah." Targus said. "Well, anyway, my thanks again for the words earlier this day. Before I fought. I won."

"I figured you did." Halm smirked. "No cuts on you."

"I killed him."

"Your opponent?"

"Aye that."

Halm shrugged and slowly turned his pitcher around with a finger. "It happens."

"I didn't mind."

"No?" Halm regarded the man across from him with a sly eye. "Get a taste for it, did you?"

Targus thought about it. "Maybe."

"I tell you what that is." Halm leaned forward. "That's *pride* whispering in your ear, telling you, 'You're a *warrior.*'

A name to dread, and rightly so, but listen—pride's no friend, and when a lad sticks you with his blade and reddens it—and that day will come—pride will throw you to fear. You remember that."

Targus reflected on the words, features twisting as if he'd eaten something rancid. Then he remembered his wine and raised his mug. "Well, I drink to success at this season's games."

That was something Halm could agree with, and he joined the younger man in his toast. He drained the rest of his drink, and when he lowered the vessel with a gasp, he snarled at the lovely burn. *Beer.* Right then, it was exactly what he needed.

They drank, ordering pitchers at whim. For every one Halm downed, Targus matched him. The Zhiberian bought his new companion a round, and Targus reciprocated.

They talked about their fights, others' fights, and the history of the games. Targus was new to the arena—his first season as a pit fighter. And even with the war on, he had elected to avoid the ranks of the Skarrs and Sujins and had learned what he could with a blade on his own time.

The night became soupy, smeared with laughing faces and slurred speech, and their command of their limbs slackened until they had to concentrate to even lift mugs to their lips, which wasn't guaranteed to work, even then.

"The day'll come," Targus said with a vengeful finger pointed at the Zhiberian. "The day'll come when… when none of us will, will be fighting in the Pit. It'll be—" He paused and stifled a belch. "It'll be on the *walls*."

"Sunja's walls?" Halm asked, not quite as pickled as Targus, but gaining.

"Sunja's walls." Targus nodded like an appreciative

horse, his lips a tight line under wide eyes. "You just wait. Juuuusst wait. The Nords will be at our throats in a year."

"I have faith in Sunja's Klaws," Halm said honestly. "They'll keep shem—them, I mean, apologies—they'll keep them at bay."

"Sunja's Klaws are being smashed," a dire Targus countered. But then a shapely woman arrived bearing two full pitchers and placed them down at their table.

"Marry me," Targus gushed, at which she frowned, then smiled, and shook her lovely head. "Then how about just holding onto my topper for a bit?"

The server's scowl deepened as she gathered up the empty vessels and walked away with a very drunk Targus clawing for her dress hem. Giggles erupted from Halm, hard enough that he had to drop his drink on the table and hold onto his bare belly. The lad was similar to Pig Knot in many ways but nowhere as successful with the ladies.

"She'll be back," Targus declared with a confident nod.

"It's her job to be back."

"No, I know, but she'll be back anyway. She liked me."

"Ah yes," Halm agreed. "I see her talking to her friends about you right now."

Targus waved a hand at three ladies, who all turned away. "Agh, a man needs his lad to be dipped in gold in this place."

He reached for a new pitcher and looked puzzled when he realized he still had his mug in hand. Halm chuckled again. It was fast approaching time to hold onto drinks with both hands. The women serving the crowds were attractive, and one in particular caught Halm's eye, a fair server with her dark hair tied back in a familiar knot. *Miki.* He blinked, disappointment suddenly burning his insides. The woman wasn't her.

"Not the prettiest about," Targus commented, focusing on the center of Halm's attention. "But then again, neither are you."

"You get braver with each mug," Halm said with a friendly frown, absorbing the not-so-friendly jab.

"So who is she?"

"Her? I don't know. But she reminds me of another woman. Outside of Sunja."

"A wife?"

That startled the Zhiberian. "Lords above, no. Not that. I don't believe I'm the marrying type."

"Why?"

Halm glared questioningly at his drinking companion but then saw no harm in answering and palm-wiped his brow. "No. Not for me. My hide's too unfit for a wife."

"But it's fine for the Pit?"

"For now, it is."

"You can't keep fighting forever."

Halm chuckled. "None of us can."

Targus scoffed at that and took a steadying breath. "I fully expect to perish in the Pit. If not, I'm still young. If I'm not pressed into the defense of the city, and by Seddon's blessing survive the games, I'll leave this place and travel east. Or… south. One of those directions. You, however, how many years you have left in you for this?"

Halm scratched at an ear. "Not long. But I have plans."

Targus scoffed again, spraying flecks of beer. "What?"

"Some lads and I have just started our own house," Halm said, the drink softening his tolerance for such a crude reaction.

"Free Trained?"

"Aye that."

"The other houses will punish you for that, you know.

Even I know that."

"We'll see."

Targus shook his head and grinned, swaying in his seat. "You're different, Zhiberian. I'll say that… that for you. You're different."

"My friends say the same thing."

"Make many of them here?"

Halm shrugged. "I have, actually, which saddens me. All of them are sliced to bits. Either in the Pit or out of it. Harsh business, lad. Harsh."

"Lesson to be learned there."

"Aye that." Halm snickered. "Don't make any friends of gladiators while the games are in session."

Targus didn't join his laughter but rather regarded him oddly.

Drunk, Halm continued, his ugly smile beaming. "You paid heed to that bit of advice. Keep to yourself while in the games. That way, you'll never have to meet one on the sands. And there'll be no hesitation if you have to put four hands of steel into him. "

"Like you've done?"

"Like I've done," Halm nodded, the room beginning to spin. "Only I fought a man and won a friend. Unfit, eh?"

Targus's mouth hung open in a drooling gash, but he didn't respond to that. His beady eyes focused unsteadily on Halm. Then Targus grasped his pitcher and chugged it down, the apple of his throat working furiously. When he finished, he slammed it down hard enough to draw the attention of those nearby and thrust out his fist. Halm reluctantly pressed his own into it. Targus shoved it back hard and smiled with drunken superiority.

"How's that for brave?" the Sunjan slurred and precariously managed to stand, leaving Halm momentarily speechless.

"I'm off, then," Targus announced and slapped Halm on the shoulder as he walked by. "Luck to you, young man. You and your house. Luck to you all."

Targus staggered away, leaving Halm still feeling the sting on his shoulder. He didn't like the Sunjan's last few remarks, feeling them too personal for someone he'd only just met, despite his resemblance to Pig Knot. In the end, Halm shook his head and finished his beer. The alcohol hadn't worked its spell entirely over him just yet, and if he saw Targus again, he wouldn't be so dull as to react to a strong push of the fist. Or so he told himself.

Right then, he felt like sleeping.

The bench he'd been sitting on fell over as he stood, and he awkwardly smiled his apologies at the patrons nearby. *Beer. More like sorcerous piss.* Still, he enjoyed its magic far too much to give it up. Those and other thoughts swirled in his mind as he walked to the bar and got his key from a busy barkeep.

On his way to the stairs, the server with her dark hair tied back caught his eye. This time, she felt the weight of his stare and caught him with a look of her own. Halm blinked and smiled, keeping his teeth hidden with his lips, and gave a nod.

And to his surprise, she nodded back, her fine figure setting his heart to skip. A good sign, but Halm didn't act on it. His spirits soared, however, as he reached the stairs. *A man doesn't need his topper dipped in gold after all.*

A friendly smile did it best.

With that, the Zhiberian labored toward the second floor. When he disappeared from sight, a man who had been following him for most of the evening lowered his warm drink. He straightened up from where he had been leaning against a thick timber and placed his mug on a nearby table. Then he left the crowded confines of the drinking establishment, intent on making his report on the one known as Halm.

Only three beats after he'd gone, another man rose from another table. They were unknown to each other, but both had been charged with watching the Zhiberian by different masters. Mindful of avoiding fights with the patrons, he threaded a path to the latrine, already aware that Halm had rented a room—that information had come straight from the barkeep at no cost. The Zhiberian lout was probably finished for the night.

Thoughts of emptying the bull and then making his own report filled the mind of the second spy.

*

Caro stepped out into the night air and looked about.

He saw the back of the staggering man, weaving an unsteady line up the lamplit street. Caro quickly caught up with the drunk pit fighter. When he came within a few paces, Targus's legs gave out, and he plopped into the street.

Caro stopped and put on a friendly face. "Well, you can't stay there for the night."

"Uh?" Targus grunted, bewildered by the other man's appearance.

Shaking his head, Caro extended his hand, and Targus took it after seeing it was indeed empty.

"Thank you," he mumbled.

"Not at all," Caro said. "You're the one called Targus, yes?"

Targus nodded, his eyes bleary. "You know me?"

Caro's smile was genuine.

15

In another part of the city, in another alehouse, Brakuss crossed the threshold and approached the bar. Glass lamps perched on shelves attached to round support beams, revealing a crowd of customers smoking pipes, eating, and drinking. Serving wenches moved amongst them with huge platters of mugs or roasted pork that spiced the air. Brakuss's boots scuffed on the clean-swept floor. He didn't expect the place to gleam so in the smoky lamplight. Based on Grisholt's description and instructions, he thought the establishment would be more... sinister.

The dizzying aroma of a freshly roasted haunch of pork caught his attention, distracting him just for a second. He waded through the evening's customers. A young man, his white shirt still clean, stood behind the counter and arranged brass mugs. Brakuss stopped in front of him and glowered with his one good eye, daring the barkeep to ignore him.

The man didn't try. "Yes?"

Brakuss's fist rested on the pommel of his shortsword, sheathed at his waist. "I'm looking for a lad called Linfur."

The barkeep's expression became sympathetic. "Perhaps you're in the wrong place. There's no Linfur here."

"I was told that if I wanted to purchase wares from the Sons to come here."

The smile on the barkeep wilted at the edges. He composed himself and leaned forward. "What sons are you talking about?"

Brakuss chewed on half his lip and adjusted his eye patch. "Cholla's, of course."

"I think you're mistaken."

"I'll probably say the same thing when I'm pulling a foot of steel out of your gullet."

The barkeep blinked and straightened. "Wait here," he said and quickly vanished behind a red curtain.

Brakuss gazed about the bar. Rich tapestries depicting boar and bear hunts hung above a row of barrels laid on their sides, reminding him of his father's den. Some of the spouts dripped steadily onto the floor, and Brakuss frowned. He enjoyed a drink as much as the next bastard, and seeing it go to waste bothered him. A table of patrons near the center of the room exploded into laughter over at a joke he hadn't heard. A young woman with deep lines underneath her eyes skirted the length of the bar from behind it, taking orders from the serving wenches. She took coin at times and tossed them underneath the counter, where Brakuss thought he heard the rattle and slide of metal on metal. Two burly enforcers appeared at either end of the bar, massive arms folded. They weren't the biggest men, but the years had raked scars across their flesh, making them hard looking, intimidating. One even had black ink drawn into the shapes of wrestling serpents on his upper arm, writhing all the way to his chin.

Someone tapped on Brakuss's shoulder, and he turned around.

There stood a stick of a fellow with flesh the color of a fish belly. The sickly lad wore sandals and tight black breeches and nothing else from the waist up, revealing a torso that looked nothing more than bones with skin stretched drum-tight over the frame. Eerie black eyes that seemed unnaturally wide met the once-gladiator, rendering Brakuss speechless. Tattoos covered the man's shoulders in evil-looking twirls and patterns, and about his wrists were inked shackles.

Then the odd fellow smiled, revealing a maw of needles beneath those unnerving eyes, as if he'd had his previous teeth smashed out with a hammer. "Follow me," the mouth whispered. With that, he walked around the bar and out of sight. Brakuss followed, seeing how more ink lashed the fellow's back.

Brakuss wasn't one to scare easily, however, which was why he had elected to come to the city—alone—on behalf of Grisholt. Now, however, he saw the mistake for what it was. He wished he'd brought along a handful of the lads, armed to the teeth, just for appearances. And to crack some heads if needed.

The unusual guide slipped through a door at the back of the alehouse, leaving the way open. Brakuss closed it upon entering, eyeing the little man now at the end of a lamp-lit hall. Closed doors lined either side, and the air was redolent with unwashed sweat. The emaciated bastard turned and smiled his nightmarish grin once more, which from a distance appeared as wet, stretching stitches. He opened another door, the hinges squealing weakly, and went into a dark room.

Brakuss stopped not three strides away. Something warned him not to enter that beckoning vat of blackness, to forget about it all and any sense of loyalty he might have for Grisholt… to turn around right then and *leave* while he still could.

"Enter or be gone." The whisper floated from that ebony opening. The distant sounds of merry drinking tempted the once-gladiator to leave and join it more than he imagined, but in the end, he gripped the hilt of his sword for courage and stepped forward.

The door slapped closed. Someone giggled.

Brakuss spun around with his sword half pulled when bodies slammed into him and braced him against a wall, rendering him helpless. A length of steel pressed against his chin and lifted it, turning his head and making him grimace in anger and fear.

A beam of light from a bull's-eye lantern shone into his contorted features.

"Relax," a voice spoke. "Relax. That dagger isn't going to cut anything unless I say so. So relax."

Huffing, Brakuss stopped struggling and side-eyed the darkness.

"Fear," the voice went on. "You can smell it, you know. Sickening. Ripe and pungent. As fragrant as unwashed flesh. Especially when a man has a blade at his throat, held by an unknown foe. As you do now. A man's pores virtually open up and heave that stench into the air. Like… like mouths trying to scream. Now, relax. Relax, I said. I have some questions for you, and I assure you nothing will happen if you give me my answers. Agreed?"

"Aye that," Brakuss got out, practically foaming at the mouth.

"Excellent. Ah. I see you only have the one eye. You lose that where? In a fight?"

Brakuss struggled with his breathing. "The Pit."

"Oh, you're a pit fighter?"

"Once."

"No longer? A shame. Why is there is no penalty, no punishment, for the years which so brazenly rob us of our youth and pleasure? I'm assuming, of course, you enjoyed being a gladiator?"

"Yes."

"But it left you half blind! A shame. Like a one-sided love, I suppose. But then, we don't always choose our talents. Our professions. They reveal themselves to us, and we must only recognize them for what they are, no matter how… painful. To ourselves or at the expense of others. Tragic. Now then, tell me…" A hand, thick with veins, came forth and gripped Brakuss's jaw while another dagger, this one sharpened down to almost the width of a blade of grass, grazed the baggy flesh under his remaining right eye. "And let it be the truth. If I scoop out your other eye, what might become of you?"

"What?"

The tip of that tanner's nightmare licked his tired skin. Pain lanced his face. Blood beaded and flowed. Brakuss grimaced, holding his tongue.

"Don't make me repeat my questions," the voice warned.

"Nothing. I'd do nothing."

"Nothing at all?"

"No."

"Not even beg in the streets?"

"Maybe?"

"Maybe?" the voice chided. "For one looking for the

Sons, you seem quite shortsighted. You really haven't thought any of this out, have you? Unless you're the messenger for someone else. Are you a messenger?"

"I am!"

"Whose?"

"Grisholt!"

"Grisholt? He's still alive?"

"Yes. Yes! He wishes to talk with… with the Sons of Cholla. He wishes to purchase their services."

"This is the same Grisholt who owns a gladiator house? Outside the city?"

"Yes." Brakuss panted, feeling his muscles cramp. He'd forgotten to relax, and the knives at his eye and throat weren't helping.

"What is it he wants?" the voice asked, interested now.

"He wants… he wants…" Brakuss grunted and squeezed his eye shut. Another bead of blood dribbled down his cheek, dangling at the curve of his chin before falling away. "He wants to *win*. At any cost. He wants you to help him. For our mutual… *profit*."

A dark, wheezy chuckle then, wicked with mirth. "Ah, dear me. You had me concerned for a moment. I truly thought you might have been something else. Well, no matter. My apologies for the dramatics, it isn't every day a person seeks out the Sons of Cholla. Especially *here*. Usually *we're* the ones seeking. Well. You're here to talk business."

Brakuss was very much aware that the knives at his face weren't removed. "I am."

"Grisholt wishes to win a fight?"

The once pit fighter closed his eye and swallowed. His gullet made a clicking sound, so dry had it become. "Yes. Well, no—he wants to win most of them."

"Ahhh. *Most* of them. I see."

"Are you willing to—"

"Make such things happen?" the voice finished for him. "Yes. I'm in a position to say so. The Sons are *always* willing to look for new opportunities. And thinking on it, yes, this does have the makings of something very profitable, yessss. We've been involved with the Pit before, actually. Blood sport isn't something new to us. Even arranged our own fights—in an arena of our choosing, of course. You might have heard about it."

Brakuss couldn't see anything beyond the blinding glare of the lantern. "Yes."

"I thought so. But we only bring in a beggar's hand of coins compared with the great Pit! Oh, we've managed to persuade the odd pit fighter to battle on our behalf on those golden, golden sands, but such arrangements never really worked out in the end, and always a one-time affair. Oftentimes, people had to be punished. Not that we had any qualms about punishing people, you understand. Don't mistake me in that regard. We... *delight* in making such examples, but ultimately it isn't good for business. Drunk tongues wag. Trails are left. The Sons wish to remain in the dark. The Sons wish to remain hidden. It's best that way. For all."

Brakuss licked his lips. His face continued to bleed.

The voice cleared his throat. "So, Grisholt wishes our help, does he?"

"He does."

"I commend you on your negotiation skills. He wishes to win his future battles in the Pit? It can be done, I can assure you. It *will* be done. Easily done, when one thinks of it. The Sons have many ways about them, all which can attain victory on the sands. Go back to your master and tell him the Sons accept his offer. We'll let you know our price later."

"Price?" Brakuss's eye widened. These dogs would make a fortune on wagers alone once they had a gladiator willing to work with them.

"Yes, price. Always a price to pay. You remember that. You tell *him* that. We'll talk again about the sum. And about how we'll deliver victory. To you."

"When?" Brakuss gasped.

"Anxious, are we?"

"He'll want to know."

"Agreed. He will. When is it your next match?"

"Tomorrow."

"Too soon."

"The day after tomorrow."

"Better. Your name is…"

Brakuss didn't want to give it up. When dealing with Saimon's hellions, one's name was the very *last* thing one revealed. Still, he swallowed and gave it.

"*Brakuss*," the voice repeated unpleasantly. "Who is your man fighting the day after tomorrow?"

He gave that as well.

"When next we meet, *Brakuss*, you'll provide us with the names of *all* of your fighters entered in this season's games. We'll do the rest. We'll contact you the day after tomorrow, at the Gate of the Moon, just before noon. And have no worries, whoever you have on the sands that day will win. Victory shall be yours."

The relief in the once-gladiator's face was unmistakable.

But then the voice hardened. "However, make no mistake. We know who Grisholt is. We know where his estate is beyond the city walls. He knows our reputation and our… appetite for vengeance. Remind him, will you, if he dares to betray the Sons… we will come for him. And you. And *all* in your vicinity."

An exhausted Brakuss closed his one eye. "I understand."

The presence lingered for heartbeats, and for a moment, Brakuss didn't think he would live to relay that message to his employer. Then the light went out. The arms released him. He opened his eye and saw the door was open, and the long hall beckoned. He blinked at the sight and put a hand to his bleeding cut.

"Leave us," a voice whispered from the dark, sounding as if it was eating something.

Brakuss did just that.

16

"Well, then, I have you now, don't I? I have you right and proper. You miserable sacks of maggot shite. You diseased punces. Lickers of fine cracks. I hope you slept well, for after this day is done, you'll drag your near-dead carcasses back to those boxes and lick your hurts like mauled cats." Machlann blared at the six men standing at attention before him, his bushy moustache and beard shaking with every gust. The new recruits waited in the middle of Clavellus's training area, on sands simmering with the sun's increasing heat, wearing only sandals and loincloths. They all stood at near equal height, with the exceptions of Sapo and Brozz. Machlann glared at them all in turn, sparing no one, his hands behind his back and a sneer on his lips. Koba lurked off to one side with his head cocked, showing his horrible scar already gleaming from sweat and the fleshy hole where his left ear had once been.

Sitting above it all, on the second-floor balcony of his house, was Clavellus with his silver mug flashing in the sunlight, already two drinks into the morning. A pensive Goll leaned forward and folded his arms on the railing. He glanced at his taskmaster, who merely took a lengthy sip of Sunjan black while watching the proceedings, unperturbed by the verbal lashing.

Machlann stole the Kree's attention with his next barrage.

"*Some*how, Master Goll feels that you lot got push enough to be on my sands. I'm here to prove him wrong. Koba's here to prove him wrong. Matter of fact, we have coin wagered you'll break before the sun drops behind those walls. Eh? Coin wagered! No lie. A sure thing in my mind since we're both here to shave the bark from the wood. *Motivated* to break you. You were Free Trained before, veritable horse shite of the games. You existed only to be trod upon by the House gladiators, to be bled and butchered at their whim. Why? Because you were simply *you*, taking up space and arms in a profession which *real* men had spent years training for, strutting in places you had no place being. *Eeeee!*" He growled as if lifting a boulder, drawing looks from some of the men, but Machlann raged on. "You had no reason for being in the games except the Gladiatorial Chamber—in all their grand wisdom—saw you as a bloody warm-up to the *real* sport. Perhaps even figured they might profit from your deaths. *Eeeee!* Perhaps they wanted to show the difference between drunken louts hacking at each other and two fully trained hellions battling to bloody conclusion. No one cared if you won or lost, lived or died, because you were *alone* on the sands. There was no one behind you. Now, however… you *have* someone behind you. You have each other. *You* have *us*."

At one end of the line, Torello shook his head

skeptically and looked at his feet.

"*Eeeee*, more to the point, my young missuses," Machlann growled, his blue eyes flashing, "you he-bitches are *mine*, and here's what you need to know. What I say, you do. If you don't, pain will be yours. What Master *Koba* says, you do. If not, pain will be yours. In my eyes, you are not worthy to be here. Dried stains of horse shite have more right to be here than you do. I've already voiced my opinion to Master Clavellus and Master Goll, and this morning... I'll prove it to them."

An odd sense of having heard and seen this all before swept over Goll, and not so long before. While the trainer below droned on, he leaned over to Clavellus. "Does he always say the same thing to the men?"

"More or less," the taskmaster replied mildly, studying the remaining contents of his mug. "Probably recites it in his sleep rather than snore. Not that it should lessen the truth behind the words. Remember, Master Goll, Machlann and Koba are training these lads to survive. The games have already started. Staying alive for the duration is his—*our* first objective. Then, maybe, we can prepare in earnest for next season."

"I want them to win."

"Oh, winning is secondary. If they survive any of their matches, chances are they'll have won. You have to remember, you are—we are sending in a troop of Free Trained dogs who answered your call. There was no scouting. No selection process. We don't know who we have here or the extent of their skills. And we have the gall to establish ourselves as a house amongst those who have taken this sport very seriously for a very long time—a topic for another day. I have no worries about facing Free Trained warriors, but we are, *will* be, at war with every house competing in the games just because of our impudence—at least, until we prove ourselves otherwise. And even then, they'll be looking for our heads in every match. Worse, we can't afford to kill any of our opponents, except the Free Trained. We simply don't have the coin or the men to absorb a war between houses."

A scowling Goll faced the taskmaster. "I've hired you, isn't that right?"

"You have," Clavellus granted.

"And wasn't it you who chastised me for sending in one of my fighters to lose? Just for profit?"

Clavellus's expression soured just a tad.

Goll continued. "And didn't you say something about training gladiators to win? Or something to that effect? Training our lads to win? No, apologies, '*our* lads train to *win*' is what you said. Ah, yes. *That's* what you said. Our lads train to *win*. I remember it now."

The taskmaster squinted at him in a new, appraising light, absorbing the rebuke.

"Train our men to win," Goll rebuked, eyes locked onto Clavellus. "Nothing less. They're house gladiators now. Victory *is* survival. Victory first."

Clavellus flexed his bearded jaw and looked toward the sands. "Understood," he conceded quietly.

Goll nodded, anger subsiding and pleased he'd won the exchange. It was far too early in the day to have at his own taskmaster's throat, but a moment later something troubled him. "Why can we afford to slay Free Trained?"

Clavellus regarded him wearily and sighed. "Because they're Free Trained. They're alone. No one cares if a Free Trained falls as there's no one to avenge them, unlike a proper house where blood usually demands blood." He shrugged and went back to watching Machlann.

Goll digested that and did the same.

"Now then," Machlann was finishing up, "you toppers are all rested up. Time for your first day of work."

"I'm bored already," Torello said. He sighted Goll and cried, "You never said anything about listening to this old pisser."

Torello's insult to the trainer momentarily left Goll speechless.

"Always one in every pack," Clavellus muttered and sipped his wine.

But Machlann bared his remaining teeth in a ferocious smile and gave all of his attention to the younger pit fighter.

"Not impressed with me, are you, my missus?"

"No, my *missus*." Torello mocked with a cold leer. "I'm not."

"*Eeee*, come at me, then."

That arched Torello's brow.

"Come on," Machlann repeated and stepped back a few paces. He wore only a thick bundle of linen about his waist while his wiry upper frame, drizzled in gray hair right up to his beard, was shirtless and tanned to near leather. Though showing his age, he was far from frail looking. In fact, scowling as he was, he looked damned threatening. He flicked a hand at Koba, who tossed him a wooden practice sword. The trainer then threw a similar weapon at the feet of Torello, who regarded Machlann with disbelief.

"You're unfit, you dusty crack."

"And you're scared now, my missus." Machlann jeered. "Pick up that weapon and come at me, or by Saimon's black hanging fruit, I'll make you howl if I have to walk over there to you."

Anger colored Torello's face. His companion, the beefy

Kolo, appeared very ill at ease with the challenge. Torello wasn't a small man. Near naked as he was, like them all, he was clearly in fine shape. He rubbed at the black stubble on his chin, shrugged, and snatched up the wooden sword.

"Apologies, lads," he said, but a cruel eagerness covered his face.

Three heartbeats later, Torello collapsed on his back, nose bleeding and blinking in astonishment while the trainer towered over him. The speed Machlann displayed in disarming and smashing Torello startled his students and made them take greater stock of the older man. Chuckles rang out from the scattered guardsmen from the outer wall.

Machlann scorched the air with insults and primitive, throat-clearing snarls of *Eeeeeee!* directed at Torello.

"Always one," Clavellus muttered and reached for the pitcher on a table just behind him.

The only thing surprising Goll more was the speed with which the taskmaster attacked his spirits. "Bit early in the morning for that, isn't it?"

"No," Clavellus said pointedly, cocking an eyebrow while pouring the drink. He took a quick sip and glanced into the shaded interior of his house.

"Good morning, my sweet." He lifted his shaking hand in greeting.

Nala, wearing white-and-green robes she made regal, appeared in the entryway. Her gray hair was tied back, and a heady scent surrounded her that distracted Goll from Machlann's barking.

"Whenever you say that," Nala spoke, "I've found you want something. Good morning to you, Master Goll."

Goll nodded in disarmed surprise. He hadn't formally met the woman.

"It continues, I see," Nala said, gazing down at Machlann while holding out her hand.

"It does," Clavellus answered, dejectedly handing over his mug.

"Where's the one I gave you?" she asked.

"I'm training now. You don't remember? I use the silver when training. Unless I can't find the other."

"Hm." She sipped delicately at the mug. Her hazel eyes became slits of distaste. "Black. Haven't you got any wine?"

"You knew it was beer before you tasted it."

"Hmm. I could hear him from far back in the house this morning." Nala deflected her husband's point, indicating Machlann with a nod. She took another sip, longer this time.

"Still hate it, I see," Clavellus observed sardonically.

"I was thirsty."

"Oh, well then. Seddon forbid."

Nala frowned at him. "I'll be leaving for Pynn's Brook, shortly."

"With who?"

"Maro and Ailsha. I'll leave you to your tasking. Try not to have anyone killed. I don't want the smell drifting through the house." With that, she took one last drink before returning the mug. She kissed his head and disappeared back into the house.

Clavellus looked into its silver depths and frowned. "Wench," he muttered and reached for the pitcher.

"You allow her to travel by herself?" Goll asked.

The taskmaster cocked his brow. "You mean without me? I have no worries there. You know this isn't Kalikos. Or Zuthenia. She has a capable guard and another servant with her. The road to Pynn's Brook is also patrolled by

Skarrs on a regular basis. She... doesn't really care for what we do."

Clavellus turned his attention back to the sands. Goll did the same.

An indignant Torello was in line with the other recruits, nursing his hurts.

Machlann resumed bellowing.

17

The morning became hellish for the six recruits, and Goll struggled not to show his disdain for some of the men's lack of endurance. With redundant, commanding growls of "Do as I do!" Machlann got them to perform his burning squat, lowering his rump to the ground as if perched on an unseen chair with his arms straight before him for balance. The trainer dipped and rose time and time again until he held it and moved no more. The others complied, with Koba stalking around them like a dangerous bear, a menacing club in his fist. Sapo, the most physically imposing of them all, with his tremendous size and heavy muscle, crumpled after only a count of thirty-two and had no qualms screaming about it… until Machlann ordered him to shut up.

"Big man, that one," Clavellus confided while sipping on yet another mug of beer. "Has arms like legs and legs like tree trunks. Impressive, but all power, no endurance. At least in the legs. Noisy about failing as well. Didn't like that at all. Embarrassed."

Tumber, the Vathian with the shaved head and great black beard, faltered at the forty-eight mark, collapsing to his knees with a curt groan. Tumber stayed there in the sand, grimacing while rubbing his thighs and watching the others.

"He did well," Clavellus muttered loudly enough for only Goll to hear.

Torello's scarred face contorted in pain at the fifty-four count.

"Stubborn, that one," the taskmaster whispered and scratched at his beard. "His companion there is only waiting for—"

Torello buckled and sat down heavily on the hot sands. Kolo followed almost immediately, rubbing his short, prematurely graying hair. Goll noted that Clavellus didn't say much about that.

That left only two: the Perician and the towering Sarlander. Brozz was easily the tallest of any of the others, edging out even Sapo, and surprisingly broad in the shoulders. He squatted with his arms straight out, his long pitchfork of a moustache quivering with mounting exertion. Junger actually looked serene as he continuously matched the trainer. Goll wondered if it pleased Machlann when a student fell.

Then, with barely a sound, Brozz dropped onto his backside. He exhaled, sat up, and hung his dark head between his knees.

Goll noted the ugly smile stretched across Torello's face.

Then there was only Junger and Machlann. The trainer made fists in the air at times while Junger squinted in the bright sun.

"That one's done this before," Clavellus said, peering over his mug.

"You believe so?" Goll asked, catching a flash of light off the silver.

"Oh yes," Clavellus whispered with interest. "Oh yes, indeed."

"Well," Torello said, "If there's ever a contest for this foolishness, you'd both do well."

Beside him, Kolo chuckled obediently.

Koba walked over to the pair and cracked their shoulders with his club, producing surprised grunts of pain. The scarred trainer loomed over them, and both Torello and Kolo kept their mouths shut.

The contest went on.

"My legs are about to fall off just watching them," Tumber remarked gruffly after some time, squinting at the sun and smoothing out the impressive bush of his beard.

Surprisingly, Koba did not strike him.

"How long is this supposed to go on?" Torello groaned, probably encouraged by the fact that Tumber hadn't been punished at all. That time, Koba ignored him.

Parts of Machlann's bare legs twitched with the growing strain with each successive dip. His movements became slower, increasingly painful. His cheeks puffed out, but the trainer kept his fierce blue eyes on the Perician, who squatted with his eyes closed, shutting out the world. The chests of both men worked. Sweat beaded down their faces. Machlann's beard looked soaked.

"Here's a lesson for you," Clavellus said to Goll and then cleared his throat. The taskmaster spoke loud enough to be heard by all. "I think you have a winner, Master Machlann. Best move on to the next task."

The trainer stood up stiffly after a count of seventy-two. A low rumble of a growl left his tired face, perhaps the only clue as to how close he had been to breaking. Grimacing, Machlann peered up at the balcony and took a deep breath.

"Move them on, Master Koba," he struggled in a labored voice and turned back to Junger. "Straighten up, boy."

Only then did Junger open his eyes and leave the squat. He flexed his legs, still springy, still strong, kicking them up and shaking them out. Upon Koba's commands, the new men paced around the open sands, all the while eyeing the Perician with something akin to distrust and wonder.

Clavellus shook his head and leaned over to Goll.

"Our lad Machlann, as old as he looks, would have stood there like that until both legs snapped off and he fell over. Can't have that. Too damaging for his pride and sends the wrong idea to any one of them lads. The trainer must impose an image of strength, always."

"What wrong idea?" Goll asked, smelling beer on the taskmaster's breath.

"Like it's possible to kill him, for one," Clavellus replied, gripping his mug. "If you feel brave sometime, ask Machlann about some of those old scars of his. But remember this. The trainer *must* have an aura of invincibility about him. And it's my task to preserve that aura, that image, when I can."

Below, Koba instructed them to pick up wooden swords from a nearby rack and got them working on striking "wooden men"—upright timbers with outstretched poles in the shape of welcoming arms, all for practicing strikes. Machlann stood apart, recovering like a winded, wounded wolf.

"Watch me, watch me," Koba instructed the six,

brandishing his club at the practice target. "Basic cut. Chop down on the left arm." This he demonstrated, his club clacking off the wood. "Then follow through. Bring the sword up and cut across the gut. Twist your hips for power. Watch me!"

The courtyard soon erupted with the irregular beats of wood on wood and the anguished shrieks of Machlann.

Mug in one hand, Clavellus placed his folded arms on the balcony's railing and rested his chin on top. "Music," he whispered, the word almost escaping Goll's ears.

The Kree watched the six men lay their wooden swords into the upright targets, belting out harsh notes that carried. Machlann strode up and down, barking instructions while Koba stepped in for a more personal touch.

"How long will they do that?" Goll asked.

"Until they drop," Clavellus answered and let it hang in the air for a moment before smiling. "Pardon me. Until they drop or the count reaches two hundred swings. Those swords aren't weighted. The lads will keep them at it for a bit, until their muscles remember it in their sleep. In time, those two strokes will happen without thinking. In an instant."

Goll knew about repetition until one's own limbs seemingly possessed a mind of their own. He'd done enough of it in his own training regime when he studied under the Weapon Masters of Kree. It was work, repeating itself every dawn, and sometimes the count would reach a thousand strikes in a day. On those evenings, he all but dragged his body back to his cot. In the beginning, anyway. Then it became more interesting, when his masters added different cuts to the existing ones, then fight tactics, finally combining it all in sparring matches.

HOUSE OF PAIN

As the men of the House of Ten journeyed on their paths, Goll recalled his own.

Machlann interrupted his memory when, standing behind the line of fighters, he lifted a hand and pointed to one in particular.

Junger.

The Perician laid his wooden sword into his unfeeling foe with an energy that seemed oddly out of place amongst the other five. His movements were short and conservative of energy while using the natural strength of his hips to power home his strikes. Machlann then pointed to the sweating back of the tall Brozz. The Sarlander attacked his target with economical but powerful blows that rang off in a steady, punishing rhythm—much like Junger's but not quite as smooth flowing. The others did as told but lacked the finesse demonstrated by the pair. Both men had done such drills before, had done them *well*, and Clavellus nodded at the trainer for bringing them to his attention.

"They've done this before," Goll muttered. It was as glaring as the sun in the sky.

"They have."

As the drill went on, the energy of four of the fighters wilted. Junger and Brozz rattled on. Even Goll caught the knowing looks exchanged by Machlann and Koba, and he felt his spirits lift. *Two*. The house had potentially leashed a pair of hellions. The thought of *where* they'd learned to fight popped into his head.

Glancing at Clavellus, who combed his fingers through his beard, Goll saw the taskmaster wondered the very same thing.

*

At the end of the day, four of the six men staggered back to the bathhouses at the edge of the training grounds. The physical challenges given them and the constant mental barrage from the trainers, especially the incessant bawling from Machlann, had exhausted them.

Brozz and Junger, however, walked to the baths—wearily but by no means exhausted.

They removed their sandals and loincloths before entering, clouds of steam enveloping their nakedness as they went into the chamber. Flagstones warmed their feet. Ahead, barely seen through the mists, lay a low wall holding back the waters of a large bath, the still surface smoking in nearby lamplight. Round beach rocks ringed the bath while before it was a depression in the floor, dotted by long, low tables.

"Not as nice as the bathhouses in Sunja," Torello griped as he stepped on one of several drain grates set into the floor.

"No, they're not," Kolo agreed, but they followed the other four to the low wall of the bath.

"Wait," said one of three manservants.

"For what?" grated Torello with a dismissive scowl at Brozz. "I'm not waiting."

"First we wash; then you soak," instructed the man and gestured to the tables.

Without a word, Sapo lumbered toward a table.

Torello looked at him, then at the water. "Well, I'm not waiting."

"You go into that water stinking as you are, and I'll split your back over my knee," rumbled an equally filthy Sapo as he lay down.

"I meant the tables." Torello thrust his chin out as he climbed onto one. Without asking, Kolo lay down on the table next to his friend.

"Well." Tumber sat down on a long bench jutting from a wall of black wood. "I can wait a bit longer," he muttered.

Junger and Brozz sat down as well.

"I hurt," Tumber groaned and hung his head. "After today, I hurt everywhere."

"It'll get easier," Junger said.

"Will it? Not sure I believe you. You seemed to be doing well enough out there."

Junger's brow shrugged. "Just concentrate on what they tell you to do. And do it."

On his table, beneath a coating of soap and water and being scrubbed by a servant, Torello actually snored.

*

During their fighters' training, Clavellus and Goll left the balcony and made best speed through the taskmaster's bedroom (which he informed Goll to pay no mind to) to the training grounds. There, they meandered along the walkways of brick surrounding the sands. Clavellus, silver mug in hand, showed the facilities of his villa in greater detail. Goll hobbled along at the older man's side, and at times, they paused to watch sweat fly off the practicing pit fighters.

When the time came, the pair ate their meals with the trainers. They later concluded the day with a meeting before the open-air smithy while the exhausted gladiators filed off the training sands.

"Well?" Clavellus asked Machlann and Koba. His voice possessed the barest of slurs from a day of steady drinking. The amount of beer and—later—wine he had consumed was offset by brief interludes of water a servant brought him. Goll didn't care for the taskmaster armoring himself with constant alcohol, but so far, he couldn't discern any impaired judgement. The Kree didn't know if he should be impressed or worried. Clavellus enjoyed his spirits.

"Two of them show promise," Machlann reported. "The others are shite."

Goll's innards shriveled at the news.

Clavellus apparently wasn't bothered at all. "Koba?"

The hulking trainer frowned and nodded agreement.

"That one called Junger. And Brozz? That's his name?" Clavellus said.

"Aye that," Machlann said. "A Perician and a Sarlander. They've put in the time elsewhere. Might move them along. They'll outpace the others."

"What about the big one?" Goll asked.

"Shite," Machlann quietly declared. "As I've said. The man uses an axe in the Pit. An *axe*."

"I take it you don't care for axes," Goll commented.

"No, I don't. For one, they put all their power into one swing, looking to take off the head or limb or whatever's offered in one cut. All that muscle burns up energy. There are some axe men who are formidable, but he's nowhere near, say, the slayers protecting the King. He's a, what's the word? A novelty. That boy is too large for this. Too slow on his feet. Feeding him alone is going to be a cost to you."

"The Sarlander's a large one," Goll pointed out.

"He's trained."

"The others?"

"The Vathian…"

"Tumber," Goll supplied.

"The Vathian," Machlann repeated dourly. "Might be

something there. Certainly kept at it. A couple of instances, I thought he was going to drop. Didn't, though. None of them did, truth be known, so that's something. But that Torello bastard and his daisy are near hopeless."

"Kolo is a daisy?" Clavellus chuckled.

Machlann soured and shrugged. "Truth be known, no, I don't think so, but the punce keeps close to Torello, the mouthy topper. That one's going to be a nuisance, I tell you. The type I see myself punishing every day until he runs for the hills."

Goll didn't like the sound of that.

"Well, then," Clavellus started. "Thank you for the effort, lads. Clean up, have something to eat in the kitchen, and we talk some more."

He then fixed Goll with a bright expression. "The first day has finished, Master Goll. And I'm feeling better about it than I did this morning. Seems we might have some potential here, after all. Let's tip a round of Sunjan black to mark the occasion."

More drinking? Goll hesitated before limping after the taskmaster in the hot evening sun.

18

Open fields of tall grass rustled and shimmered in a breeze. The sun dipped into banks of deep, purpling clouds, and the mix somehow colored the sky pink. Pig Knot had never felt better—never more relaxed. Nestled at his arm and on her back lay a fair, red-headed woman, her green-and-white dress pulled down to her waist. Freckles dappled the flesh between her breasts. He couldn't remember her name, but he felt he'd known her all his life.

She looked into his face, alarmed. "They're calling you," she whispered, her warm breath tickling his arm.

"They can wait."

"They're calling you."

Pig Knot gazed into her eyes, seeing sadness there.

"I'm not going anywhere," he assured her.

She lifted herself up on an elbow. Her hand splayed over his flat belly. It pressed down as if he might blow away.

"Pig Knot."

Strange. That time she sounded a lot like Muluk.

"Pig Knot."

He groaned and clapped a hand over his eyes.

"You awake?" Muluk croaked.

Pig Knot's flesh sweated in the shade of the living quarters. In reality, they were only sleeping quarters with a shuttered hole in the wall and a simple straw bed covered with a rough-spun blanket. Sunlight traced the lines of the shutter. A cloth hung across the doorless opening, granting him some privacy. Muluk really was calling his name. That left him with a raw feeling of disappointment. Pig Knot lifted his head and gazed down toward the foot of his bed, for he no longer trusted what his brain reported.

His face slackened with regret. His legs. His damn, damn legs.

Gone.

Even though his mind *insisted* they were still there.

Pig Knot screamed. Thrashed. He pressed himself against the nearby wall as if attempting to escape his crippled existence. Then he realized he couldn't open his mouth, feeling bandages looping under his chin and up over his head, and was screaming through clenched teeth.

"Pig Knot," rasped Muluk from beyond the drawn curtain.

The Sunjan calmed, huffed, and grimaced, and scanned the timbers of the murky ceiling.

"What?" he grumped.

"You're awake."

"Aye that," Pig Knot said, biting back a much more scalding reply. He remembered the beauty of his dream.

"You all right?"

What could he say? Pig Knot grinned like a skull

behind his curtain and lifted one bandaged stump and then the other, each looking like a trussed-up chunk of meat. No, he wasn't *all right*. He doubted he'd be *all right* for the rest of his days.

"Where are we?" he asked through clenched teeth.

"Where?" Confusion filled Muluk's voice. "Can't you hear them?"

Pig Knot frowned and listened. He could, indeed. "They're training."

"Aye. How are you feeling?" Muluk tried once more, weakly.

Pig Knot remembered seeing him the night before. Though he had his legs, they had still carried him upon a stretcher. A hazy memory.

"I feel like a sore shite trough," he answered truthfully, sitting up and eyeing the curtain to the hall.

Muluk chuckled and muttered something in Kree. "It must be the healer. That medicine he forced into us."

Pig Knot remembered. That was good stuff.

"The heat is too much," Muluk muttered. "I need fresh air."

"Open your window."

"I have. There's no breeze. At all. *Aaagh*."

The groan caught Pig Knot's attention. "Hot?"

"No, I'm… I'm seeing how I'm cut up. Look like a whipped haunch of beef."

That made Pig Knot smile just a little. But then he remembered his legs.

Someone walked toward them.

"Good morning," greeted Shan the healer, the joviality in his tone making Pig Knot cringe. A moment later, the sandy-haired man pulled back the curtain and beamed at the Sunjan. "And good morning. You're both awake, I see.

Now, who screamed?"

From the other side of the corridor, Muluk pointed at Pig Knot.

"You frightened me," the healer said softly to the legless Sunjan.

"We slept fitfully through the night," Muluk croaked.

Shan paused. "Oh, you slept longer than that. You slept through the first night and all day yesterday, right up until now."

The news made Pig Knot's eye widen. He twisted about to face the healer. "Two nights?"

"Two nights," Shan affirmed with a little smile. "I'm afraid it was that last drink I gave you, for the pain while travelling. It was a bit too powerful. I won't do it again. Unless necessary. Now then, let's have a look at your bandages."

"Where are the others?" Muluk asked.

"Outside, training. You've no doubt heard them."

"How are they doing?" Even Pig Knot lifted his chin at the question.

"It's not for me to say, really," Shan answered, inspecting Muluk's wrecked body. "You can hear the older one yelling. The one with the beard."

"Machlann."

"Yes, that's him. He's frightful."

Both wounded men muttered agreement.

"The other one—Koba? He's not as loud but, well, they're none too gentle with the lads."

"It's a none-too-gentle sport," Pig Knot grated, spittle spraying between his teeth.

"Yes, well, since you're awake." Shan paused as he peeled back a lengthy strip of bandage from Muluk's shoulder. Maroon blotted the white. "Since you're awake,

I'll get someone to move you out onto the grounds. Somewhere in the shade. You can't stay in here all day."

"That's a fine idea." Muluk brightened. "Any chance of getting something to drink?"

"Water?"

"No, beer, ale, wine…"

Shan *tsked*. "That won't help the healing."

"Can't hurt the healing," Muluk pointed out.

"It'll sure as Saimon's hell help *my* healing," Pig Knot grumped. "And what's this?"

He pointed at his chin.

"You had moments when you almost surfaced to consciousness. You complained of your chin. I believed it was broken, so I made sure the bone was where it should be and lashed your jaw to your head just as a precaution."

Pig Knot's eyes widened like dirty puddles.

The healer considered the pit fighter's missing legs. "I suppose a little won't hurt. The spirits, I mean. Keep your morale up."

"Well said," Pig Knot hissed.

"Very well said." Muluk's bearded face split into a yellow grin. "Can't hurt."

Then they heard an angry stream of curses from outside.

*

The morning had gone well enough.

Four of the six complained about stiffness from the day before, but that was expected. So Clavellus instructed his trainers to go easy with them as the morning aged. Under Machlann's critical eye, the men practiced the cuts learned the day before, and the sounds of wooden blades whacking their targets rang out over the sands.

"Those are weighted sticks," Machlann growled as he walked behind the line of men. "Don't fear breaking them. We'll get more. In fact, break them if you can, and we'll get you proper ones—dulled but serviceable. Master these strokes, and we'll show you a few more."

He stopped behind Sapo's heaving, sweating mass. The big man's pale skin had burned underneath yesterday's sun, and every move seemed to bother him. Machlann watched the large man work. Sapo grunted dramatically with every cut and as he struggled back to a starting stance.

The scowl on Machlann's face deepened with each swing Sapo made.

"*Eeeee*, that's not some stupid cow you're butchering," the trainer snarled. "Flow with your strikes and get your ass back into position faster than that, in case your foe actually gets out of the way."

Sapo slowed and glared at the trainer.

"Don't be looking at me with love in your eyes," Machlann near shrieked. "Focus on the cut and follow through. *Think*, you blistered ass licker."

Sweating as if the sun itself hated him, Sapo took a deep breath and applied himself again.

"Twist them hips," Machlann shouted above the racket. "Twist and take out the gut with the follow-through cut. You're cutting for the backbone. The thing isn't moving on you right now. If you can't master this, what in Seddon's bounty will you do once you're in the Pit? Lords above. Sick cows move better. Sick. Straighten up and do it again... *now*... What was *that*? *What was that?* Dying Seddon, you're not shovelling *shite* at that target. Look at that Perician there. Look. Go on. He's got it. See how he makes the cuts and readies himself for more. He even dances back, which isn't something I taught him, but it works all the same. Do it again and don't so much take the arm *off—what* was that *gurry*? Saimon's black pisspot! Have you even *listened* to me?"

Sapo stopped swinging and drew himself up to his full height. His shoulders heaved with each cavernous breath as sweat ran down his frame in rivulets. "Put me in the Pit, and you'll see," he warned.

Machlann's eyes widened. "Oh yes, I'd damn say I'd see. I'd see you be butchered by any pit dog who knew what to do. Oh, what's that now? You look angry, my missus. Are you angry? P'rhaps the sun's cooked you one shade too many?"

"I haven't been in the shade, old man."

"Is that's what boiling you?" Machlann asked. "The sun's too hot?"

"You're good for shouting, but you haven't taught me anything yet."

"Then we'll have to straighten that out. *Stop!*"

The clattering of wood on wood ceased.

Machlann turned away from the practice dummies and strode onto the open sands. "We have a disbeliever here. One who's failing to see the worth of what's being done."

The trainer walked to a rack of weapons and picked up a pair of wooden clubs. With these, he faced the men and strode to the center of the open sand, scowling and gesturing for the larger Sapo to follow.

From the balcony above, Goll felt a twinge of fear for the old trainer. The size difference between the two men was considerable. Clavellus didn't appear too concerned, or perhaps he'd already downed too much beer too early in the morning.

"I'll smash you, old man," Sapo warned, brandishing

his sword while swaggering toward the trainer. The other gladiators stopped their drills and watched with interest. Torello's dark face in particular was unmistakably eager.

"Lad," Machlann said. "You'll not smash *me*. You'll not smash *anyone*. That's my *point*. You're unable to even touch anyone who's had proper training. Look at me. I'm an old tit, and yet I'm calling you onto the sands to teach you a right and proper lesson. You're eager enough to inflict pain, but you aren't so eager to listen on how to do it *right*."

"I'll beat your head open and piss in it," Sapo vowed, lifting his weapon to his shoulder.

"See, you're still not thinking," Machlann hissed through what teeth he had remaining. "*When* I smash you, you'll have to endure the ridicule from the others here. *Then* you'll have to listen to me all over again and, truth be known, if you aren't listening now, I doubt you'll listen with half your skull bashed in."

"I don't think you can reach that high."

Machlann shook his head. "Come at me, my son. I can see you're a rare kind of stupid."

Sapo trembled with fury.

"Come on, then!" Machlann screeched.

And the big man charged, swinging his sword as if he were about to sweep aside a mountain.

Except Machlann was no longer there.

The old trainer ducked under a meaty arm and hooked a foot with his own, tripping the larger fighter. Sapo flew into the sand, sending up sheets of it. Roaring, he stood and wiped at his face, clearing eyes that blazed. But he didn't charge Machlann that time. That time, Sapo walked in, hunched over and furious.

Sapo swung for Machlann's head and missed. The

trainer bobbed in and cracked his larger foe's bare elbow while spinning out of reach. But instead of countering, Sapo dropped his sword and wailed in dramatic fashion while his face underwent deathly contortions. Machlann retreated a few paces, giving up ground. Sapo bellowed again as if he'd been skewered through the middle. He cradled his arm in great discomfort.

"Nerve strike," Clavellus confided to Goll. "If that was a real blade, that arm would be half shorn away right now."

But Sapo wasn't finished yet. Fuming that his arm refused to work, he snatched up the fallen sword with his left hand and charged.

Machlann sidestepped the rush, clubs flashing, smashing red flesh in a combination of strikes Goll had witnessed firsthand before. Sapo flailed a backhand, but the trainer was no longer in range. The big warrior slowed and swayed on his feet, grabbing his jaw this time and sluggishly bending over at the hips. Another miserable roar left the brute, but he straightened, fury twisting his bearded features.

If there was one thing Goll could say about his biggest recruit, it was that he didn't give up easily.

Another bull-like roar erupted from the stricken pit fighter. He faced the trainer, red-rimmed eyes narrowing into hateful slits.

Machlann didn't flinch. Instead, he strode ahead with his clubs at guard.

With a grunt, Sapo punched. It was a huge, arcing right cross, the previously frozen arm no longer hurting quite as much. The trainer ducked, but that mallet of flesh and bone grazed the older man's skull, knocking him off balance. Sapo thundered victory at the connection and the results.

Both Koba and Goll flashed looks at Clavellus… who sipped at his drink.

"Feel that?" Sapo grated, the side of his head and ribs red and tender from Machlann's strikes. He grabbed the stunned trainer by the neck, his huge hand almost completely enclosing it, and wrangled the older man's face up to see the poised fist orbiting Sapo's head. The "Hill" held the stance for a fleeting instant, savoring the moment, and smiled.

Machlann jabbed a club into Sapo's linen-covered balls.

The contact bleached the brute's face. His beast-like puffing became a whimper. All strength left him as he crashed to his knees, cupping his screaming testicles. Like a tree, he toppled over in sickened agony and drew his legs close to his chest.

Machlann staggered a step back, straightened, and smoothed out his tufts of gray hair. "Your pardon. I almost nodded off there, my missus."

Machlann turned and tossed one club after another to a smiling Koba.

Goll was speechless.

Clavellus smirked. "You think I'd have just *anyone* training my lads?"

Below, Machlann dabbed at his head and drew away blood. "You broke skin, you mountainous bastard. I'll give you that."

Sapo hid his face in the sand, paralyzed with agony.

Machlann straightened and regarded the recruits. "Why did this man fail to defeat me? *Eeee?* Because I'm faster? *No.* Stronger? *No.* So then why?"

No one answered.

"He lost because he looked upon this"—he swept a

hand up and down his person—"as old meat. Done. Spent. *Weak*. He allowed himself to get angry when he should've been alert. He was overconfident in his attack, underestimated his opponent, and worst of all, he had me and did *nothing*. You all saw it. *Eeeee*, he had me by the damn *gullet* and took a pissing heartbeat to relish my impending death… when he *should* have been killing me. That was fatal. When you have your foe at your mercy, especially an opponent much more capable than yourself, *finish him*. Save the posturing for after the match. And by Seddon's hairy crack, do *not* do as he's done. You might not be as fortunate to get away with only your bells rung."

Respectful silence.

"That was your rest." Machlann glowered at his students. "Get back at it."

Torello and Kolo resumed practicing while Brozz took a moment longer. Junger lingered, however.

"Impressed, are you?" Machlann demanded, pressing a hand to his bleeding head. To his surprise, the Perician pleasantly nodded back. And for a moment, just the barest flash of time, Machlann sensed the man truly *was* impressed.

Then Junger returned to his preparation.

Machlann winced and gazed down at Sapo's paralyzed mass, still powerless on the ground. The trainer's stern expression softened just a fraction.

The dark-bearded Clades stood at the edge of the sand. The retired Sujins Pratos and Valka stood behind him, lowering a legless Pig Knot onto a straw mat situated underneath the shade of the bathhouse's eaves. The healer hovered nearby, but the crippled Pig Knot didn't seem to notice. His eyes locked on Machlann.

The venerable trainer sighed.

Sapo groaned then, distracting Machlann, and he nudged the fallen giant with a sandaled foot. "Get up, you sorry hellpup," he said without heat. "Get up and grind it out. They'll grow back."

Slowly, Sapo struggled to a sitting position, his hands cupping his tender bits, half his face crusted with sand.

"You'll do what I tell you from now on," Machlann warned over the resumed clatter of swords on wood. Sapo winced and nodded.

"Get on, then. Join the line when you're ready," Machlann grumped and strode toward Pig Knot.

When the trainer got close enough, Shan observed, "You're bleeding," and rustled through a leather satchel hanging off his hip.

"Men do that. From time to time." Machlann stopped and stared at Pig Knot and his missing legs. "Back from the grave, I see."

"And in Saimon's hell," Pig Knot answered.

Machlann kept his tongue as the new guards helped Muluk outside. They sat him down in the shade, next to Pig Knot.

"The biggest set of unshaven dog balls I've ever seen." The trainer smirked with just a touch of fondness.

"We're back from the dead, and that's the best you can say to us?" Pig Knot said, heat in his voice.

A frowning Machlann snatched a cloth bandage from Shan's hand before the healer could apply it to the trainer's head wound. Machlann gave the healer a withering look before directing his attention back to Pig Knot.

"I just said it. You're back from the grave. What more do you want?" The trainer pressed the bundled wad to his wound.

"Should've expected this." Pig Knot spat.

"What? Pity? From me?" Machlann asked in a voice of iron. "*Eeee*, that spring dried up long ago, my missus. Just be glad you've a roof over your bed at night."

The bandage tight against his skull, the trainer walked away, back to his new recruits.

Goll watched and heard the exchange and didn't like it.

"You'll have a handful with that one," Clavellus said. "He's done for."

"Without him, there would be no house," Goll stated quietly, picking at the balcony's railing. "I'll find something for him. Even it's just sitting and cursing."

"Perhaps it won't come to that."

The Kree glanced at his taskmaster. "What do you mean?"

But Clavellus changed the subject. "You'll need armor and weapons soon. What was your plan again?"

"We'll get what armor they need. They have their own weapons."

"That smithy down there has a good forge. When your man is ready—Muluk, is it?—He can fire that pit up. But it'll be too much work for one man alone. Especially if he has to put together armor. If he can do that."

"He can do a little."

"Then you'd best find another armorer and weaponsmith. Just to help. Armor takes time to fashion to exact measurements."

"Then we'll buy it."

"More coin," Clavellus pointed out, smiling into his silver mug.

Goll stood.

"Where are you going?" Clavellus leaned back.

"To speak with Pig Knot."

"Ah, well then, I'll have one of the servants look after

both of them lads." He lifted his beer for another sip.

"Are you going to drink all the time?" Goll had to ask.

Clavellus stopped. "Weren't you here yesterday?"

"I was."

"Then, there's your answer."

"I won't stand for a drunk taskmaster."

The air thrummed with unseen tension until Clavellus broke it by deliberately taking a larger than usual gulp of his drink. He made a scene savoring it. Goll lingered for a moment, absorbing the defiant act, before turning to leave.

But Clavellus wouldn't let him go just like that.

"My property. My trainers," the taskmaster stated quietly, freezing the Kree in his tracks. "*Mine*. You've convinced me to take the chance on you, but what I do *here* is my business. All mine."

Goll didn't bother turning around. He left, sensing another confrontation in their future. Goll passed through the house, where sunlight dappled the cool floor stones, and entered day. He limped on the dusty brick path bordering the sands. The men paid him no attention, and with the likes of Machlann and Koba stalking about, they probably realized it was best not to pay the house master any heed.

Shan had just gone back into the barracks, but Muluk and Pig Knot sat and stewed under the shade of the bathhouse eaves. The pair resembled warriors fresh back from the Sunjan-Nordish front. The Kree countryman brightened, and his wild mop of hair and beard bounced in Goll's direction. Pig Knot glanced over, scowled, and looked toward the sands.

"Lads," Goll greeted.

"Goll," Muluk returned. "See you're not using the crutches anymore."

"Day by day. There's a limp, however, but I'm getting by."

"That's what you do isn't it, Kree?" Pig Knot seethed, his face swaddled in cloth and simmering into a harsh shade of red. "Get by. You'll always get by. No matter what, eh?"

The scathing tone silenced both Muluk and Goll.

"Not you," Pig Knot muttered apologetically to Muluk. "Him."

Goll took a steadying breath. "Thank you, Pig Knot. For losing the fight. Because of you, we're bound for bluer seas. Because of you, we have a house. A formally accepted house. We're established solely due to your sacrifice… and for that, I thank you."

"I thank you, too," Muluk muttered, somewhat in awe of Goll's short speech.

Pig Knot's lips became a bloodless line. "Sacrifice. You're right about that. Look at these." He thumped his stumps on the mat. "Seems to me the only one not sacrificing around here is you, *good* Goll. Or perhaps, with my little mind, I'm missing something."

"I've sacrificed," a stoic Goll stated, keeping his eyes on Pig Knot. "If you think about it, you'll discover what."

"I'll do that. I have plenty of time to do just that, thanks to you."

Goll could've pointed out many things to the surly Sunjan, things he thought obvious. But that would be petty and, in the end, time-consuming.

"Well, I'm sorry about your legs."

"Aye, you look sorry."

"But I am grateful for what you've done for the house. You'll both be taken care of. I promise you that."

That brightened Muluk. "Well, that sounds good."

But Pig Knot didn't seem too convinced. "Taken care of. That is a good idea. Why not take care of us this instant, eh? You don't seem terribly busy. Why don't you get something for us to suck down while we're here. Might as well drink and watch, eh? Something to pass the time."

The dislike for that idea showed on Goll's face.

"Thought so," Pig Knot said with a leer. "If it's not for you, it's not for the rest of us, right? Not even the pair of us."

"I'll send you something."

"I'll believe it when it happens."

"I said I'll send you something," Goll said with heat. With a dark, departing nod at Muluk, the house master walked away.

"I'll believe it when I have it in my hands," Pig Knot fumed, not bothering to watch the Kree go.

19

Just before noon, Halm stood outside the Gate of the Sun, scouring the crowds entering Sunja's Pit for Skulljigger. The best place to catch the man would be below, in general quarters, but truth be known, the Zhiberian didn't want to wait for a lengthy period down in that foul-smelling darkness. Fresh air was more to his liking.

He was only a little hungover as he drained what water was available at the alehouse. And he managed to keep down a light breakfast of cold pork and cheese, which settled his stomach enough to walk. Though not at his best, Halm didn't think he needed his best to face Skulljigger. He *would* need to restrain himself from killing the man outright, however. He would save that until they met on the arena sands.

As on any day while the games were in progress, people filled the fairway surrounding the Pit. Long lines waited at the windows of the Domis. Halm sized them all up, lingering on the more attractive women, regardless of whether they were with a man or not. Looking wasn't an offense in the Zhiberian's mind.

The men placing their wagers and a dark-haired wench were dividing his attention when his guts froze. One lout stood tall amongst the other, shorter men.

Skulljigger.

Though the brazen bastard didn't wear a helmet, Halm still recognized his smiling face as he nodded and talked to someone unseen. That he was in plain sight, enjoying himself while Pig Knot suffered, made the Zhiberian's blood boil. A scowl darkened his face as he pushed off from the wall, making a tight fist over the hilt of the Mademian steel at his bulging waist. The people in his way shrank back, nervously taking stock of the bulky warrior.

A smiling Skulljigger stood unawares, talking and looking toward the distant window of the Domis. Halm meant to grab the killer by the shoulder and rattle a fright into the pit fighter, a taste of things to come. Halm wanted to tell him eye to eye that he intended to gut him on the sands, before screaming thousands, for what Skulljigger'd done to Halm's friend. All manner of grisly visions played out in his mind's eye as he closed the gap between his unwary foe, pushing aside a few protesting souls.

Fading bruises marked Skulljigger's face, but he wouldn't have to worry about those soon, not after Halm exacted his revenge.

Three arm lengths away, Skulljigger tipped his head back and chuckled at the sun, perhaps hearing a grand joke. He staggered a step as if pushed, and in the resulting gap, Halm saw his hated foe holding the hand of a small boy, his round face beaming at the larger man. The lad's hair and eyes were as dark as those of the bruised gladiator next to him.

As quick as that, all fight left the Zhiberian, and it showed on his face.

Sensing danger, Skulljigger glanced over his shoulder. The unmistakable smile of a father frosted over, quickly replaced by the promise of a proper beating.

"What's this, then?" Skulljigger hissed, yanking the boy's hand and pulling him close to his thigh.

Halm released his sword and held up both hands. For the life of him, he couldn't summon words.

Skulljigger's face twisted in anger. "What're you about? Can't wait for the arena? Fearful enough to stab at me while I'm with my *boy*?"

That simple, chilling word repelled the Zhiberian's bulk, and he hastily retreated a step, backing away from the line and the many faces. "No… not at all."

"And in broad daylight? Not fearing much, are you? What were you going to do, you brazen punce? What's in that unfit skull of yours?"

"Perhaps he was going to cripple you?" one nearby man suggested, pointing at the sword.

"Oh, he's a killer," another declared. "I've seen him in the Pit. Right vicious, that one."

"Aye that, don't let the fat fool you."

"He's quick. He's quick."

"I wasn't going to do any such thing," Halm barked, chagrin coloring his face. "Not at all."

The boy peeked around his father's leg and stared with distrustful eyes. Nothing could have more effectively leeched the will out of the Zhiberian.

"Get away from here this instant, or I'll punish you, right and proper," Skulljigger warned. Eager faces turned to see what Halm's reaction would be. He disappointed them, nodding profusely and spinning around to leave. His elbow caught a brown-robed man in the chest, buckling the bystander in pain. Halm apologized with a look and a pat on the grimacing spectator's back.

"Away with you!" Skulljigger stepped forward and shook his fist, banishing the Zhiberian from the light as if he were one of Saimon's hellions. Similar cries erupted from the line, enough to draw the attention of the guarding Skarrs.

But Halm turned about and hurried away. Insults and jeers pelted his ears in his hasty retreat. *Mobs.* He cursed. *Nothing braver when they're hounding only one man.* But what *was* he going to do just then? The boy's face had eclipsed his plans, making them unclear. He had never thought to kill the boy's father—Skulljigger, he corrected himself—or did he? But in a public area? His vision narrowed. His breath quickened. He skirted the southern curve of the arena walls, ignoring calls from merchants in their booths, placing distance between him and the Domis and just wanting to get out of sight.

A short time later, he leaned against a red brick wall of the inner city, off a street and in the forgiving shade of an alley. Robed people passed by its mouth, and a few walked by the large man, ignoring him.

Halm caught his breath, turned around, and placed his forehead against the cool surface of the brick. Skulljigger had a *son?* Who would've thought the he-bitch had a family? A groan burst past Halm's lips, and a terrible sense of loathing wrenched his heart. He knew he could be a hard man, and he wanted to revenge Pig Knot but, Seddon help him, he wasn't about to leave a boy fatherless. And he'd only barely noticed the lad! Worse, Skulljigger might be a father to even *more* children. He certainly had a wife, for that matter. The horror of the revelation fattened in Halm's mind, pressing thoughts against the roof of his skull. He had never considered the fighters participating in the Pit as being family men, and he realized how *myopic* he'd been. The notion he'd been executing *fathers* all that time made his bandaged belly lurch in horror. He bent over at the waist and opened his mouth to retch, the shock rendering him queasy.

No. They weren't all fathers, he argued against the stormy swells in his gut. It wasn't possible. And if they were, they had no qualms about carving slabs off his person. But Halm could see only Skulljigger's son, and all hate leaked away. Dying Seddon, even just fighting the man ran a fair chance of somehow crippling him…

Halm spat onto the fitted stones and gasped for air. His mouth hung open in panic.

Lords above.

He'd issued a blood challenge to the man.

One of the arena gates wasn't far away, but the Madea wouldn't allow him to retract the challenge. He'd learned that seasons ago. Blood matches couldn't be done that way, else the arena official would spend a season issuing and then cancelling such matches as drunken men sobered. Once Skulljigger checked with the Madea, all would be sealed, and Halm would have to battle the father to the end or be executed himself.

Choices. There were always choices. Skulljigger might not accept the challenge, and that naïve idea went through Halm's mind like a bird fluttering through a house. The man saw him as a threat now and no doubt wanted to butcher him.

Halm could forfeit the games and leave the city, as it was unheard of to carry a blood challenge over to the next season. Yet not even that would work. To run meant forsaking his own run of victories, the best showing he'd had in any season of the games. The newly established house itself, of which he held the formal title of master, also entered his mind.

A quiet stream of oaths left him. No, he wouldn't leave the games. Halm rubbed his chin. Talk. He had to talk to Skulljigger. Had to convince the murderous bastard to not accept the challenge. Even that seemed improbable.

Gold.

Halm exhaled in a hiss, his breath sawing on ruined teeth.

Coin might be the only way.

A voice whispered that it might be easier just to kill Skulljigger and have done with it. Halm cringed at the notion. There was no way he'd knowingly rob a whelp of his father, despite the man being a right and proper king of a ball-paddling he-bitch. Taking a breath, he faced the alley mouth and strode toward the river of people passing by, reasoning that if Skulljigger had the boy with him while in line for the Domis, there was a very good chance he wasn't fighting that day. And if he wasn't fighting, sooner or later he'd be leaving the arena. Maybe even from the Gate of the Sun.

Halm believed it was as good a place to start as any. He returned to the brick archway of the gate, spotting a large strip of parchment, covered in the mysterious scrawls and symbols, hung just outside for all entering to see. Halm stood and fumed at what he knew was the schedule. He stopped a man going inside and asked if the name Skulljigger was present on the parchment. After a quick inspection, the fellow reported it wasn't.

Relieved, Halm thanked him and moved away from the

gate. He placed his back against a mighty column of black-veined Vathian marble, which was large enough to partially conceal him from anyone exiting. Behind him, on the arena's wall, gloriously painted murals depicted battle scenes from a bloody past, the images stretching all the way to the next magnificent column and beyond. Halm stole glances at the artwork, appraising the drawn heroes and beasts in ferocious poses. Every so often, cheers and applause of startling power erupted from the arched heights, causing Halm to look heavenward.

Time passed, and Halm's belly rumbled as suppertime drew closer. Before long, a great gout of people exited the arena, talking excitedly about the day's events. A rush of panic shot through the Zhiberian, fearing he'd miss Skulljigger in such a flow of bodies. He almost did, except for the boy.

Skulljigger left the arena with his son perched on his shoulders, keeping high him above the tide. The lad bounced on his father's shoulders, his little hands wrapped around Skulljigger's forehead, delighting in the view. Minding the crowds, Halm merged with the sweaty deluge of flesh and kept the gladiator and his boy in sight.

They walked through the main streets, passing by tall wooden homes and stone walls. The taverns and the alehouses had opened their doors and windows, and people bled into them in spurts. The smells of spiced racks of lamb and beef assaulted Halm, and his belly protested. When Skulljigger and his boy turned down a side road, the Zhiberian's spirits spiked. He rushed to the corner of a tailor's shop and peeked before proceeding, drawing attention from the men and women working just inside the shop's open windows. Halm ignored them and hurried down the smaller road. Skulljigger was far enough ahead, and a small tributary of people walked behind him and his son. Walking briskly, Halm cut the distance in half, using the crowds as best as he could to conceal himself.

The pursued pair took another turn down an alley, and Halm suddenly found himself trying to get around two men pulling a cart of melons. An opposing current of people attempted to get around them from the other side. Yelling erupted, and moments passed before the men hauled the cart to one side, allowing the pent-up traffic to gush past. Halm rushed, bumping people and hearing the curses flung at his back as he rounded the alley's corner. He found the next path much less populated, with heavy tarps stretched overhead in places, casting shadows and breaking the heat. In the gloom, weary boot- and shoemakers worked to the dull tune of *tap-tap-tap*, bent over with awls and leather. Old vendors beckoned, urging Halm to sample their displayed goods. He strode past, ignoring cooked chickens glistening on skewers. He reached an intersection, backed up, and peered left and then right.

There. A glimpse of Skulljigger turning a corner, his son at his side.

Halm picked up his pace, heedless of how narrow the alley became. The stone walls of the buildings pressed in and towered overhead, connected by bare clotheslines. Halm's arms grazed the walls, rasping against his flesh. Halm pushed on, focused on the approaching corner, intent on catching Skulljigger before he could get too far ahead.

Halm rushed around the bend, and a hard fist greeted his jaw, snapping his head back in an explosion of black light. He staggered, kept standing only by the confines of the passage. A second fist cracked into his face. A crushing jab deflated his gut.

"Couldn't wait, eh?" Skulljigger hissed.

"Kill him, Father!" yelled a boyish voice, all too eager. "Kill him!"

Skulljigger grasped Halm's forehead, shoved him against the alley wall, then grinned and cocked a fist. "Lad wants you dead—"

Crack—hard knuckles hammered into Halm's right cheek, splitting flesh.

"And I'm in favor of—"

Smack, to the left cheek, plastering the Zhiberian flat.

"*Doing* it." Skulljigger's voice strained as he gripped Halm's jaw and straightened it for an overhand fist intended to flatten the fat man's nose.

He punched, but Halm got up both arms, blocking the blow.

"Kill him, Father! Smash him!"

Halm knocked away the hand on his face and lashed out. Skulljigger deflected and countered, smashing Halm's belly and making him yelp. The Zhiberian pressed ahead, throwing his greater mass into his foe and smothering him against the other wall. Both men hissed and grunted with exertion. Halm splayed fingers over Skulljigger's mouth, who attempted to bite through them. Halm squealed. Blood spurted. They twisted and rolled against the building, exchanging short, brutal punches. One fist bludgeoned the Zhiberian behind the ear, and he staggered. Another hammered across his jaw. He punched back and heard Skulljigger grunt in pain. An instant later, Halm saw his foe's eyes blinking back a ribbon of blood.

They grappled again, without any style, seeking only vitals, rolling along the wall and leaving a dark smear of red.

Halm stopped a hand groping for his crotch, caught it, and twisted the wrist.

Skulljigger winced and momentarily dropped his other arm. Halm hammered an elbow across the pit fighter's face, hitting him repeatedly, bouncing the Sunjan's head off unyielding stone. All fight left Skulljigger then, and his legs gave out. His shoulders slumped. Relentless, Halm grabbed his tuft of dark hair and lined up a fist, suddenly very intent on breaking every white bone in the bastard's face.

"Father!"

The boy clawed and kicked at Halm's back and legs with a frantic energy that momentarily stunned Halm. He turned and shoved the attacking boy back on his rump with a yelp. Red eyes were framed in a contorted face.

Those eyes defused the Zhiberian's blood lust. He stared at the weeping yet outraged face for a heartbeat before releasing Skulljigger, allowing the pit fighter to crumple as if he were a handful of steaming offal. Halm leaned against a wall, grateful for the support, and eyed the youngster, whose jaw trembled while water leaked from his wide eyes.

"Go on home," he told the boy.

"No!"

"Your father and I have some talking to be done."

"No! No!"

Dying Seddon! "Get on, or…" Halm fumed and raised a bloody fist.

"Don't."

The voice arrested the Zhiberian, and he looked down into a bleeding mess of a face. A single eye, bright in an otherwise blackening mold of flesh, blinked. Skulljigger spat blood, grimaced, and took a very deep breath. He tried to sit up from where he'd collapsed against the wall. "Don't... hurt him. Please."

The sight of this father begging for his son's safety turned Halm's guts on himself, as if he'd been dumped into a vat of shame, set afire, and left to howl. He hung his head and exhaled mightily, regaining some energy spent in the fight.

"All right, then." He panted and focused on the battered Skulljigger. "Listen. You can't fight in the arena. Your season is done."

Skulljigger's eyes, even the one swelling shut, widened.

"I made a blood challenge," Halm admitted.

"You *what?*"

"Aye, but it's only if you accept it."

"Oh, I'll accept it, you fat, unfit pisser."

"Listen," Halm cut him off. "I... I didn't know you had the boy. Truthfully, I thought a brute like you probably had to..." he let the thought go unsaid, mindful of the nearby child. "Anyway, I didn't know. It changes things."

"Changes *nothing* in my mind. I'll fishhook you on the sands."

"No, you won't. You're done."

"The season is everything to me," Skulljigger gasped and spat out a gob of blood. "It's work! I've a family to feed, you fat prick."

Halm shook his head and came to a thought he wasn't sure he liked, but he threw it out there anyway. "How far do you think you would have gotten?"

"What?"

"In the games. How far you think you would've gotten?"

"To the last."

Halm chuckled cruelly. "You wouldn't have gotten to the *last*, lad. Stop thinking with your ass for a moment."

"I'm undefeated."

"You haven't fought anyone of note yet. Not even the house gladiators."

Skulljigger prodded his nose with red fingers, wincing.

"Truth is," Halm went on, "they would've cut you up. And then where would your family be? Eh? Your son? Your wife?"

"Wife's passed on," Skulljigger whispered. "Died during the last childbirth."

Halm balked. "You miserable bastard. And here you are fighting in the Pit?"

"I've four children. Three girls. One…" He pointed weakly to his son, now standing and ready to charge if needed.

"One hellion." Halm eyed the boy warily.

"One… hellion." Skulljigger smiled weakly, his pride shining through his bloody teeth.

"Well, regardless, your season is over. The Madea won't take a refusal. You know that. That's the frightful thing about a blood challenge. Once it's out there, it's there."

"I'll butcher you on the sands."

"*Listen*," Halm talked over him. "I made the challenge. All you have to do is stay away from the games for the rest of the season. Nothing's carried over to next year. Stay away and… and I'll pay you gold for the next three matches, just supposing you would've made it that far."

Skulljigger's bruised face was in full hideous bloom now, and Halm wasn't certain whether the man had heard him or not. "Well?"

"Six," the battered Sunjan finally countered.

"*Six?*" Halm almost shrieked. "Who do you think you are, Seddon's fist?"

"Six or nothing."

"I should've grabbed your bells from the start of the fight. How could I miss those kegs?"

Skulljigger released a lungful of air, deflating himself. Blood lined his teeth.

The sight weakened Halm. He braced himself. "All right… five."

A considering pause. "Done."

"Done," Halm agreed, glad of reaching an agreement. "And you're finished for the season. You just… just stay with your youngsters. Think of them, now."

Skulljigger weakly nodded.

"All right, then." Halm extended a hand. The battered Sunjan studied it for a moment before taking it.

Halm gripped the hand with both of his own, captured a pair of fingers, and snapped them back with a grisly pop of bone and flesh. Skulljigger howled. The boy shrieked and flung himself at the Zhiberian, who stopped him with a flat palm to his chest, dropping him again on his rump.

Making sure both were out of the fight, Halm regarded Skulljigger cupping his wrecked hand. "That's just in case you changed your mind."

Skulljigger mewled in agony as he righted the pair of fingers on his sword arm. He gulped great lungfuls of air at the crackle of bone.

"Now look," Halm explained, not dropping his guard around the wounded pit fighter, "I'll walk you home. Or to a healer. Your choice. But have no worries. I did that to make sure you did as told. I'll get that coin for you. And I'll get it soon."

Halm abruptly became aware of his left hand and saw

with disdain that Skulljigger had, at some point during their scuffle, bitten through the flesh of his middle finger. A gob of meat hung off the bone. "Seddon above," he muttered and, with trembling fingers, fitted the chunk into the wound as best as possible. Thankful, Halm believed it could all be stitched. He made a fist, and a sharp throb shot up to his elbow, but he believed he could still use it.

"All right?" Halm grated.

Skulljigger took a few moments before he nodded.

Halm held out his hand again. Skulljigger eyed it as if it were a smithy's set of red-hot tongs. The beaten man avoided the offered help and struggled to his feet. Halm didn't fault the Sunjan for that. The boy rushed in and hugged his father's waist. Skulljigger rested his good hand on the lad's shoulder with a gentleness that made Halm feel like the underside of a sun-scorched cow kiss. Who would've thought the bastard had a family? Not he.

"When will you have the coin, then?" Skulljigger whispered pitifully.

Good question. "Soon," Halm answered, evading the man's penetrating gaze.

"I'll need it soon."

"You'll get it."

"I'll... wait for you, tomorrow, outside the Gate of the Sun," Skulljigger said. "At noon. Bring me the gold then."

Or else... was left unsaid. Halm sensed the warning. Pig Knot had the Zhiberian to exact revenge upon the Sunjan. Halm guessed Skulljigger might very well have a few friends of his own.

"Tomorrow will be difficult."

"Not like mine, I imagine."

Good point.

"Tomorrow, then," Halm agreed, hating himself for the

lie. There was no way he could obtain that amount of money so soon.

"Until then." With that, Skulljigger walked away steadily enough, forgoing any help and guiding his son with his good arm. Neither looked Halm in the eye, and for that, he was thankful. He tightened his bleeding fist and rubbed at his face, his jawline clenching in pain.

"Your father's a fair puncher, lad," he called out to their backs but didn't get an answer. Instead, father and son disappeared around a stone bend.

Halm didn't blame them in the least.

20

Borchus noticed him almost right away.

The Zhiberian stood out like a boil on a sick cow's ass. There was nothing harder on the eyes than an unshaven brute of a foreigner, bruised, cuts crisscrossing his chest, his waist bandaged tight. It further amused the agent that Halm, his dark features pensive and hawkish, scanned the masses lined up for the Domis, obviously searching for someone. The very sight of him made Borchus wonder what in Saimon's name might have lured the topper from the sewers. He had better things to do, though, and actually made it a point to join the people walking past the Zhiberian and head into the arena under his nose. Whatever the punce *thought* he was doing, Borchus would leave him to it. He and Garl had left the cellar that morning and parted ways near the Pit. The spy was a nervous kettle, but he went off to do his job, mostly because Borchus promised him he'd be watching.

That lasted only a few moments.

While Borchus felt somewhat guilty for deserting his spy, he still had to consider his primary task for Goll. The stairway leading down into the hell known as general quarters could have been found by smell alone. The stench issuing from the dark below made Borchus wonder if the sewers to the massive underchamber had been somehow damaged or blocked. The air smelled as if an entire pack of dogs had voided somewhere down in the blackness, ripe enough that Borchus wanted a rag for his mouth and nose. Still, he descended, loathing how hot the air was becoming, feeling the sweat ooze from his pores. He passed under flickering torches mounted in sconces and followed the passage deep beneath the surface.

The tunnel opened into the shadow-gorged underworld sheltering the homeless of the games. Light from torches revealed masses of pit fighters moving about, teeming around stone columns and walls. Hundreds of voices meshed into a constant and ominous vibe Borchus could actually feel on his sweaty skin. The faster he got out of this hell, the better. Next time, he'd send someone else. Holding his breath at times, he threaded through the fighters to the station of the Madea. As always, a wall of Skarrs guarded the arena official, ensuring his safety. Borchus stopped a few paces away from the Madea's heavy desk and gazed up at the monstrous matchboard. Fights had been posted for that day and the next, and Borchus strained to read down through the pairings. As far as he could see, none of the names belonged to the House of Ten.

"Madea." Borchus stepped up to the desk of the seated man, admiring the straight-cut parting of his white hair, right down the middle. The older man regarded the agent with mild puzzlement. As the desk was on a raised platform, Borchus appeared shorter than usual.

"I'm looking for gladiators of the newest House."

"The newest?"

"The House of Ten."

"Ah, the Free Trained one."

Borchus didn't correct him. "That's the one."

"One moment." The official pulled out papers and rummaged through them. While most of the general quarters had torchlight, bright oil lamps illuminated the Madea's charts and documents as well as his mighty matchboard.

"Ah, yes. They fight five days from now."

"Who exactly?"

"All of them. Their matches will be split over two days."

The news surprised Borchus for a moment, but he hid it well. Then he reminded himself the house only had seven fighters, unlike the more established ones. "Who are the opponents?"

In answer, the official turned his chart around and pushed it toward the edge of his desk. "You're early, but those fights will be on the matchboard later."

Borchus quickly scanned the list of opponents, noting they were all Free Trained. He saw Halm had no challenger listed, yet his name had been circled. The agent memorized the names of the six warriors to fight the House of Ten before sliding the chart back to the Madea.

"Pardon me, Madea, but what about the blood challenge to Halm of Zhiberia?"

Not appreciating being interrupted while working, the Madea scowled. "Nothing just yet."

"Nothing?"

"The House of Curge hasn't given me a name for their

fighter. It's their right to decide who they'll send to fight and when—if they decide to continue challenging the Zhiberian. However, if they don't send word soon and provide a fighter, I'll find another opponent for the Zhiberian. But that one issued a blood challenge of his own. To one called Skulljigger."

That didn't surprise Borchus in the least, but he wondered if Skulljigger was the object of Halm's search outside. He thanked the Madea and departed for the surface. In the future, with a little luck, he'd employ someone to keep an eye on the matchboard.

For the remainder of the day's fights, Borchus climbed the stairs and mingled with the masses of spectators, for where better to grasp the pulse of the games than from the common folks? He listened to men argue over favorites, stood in shaded arches, observed the day's fights, and even spied a couple of women flaunting their wares at warriors. The heat, the energy, the excitement, and of course the honey pots all brought a smile to Borchus's features. He enjoyed the season as much as the next person.

At the end of the day's bloody entertainment, the crowds milled toward the exits in thick torrents, and the agent once again merged with the flow of bodies. It carried Borchus through the Gate of the Sun, and he struggled to see through the people to where he'd seen Halm earlier. Despite knowing he should be gathering information on the fighters facing the House of Ten, the notion of startling the burly topper amused him.

However, Halm was no longer there.

Borchus frowned. Count on that Zhiberian bastard to ruin a plan.

The agent pressed through a fragrant mess of torsos and limbs, searching for the half-naked, bandaged he-bitch.

Then he spied the foreign warrior, walking just ahead and acting more than a bit odd. If Borchus didn't know any better, he'd think the hellpup was following someone. Curiosity piqued, the agent kept Halm in sight, even when he went off the main street and started down narrower lanes. Watching the bulky warrior's attempts at being stealthy made Borchus smile with contempt.

The alleys became narrower, touching Borchus's wide shoulders. Ahead, a corner beckoned, and Halm went around it—right into a fist that slammed him against a white wall.

That stopped Borchus in his tracks.

He recognized the man pummelling Halm's face. A boy shouted for his father to *kill him!* Borchus pressed himself against the alley, paralyzed over whether to join the melee, and watched as the Zhiberian took the offensive and pushed his attacker out of sight. Grunts and growls burst from the corner, and Borchus felt his belt buckle and the blade hidden there. He edged closer to the battle, only to hear it finish and dissipate into words riding on great, jagged gasps of breath. As they seemed momentarily civil, Borchus decided to listen rather than interfere.

"I'll pay you gold for the next three matches…"

The agent's eyes bulged at the Zhiberian's words.

The punce was *mad*.

Borchus leaned closer to the corner and shook his head at the combatants' weary conversation. In time, the talking stopped, and someone walked away. He heard a smattering of Zhiberian and knew Halm rested just out of sight.

Borchus waited a few heartbeats more before revealing his presence.

"'Until then,'" he repeated with bitter disbelief, but

pleased at the shock on Halm's battered face. "'Your father's a fair puncher.' He must be, for you to agree—to even *offer* such terms. Gold equaling five victories? You know that's a hundred gold pieces? Where are you going to get that kind of coin? Hm?"

Halm recovered from his surprise and inhaled deeply. "Why didn't you help?"

"I just got here," Borchus lied. "But I heard your conversation, and I must say, one word and one word only comes to mind when I think of what you've done here—*unfit*."

"The boy was right there. I couldn't think of anything else."

"Have you looked at yourself?" Borchus's tone peaked. "I'm surprised any thinking is going on at all in that smashed melon you call a skull."

Halm touched his bruised face. "Is it bad?"

Borchus shook his head. "Oh no, it's much improved from before. Look. Listen to me. You can't afford this. There's no way you can get that kind of coin by tomorrow afternoon."

"There has to be a way."

"No, you idiot, there isn't."

"There *must*."

"Well, there *isn't*. Unless you start milking kogs for whoever'll drop a coin at you, and I doubt you'll find that many between now and then. And did I mention unfit?"

Halm stood and shrugged by the smaller man. "I'll find something. I'll go to Goll."

"Goll?" Borchus nearly exploded. "You think Goll will give you coin for this?"

"He will."

"He *won't*."

Halm spun on the agent. "Why don't you start helping instead of annoying? Hm? Can you do that down there?"

"I can see the vat of shite you're hip deep in from down here, though I don't believe you care."

"Of course I care!" Halm barked and blinked in embarrassment a beat later. "You heartless bastard. That man is wifeless and has four mouths depending on him."

"I heard all of that. And I know the dog blossom probably had enough wits to say anything to get out from under your fists. That's what irks me the most, by the way—you damn near *crumpled* when he said that. I'll remember it if we find out his missus is in fact still alive."

"I'll deal with that when I see it," Halm vowed. "But I don't think I'll have to. He was telling the truth."

"So you're going to pay him off?" Borchus asked in stunned dismay. "If this tale surfaces, you can wager that it'll give you a very bad name."

"Like I care," Halm rumbled, grimacing and inspecting his still-bleeding hand.

"What's that?"

Halm opened his fist and showed him his damaged finger. Borchus made a face.

"The he-bitch certainly snacked down, didn't he?" the agent said softly. "Any other gurry to show me, then?"

"That's it."

"You've got to fight in five days, you know."

"I didn't," Halm said. "And I don't care about that right now. I *do* care about finding that coin by tomorrow."

"You know anyone who might loan you the money?"

"No."

"Give?"

"No."

"How do you feel about stealing, then?"

Halm smirked and looked away.

Then Borchus remembered something. It was the season for the games, after all. And Sunja's Pit wasn't the sole venue. The Zhiberian would have to be mad to attempt it, but then again, he wasn't a friend, and Borchus didn't really care what became of the pig-bastard.

"You really want to pay this man? You really want to buy him out?"

Halm blinked, took a breath, and thought about it for a moment. "Aye that."

"It'll be easier to just kill him on the sands."

"Skulljigger? No. As I've said, I'll not make four orphans."

"What will Pig Knot say?"

"What is it you want to say?" Halm burst out. "I can see you're about to piss it out, so let's have it, or just shut up or leave."

Borchus allowed himself a little smile. "Very well. There *might* be a way out of this. Just might. You fight in the Iron Games."

That revelation rendered Halm speechless, and he regarded the agent with a look of horror. "And here I was thinking about wagering away the few coins I have."

"Oh, you'll need those coins—I guarantee it."

"I've heard of non-commissioned fights beyond the Pit, but I never knew where they were. The Pit pays better, anyway."

"Well then, you don't need my help, do you?"

"Wait," Halm grated. "You miserable stain of maggot shite. Lead on. I know you're biting at the chance to see me take more punishment, so lead on."

Borchus didn't bother replying.

He had to remind himself the Zhiberian was smarter

than he looked.

*

A short time later, Borchus located Garl leaning against an alehouse wall and keeping to the shade. The once-beggar wore new-looking breeches and a shirt and, shaven as he was, appeared almost respectable. Borchus led Halm past his spy before looping around back, through the next side street.

"Where are you going?" Halm asked more than once, but Borchus wouldn't answer.

They snaked their way through a second alley until the agent stopped amongst walls of white stone and brick. A nearby sewer grate gorged with offal soured the air. Borchus caught sight of a tail disappearing down a black pipe.

"Can't stay here," Halm said indignantly, studying the garbage and the panels of stone fitted into the ground, split by age.

"Seems fitting for the situation you're in," Borchus retorted.

"I'm waiting over there," Halm pointed to the last corner, just on the street.

"I didn't ask you to stay."

Halm ambled off, got halfway, shrugged, and then meandered back, appearing none too pleased. That pleased the agent. In his mind, the fat man *should* squirm.

Then Garl appeared, swinging himself around the edge of the building and stopping within the gloom of the deepening evening.

"Where were you?" the spy asked, balancing himself on his crutches. "And who's he?"

"He's one of the fighters in the new house," Borchus said.

"Oh." Garl hesitantly raised a hand in greeting. To the agent's surprise, Halm waved back.

"I thought you'd be around." Garl turned his attention back to Borchus.

"I had work to do as well."

"Anyone could have knifed me back then."

"But they didn't. Keep that in mind."

"Not this time."

"No one is going to hurt you," Borchus insisted. "But we have a new problem."

"What?"

"Him."

Garl studied the Zhiberian once more. "Unfit to look at, if you ask me."

"I'm not, but I will ask this… are the Iron Games still happening?"

"They are, but I don't know anything about them."

"You know where they are?"

"Aye that. Where all the old warehouses were. There's a few streets that are abandoned now. Not even the Street Watch goes there, from what I understand. Anyway, I've heard of fights happening over there, somewhere. Go and ask about. You might find something before nightfall."

"We don't have the time," Borchus said. "You'll have to walk us over there."

"Me?" Garl jumped at the notion.

"You. Make your way through the back alleys if you can. Stay away from the main streets. We'll follow you far enough back that no one will notice."

"The city has *eyes* about, Borchus."

"There's coin in it for you."

"Gold's no good if I'm fishhooked."

"He'll pay you." Borchus pointed to Halm. "Won't you? You shameless ass licker."

Halm raised his hand again and eyed the passersby.

"See?"

Garl mulled it over, running his mutilated hand over his trimmed beard. "This is gurry. You said I only have to get information on fighters."

"He'll toss you a few coins."

"He means to fight in the games?"

"Aye that."

"What if he dies?"

The agent sighed. "Then I'll pay you out of my pocket."

Garl's expression soured, but Borchus suspected he'd do it.

Moments later, the crippled man led them through the darkening veins of the city.

21

Just at dusk, they arrived at the back door of a healer's house. Halm's finger had stopped bleeding, but it needed stitches. Lamplight glowed behind shuttered windows. An old tomcat perched on a nearby wooden crate garnished with a few stray feathers eyed the three men with disdain. Borchus knocked while noticing Garl, who was becoming increasingly uneasy.

"What's the matter?" Borchus asked.

"Just nervous—with night coming on," Garl muttered.

"Well... relax."

That didn't calm the spy, and he fidgeted on his crutches.

"What's the matter with him?" Halm asked, slow on the exchange as he'd been inspecting his finger.

"Nothing's wrong with him. Garl's just fine."

But Halm could see that Garl *wasn't* just fine.

The door opened as Borchus was about to rap once again. The healer, chewing on supper, stuck his head out and cocked an eye at the lot of them. A great white beard flowed to his chest.

"We have a man who's been in a fight."

The healer, pudgy jowls working away, peered at Halm.

"What's for supper?" the Zhiberian asked him good-naturedly.

"Rabbit," the healer replied in a voice that might've needed a drop of oil. "What's the matter, precisely?"

"He had his finger bitten."

"His finger bitten," the healer repeated stoically.

On cue, Halm held up the afflicted digit in a one-fisted salute, twisting it this way and that. The gesture put a frown on the healer's aged face, who didn't take kindly to the display.

"Come in, then," the healer grumbled.

The old man worked his art. He sterilized the wound with a dollop of firewater, stitched it up while Halm made bad jokes, and rubbed a gob of onion-smelling saywort over the area, which screwed up Garl's face. The finishing touch came with a linen bandage wrapped three times around the area and knotted. Once done, the healer stood back and admired his work.

"No more fighting for you," he declared.

"No more," Halm promised earnestly. "I swear. Pay the man."

Borchus scowled jagged daggers at the Zhiberian.

Halm shrugged and dug out a gold coin. "It was a *joke*. You'd think you'd have a better sense of humor with them long forks of wool on your face."

"When I hear a better joke, you'll see my sense of humor."

They thanked the healer and were off, following Garl through a maze of stone and wood.

Somewhere in the western section of the mighty city, off a side street and down the throat of another, a single lamp flickered. No honest lamplighter with a family tended to that solitary beacon, which sometimes creaked a nonsense tune in the night's wind. It hung off a wooden arm attached to a dilapidated storehouse front, and no one ever saw exactly who or what refilled the glass fixture when it burned out. Few hardworking Sunjans ever dared to venture down that particular forbidding road for fear of being knifed and robbed… or just knifed. Whispered stories said some citizen had complained to the Street Watch about the area, prompting the authorities to investigate the narrow strip, but nothing was ever found during the day. The same whispers said those who had summoned the Skarrs were later found dead, their loved ones also murdered.

No one summoned the Street Watch ever again.

The businesses there that had once thrived—weavers, clay shapers, wagon carpenters, barrel makers—shriveled up and relocated. Honest families moved, abandoning that short belt of crumpling stone to time and the elements and the vermin.

Sometimes shrieks stabbed the night air from beyond the eerie radius of that one lamp—frighteningly muffled sounds that emanated from the tomb-like interiors and reverberated off the foreboding heights of the nearby buildings. Those close enough to hear such cries quickly got on their way.

At a glance, a two-story warehouse seemed tethered to the street by impenetrable shadows. Roof slats and crumbling clay tiling lay in the narrow alleys about the building's sides. Ribbons decorated its heights, hanging like dead strands of hair about a weathered face. Straining planks partially blinded the windows, giving the feel of a prison about to burst at its seams. Two doors marked the entrance, placed in the middle of the ground floor. One was closed and nailed shut with wood pried from neighbouring structures while the other door had a man-sized oval hole in its lower half, as if rats had chewed through it. Through this ragged mouth, the breath of something rancid drifted.

Night had fully descended by the time the three men stopped in front of the entryway.

"Place is a pisspot," Halm commented.

Borchus ignored him and looked at Garl. "Can you find your way back?"

The beggar nodded.

"Pay him," Borchus whispered to Halm.

"What's that?"

Borchus glared at the Zhiberian.

Frowning, Halm dug into his purse once again, withdrew two coins, and placed them into the hand of Garl, who made the gold disappear.

"Now, get on your way," Borchus instructed his companion. "I'll return when I can, and when I do, you'll hear four slow knocks, so…" He trailed off, indicating the crutches.

His expression smothered in the unsettling gloom, Garl bobbed his head and got moving without protest.

"You think that's wise? Him by himself?" Halm asked quietly, watching the crippled man shamble off.

"No," Borchus admitted, "and neither is this."

"Aye that. You're right there."

"You can still kill this Skulljigger in the arena."

Halm faced him as if catching a whiff of something foul. "Already told you. I'm not about to orphan four whelps. Leave if you like. I'll carry on from here."

With that, he went to the door. Borchus followed after the barest hesitation, knowing full well what Goll would say to him if he allowed the House of Ten's prize gladiator to carry on without supervision. He sized up the building. It sagged in on itself, as if its wooden bones were about to splinter and break.

Halm stopped the door, tugging on a handle that would not give. He hunkered down, placing a hand to his bandaged gut and peered inside. "This looks to be the way in. There's a line of light inside."

"In you go, then," Borchus said.

Wiping his face, Halm got down on all fours, grimacing as he went, and wormed his bulk through the hole. Borchus waited until the man's large posterior disappeared inside before following… into a wooden tunnel.

Something slammed into the floor behind Borchus once his feet cleared the threshold. A toe tap informed him the way had been closed off.

"What was that?" Halm whispered from ahead just before hands yanked away the tunnel's ceiling. Torchlight flashed. Hard-looking men stood above them, their features in shadows. Their swords gleamed, poised over the exposed trough filled with the frozen forms of Halm and Borchus.

"Yes?" someone asked.

A startled Borchus hunched over like a cat and glanced up, well aware of his perilous position. He figured if he made one wrong move, about a half dozen blades—including one or two spears—would skewer him. "We're here to fight."

"Are you, now?"

"Well, truth be known, he is," Borchus said, nodding at Halm while eyeing the blades. "I'm here to watch. And wager."

"Well…" the voice spoke. "Let them up, lads."

The swords fell away. Halm rose from the wooden channel, studying the dark faces and being careful with every movement. His Mademian blade was at his waist, but he made no move for it. Borchus didn't blame him for being careful. He got to his own feet and dusted himself off, wary of the individuals surrounding them both.

"Your man's cut up already," one of the shadows remarked.

"I'll do fine," Halm stated with a grim smirk.

"That one." Borchus took a breath and gestured at the Zhiberian in grand fashion. "Has the House of Curge after him. And he's put down three men already in this season's games. He might look like a fat slice of ham, but I assure you, damn near every pit fighter he's met thought the same thing. And perished because of it."

"Well, except one," Halm corrected.

"Except one," Borchus cut him off with a glare. "Who even now is crippled for life."

Halm's expression furrowed but then lightened upon realizing what Borchus was attempting.

"The Zhiberian?" one of the shadows muttered, recognizing him now. "Seddon's crack, he's the *Zhiberian*."

"You know him?" another asked.

"Oh, aye that. Man's a killer. A right unfit beast."

"You're *right*," spoke another shadow. "Should've recognized that gut first off. Oh, let him in! They'll enjoy this butcher!"

"He can fight?"

"Saimon's hell, he can."

"He's cut up." One pointed at the cloth bandages looped around Halm's midsection.

"Don't mind that." Halm dismissed him with a vicious smile, playing up to his audience.

A man with a wild bush atop a pasty, round face cleared his throat and got Borchus's attention. "Well, since the lads know you, I suppose I can allow it. It's not every day we do this, you understand—make, er, exceptions."

"Understood."

"First time at the games?"

"Ah, yes," Borchus admitted.

"Well, then, you're in luck. It just so happens we are holding fights this very night. Walk with me," Wild One invited, holding out an arm as the wall of swords split and faded away.

Halm and Borchus swung themselves over the sides of the opened tunnel. Once it was clear, two men covered the top with slabs of wood. Borchus liked the arrangement. Anyone crawling into the place would be caught unawares when these louts cracked open the top. Scattered torches revealed little of the interior, arranged to conceal guards in pockets of shadow. Their boots scuffed over planks, and Borchus detected cheering underfoot.

"Well," Wild One declared, halting near a set of doors framed into the floor. A pair of thugs stood on either side, holding the ends of thick ropes.

"These are the rules. To enter the Iron, you must pay two gold coins apiece. Once you are here, we expect you to wager. If you aren't wagering, you're fighting. If you aren't doing either, then you shouldn't be here, unless we know you—which is another matter entirely. Fights on the Iron are somewhat different from the Pit—our battles are usually to the death but not always. Fights continue until one man cannot continue."

"Pay the man," Borchus muttered out of the corner of his mouth. Halm frowned in annoyance before fishing out the last of his gold and handing the fee over.

Wild One nodded his thanks. "Excellent. I suppose you're fighting?"

"I am," Halm muttered.

"And you are?" he directed at Borchus.

"His keeper. For the night anyway."

"Very well. Now then, unlike the Pit, we aren't financed by the king himself, hence the gold to enter and required wagering. There's no armor to be worn. No helmets. Fighters use only the weapons they are given, and we choose them. Because of this, we obviously are not, uh, wholly supported by any Chamber official, and thus, we appreciate you taking care when speaking about the Iron at the end of the night. Our battles are not the highlighted ones of the season, yet they are no less spectacular than those supported by the king. The Chamber dislikes us for other reasons, mostly concerning coin, but also because of our preference for a more… *fulfilling* touch to our combats. Understood?"

Wild One finished with the chilling timbre of an unspoken threat. He locked gazes with both newcomers. A violent burst of cheering erupted from underfoot, drawing attention to the floor. The sound peaked and then ebbed away to a dull roar.

Halm's face darkened pensively, and he flexed his fist with the bitten finger. Borchus didn't bother asking if he'd had a change of heart. They were well past that.

"Everyone gets the same speech?" the agent asked, his attention divided.

"The new ones, yes," Wild One answered.

"How do people learn of these matches if you caution them about speaking?"

"Oh, there's an… undercurrent in Sunja, where if you listen long and hard enough, you'll know. Or we'll tell you. And then there are those, the dedicated ones, like you, who simply find out."

The cheering seeped through the floorboards, splitting Borchus's attention. "Let's see it, then," he said grimly.

Wild One smirked evilly and waved a finger.

The very ground split apart with a gash of light and the sound of a thousand throats.

22

A smoky, acrid puff of air escaped like a rupturing bubble of sewer gas, stopping them cold upon the threshold. Wild One gestured toward stone steps descending at a sharp incline, down into the earth, well below the floorboards, where spidery veins of dirt crumbled from cracks between ancient brick. A torch beckoned, flickering above the first landing some twenty steps away. People clustered there, sitting on the stone and pressing against wooden railings, their legs dangling. A dozen pallid faces lifted to see who was about to descend into their domain. Halm could barely make out the dark knobs of heads farther down. Another roar erupted from the thrown-back doors in the floor, unmuzzled and frightening, the heckling and chanting of hellions.

"Seddon above," Halm whispered in horrified awe. He wanted to ask if they were really going to go down there, but Borchus immediately followed Wild One below the floor. Taking a steadying breath, Halm went down after them.

They descended, hunkering down to clear the lip of the entrance, careful with every step. Borchus leaned against the wall as another round of cheers exploded from the spectators. Not knowing what he'd see, Halm peered over the railing. Six points of lamplight burned three levels below, an uneven ring of light holding back an undulating blackness. Figures pumped fists and shouted in a rippling tide of excitement while the very walls pulsed with people.

People. The edges of the darkness teemed with limbs and screaming faces devoid of bodies. Reluctantly, Halm followed Borchus to the first landing and weaved a path through the thickening clutter of men and women perched on the stairs. The agent wasn't happy in the least, being so far beneath the ground. The short man reached out and grasped the railing for balance at one time, making a few heads turn questioningly in his direction. Borchus withdrew his hand from the wooden rail and pointed below.

Halm looked. And swallowed.

Two half-naked men fought on a checkered floor, but as Halm descended, he could see it was a huge grate of iron. They punched at each other with fists that gleamed in the hot light, the meaty connections creating curt echoes an instant before the crowds shrieked bloody approval. Grunts of pain and effort reached Halm's ears as the pit fighters struggled against each other, their muscular torsos dripping black.

One warrior slipped, the flesh of his back cut several times over. Halm realized why they fought over a grate—it was a massive drain, perhaps situated over the city's sewer system, and the combatants bled into it, which probably made cleaning easier when the time arrived.

HOUSE OF PAIN

The standing fighter smashed three short jabs into his off-balance opponent. Each brazen smack of fist on flesh ripped cheers from the crowd. The first punch buckled the fighter, the second one lifted him off his feet, and the third dropped him to the iron floor. Then the punisher dropped on the fallen man's chest and rained down blow after devastating blow.

The onlookers damned near blew out their throats roaring.

Halm, Borchus, and Wild One were perhaps five steps from the floor when the victor lifted himself off his twitching opponent; the dying man's face was a broken bowl of red pulp.

The winner raised his fists, accepting the crashing approval from the spectators. Two ratty fellows grasped the pit fighter's sides and led him away off the Iron, through the parting crowd, and out of sight. Three others moved in and dragged the carcass of the fallen to one edge of the grate, where more brutes struggled with opening a broad lid. Hinges squealed. Once it was opened wide enough, they stuffed the body into the hole and dropped the cover.

"Dying Seddon," Halm whispered as he watched, catching a whiff of something other than spirits on the air.

"Over here." Wild One led the way through a gulf of faces, several of which brazenly sized up the newcomers.

"Who you have there, Calagu?"

"More meat for the butcher?"

"Seddon's balls, man—that one's already *been* in a fight!"

"Who're the babes, Calagu?"

But Wild One—Calagu—ignored the questions and the leers and led Halm and Borchus to an open door. They entered a solid brick room, and Halm could smell fear, a rank bodily stink, ripe of sweat, that almost stole his very breath. Four men, stripped to their waists, stalked a large inner chamber, passing through torchlight like snowy ghouls rethinking past lives.

"You sit here," Calagu said. "I'll call you when it's time."

"Wait," Borchus held out a hand. "What are the conditions?"

"Conditions?"

"Armor? Weapons? That sort of thing."

Halm became pensive, knowing he wasn't going to like the answer, and Calagu's pale smile, half concealed by shadow, made him curse coming here.

"Forgotten so soon? I've already said there's no armor. And ultimately, we choose the weapons. Tonight, our warriors use these." Calagu snarled over his raised fists. "You can find a pair there, along the wall. Find ones that fit. Or don't wear any at all. But give that sword at your waist to your keeper as you won't be using anything else."

He turned to depart and stopped in the door. "Good luck, Zhiberian. I look forward to seeing you fight."

Halm regarded Borchus, feeling none too happy about any of it anymore. "What in Saimon's black bag have you gotten us into?" he asked, undoing the belt just below his belly and handing his sword and scabbard to Borchus.

"Me?" the agent exclaimed, eyeing the other unchained brutes in the room. "*You* came to me! Oh, *I'm not about to orphan four whelps,* you said. And what did I say? Hm?"

"All right, all right."

"No, what did I say? I want to hear it."

An uneasy Halm turned away, scratching his brow and not meeting the faces of any of the pit fighters moving about the chamber's charnel gloom. The weapons Calagu had mentioned caught his attention, next to the doorway. Three rows of metal gauntlets lined the brick wall like an executioner's trophy rack. For a halting moment, Halm thought he was staring at hands before he realized the grim reality. *Fists.* They wore studded gauntlets that night. He stopped before the rack and sighed. A wooden bin full of linen bandages sat next to it, with a spool of catgut for stitching. Needles sprouted from a ball of string.

Outside, a voice barked and stirred the crowds into a vicious heat, introducing the next match.

"Dying Seddon," Halm breathed, examining his choices.

Three racks. Ten sets of gauntlets of varying sizes, all extending perhaps halfway up the forearm. Three different styles of weapon. The first rack had gauntlets studded with brutal spikes. Meat clung between the fixtures. Halm's face screwed up in horror at the sight. The second rack's had blades attached, like an animal's claws. The third rack…

Halm blinked.

The third rack's gauntlets made him shiver. Briefly. He hoped Borchus hadn't seen.

Broad sickles of flat-edged steel grinned at him. *Cheesecutters*, he knew them to be called in jest, but he didn't know the real name. Cumbersome because of their length and weight, frightening to behold, and above all, brutal. The cutting edges longed for flesh like the blood fish of distant Harudin.

The notion of wearing anything from such a butcher's selection twisted his guts… but he knew his foe most certainly would.

"Who are you here for?" a voice asked. Halm turned and faced a near-naked brawler of a man, wide eyed and quivering with suppressed energy. His clamped jaw showed too-white teeth, as if he'd just finished biting through leather.

"What's that?" Halm asked, having difficulty in understanding the Sunjan's speech.

"*Who* are you here for?"

A sudden gush of cheering made the speaker shift his eyes to the door. Halm took the opportunity to glance at Borchus, who shrugged.

"I don't understand," Halm finally answered, noting the spikes sprouting from the fighter hands.

"*Heeeee*," the lout wheezed an evil giggle. "I fought in areas of Pericia. Bled men amongst the snowcapped peaks of the Chains. I brought the Paws to their knees at Three Rivers and slaughtered Dezer throughout the halls of the Vathian wild." The pit fighter sucked in a deep steadying breath and then took a step closer.

Halm saw madness in his eyes.

"I executed barbarians in the Ice Kingdoms and whored in the pleasure palaces of Zuthenia and Kalikos. So *who* are you *here* for?"

Halm stood at an utter loss.

"I'm here because I want this," the warrior hissed, evil emanating from the man as rank as foul breath. "I. Want. *This*." His spiked fist thumped his muscular chest and left a bloody print. The warrior paid it no heed, trembling as if ready to burst.

A voice outside shouted a name, "Amessar!" and the warrior's bravado faltered.

But only for a moment.

Amessar shook his limbs and barked at Halm, making him flinch, before tearing through the doorway and out onto the iron grate. The wall of bodies sealed up after his passing, and cheering harsh enough to split stone flooded the chamber.

"Unfit," Borchus muttered.

Halm regarded him with a sour look. "Try not to piss yourself, Sunjan."

"Nowhere near pissing myself, fat man."

"Where were you when that unfit topper was threatening me?"

Borchus squinted. "Well out of reach of that insane shagger, that's where I was. Besides, the great Halm needs support? That lad was pickled. I could see it in his eyes."

"Pickled?"

"Aye that," Borchus said. "Pickled. Unfit. Warped. Can't you smell it? Some of them out there are chewing the Tar. *White* Tar. Although damned if I understand why."

"What's Tar?"

"A weed you chew. Takes one away to places without leaving your bed. Wide awake dreaming, they say. I'm not sure why they're chewing it here, not that I'd understand the appeal of Tar in the first place, but that one spewing at you was pickled on something else."

"What?"

Borchus rolled his eyes. "I don't *know*. I'm not an authority on such."

"Sounded like one to me."

"Yes, well." The agent glanced over his shoulder at the other occupants. "You're a fat tit three heartbeats from being a slab of gurry. You should be thinking about other things. You there!"

One of the pacing men stopped and regarded them, his frame shivering with barely suppressed fury.

"What was wrong with that one?"

The vibrating figure ignored the question and resumed pacing, stomping hard enough to splinter shinbones.

Borchus could only stare before dismissing the warrior with a hand. The agent stepped toward Halm. "Seddon above. These poor pissers aren't in their right minds at all. Look at them. Pacing like that. I'd wager they're *all* fermenting on something."

"*What?*"

"I don't *know*."

Outside, the cheering spiked in a crescendo before ebbing away like beach rocks pulled by the surf.

"Fight's done," Borchus stated, his eyes on the masses beyond.

"You'll have to put coin on my head," Halm told him. "I've none left."

"*I'm* not placing any coin on your considerable ass! This was *your* choice. Win the fight, and you'll have plenty to play with. Or at least more than you do now."

"When do I fight?" Halm asked.

In reply, Borchus pointed to the racks of gauntlets.

Halm chose a pair bristling with spikes and pulled one of the gruesome things on over his hands. It actually fit quite well, so he quickly donned its twin and made fists.

"I can feel it against the cut," he said, adjusting the fit.

"Your finger?" Borchus asked. "You're going to feel it. You've got that roll of bandage around it."

"Perhaps I should take it off?"

"Perhaps you should just chop it off and have done with it."

Halm frowned. "Only saying. Saucy bastard."

"Only answering, spraying pisshole."

Before either of them could really get started, the doorway filled with a tall stick of a man. A leather vest, opened down the middle, draped his cagey chest. "Bohem!"

One of the remaining warriors straightened and charged the door, bladed fists swinging. Bohem bellowed as if about to leap to his death. The onlookers cried with wicked glee when he burst forth from the door.

Borchus rubbed his eyes and put his back to a wall, alternating between looking outside and squinting at those who remained in the chamber.

"I think I prefer the Pit," Halm said quietly.

Borchus nodded. "Amessar didn't come back."

"No. He didn't."

Halm breathed in air flavored with a hint of some exotic spice and studied his spiked hands. He punched shadows, loosening out the knots in his arms and frame. Borchus watched him and spoke not a word.

The third fighter hadn't mentally prepared himself when the Stick with the open leather vest reappeared, shouting his name. The Stick yelled for "Stuhun" twice, but the fighter pressed into a back corner as if it were sucking him into the cracks, not as eager as the others before him.

"I'll go," Halm said.

The Stick's united brow arched at him.

"I'm ready," the Zhiberian stated.

"This way, then."

Halm followed the Stick into the mob.

Borchus trailed at their heels.

The walk to the iron grate was a startling experience, as never before had Halm been within arms' reach of the audience. They slapped his shoulders in an outpouring of support, reddening his flesh. Some cursed, but that was expected. Stick guided him to the edge of the iron floor, and Halm spied a wide smear of blood staining a path to the lidded sewers. No barrier existed between the eager spectators and the combatants, and that made Halm nervous. Armed men stood facing the crowds, containing them with fierce looks. Halm had no confidence in their ability to stop anyone should a drunkard become violent. The fighting ground itself was a smaller, more intimate, and infinitely more brutal arena hemmed in by flesh, woefully inferior when compared to the grandeur of Sunja's Pit.

As far as Halm was concerned, the Pit was superior in every way.

They introduced him, but he listened only remotely, focusing on the parting of bodies directly across from him, not ten paces away.

Then Halm's opponent appeared to the crowd's rising cries of evil exultation.

The pit fighter's shoulders rose above the crowds. Frightening gray eyes fixed upon the Zhiberian with all the menace of an angry butcher rising with the dawn. The brute's features contorted with hate and something more, a feral intensity, an eagerness Halm hadn't witnessed anywhere before.

Then he realized that wasn't true.

The same vicious guise had contorted Amessar's face.

The crowd chortled and leered with wicked delight, seeing Halm's hesitation and smelling fear.

A smiling Stick allowed a few short moments for wagers; then he took the center of the Iron and waved a hand at the beast on the other side.

"For the second time this night, Drajen! Are you ready?"

Drajen shook like a dog drying off from a swim. "Aye!"

And the crowds shouted with him.

"Are you ready?" Stick asked Halm. The Zhiberian gestured he was.

His job done, Stick quickly got out of the way.

And Drajen charged, his spiked hands flashing in the torchlight, mesmerizing. He swung for Halm's head. Halm ducked and crushed his own weaponized hand into an exposed set of right ribs. The entire side of the fighter body shivered under that mighty punch, and Drajen staggered sideways a few steps, almost touching the wall of people. The man hissed like a full pot, bent over his ribs. Halm stood at guard while Drajen composed himself, awash in the goading from the crowd. They cursed him to move, to fight, to do *something*.

Drajen grimaced and kept his right arm close to his side, protecting the dribbling red holes speckling his ribs.

Halm waited with his fists held high. He didn't wait long.

Drajen collected himself, yelled gibberish meant to intimidate his foe, and attacked.

Halm stepped inside his opponent's guard and destroyed Drajen's jaw with the first punch, stretching skin, the bone twisting grotesquely to the side, before uppercutting a second blow to Drajen's reeling head.

The fighter crashed to the grate and did not get up.

"Kill him!" the onlookers demanded. "Kill him!"

One fellow dressed in a stained white shirt slipped past the guards and rushed Halm. The Zhiberian parried the knife meant for his kidneys and fired a punch from over his shoulder, breaking another chin and dropping the attacker in a heap.

Angry and on the defensive, Halm made a wary circle, waiting for the next one. None came. The people roared an unsettling mix of happiness and hatred—the winners and the losers. At least that was the same as the Pit.

Stick appeared then, none too happy with the fool cradling his face and crawling toward the sidelines. The guards gripped the wounded knifeman by the shoulders and hauled him out of sight while Stick inspected the still-unconscious Drajen. Stick rubbed his chin, straightened and chopped a hand in Halm's direction.

"Victor!" he shouted.

Hundreds of throats opened up, charging the air with unruly sound. Halm gazed around, seeing coin being exchanged. He located an impassive Borchus being jostled by those around him. Then Stick caught the Zhiberian's attention and tossed him a small cloth sack. Halm caught his winnings with spiked hands dripping red.

"Again?" Stick asked.

Halm hefted the bag. There wasn't near enough in it for his needs. "Aye that."

"Stay right there, then." Stick turned away and waded through the crowd.

That surprised Halm, and he looked at Borchus, who appeared equally startled. Guards grabbed the limbs of the unconscious Drajen and dragged him off the Iron. As they worked, Halm strode over to the agent, standing amongst a clutter of limbs and faces.

"Take this and wager it on my head."

Borchus took it. "You're fighting again?"

"Aye that, the only way I'll come away with enough gold this night."

"You're a glutton, Zhiberian."

"It's what I do."

"Try not to piss yourself, then."

Halm would keep that in mind. He went to the center

of the underground arena and lifted his arms, burning off excess energy with a guttural bellow and letting the onlookers know he wasn't done. He strutted around the iron grate, ignoring how his boots stuck briefly with each step. Some watchers cursed him for his arrogance. Others reveled. Borchus stood to one side, talking with a couple of dogs eager to take a wager. Halm inhaled and tasted something strange over his tongue. He wished Pig Knot were present. The Sunjan would have been able to identify every smell in that hole.

Screams of approval cut the tepid air, yanking him back to the present.

Halm swung around, facing the other end of the grate, to see Stick leading a new fighter into the fray.

It was a warrior from earlier, the one who'd mashed a man's face into the floor and left him for dead. Dark eyes gleamed in the torchlight, and the baleful grin splitting the bruised face resembled a hellion's. Stick got out of the way of the pit fighter, who gazed upward for a moment as if checking for rain, before leveling his attention at the newest challenger and shaking out muscular arms ending in frightening cheesecutter blades.

Steeling himself for the fight to come, Halm backed up unconsciously. His adversary had exchanged his gauntlets for those curved nightmares. The notion of fighting someone wielding such weapons—and using them well—nearly unnerved him. He got the sensation under control right and proper. The Iron was no place to show fear.

Stick stepped between them, and Halm didn't appreciate the eerie calmness of his opponent.

"What's your name?" Stick asked.

"Halm of Zhiberia."

"The Zhiberian will face…" Stick's hand flashed in the

direction of the hellion. "Surugar!"

The underworld audience approved as all sides of the iron floor erupted in wagering. Halm didn't take his eyes off Surugar. He didn't like the sly light in the killer's eye.

"Now…" Stick lifted his hand and backed off the Iron. "Begin!"

Halm shifted, staying light and moving, while Surugar circled to his right almost casually, sizing up the Zhiberian like a cut of meat. The people chided Halm for his little dance and jeered even more when he retreated from Surugar. The man stood at the same height as the Zhiberian, but Halm knew *unfit in the head* when he saw it. He supposed any gladiator was a touch insane to fight in such a hell.

Surugar brought his arms up to guard, the sickles near his head like twin moons. Then he feinted, stomping the iron and making it echo like a thick gong. Halm darted backward, but when Surugar didn't pursue, he reclaimed a step.

A cheesecutter lashed out, scything the air and making Halm jerk himself backward several steps. Surugar didn't press the attack, but a malefic smile widened upon his face. A beat later, Halm felt warm water cover his face, leaking into his eyes.

Blood.

Lords above, the bastard actually connected!

Surugar leapt at him, and Halm ducked under a blurred streak of steel. Both men whirled about, but the Zhiberian was faster. He charged forward, got under the twin blades, and wrapped his arms around Surugar's bulk. With a growl, he heaved Surugar up off his feet, to the immediate awe of the crowd. Surugar's smile wilted as his feet left the floor. He swept one of the cheesecutters down, slicing

Halm's bare back in a straight red line, and the Zhiberian went rigid with pain.

Baring his teeth, Halm tightened his mighty grip around the small of his opponent's back. A surprised grimace flashed across Surugar's face, and his head thrashed backward. He drew back an elbow to smash into Halm's head.

But the Zhiberian slammed the man into the unyielding Iron, braining him like a slippery fish.

Surugar's arms splayed wide, and he arched his back as if impaled on nails, his face livid and twisted with pain.

Halm stood back, ignoring the deafening hollering of the people, and wiped his bleeding brow with a forearm. Rivulets streaked down his back.

In a defiant display of strength, Surugar sat up, to building cries of surprise and approval.

Halm took two steps and kicked the man squarely in his face, straightening out his neck and flattening him on the grate. The crowd drew back as if feeling the violent connection and groaned as one. But to Halm's dismay, Surugar rolled onto his belly only an instant later. The warrior unsteadily hefted himself to his knees and elbows, broad back trembling with the effort. Then he flashed a look at Halm.

Surugar was smiling once more.

"Unfit," Halm muttered in horror. He launched himself at the rising warrior, placing every drop of strength into one final punch flying from the shoulder. Halm's spiked fist exploded into Surugar's jaw, snapping the pit fighter's head to one side. The unbalanced fighter collapsed on the Iron, flattened out as if stepped on. A bloody fury took Halm then. He jumped on top of Surugar, grasped his skull in a punishing grip, and twisted.

The crack of bone whipped the audience into silence.

Halm stood, torso heaving, blood spattering his face and chest, waiting to see if Surugar would somehow defy death and rise again. He didn't, however, so Halm took the center of the floor, dabbing his forearm against his scalp, shaking and blinking away blood while the crowd raged with glee and disbelief.

Halm didn't care. "Give me another!" he shouted, dark specks flying from his lips.

People drew back from the Zhiberian. They'd heard stories...

Stick stepped onto the grate as if it were a thin sheet of ice, mindful of the frightening foreigner making hateful faces at the spectators. He knelt at Surugar's side, grasped a fistful of hair, and pulled the head off the floor. An instant later, he released it with a thump.

"Victor!" the Stick announced, and the masses truly went wild.

Without waiting, Halm turned about and stalked off toward the entry of waiting chamber, every breath a mist of blood. Not surprisingly, the people melted away from his path.

Once inside, Halm leaned against the nearest wall for support. He took massive breaths, and with each lungful, his fury dissipated. He wrenched the gauntlets from his hands and let them fall. Shoulders trembling, he felt his face and discovered the cut from Surugar's initial slash. Halm hissed. The slash went to the bone and ran at least the length of a finger. Even as he dabbed at it, fresh blood dribbled down, causing one eye to shut. He didn't have to check his back to know it was bad as well, but he reached around anyway. The blade had sliced through skin and a loop of cloth bandage. Another sliced dressing hung off him, dark as if dipped in vibrant dye. Halm sighed and drew back red fingers.

"You're doing well," a voice remarked.

Borchus.

"I'm bleeding… like a…" Halm couldn't finish the thought.

"Yes, well, I think we both knew what fighting here meant," Borchus remarked. He stepped in front of the gladiator and held out a handful of cloth. Halm regarded it through a gory squint and snatched it away, applying it to his forehead.

"Wasn't fast enough in that last one."

Borchus shrugged. "Oh, you were fast enough. From what I saw, you merely misjudged the reach afforded by those blades. You got it right the second time. I have your gold, by the way."

"How much?"

"Not quite there. About a third, by my count. But…"

"But not quite there," Halm growled. His wounds quickly saturated the cloth, and he studied it somberly. "You have any more of these?"

"Oh, yes," Borchus muttered with a little jolt. He went to the bin next to the door and fished out a handful of bandages. When he returned, Calagu and the Stick entered the dim chamber. Both men stood well away from the Zhiberian.

"You truly are a butcher, Zhiberian," Calagu said with admiration. "A true monster to behold. Such speed. Such strength! Can no one match you in ferocity? In power? In skill?"

"In bleeding," Borchus quietly added.

"Well," Calagu amended with a considering expression. "Men aren't tickling one another out there."

"Ready for another go?" the Stick asked.

"Another?" Halm's brow knotted together as he peeked past his bandage.

"He's barely finished bleeding," Borchus pointed out.

"How many times can I fight?" Halm asked, speaking over the agent.

"As many as you like," Calagu informed him. "Provided you're able, of course. It's plain to see you need a little time to clean yourself up, but truth be known, you should leave a bit on you. For color. The people enjoy the blood, the theatrics. They'll wait for you if you decide to fight again."

"The floor is ruled by one fighter until he can't rule it any further," Stick added.

"What?"

"He means," Calagu explained, "you fight until there are no more challengers or until you decide to stop. Or you're dead. Whichever way, it's gold for you. A spectacle for us."

"I'll wager it is," Borchus commented, unimpressed.

"Well," Calagu said, "we'll arrange a few more matches. When you're ready, send your manservant out."

Borchus scowled at the jab.

"Wonderful work, Zhiberian, *wonderful*," Calagu exclaimed as he and the Stick backed toward the door. "Worth every coin. Marvelous!"

They left Borchus and Halm to themselves in the poorly lit room. The agent rolled up some clean cloth, pushed Halm's hands down, and pressed the bandage against the flowing cut.

"Now then," the shorter man said. "Hold it here, firmly."

"I know how to stop bleeding."

"Well, then you can stitch yourself. You can also have fun applying the saywort that's over there as well. And know full well I'll laugh when you get around to sewing up your back, or have you forgotten about that?"

That silenced the other man. "Apologies."

The cries from the people distracted the pair as Stick herded two more fighters onto the iron floor.

"Not needed," Borchus eventually said in a quieter tone, the shadows playing across his features. The agent met the dull stare of Halm's red eyes as his mouth hitched into an approving smirk. "I'll say this, however… you certainly paddled some balls out there."

A weak smile spread over Halm's face.

Outside, the cheering intensified.

23

Upon the agent's instructions, Halm sat closer to the torchlight and kept wads of cloth against his scalp and back. Borchus went to work, thumbing a gob of saywort into the cut. Having done that, he threaded the needle he'd use to stitch the wound shut. The blade had taken Halm right at the hairline, opening it like a messy mouth. When Borchus threaded the needle through the parted skin, he quietly gave thanks the man's hair was short.

While Borchus sewed, Halm remained still and kept the cloths in place, hissing at the prick and passing of the needle. He caught himself thumbing the bandage covering his sewn finger and cursed himself for doing so.

"Goll won't be too pleased with me," he finally muttered.

Borchus stopped stitching. "Oh, *now* you remember the Kree? After you've been bled like a sick sow? Well, given what little I know about the man, and all of that isn't flattering in the least, no, I don't think he'll be too happy with you or any of this at all. I only hope I'm around when you try to explain yourself."

"I'd like to see me explain myself."

"He'll…" Borchus let it hang. "Well. He won't be pleased."

"What were you going to say?"

"Nothing. I just remembered you intend to go out there once more."

"At least."

"One more fight will be enough, I think. If you haven't already convinced the punces into wagering on you. On that thought, if the odds are equal… well, it'll be dangerous."

"Think so?"

Borchus paused and stared hard into Halm's skull. "It's what I do. Think. You might try it sometime. Especially before going out, making promises you shouldn't be making, and pursuing nights like these."

The agent got back to work, leaving Halm to simmer. Borchus finished the scalp cut and reached for a jar of saywort. Meanwhile, two other men from their chamber had been invited to the iron floor and did not return.

"You're fortunate," Borchus said as he rubbed the pungent ointment into the wound on Halm's back.

"Why's that?"

"Your blubber saved you."

Halm smiled at that. "Better than armor."

Borchus snorted. "Gurry is what that is."

"I can still feel my ribs at times."

"Your ribs?"

"Thought I might have broken some a while back. Now, I'm not sure."

"Does it pain you to breathe?"

Halm shook his head.

"Then either you didn't or they're healed."

"Don't think bones heal that quick."

"You just get your breath back and concentrate on the next fight," Borchus ordered. "You get this next one, and we can leave these games of blood."

"They're all games of blood."

"But three fights or more in one *night?*" Borchus questioned. "Against animals like these? A Free Trained might do it, but not a house gladiator. They'd stay away from such savagery and with good reason. And if one actually *did*, I wager he'd smash whoever they have pickled enough to fight him."

Halm smiled darkly. "*I'm* a house gladiator."

The grim sincerity in his tone made the agent pause. "So you are. Apologies."

That word became a memory as Halm felt the sting of the needle in his back. He inhaled at the pinch, wondering if the little man was torturing him in some fashion. He didn't bother asking. Borchus would only laugh in his face or jab with a cutting remark. Or give a deeper thrust of the needle.

"You best watch yourself now," Borchus cautioned. "These stitches will hold, but any harsh moves will rip them all free. And if that happens, I won't be the one putting you back together. Whoever you face next, whatever you do, finish it quickly, as if your very ass was on fire."

Halm regarded the agent with a cocked brow, then stood and placed a hand against the wall. He stretched lightly, feeling weary and sensing how the thread pulled his skin. *Madness. All madness.* He shouldn't have done these secret games. Outside, the crowd's chanting swelled, bloated with a lust for more blood. Halm closed his eyes and focused for one more fight. The face of Skulljigger's son, angry yet pitiful, formed in his personal darkness, accompanied by the floating words, *Don't... hurt him. Please. Don't... hurt him.*

Halm mentally pushed the boy away.

Then Miji's face appeared, dark hair tied back, tending to her tiny tavern in Karashipa, and that lifted his spirits greatly. Not even the din from outside could break the spell she cast over him. A smile touched her hazel eyes, but no words came. It seemed as if she were waiting.

"Zhiberian?"

Halm was pulled back by Stick's voice to the present, where the air stank and his wounds throbbed.

"Ready for another?" the man of the iron floor inquired.

Halm nodded. "One more and I'm done."

Stick's face remained unchanged. Perhaps he'd heard it many times before.

"Come on, then." The iron official beckoned.

The crowds screamed at the Zhiberian—no surprise there—but a few simply *shrieked*, riled to a fever pitch of insanity Halm hadn't thought possible. Some threw beer over his shoulders, which only annoyed him since they missed his mouth. Borchus slapped him on the back and shouted, but he couldn't hear. Halm stood at the edge of the iron floor, feeling the stickiness underfoot and not enjoying the sensation in the least. *One more.* He fought to distance himself from aches and pains all over his person. The bandaged knot on his finger felt wet. Perhaps it was bleeding. The whole digit felt bloated and uncomfortably stuffed into the spiked gauntlets. *Seddon above*, the prayer flashed in his skull. Halm wasn't at his limit yet—not yet—but he would've slapped down gold for a pitcher of beer or mead or wine or anything with bite.

Movement in the torch-born shadows made him glance to his left, into a dark wall of faces and torsos, and he caught a man leaving for the stairs. The sight pawed at a memory, but it wouldn't surface. Halm shrugged just as the crowd opposite him split apart, allowing his opponent to walk onto the Iron.

The pit fighter stood half a head shorter than Halm, but he was lean, with ropy cords of muscle whipped onto his powerful frame and lashed with flesh. Bandages covered his arms and lower body as well, and the torchlight gleamed off stitched cuts glazed with saywort salve, making it clear the man had had a busy night himself. His hair was slicked back, a fork of a greased beard hanging off his chin, and as Halm judged him, the Zhiberian was judged in turn. The chilling warrior's eyes raked over Halm from feet to forehead, studying his mass and the bandages keeping him together. Halm put his best face on, presenting an indifferent scowl.

The short hellion grinned in return.

Sweet Seddon. Halm blinked in shock.

The brazen bastard opposing him had filed his teeth down to points. Shivers coursed down the Zhiberian's spine. The shark-toothed prick smiled all the wider, sensing fear.

Shark Tooth held up his fists: spiked. A bit of Halm's apprehension slipped away. At least the savage wasn't wearing a pair of cheesecutters.

Stick stepped between them while the very air hummed with wagering.

HOUSE OF PAIN

"The night grows old and saves the best for now." The gaunt ring official threw his long arms wide, dampening the crowds. "Once more, the Zhiberian comes to fight, eager to take down another foe. While here"—he gestured to the still-leering cannibal—"*Sibo* has *also* returned, looking for his third victory this night, in these grim games. Only one of these men shall walk away victorious this night. Only one shall take away a purse of coin. Who among you wishes to see these beasts clash?"

The very walls trembled with the thunderous response.

Halm rolled his eyes and set his jaw. He hadn't counted on being rendered deaf amongst his other hurts.

"Then, Halm of Zhiberia… Sibo of Sunja… *begin!*"

The Stick all but leapt out of the way of the two fighters. The audience simmered and heckled in anticipation of these two killers swinging.

And to Halm's surprise, Sibo held out a spiked fist. The formidable Sunjan nodded at his hand, indicating he wanted it pressed. Halm blinked, uncertain whether to accept the warrior's display of respect, as the very act momentarily disarmed and shocked him. Confused, he searched faces until he located Borchus. The agent cringed, his eyes becoming slits, his expression all but shouting his feelings—*he* wouldn't press fists with the filed-toothed hellion. To further his point, Borchus shook his head.

Not feeling any better in the least, Halm faced Sibo, who waited with an outstretched knot of a hand.

Saimon's black hanging fruit. Halm groaned, knowing it would be the end of him, but there wasn't a Sunjan alive who was going to make him out to be the villain. Not this night and not ever. Inhaling deeply, he reached out and tapped the offered fist with his own, knuckle to spiked knuckle, and pressed firmly.

Sibo responded with an equal but not overpowering amount of pressure, nor did he violate the gesture with a dishonorable blow. Relief coursed through Halm for that, and even the crowd appreciated the show of respect with *ooohs* of awe.

Apparently satisfied, the Sunjan nodded and stepped back. Halm did the same, shooting one final glance at Borchus.

The agent shook his head, this time in contempt.

Halm raised his fists to guard, feeling suddenly good about the exchange and showing the little bastard agent he could think for himself.

Without warning, Sibo rushed in and swung, so fast the Zhiberian was caught off guard. Halm lurched away, the mighty wind from that sudden flash of steel batting his eyes. Sibo swung again, seeking to batter Halm's meaty head from his shoulders. The Sunjan got in close and immediately unleashed three punches, as quick as a bowshot. Halm retreated from each swing, feeling his stitches pull with every movement.

Then Sibo swung and overextended himself. Halm counterpunched at that washboard gut.

Missed.

The smaller man danced away.

Sibo retreated all the way back to his side of the iron floor, nodding with approval at the Zhiberian. Halm wasn't sure what the greased kog was so pleased about, but he'd give the Sunjan something to consider soon enough. Measuring up the little man from between his fists, Halm cautiously waded in.

Sibo blurred forward, roaring and swinging from the shoulder, and Halm only just got his hand up in time to partially absorb the impact. Metal clanged, the force powerful enough to bash the larger man off his stride, staggering him, to the delighted howls of the onlookers. Halm regained his balance and kept his hands up, but the left side of his face burned as if branded by hot iron. He realized his own spikes had been deflected and driven into his jaw and ear.

Halm straightened, and Sibo lunged straight-armed, his fist blasting through the Zhiberian's upraised hands and crunching Halm's nose which burst like a grape. Blood sputtered over his lips as he stumbled backward. Sibo got in close and pistoned two fists into Halm's gut, crumpling his side and causing him to bark in pain. An overhand punch barely missed crushing the Zhiberian's right eye socket, but the following uppercut snapped Halm's head back on his shoulders, the spikes tearing gory arcs out of his chin. Sibo swung twice more, agonising power punches hurled from his shoulders, both absorbed on the mail sleeves of Halm's raised gauntlets, but the blows doubled the Zhiberian over like a terrified boy.

Sibo whirled and kicked him square in the gut.

The force buckled the Zhiberian, despite his padded fat and set muscle underneath. He dropped to a knee, his whole belly quivering as if it had just stopped a battering ram. Somehow, Halm threw his arm up in pure reflex and stopped the spikes aimed at his right ear. The impact rocked Halm into the crowd. A rush of voices cried out and heaved him back toward Sibo. The Sunjan feinted, closed quarters, and wrapped his heavy arms around Halm's skull. Sibo bared his frightening maw, hissing like a hellion, only to have an armored forearm shoved into it. Sibo chomped into metal, released, and bit down into Halm's unprotected flesh closer to the elbow. The Sunjan reared back, blackness misting the air, and spat out a white chunk ripped from the Zhiberian's arm.

Howling, Halm stood and shoved the savage away three steps, not wanting any part of him. Sibo regained his balance, glaring at his foe from under a darkened brow, and bared hellish teeth.

The crowds loved every moment.

Halm withdrew to the edge of cheering and swearing faces, cringing over his newest wound and suddenly fearful for his life.

A bloody Sibo stalked the center of the floor, inspecting his handiwork and appraising his opponent with a grim eye, like a butcher determining the next best cut. Halm's guard trembled, blood pattering the iron floor in fat drops, spilling through holes and plunking into the dank sewer below. He took quick, shallow breaths, feeling his strength leaving even as he struggled to summon it.

That he looked every bit a squashed cow kiss, he had no doubt. The punces watching him knew it, and half of them shouted and swore upon Sibo to finish the fat man.

The Sunjan responded. He walked left and right with predatory grace, grin widening as he eyed his victim top to bottom.

Despite feeling otherwise, Halm smiled back... and even winked.

Sibo's eyes widened at the slight and immediately rushed in, right fist flying from his shoulder like a red meteorite, the torchlight blurring the flash of the spikes. Sibo charged like a Dezer on a maddened stallion, and the whole watching mass nearly choked on its collective breath as Halm put his head down and barreled into the oncoming man, embracing the smaller Sibo and lifting him up with a determined roar of his own. Sibo shrieked as he left the floor. He kicked, raked Halm's back with his spiked fists, clubbed him, and even struggled to bite.

Halm whirled him around—once, twice, three times—making a spectacle of the shrieking hellion held high in his arms. Sibo's glittering limbs shredded air before Halm reared up and slammed the Sunjan flat onto the iron. Sibo landed in a devastating clap of bare flesh and bone on unyielding metal, stunning the crowd to an incredulous whimper. The pit fighter's arms flew wide as his spine arched, a bloody snarl on his lips, before his whole body softly collapsed. Scarlet oozed from the Sunjan's skull.

Sibo did not attempt to rise.

But his wide, terrified eyes flicked to the looming Zhiberian. Then Sibo blinked, meaty cords straining about his neck, and an agonized pleading replaced his fright.

Halm recognized the request in the fallen man's gaze. He remembered the touching of fists at the very beginning of the fight. Whatever Sibo might have been, he was not a dishonorable man, and Halm had no wish for him to suffer.

While some onlookers began celebrating riches not yet claimed, Halm dropped to his knees, sighed heavily and, with whatever strength remained, crushed the warrior's windpipe with a chop of his hand. Then he broke the man's head with one punch.

Sibo departed, and Halm of Zhiberia, fists dripping raw carnage, stood on unsteady feet.

To bewildering cheers.

"Well done!"

"Right and proper!"

"Hellpup, Zhiberian! You're a hellpup!"

Squinting in discomfort, Halm gazed about, noting not all were rooting for him, not that it bothered him much. Then he found Borchus, and the flattering little smile on the agent's face was as good as being dipped into an entire vat of healing ointments.

"Victor!" the Stick cried, clapping a hand on the Zhiberian's shoulder.

And the doors above almost lifted from the explosion of sound.

24

They paid Borchus coin, given in a small cloth bag, and he heaped the wagers won on top as the next fight got underway, the crowd eager for the next round. Once every piece was collected, he met Halm in the waiting chamber. The overweight pit fighter had slumped against a brick wall, weak from blood loss and battle fatigue. He'd shaken off his spikes, grabbed a handful of bandages, and pressed a clump into the bite wound on his left arm. The mess of his nose and chin remained untouched, and Halm hung his head and simply allowed the blood to drip to the floor.

The agent stood back from the wreck of a man and shook his head, *tsk*ing.

At the sound, Halm lifted his bleeding head, his face pale in the torchlight. "What?" The word specked his lips with blood. "Ah. You."

"Aye that. You're a mess."

"Did you… get the coin?"

"I did, I did that."

"And?" Halm's chin drooped.

"I'd say you earned close to a hundred and forty pieces of gold for this one night's work. Surprising, considering the level of competition here."

"In your hole," Halm growled with a warning smirk. "I didn't see you. Out there. On the Iron."

"That's because I don't make bargains I can't keep."

"I kept mine."

"You did that. Seddon above, you certainly did."

"Don't... worry. One day, you'll grow up..."—his gruesome smile was lined with blood—"and do as I've done here tonight."

Feeling a sudden mix of wonder and, dare he admit it, *respect*, Borchus decided to let that one go.

"If you can..." Halm took a breath, closed his eyes, and thumped his skull against the bricks. He didn't speak for moments, and Borchus thought he might have lost consciousness. Then the Zhiberian's eyes creaked open. The small movement struck the agent as being very, very tired. "Bind my wounds. And we'll be off."

"You can walk?"

"We'll see in a few moments."

Borchus supposed that was true. He placed the sack of coin near the gladiator's leg and got to work, bringing what was needed from the nearby bin of healing supplies. He dabbed saywort into anything bleeding, stitched what he could—once more sewing up cuts that had broken open—and wiped away excess blood. The bite wound couldn't be closed, so he filled it with salve and bound it with thick bandages, hoping it would be enough, at least until Halm got to a healer. It took time, and Borchus felt clumsy in his administrations, which got on his nerves. When all was done, the excitement outside the chamber seemed to die down. The last fight had finished.

"Thirsty," the Zhiberian muttered after some time.

Borchus glanced around. "Doesn't seem to be any water about."

"Saimon's hell with water. I want something with bite."

Borchus knew then the Zhiberian monster would live.

"Can you walk?" the agent asked.

Halm opened his eyes. With a grunt, he labored to his feet and nodded, holding a hand to his ribs. To their mutual surprise, he walked in a slow, straight line without a stagger or a limp. The audience had all but departed, but a few dangerous-looking types hung back, hesitant to return to the streets. Some watched the pair. A couple even nodded with approval.

"Come back again," Calagu called out when Borchus and Halm reached the stairs leading to the surface. "In five days, we should have enough men for another tournament."

Neither man from the House of Ten answered him.

On the surface, the lamp had burned dry, and darkness ruled. Dim light beckoned over rooftops, and shadowy figures walked the side streets—the same people who had watched the fights under the street. The night felt late, and Borchus and Halm paused outside the storehouse, quietly watching dark figures bleed away into the pitch.

Borchus walked alongside his companion, keeping an eye on him in case he fell.

"Air's sweet," Halm muttered.

Borchus regarded the sky and took a breath. "Compared with what we just left, I suppose."

"Air's sweet," the other reaffirmed, making Borchus wonder just how badly the man was hurting.

"We'll get rooms at an alehouse."

"We will?" Borchus asked, mildly surprised.

"Aye. You…" Halm composed himself. "You helped. Wait."

With that, Halm stopped in the middle of the street, heedless of shadows lingering in nearby alleys. He pawed at the cloth sack he carried, opening it. The agent glanced about nervously, but no one moved upon them. With the performance the Zhiberian had put on that night, Borchus wasn't really surprised.

"Here," Halm repeated, held out a fist, and dropped a dozen or so coins into Borchus's hands.

"What's this?"

"You don't want it?"

"Didn't say that," Borchus scoffed. "I'll take coin from anyone who offers it. Including corpses like yourself."

"For your troubles."

At the moment, Borchus couldn't think of one.

"And your time," Halm went on. "For watching my back down there."

"I didn't watch your back."

"Well, whatever you… you want to call it. You did it anyway. And the sewing." The familiar, horrid smile gleamed.

"Well, there was that," Borchus admitted, forgetting his earlier irritations.

"Let's find that alehouse, Borchus," Halm rumbled in an exhausted voice. "Seddon above, I'm thirsty."

They got moving. And neither man spoke afterward, not even after they found an establishment and bought and rented their well-earned luxuries.

*

HOUSE OF PAIN

Standing in a nearby alley of the storehouse, concealed by the darkness, a stranger watched the Zhiberian and his stocky companion leave that building and meander off into the night. An itch took the watcher in the nose, demanding attention. He scratched at the misshapen lump of flesh, cartilage, and bone in the middle of his face and wiped a forearm across it. The Sons of Cholla had no idea who the hunched-over individual was or which clan he belonged to, but the Zhiberian might. And the watcher had learned long before that a person's memory, no matter how much time had passed, could be triggered by just a glance.

Because of that, Zamek had retreated, hiding in that rippling mesh of bodies below when the Zhiberian pit fighter had seen his face in the crowds. Zamek had only barely concealed his own surprise at seeing the fighter at the Sons' event. Only the dregs and the animals fought below the streets.

Though the fat warrior might not have recognized Zamek as the quartermaster who'd handed him the poisoned sword—the very weapon that had aided in killing Vadrian—Zamek took no chances and immediately left the Sons of Cholla's crumbling underworld and their bloody entertainment. The night had been a success despite the appearance of the Zhiberian.

Zamek had learned what he needed to know.

25

Nordish Front

In the darkness that had seized his consciousness, Arrus felt his arms and legs being pulled. Nightmarish voices whispered in his ears and rumbled in the distance. Things crashed into him at times, spinning his body like dust playing upon a breeze. With more pulling, the walls of the dark trembled as if being buffeted by mighty winds. Then these sensations subsided to the curious feeling of sinking into peacefulness, a stillness as warm as bathwater, which puzzled him in a dreamlike sort of way.

Waking reality crashed upon his senses, twisting his arms in his sockets. Arrus cried out, a throaty whine quickly spent of breath. Laughter brayed over his head, and a stab of pain in his shoulders took his breath. More guffaws delighted in his agony. He opened his eyes and saw a forest floor trampled into a paste of decaying leaves and mud. They had planted him on his knees, and he realized his hands and feet were tied.

A Sunjan spoke, causing Arrus to lift his head. Something hard smacked him just above his right ear, stunning him, while a second blow toppled him forward. Dirt plugged his mouth, and he realized with a sputter that they'd unmasked him. A hard boot caught him in the stomach, and his wind left in a gush, paralyzing him. Hands roughly gripped his arms and shoulders, pulling him back into a kneeling position. A man planted a meaty palm on Arrus's forehead, forcing it back so he had no choice but to look upon his captor. The Sunjan, black of hair and beard and possessing both a green and a blue eye, squinted back angrily. The soldier breathed into Arrus's face, daring him to speak. When he didn't, the Sunjan removed his hand with a derisive shove, nearly upsetting Arrus once again.

Arrus righted himself and glared at his captor, and a soldier standing behind him slapped the back of his skull hard enough to make it ache. That time, the message received, Arrus kept his head and eyes lowered.

Armored Sujins moved about Arrus. Horses walked by. Sounds of metalworking rang out, as well as the chopping of wood. The sounds of activity surrounded Arrus, suggesting he was inside an enemy camp. Peering out of the corners of his eyes, he saw other Nordish men spread out in a line on either side of him, all on their knees with their hands bound behind their backs. Arrus took a breath and became aware of a *slap… slap… slap* from just ahead—the sound of flesh hitting something. Sujins muttered nearby, but Arrus couldn't understand a damn word of it.

Someone shouted, heat in his voice, followed by the unmistakable crunch of metal on bone. One of the captured Jackals lay on his belly, his head split open to the jawline. A Sujin towered over the corpse, red faced and scarred, not bothering to clean the broadsword he had used to execute the prisoner. The warrior growled a few choice words at the body and sniffed hard enough to clear his sinuses before stalking off to a tree. Another soldier sat on a chunk of wood, casually flipping a dagger into the air and catching it, the hilt slapping his bare palm.

Grim Sujins wielding axes and swords stood guard all around, their faces full of either contempt or cold indifference as they gazed upon their Nordish captives. Scratches and chips marred their weapons while torn chainmail links needed repair. Danger permeated the entire worn-looking lot, and Arrus understood he and his countrymen had been taken by experienced, battle-tested soldiers. What Arrus didn't understand was why they were still alive. It wasn't that kind of war for the Nordish, having put that point to their enemy at every opportunity. The Ivus had decreed *all* Sunjans to be put to a sword's edge–commoners, soldiers, women, and children–and the Ikull's commanding Kalash reminded his officers at every opportunity.

The war was no longer for territory or riches.

Prisoners. Arrus shook his head and lowered it, staring at the ground and the thin trickle of blood threading its way past him. The Sujins had taken them as prisoners, and only the all-knowing Curlord might discern what the devils had planned for them. A chill overcame him. The Sujins would torture them, discover no officers amongst the lot, and slaughter all. Arrus remembered the pale face of his dead brother and set his jaw in grief. They would meet again before long.

A rustle of leather and mail caught his attention, and Arrus glanced up, as did some of the other Nordish men.

HOUSE OF PAIN

There was no mistaking the new figure standing before them.

The Cavalier regarded the prisoners impassively—the same man who had slain his brother and several other Jackals. The warrior's shoulders quietly heaved, the dark stains covering his leather armor every bit as menacing as the blades hanging from his waist. His helm had no visor, and a black beard, fashioned into a hammer-like square, hung off his iron chin. Lines crossed the flesh of the Cavalier's callous, swarthy face, reminding Arrus of the surface of a butcher's old cutting board.

Arrus knew this was his brother's slayer, just from the way the warrior lorded over them.

The surrounding Sujins quieted in the Cavalier's presence. Even the dagger-tossing Sujin caught his weapon by the hilt and stood warily, minding his manners. None of the fearsome soldiers spoke in the Cavalier's presence, adding further dread to the scene.

The Cavalier—Blackbeard—lifted hands to hips, leather creaking as he did, and studied the assembled prisoners. He stood poised like death itself, daring anyone to give him reason to take a life. Arrus remembered the hill and avoided the warrior's eyes.

Blackbeard then reached up and pulled his helm off. He let it drop to the ground, revealing a scalp shorn to a stubbly rash, every bit as black as his beard. His face screwed up in distaste as if daylight on his flesh displeased him. He faced the prisoners as if they were an annoying side task needing resolution before he could carry on with more important matters. Grinding his jaw, the Cavalier glanced to one side and beckoned to a Sujin.

This new man regarded the Nordish captives with a troubled expression. He wore no helm, though his chainmail shirt appeared tarnished but well kept. Pale-green eyes studied the Jackals for a moment. He took a breath, rubbed his dirty face, and glanced over at the Cavalier before asking a question.

Blackbeard replied gruffly, and the Sujin got busy. He turned to the assembled prisoners and cleared his voice.

"Officer? Officer? Who officer?" Green Eye asked and pointed at them in a raw slaughter of the Nordish language. Arrus could barely understand the words.

"What's he saying?" Arrus recognized Kestimir's voice.

"The poltu can speak," said another. "To a point."

"That's speaking?" exclaimed someone guardedly. "My ass can speak better."

"Your ass gets plenty of practice," said one of the Jackals, putting a smile on Arrus's face and causing others to giggle softly despite their predicament.

The Sujin paused for a moment, visibly flustered at the chuckles from the prisoners, and glanced at the Cavalier. Blackbeard stood with a thundercloud of a scowl on his gouged features, clearly not impressed with his interpreter's results.

"That one looks ready to shite," Kestimir observed.

"He does," agreed someone. But something in the Cavalier's demeanor killed the smile on Arrus's face.

Then, with ominous purpose, the Cavalier motioned toward another Sujin.

An armored giant of a man stepped before the line of Nordish prisoners, walking almost without a sound. The ogre held a massive battle-axe, the edges chipped in places from repeated sharpening. A full visor covered his face save for his sinister eyes, which studied the nervous captives to a man, those eyes a chilling, faded blue.

Blackbeard rumbled a curt stream of syllables, and the

executioner thrust his weapon's head into the ground. He adjusted fearsome metal gauntlets covering his hands, ensuring the spiked knuckles fitted properly. Terror swept over Arrus then. The prisoners stayed as still as they were silent—no joking then, for fear of drawing the attention of that monstrous axe.

The Sujin executioner questioned his commander with a look, and the Cavalier allowed a tired nod.

Without a trace of emotion, the spike-fisted slayer approached the nearest prisoner with a bored swagger. The executioner studied the man's face for a moment, sizing him up from various angles, taking all the time in the world…

Before swinging from the hip and pulverising the man's jaw with one punch.

The Nordish fell over flat.

Not yet finished, the executioner stepped away from the fallen man, whose legs kicked weakly. The Sunjan quietly retrieved his battle-axe. With barely a breath of effort, he lumbered back to the unconscious man. He hefted the axe and, almost casually, drove its razor edge five fingers deep into the prisoner's skull, splitting it with a clay-like crack. The executioner planted a boot on the corpse's head and freed his weapon with a lurch. His example made, he backed away a few steps and stopped in the mud, becoming inanimate.

The surrounding camp sounds flowed into the silence of the execution's wake.

Not surprisingly, the rest of the Jackals became very mindful of the Sujin holding the battle-axe across his pelvis.

Arrus realized he was trembling. He licked at dry lips, blinking as if his eyes were crusted with grit. In truth, he was damn close to pissing himself.

Green Eye stepped up and regarded the prisoners. "Officer? Who officer?" he demanded, butchering the language with his heavy accent. "Tell I officer. Ah, no kill. No kill. We. Uh, them."

The translator paused for a moment, drawing an irked glare from Blackbeard.

"No?" a piqued Green Eye asked.

No. The prisoners maintained their silence.

Green Eye frowned, shrugged his shoulders, and waved for the executioner. The Sujin with the axe immediately looked at Blackbeard, who nodded imperiously.

Clearing his throat before sighing heavily, the executioner waded toward the line. He nodded to a Sujin standing behind the chosen Jackal, and the guard gripped the man's head with both hands. A gasp fled from the Nordish, followed by a terrified panting every bit as unnerving as the headsman's axe.

An unconcerned executioner hacked into the captive's neck, splitting collarbone and two ribs underneath. A dying gasp escaped the Nordish, weakening into a whisper of a hiss, and he crumpled into the wet ground.

The faceless executioner worked the axe free and, with a loud grunt, chopped into the grisly V once again. Bones snapped. Meat sucked at the metal, then bone scratched steel with an awful sound. He struck the dead man twice more, each wet impact making Arrus's cringe.

The executioner eventually sniffed, muttered something unintelligible, and returned to his starting position. The Cavalier wanted the remaining prisoners to see the warrior walking toward them, to see their deaths approaching. That much was clear to Arrus.

"*Vudosdizz!*" Kestimir breathed.

HOUSE OF PAIN

Blackbeard understood the Nordish curse and didn't like it. His blade flashed as he pulled it free of his scabbard. With all the nonchalance of taking a walk in the forest, Blackbeard strode forward and snapped the pommel into Kestimir's bearded face, smashing his nose.

Kestimir cried out and toppled. The Cavalier stabbed the Jackal through a thigh, the blood running almost instantly. The wounded man screamed again, twisting upon the blade, kicking bare feet. Blackbeard yanked the steel free and slashed at Kestimir's feet.

Kestimir's howling reached new heights.

The Nordish thrashed on his back, hands still bound behind him, and tried to worm away while fearfully eyeing the Cavalier. Cruel amusement seeped into the faces of the guarding Sujins.

Kestimir's frenzied slinking slowed, weakened by blood loss, and the Cavalier walked toward him. Blackbeard's shadow engulfed the stricken man, and he planted both feet at the sides of Kestimir's torso. The Sunjan officer studied the Jackal for fleeting moments before punching the sword's tip through the prisoner's guts.

Kestimir died squirming in the mud.

Yanking the sword free, Blackbeard rumbled gibberish in that harsh Sunjan tongue. Green Eye nodded immediately and chewed on the inside of his cheek.

"Officer? Who is officer?"

Arrus shook his head, suddenly wanting to save the other Nordish from the Cavalier and his dogs. "There is no officer, you *curnos*. There's only *us*."

"You?" Green Eye asked, dividing his attention between Arrus and a suddenly rapt Blackbeard.

"*Only us*, you maggot."

"Ah. Uhh, good."

Green Eye reported to the Cavalier, who had already forgotten the body at his feet. The black eyes of the officer narrowed and simmered, making Arrus swallow uneasily.

"No officer," Green Eye said sadly and shook his head. "Many question. Uh, I have. *You* answer question, or I—*we* kill. Sword. Axe. Hand. We kill."

Arrus had no doubts.

His hand resting on the pommel of his sword, Green Eye marched over and stopped before Arrus. "How many? You?"

"What?"

"You? How many?"

"How many are there of us?"

Green Eye blinked, absorbing the words, and nodded. "Yes, yes. How many?"

"Tell him nothing," someone hissed from down the line.

That brought on a flurry of movement, and Blackbeard kicked the speaking prisoner's head back, the crack of bone echoing horribly in the clearing. The Jackal had only just hit the ground when the officer's sword stabbed him through an eye. The scrape of bone and chuffing of dirt terrified Arrus and set him into a fit of shaking. He struggled to control his nerves, hating that awful sound of breaking bone. He sensed the remaining Jackals suddenly tuning in to the exchange.

"About three hundred," he sighed.

"Three…?"

"Three hundred."

"Hundred?"

Arrus looked up in dismay, shocked to see the interpreter unable to recognize the Nordish word for "hundred." "*Hundred.* You don't understand, do you?"

"I understand. Hundred."

"No, you don't. You can barely speak the language."

"What?" The Sujin's hand tightened on his sword's pommel. Arrus grimaced and licked his lips. The man wasn't that stupid after all, and Arrus had to admit, the Sujin spoke better Nordish than he spoke Sunjan.

"Thirty *tens*," Arrus tried again, flashing his teeth.

"Uh? Thirty tens? Ahhh… thirty *tens*! Yes, yes." Evil delight flooded Green Eye's features and reported to the dour Cavalier. Blackbeard replied with something unfathomable, setting Green Eye nodding.

"Yes, we kill all."

"You what?" Arrus asked, feeling his stomach plummet and the ground warp.

"Yes, yes, we kill. Uh… every dog."

Killed every dog? Arrus's heart shriveled as if doused with acid.

"Where, uh, Ikull?" Green Eye grabbed Arrus's chin and roughly lifted his face.

"Ikull?"

"Ikull. *Where?*"

"Two months. Behind us."

Green Eye shook his face, again not understanding.

Arrus gasped in frustration. "Days?"

"Uhhh, days? Ah, days! Yes, yes."

"Sixty days," Arrus grated and jerked his head what he believed was the northwest. "Behind."

"Sixty days?"

"Yes, sixty days, you miserable, piss-lapping curnos, *sixty* days!"

Green Eye searched Arrus's face, watching for a hint of a lie. Unable to detect one, the Sujin translator straightened and once again reported. Arrus felt only half a traitor. The main army was actually *less* than two months behind. With luck, the Sunjans would smack into them unawares, and the Ikull would crush them all on its way to Sunja's heart.

"Well done," a voice whispered nearby. Arrus moved his head only a fraction to meet the shifting eyes of an unmasked Jackal. Arrus couldn't place the name.

Then Blackbeard spoke, and the Sujins closed in, yanking the prisoners to their feet. They lined them up in short order and marched them from the clearing with slaps and sword prodding. Heads down, the line of men shuffled along, dejected yet defiant, knowing their doom was nigh upon them.

*

"Well, that was something," the translator said, switching back to his native tongue.

But the Cavalier, a callous man called Vogul, scowled dismissively as he returned his blade to its scabbard.

"Something wrong?"

"Two months back," Vogul spat and scowled, the lines in his face deepening. "A lie if I ever heard one. I'll be surprised if I don't find their damned army two weeks from here."

"You think they're lying?"

Vogul leveled his emotionless gaze at the Sujin. "Believe me. I speak from experience when I say I could have gutted the whole pack of them right now without any of them breaking. I only do this because there's always a chance, a slim chance, I might find one willing to talk, but I haven't yet—not in four years of hunting, killing, and capturing these bastards. Say what you will about the Nords, but they don't betray their own."

The translator absorbed this. "So they'll be executed?"

"Them?" Vogul asked and wearily shook his head. "No. This is too much of a *prize*. The Lords smiled upon us. Any other day, the Jackals would've fought to a very bloody death before being captured. I swear, they must fight the very hands pulling them from the womb. Especially *these* bastards—maggot shite that only strikes at night. That we managed to capture any is a wonder. Why do you think I ordered our archers to use blunted arrows? *These* Jackals don't wear helmets. Some still died in that first volley, but no matter. I've orders to send the survivors back to the city."

It was the translator's turn to scowl.

"At least we won't be feeding them," Vogul pointed out, briefly gnawing on one corner of his mouth, his square beard slanting askew because of it. "And at best, a man can only hope to live two or three weeks on water. Lord Winter wants starved Jackals for public torment and execution—to raise the morale of the people, according to Lord Winter's thoughts. To see these… *terrors* wasted away to nothing before having their heads lopped off."

"You believe that?"

"Doesn't matter what I believe," the cavalier muttered, inspecting his hands before looking to the surrounding camp and forest. "I follow orders. Lord Winter wanted a handful of beaten Jackals. He'll get them. Thus, those orders have been filled. Now I go back to doing what I do best."

With that, Vogul walked away from the translator with the green eyes.

The Sujin knew what the Cavalier spoke of.

26

Rumbles of far-off thunder rolled across darkened plains and slanted rooftops, waking the battered Zhiberian with a jolt, long enough for him to realize what the noise was. He lay in bed, uncovered, staring at the dark timbers and off-color wooden slabs of the ceiling. The air smelled of approaching rain. Halm made a pained face and suppressed a groan. Everything hurt that morning, and he wasn't surprised to see dark blotches staining the white linen of his feather pillow. From his chin or scalp. Or back. Or *everything* all at once. He rolled onto his shoulder and feebly moved his legs over the cot's edge, pausing there to take careful breaths and gather strength for his next feat. He studied his bandaged gut and swore at it, knowing the ladies adored such stylish and colorful designs. That thought made him rattle off a chuckle, and he immediately winced.

Seddon wanted him alive; that much was clear. For what sinister purpose, however, he had no idea.

HOUSE OF PAIN

Grunting, Halm puffed out his cheeks and pulled on his stained breeches, knowing he'd have to purchase a new pair. Eventually, he stood, straightened, and strapped on his sword. Moving slowly to avoid dizziness, he found the hiding place for the night's winnings and smiled upon checking the contents with a peek.

That was all fine, then, despite the boulders clattering in his brain. His hand found his head and held it as he willed the pounding to stop. Even the squeaking of the floor planks made him cringe and hurt. The bare metal hinges of the door whined upon closing, straining his nerves. He left the rented room, feeling quite dead. The alehouse's weathered hall reeked of spilled beer and a suspect undercurrent of piss, which wasn't what he needed to smell so early in the morning. Halm regarded the nearby stairs but shuffled along to the far end of the hall, where a square window, its shutters thrown wide, lit the rustic interior. He passed the open door of Borchus's room and didn't bother looking in. Halm knew the agent had left earlier, wanting to meet his man Garl. *Garl* sounded like a right fidgety one.

Patting his leather scabbard, Halm gazed down at the people filling the narrow street two flights below. People... writhing and pushing and stinking. He forced himself to stop thinking about all of those bodies right there.

Taking a deep morning breath and thanking Seddon for its coolness, he got moving.

He broke fast at a small food stall—a meal of fresh bread lathered in wild-berry jam with cold pork from the night before. Water washed it all down, and willpower kept it there. Halm learned from the old man feeding him that the time was, in fact, late morning and nearing afternoon.

That revelation made the Zhiberian chew on both sides of his mouth before he took off for the Pit.

After last night's hell, he dared not miss meeting Skulljigger.

Rain, he overheard in the streets. Rain would fall that day. And one look at Seddon's normally blue sky informed him a storm was brewing. Halm suspected the games of the Pit would be cancelled for the day, which suited him just fine. A day of wet weather meant the whole fight schedule would be pushed back, which meant a day of rest. A day of rest sounded right and proper to him.

Somehow, he made it to the Pit without dropping any limbs or losing any blood. A light but steady rain began to drizzle in the air, breaking the heat and prompting most people to walk just a little faster. Halm walked around the wet hide of the Pit, hearing its red brick and majestic timbers hissing under the wet weather. The open fairway surrounding the arena was nearly deserted and looked slick, and he almost slipped on the fitted stones. Food and drink merchants bent on enduring the weather busied themselves with securing canvases over their heads.

Halm reached the Gate of the Sun and placed his back against the lip of the entrance, grimacing at the contact. To his right was oddly empty space—where the day's schedule of matches would be posted. Knowing he shouldn't, he probed his face anyway while waiting, cursing his fortune. Thoughts of what Goll would say entered his mind, but he shoved them back out. There would be a time and a place for that confrontation.

"Zhiberian."

The voice made Halm look up, rain pattering his features. Skulljigger.

And three friends. Three *vengeful*-looking friends.

Dying Seddon. Halm groaned and straightened, his hand touching his own sword.

"Looking to pick up where we left off?" Halm asked.

Skulljigger's broken finger was bound up with splints and cloth, and his face was nearly unrecognizable from a thick wrapping of wet bandages. The wounded pit fighter glanced at his companions and shrugged.

"Just making certain we stay friendly is all."

Skulljigger seemed to inspect him for a moment. "You had a rough night."

Halm chuckled coldly, squinting against the rain. "Aye that."

"You have the coin?"

"You just keep your lads back a bit," Halm warned, half good-natured, half serious. He'd already counted out the hundred he'd promised Skulljigger and was keeping the sum in the same cloth sack received from the Iron Games. The rest he'd transferred to his much heavier purse.

"Pay him," one of Skulljigger's lads ordered, a right proper animal itching to club something. Halm kept an eye on him.

"Here," the Zhiberian said and held out the sack. "I can toss it on the ground, or you can take it from my hand like an honorable man. It's up to you."

Rain beat against the stones underfoot. Skulljigger stepped away from his friends and reached with his good hand. Nodding in approval, Halm released the sack while keeping an eye on the pit fighter's companions. Skulljigger fumbled with the string before finally opening it and peering at the contents. His bandaged face brightened about the mouth, the only part truly visible.

"Blessed Seddon. Looks all here."

"It is," Halm assured him, tasting water on his lips. The

skies grumbled somewhere to the south, and the rain began to truly crash down.

"Count it," one of his friends sputtered.

"Aye, count it."

Skulljigger met Halm's eyes then, the gaze unreadable.

"You watch him," he said to the two-legged animal who'd demanded Halm to pay. The beast smiled brazenly at the Zhiberian, who sniffed and immediately regretted it--snarling at the painful buzz in his nose. He kept his hand on his blade, ready to pull steel if the lout tried anything. Skulljigger ushered the other two in close and counted coins into their cupped hands.

The sky cleared its throat once again, closer this time. The rain held steady, matting Halm's short hair against his hurting head.

"All here," Skulljigger announced and started shoveling coin back into the sack. Halm saw that he left a few coins with his friends, for their trouble on such a gurry day.

"Must admit," Skulljigger said, "didn't think you were going to do it."

In too much discomfort to care anymore, Halm sighed and left his thoughts unsaid. "So we're done?"

"We are."

"Your games are finished?"

Skulljigger wasn't quick to answer, and Halm became unsure about the man—was he simply drawing things out or actually thinking dire thoughts? His hand twitched on the Mademian pommel.

"For this season," Skulljigger finally declared. "But as Seddon's my witness, I'll be searching for you when the next one happens. You can count on that."

Halm sighed again. Some people never learned. "So be it, then."

"Aye that," Skulljigger said, and Halm sensed a fight was but one word away. He drew back a leg as if to kick, wondering who would first taste his boot.

But instead, Skulljigger smirked and backed away, his lads beside him.

"Next season, Zhiberian," he barked and shook a galling fist. "Next season, I'll be watching for you."

"Watch my soaking ass," Halm muttered low enough that the departing men couldn't hear. Skulljigger's group distanced themselves a good twenty paces before turning and making speed down a street.

Halm hoped the man would put the money to good use and keep his children fed.

Only when they disappeared from sight did Halm relax and lean against the arena wall. Skulljigger would be watching for him the next season. That put a smirk on his hurting face. He wasn't sure he'd live to see the end of the *day*, let alone next season. Grimacing, Halm rested against the cool hide of the Pit and placed a hand against his side, where the stitches had burst. Then he inspected the bandages covering the chunk of flesh Sibo had ripped out with his teeth. A pang of nausea rose in the Zhiberian's gullet. His tongue curled.

"All done?"

Halm glanced up, sputtering water.

Borchus.

"Unfit punce," the Zhiberian casually greeted.

"Unsightly pisser," the Sunjan countered smoothly.

They exchanged unkind looks in the falling rain.

"Yes," Halm said. "All done."

"I was watching from over there," Borchus remarked, indicating a length of wall. "Rest assured, I wouldn't have come to your aid if they pulled steel on you."

Halm squinted away water. "Well, good thing it didn't. Very good thing."

Borchus came closer, his hair and clothes soaked. "What's your plan now?"

"Plan?"

"Yes, you thick-headed prick, *plan*. What is it?"

Halm chuckled darkly. "Try and survive the trip back to Clavellus's training grounds. Maybe that young healer might be able to do something for me."

"If not, I'm sure someone will dig a hole for you."

"You're too kind."

"Imagine you hear that a lot," Borchus muttered and frowned at the skies. "No fights today. Perhaps tomorrow. I'll walk you back to the koch bay."

"The what?"

"The koch bay. You aren't going to *walk* out of the city in this weather. You might possibly roll down the south slope and gain enough speed to carry you all the way to Clavellus's front gate, but somehow I doubt it."

"Don't you have that little man to take care of?"

Borchus became uncharacteristically quiet. "He's no concern of yours."

"Well, I don't need you to lead me anywhere."

"In your condition? You might stumble into one of the city wells. Or an open sewer. Then again, falling into a sewer might bestow certain regenerative properties upon you."

Halm didn't understand a few of those Sunjan words, but he didn't let on, and he'd certainly remember how they sounded.

"I'll get a wagon," he said.

"What?" Borchus exclaimed. "With that full bladder of a purse just waiting to be pissed away? Nonsense. A wagon will bounce you around like a slab of bad meat. A koch's better. Get moving. I've already sent word back to Goll this morning. You'll fight in five days. *Everyone* fights in five days. Including you, which is one match I'll make certain of seeing, just to see if anything important drops off. Your fight's the one where your opponent's yet undecided, but the others are facing Free Trained gladiators. And at this point of the games, they're ones who have raised themselves above the pack through strength and skill of arms. Unblemished records. Undefeated."

Borchus let that sink in.

"We'll have ourselves a little war, then," Halm remarked, palming water off his face.

"We'll have something, I guarantee it. And I'm not sure all the rain in Seddon's heavens this day or next will wash the blood away. Regardless, I'll remain here. See if I can find anything on these men we're to face."

With that, Borchus studied the sky, snarled as the rain crashed on his face, and without a word of goodbye, left for drier places. Halm watched him disappear into the thickening sheets of weather. A moment later, he smirked to himself.

Had to admit, the little bastard had a way about him.

Halm's face and bite wound throbbed, demanding attention. He got moving, knowing it was a far walk in the rain, and his hurts were many.

*

As the pair of men departed, hidden eyes from two different sections of the streets watched them go. Then they noted a single fighter emerging from the tunnel entrance, detaching himself from the shadows.

The eyes did not linger on him.

*

Targus stepped out of the tunnel, felt the rain, and withdrew just inside, watching the Zhiberian and his companion through the thickening sheets. He shook his head, replaying bits of the conversation he'd overhead.

I can toss it on the ground, or you can take it from my hand like an honorable man.

Must admit, didn't think you were going to do it.

So we're done?

We are.

Your games are finished?

For this season…

Targus couldn't believe it. Why was the Zhiberian paying another fighter to not fight him this season? What was the man afraid of? No answer came, but Targus was no longer inclined to be so respectful of the large, ugly foreigner. Word had gone around that the Zhiberian was hunting for the Sunjan, but now? Targus didn't like what he'd overheard. The fat pisser was actually bribing his opponents? Why?

Not one for deep thoughts, Targus believed he had an answer. The Zhiberian feared *losing* his blood match to the Sunjan, thus the only way out of it without losing face was paying his opponent to not compete. Given Halm looked like a walking corpse, it made complete sense.

Unfit. Targus fumed.

But the Zhiberian was no friend of his, and Targus didn't even want to be in the lout's presence. A deep-rooted anger took hold of him, simmering to the surface, and joined with another notion.

The Zhiberian was battered, obviously afraid… and entirely ripe for the taking.

27

When Clavellus awoke that morning and ate breakfast with Nala, the storm clouds churning overhead told him no fights would be occurring that day. Later on, as he sat on the balcony looking out over the morning warm-ups, listening to Machlann's bawling while Koba led the pit fighters through their exercises, the first drop of rain announced itself by slapping against his silver mug. Clavellus watched the bead of water run down the metal, feeling two more drops splatter against his bald head. He frowned at the pecks and stroked his beard with his shaking hand.

"Rain," Goll muttered from his seat next to him.

Clavellus let that go. Though he'd only been in the company of the Kree for a short time, he was noticing little things about the man: quiet, determined, and at times, almost amusing in stating the obvious.

"Rain," Clavellus agreed and sipped his morning beer. "Must fall, eventually."

"What does it mean for the games?"

"Postponed for the day. We're lucky. Or rather, those at the Pit are. It started before the days' matches, before anyone actually took to the sand. Terrible fighting conditions. Miserable. And the audience doesn't take kindly to it either."

"So a day of rest?" Goll asked. Clavellus noticed that most of the bruising on the man's face had disappeared.

"From the games," Clavellus informed him. "Not for us. Unless your Weapon Masters had you doing things differently?"

Goll shook his head.

"Then," Clavellus offered, "I'd suggest we head downstairs and watch the training under the balcony. It'll keep the worst of the rain off us."

None of the men noticed the owner and the taskmaster placing their chairs below the balcony. If they did, if they broke concentration, Machlann would punish them with his club. They stretched and did their morning exercises. Koba had them punching air, lightly at first, then with more power. Even that simple exercise wore them out before a hundred strikes.

Except for Brozz and Junger.

As with most of the exercises and drills, the trainers quietly observed the pair of men performed exceedingly well. Brozz proved himself more than capable at the tasks put to him, while Junger was a simply a wonder. The Perician flowed through every movement with a natural grace a man could only be born with, refined to perfection. Twice Machlann stopped behind the line of fighters and simply gazed upon the loincloth-clad fighter's flawless execution, studying his every movement and finding nothing lacking. He even glanced at Koba, who was standing in front of the line and met his gaze and faintly smiled his own thoughts.

The rain strengthened from drops to a steady beat. Machlann caught the questioning looks Sapo and Torello threw him, obviously wondering when the exercises would be called off. Lazy wretches. Machlann studied the soaking heavens and bared what few teeth remained in his head. He had no intention of canceling anything. Nor did Koba.

Days like those served to see who had the spirit and who merely talked.

"To the edge of the sands," Machlann shouted.

The six men stopped swinging and started running. Koba followed behind them and formed the fighters into a line at the far end of the training area, just in front of the barracks.

"You aren't going to get in from the rain, are you?" Pig Knot shouted.

Machlann knew the legless lout's voice and didn't bother acknowledging him. The crippled fighter sat on the ground behind the men, his back against a stone wall, just below the overhead eaves. Muluk was next to him, eyeing the bearded trainer with a flicker of fear, even though the trainer hadn't said much to him since returning from Sunja.

Machlann dabbed at the seven stitches Shan had put in his head—a little memento of Sapo's unmistakable power. "Ready them, Master Koba!"

The old trainer relished the expressions of dismay on a couple of the faces.

"It's raining, in case you haven't noticed, you ancient topper." Pig Knot.

Machlann brushed at his ears as if swatting an unseen bug.

"You hear me?"

The trainer regarded the pair of healing men, seeing how Pig Knot's eyes smoldered. Hateful. The lad was poisoned with it.

"Glad you didn't lose your arms, my missus, since you make this much noise with only your legs gone."

"In your hole, you bastard. Whose teeth are you going to smash in this day, eh? Who is it you're going to beat into submission while that other hairless ape there watches? Move away. Get on. I can smell you from here."

Machlann ignored any further exchanges with Pig Knot. The man could quite possibly scream shite at him all day if inclined. And Machlann didn't relish trading barbs with sour cripples, though he wasn't above it.

"Race from this end to the smithy, touch the brick pathway, then run back again. Run like your lives depended on it. In bare feet," Koba commanded the waiting pit fighter trainees.

Four of the men quickly kicked off their sandals while Torello and Sapo took their time.

"*Eeeeee*, Master Koba! If those two shite shaggers do not jump to, feel free to bury your foot in their asses."

"It's raining!" Torello bawled back.

Machlann swiped at his ears again, unhappy with missing the annoying gnat the first time.

Koba strode over to Torello and snapped his club across the man's shoulder, eliciting a cry of pain and prompting a brooding Sapo to get ready more quickly. A sulking Torello took his place as well, rubbing his shoulder.

Once they appeared ready, Koba got out of the way,

lifted his arm, and dropped it.

The men bolted, kicking up damp lumps of sand. They pounded down the length of the training grounds as the rain fell. Junger immediately took the lead, blasting ahead of the others. He burned a line to the end of the grounds, quickly stopped, tapped the brick walkway, and fired back, passing the remainder of the field as they were three strides from completing the first half.

Junger slowed before crossing the starting line. Koba watched him with slit eyes. Machlann's mouth hung open, exposing his partial rack of teeth. Clavellus could only shake his head at the burst of speed he'd just witnessed while a stoic Goll kept his thoughts to himself.

Brozz led the other four back to the starting line. As he crossed, he glanced over at Junger and shook his head. The Perician stood with his hands on his hips, already breathing easily.

Sapo lumbered over the line, dead last, and his scarlet features appeared ready to burst.

Clavellus signaled for the men to repeat.

"Have them run it again, Master Koba!" Machlann bellowed and was answered by an epic rattle of thunder.

Once again Koba's arm dropped and set the men loose, leaping from their starting positions. Junger completed the lap *faster* than before and left the remainder lagging in the wet sand. Brozz came in second, chest heaving, while the others chugged across in slow time, glaring at the Perician.

"Again!" Machlann roared.

And as the rain came down and puddled the sands, the six men repeatedly raced the length of the field. Each time, Junger excelled while the others faltered. Sapo in particular was reduced to a wheezing tower of swinging arms quite ready to die any moment. Near the end, while the others staggered over the wet sands, Sapo could only walk with hands on hips.

When Koba finally gave the command to rest easy, five of the six fighters were forever grateful.

"Never thought," Clavellus observed from under the balcony, "that the Pericians would be so swift of foot."

"He runs quite well," Goll remarked pensively, looking at the ground and how the rain marked the sands.

"Quite well? The man's a hellion on two legs. I've seen gaps before, but entire field lengths? Never! We have something very… special here, Master Goll. Very special indeed."

Goll remained silent, glaring at the drenched fighters.

"You want to see speed?" Pig Knot hollered raggedly across the field, capturing the attention of everyone. The fallen pit fighter appeared a bloody bandage with stitches. His broken chin couldn't be seen under the swaddling of cloth, the ends tied in a knot at the top. Pig Knot leaned to one side, lifting one cheek off the mat beneath him, grimaced with effort, and loudly passed gas. If the weather had been dry, the blast would have manifested itself as a dust cloud.

"Chase *that,* you wet bastards!" The Sunjan broke into an evil chortle.

A few pit fighters smiled, but in truth, they were too tired to do much more. Machlann's and Koba's hard looks lingered a bit longer on Pig Knot while Clavellus ignored him completely. Goll bit his lower lip in spite, checking his annoyance.

"Rest up! Then in pairs!" Machlann shouted and walked the length of the sands to converse with Koba.

All the while, Pig Knot grunted and roared through clenched teeth. "Aye that, rest up, you hellpups! Rest up!"

"How much has he had to drink this morning?" Clavellus asked Goll.

Goll's brow flexed, and he continued to chew on his lip. "He hasn't had any."

"Oh. Well then. So much for that thought."

Though the weather was piss poor, Pig Knot found ridiculing much to his liking. It took his minds off things, like the facts that he had nothing below his knees and that the knobby ends itched and stank of saywort, cutwort, and every other foul-smelling medicinal ointment Shan the healer could slap and rub into them. Though he had been limbless for only three days and was still recovering, Pig Knot was sick of it already.

"I'm off," Muluk said, standing next to him, the rain flattening his unruly bush of hair and matching beard. "Not sitting out here in this."

"Where are you going?" Pig Knot asked.

"Back inside," he said and limped away on his bandaged leg. Pig Knot watched him go, envious of the man's legs, of all things, and thinking black, rancid thoughts. He didn't deserve this. He didn't deserve *any* of this. Pig Knot had always been his own man and watched his own hide. The moment he'd joined this *place* was his downfall. His hateful mood bubbled to his face.

Then the Sunjan beheld a vision who brightened his mood considerably.

She carried a pitcher with the grace only a young biscuit like her might possess—small frame, tanned skin, blond hair—as pretty and glowing as wild berries. He'd seen her around before, before his world went to Saimon's hell. She kept to the eaves of the main house until the eaves ended, whereupon the rain soaked her robes, making them clingy. Pig Knot liked what he saw—she was a damn sight better than the punce who'd brought wine to him and Muluk yesterday.

With two wooden mugs in one hand and the pitcher in the other, she stopped before him, cringing in the rain, and stooped to one knee.

"And what's your name?" Pig Knot asked, dark eyes twinkling. Some men could cast spells over women using their bodily injuries. He knew he looked a mess, but he couldn't pass up the opportunity to attempt a bit of magic.

"Ananda, Master Pig Knot," she said in a miserable voice. Pig Knot didn't blame her. He took pitcher and cups from her, catching a withering look from Koba, who spied them half a field away. That tugged at a memory from before, a talk between the large trainer and him, and Pig Knot smiled, feeling evil.

"Well, thank you for bringing this to me," he said to her, ignoring the trainer.

"Where is Master Muluk?"

"I'll see that he gets this. Don't worry."

She nodded thanks and practically ran back to the house. Pig Knot sighed and blamed her quick departure on the weather and not his wrecked features and crippled body.

"I'd chase you..." he muttered through clenched teeth and trailed off, watching her escape the rain, the wet robes revealing enticing curves. He sighed wistfully and regarded his missing legs. The good feeling dissipated. Sniffing, Pig Knot peered into the pitcher, saw it held wine, and took a deep drink, hoping to drown his rising misery.

"I'd chase you..." he whispered, wine spilling down his front.

He studied the stumps of his legs.

*

A messenger from Borchus arrived at the villa late in the afternoon. The man was drenched and wretched-looking from his horseback ride through the rain. He handed the guards minding the gate a tubular, wax-sealed case. Clades delivered it to Clavellus, still sitting underneath his balcony with Goll and observing the men practice two-strike drills in the steady rain.

The taskmaster glanced at the case, frowned at the dripping, and handed it over to Goll. "It's for you."

Goll took it without thanks and broke open the seal. He spilled the scroll out of the case, unraveled the parchment, and read the contents quickly.

"What is it?" Clavellus asked.

"We fight in five days."

"Who?"

"All."

Clavellus brow arched at the news. "Well, not entirely uncommon. It happens. Who do we face?"

Goll rubbed his jawline. "Free Trained. All of them."

"Our good fortune."

"Apparently, they're undefeated thus far."

Clavellus sat back and sniffed. "So are ours. They all are at this point in the games. Relax, Master Goll," he soothed. "We have only a little time, but the dates are set. We'll have the lads prepared with a trick or two."

*

Halm arrived later in the evening.

HOUSE OF PAIN

The dripping, muddy husk of a koch pulled up in front of the closed gates of Clavellus's home and deposited the Zhiberian right on the doorstep, hunched over and looking as if he'd just escaped a butcher. He smiled his gruesome snarl at the guards, who didn't recognize him at first, but the Zhiberian's short, scathing outburst jogged their memories. The gates opened, and Halm walked through the short tunnel leading to the training grounds.

Swelling puddles dotted the soggy sands, and not a person could be seen. The rain had intensified into gray sheets, and the droning hiss smothered most sound. He stood within the relative dryness of the tunnel before eyeing the open door of the living quarters, feeling the distinct chill of the air. Taking a breath and holding his wounds, he started walking.

"Ho there," a voice called out.

Halm looked up to see the ghostly figure of Clavellus on his balcony. His upraised silver mug glowed in the downpour.

"Welcome back," the taskmaster called out. He guzzled his drink, straightened in a pickled sort of way, and bumped the door frame as he went inside.

Halm chuckled. Wet was obviously fine for the taskmaster.

Feeling better with the greeting, Halm went to the living quarters and stomped his feet weakly on the threshold before entering. The tables of the common area had already been emptied and cleared, and Halm cursed the weather for his slow journey as he'd hoped to join in at supper. He'd ask the first servant he placed eyes on if anything might be brought to him. With a huff, he dragged himself past the tables, wincing in discomfort, toward the doorway in the rear.

The man called Kolo emerged and blocked his path.

"Master Halm," he blurted. "Didn't expect you here."

"Just 'Halm' is good. And here I am. Wetter than a sick dog. Who's about?"

Kolo smiled briefly. "We're all about, just that most are in agony and have retired early. They beat us down right and proper this day. I'm just looking for the water barrel for a drink. All this rain, and I'm still parched."

Halm liked that one, and he returned Kolo's good humor as he shuffled past. A gray light shone from an open window at the end of the hall, enough to reveal all the drawn curtains. Most men were already asleep.

"Halm?" a voice whispered.

"Muluk?"

The hairy Kree yanked back his hanging cloth. "Lords above. What happened to you?"

"Been busy hunting."

"I hope the other man's in harder condition." Muluk stuck out his fist.

"Oh, he is. He is." Halm pressed his knuckles firmly against his friend's. "Where's Goll?"

"In the baths."

"Pig Knot?"

"Here, you Zhiberian shite."

Though Muluk's thick curls trembled as he frowned, Halm snorted as if the insult were nothing. "I'll talk with you later."

The Kree's face lit up.

Halm turned to his right and pulled back the curtain.

There, Pig Knot lay on his back, looking back down the length of his nose, the swelling around his eyes not so bad. Shirtless, he was trussed up with linens and smelled of onions.

"Hope you don't use that same bait for the women," Halm groaned and leaned against the frame. Having taken note of snores cutting the air, he kept his voice down.

"Daresay I'll have to pay for them from now on," Pig Knot grumped. Rain pelted the closed shutters above his head.

"You had to pay for them before," Halm pointed out.

"You're right." Pig Knot smiled feebly. "I did."

"Then nothing's changed, has it?"

In answer, the Sunjan snarled as he pushed himself up on his cot, drawing attention to his stumps.

Halm quietly regarded them then Pig Knot's face. "It'll take some getting used to."

"Suppose it will."

Halm exhaled. "I found Skulljigger."

Pig Knot stared. "The blood challenge? You punished the bastard?"

"I did. And didn't."

"What do you mean?"

"I didn't kill him."

A confused Pig Knot wiggled a finger underneath the bandages keeping his chin in place and waited. Halm told him everything. The legless man listened, and every now and then, the rain crashed against the wooden shutters. Halm didn't really know what to expect from the Sunjan warrior, whether he'd be upset with the report or even more bloodthirsty, but when he informed him about the fight in the alley, and how Skulljigger's son came to the man's aid, the Sunjan's face slumped in defeat.

Not even Pig Knot wanted to make orphans of the man's children.

Halm then revealed the matter of the gold Skulljigger wanted, which Pig Knot wasn't impressed with; nor was he impressed with Halm fighting in the unsanctioned Iron Games to secure the coin.

But in the end, Pig Knot held out a fist, and Halm pressed his own into it.

"No one else… would have done that for me," Pig Knot said softly. "I almost feel sorry for you."

"What do you mean?"

The apologetic crease of a smile spread over the man's shadowed features. "You'll have to explain all of this to Goll… and I daresay he won't be as understanding as I."

Halm's jaw clenched. Pig Knot was right.

"I hear he's in the baths?"

"He is."

"Then he can come to me later," Halm muttered. "I'm done staggering about. Haven't even had anything to eat or drink, either. I'm for one of these beds. You don't have anything to eat around, do you?"

Pig Knot's smile widened. "No."

"As always." Halm had turned to leave when his companion's voice made him pause.

"It's good to see you, Halm of Zhiberia, even though it looks as if something stepped on you."

For some reason, the words lifted the hurting man's mood.

"And you, Pig Knot of Sunja. And you."

Then to the opposing curtain. "And you as well, Muluk of Kree."

A grateful voice meekly drifted back. "Thank you kindly."

Halm wandered down the hall and found an open cubicle, the curtain drawn back. An empty cot beckoned. The grinding snores made him feel very weary. The healer was about somewhere, but Halm would seek him in the morning.

Lowering his bulk onto the cot and feather pillow, he smiled faintly at the clean sweetness of the straw, kicked off his footwear, and closed his eyes.

28

"Wake up, I said."

Roused from a deep sleep, Halm blinked at the command. Looming above and poised to strike was a none-too-impressed Goll. The Kree appeared damn well ready to pick at stitches and rip them out with his teeth, just for spite.

"Why didn't you tell me you'd returned last night?"

Unable to control a yawn, Halm righted himself and, with some effort, swung his legs over the cot's edge. That movement alone caused him discomfort. He smacked his lips and wished for something to drink, sensing warm daylight seeping in through the shutters behind him.

"Good morning, friend Goll," he rasped eventually.

"You keep your greetings," Goll snapped, like a dog reaching the length of his chain. "I'm waiting for the explanation about why you look like something nailed to a tree and clubbed with spiked mauls. *That's* what I'm waiting for. You were hard to look at before, but now…!"

"I was going to ask for the healer."

Goll's face reddened before he said, "You need *ten* healers."

"One will probably do." Shan's voice piped up from just beyond Halm's line of sight. One venomous glare from the Kree silenced the healer, and Goll held that withering look for several punishing seconds before directing his attention back at Halm.

"Let's hear it, then."

"Ease off the man," Pig Knot's voice called.

"*You* stay out of this," Goll barked. "You stay out of this." Then to Halm, "You should've come back with us instead of going on about vengeance. I should have insisted. Look at you. I mean, *look*. How is it you're still alive? Ordinarily, wounds in this place become commonplace and easy on the eyes, but *you*… You're something special."

"Not as special as me, I wager," Pig Knot challenged.

"Saimon's black hanging fruit, Pig Knot, will you *shut up*! This isn't just a business we've started here. This isn't just a gurry whim. We fight for the name of the house now. We fight to show those who wouldn't take you or me or any of the others. To show them we're worth more than they measured or could ever expect!"

"Really? I fought only for the coin," Pig Knot said.

"So did I," Halm agreed.

This infuriated the Kree, and his face boiled to a dangerous redness. He brandished one fist, ready to throttle them both, and tensed up with the threatening power of a loaded ballista. Heat emanated from the man in such intensity that even Halm became uncomfortable. Normally, he'd enjoy seeing how angry a person became before something snapped. It wasn't nearly as enjoyable with Goll. And when the Kree finally spoke, the quietness he forced into his voice was absolutely frightening.

"Pig Knot. This would not have existed because of you. You have no legs because of the house, thus the house will shelter you for the rest of your days... *if* we can make it through each and every season. *Especially* this one. The only way we can survive is if we win. Every gladiator under this roof has to bring us their share of victories, and one vital element contributing to their—to *your* victory on the sands is to be as close to perfect health as possible upon the day of battle. I'll be forever grateful for what you did and forever guilty because of your legs. But if you open your maw once more before I'm finished with this sliced rump of ham here, I'll damn well forget who you are, who *I* am, and what we've gone through thus far."

"And do what?" Pig Knot. Fearless.

Goll's mouth puckered into a furious pout, and he turned around.

"I didn't get this fighting in a blood match," Halm blurted, pausing Goll's wrath. "I got this at the Iron Games."

Goll impatiently rattled his head, not understanding.

Halm held up a hand. "They're unsupported fights that take place outside of the arena. Skulljigger had children, and he was going to accept the bloodmatch. I was certain I'd kill him, so I convinced him to... not fight... to leave the rest of the season, on condition I pay him. A hundred gold pieces."

Goll straightened as if speared in the back. Almost impossibly, his face darkened even more.

Halm blurted the rest. "I fought in the games with Borchus at my side and won. Won coin. Which I then paid to Skulljigger earlier this day. He won't pursue the blood challenge. And I don't have the worry of fatherless children on my conscience. I got cut up, plain to see and feel—I'll tell no lies—but I can still fight."

Halm lowered his eyes and peeked at the Kree. The silence swelled to a dangerous tension where a fight might start if someone inhaled too loudly. Goll controlled his base urges and finally exhaled steam.

"No mother?" Goll said through white lips.

"No mother." Halm didn't go into whether or not Skulljigger was lying. He didn't feel the man was, and Goll didn't bring it up.

The Kree stood in the doorway, contemplating, shaking his head in black dismay. Then he leveled a warning finger.

"No more of this foolishness." Goll's voice seethed. "No more. From here on in, you fight when the Madea tells you it's time. You avoid confrontation outside of the Pit. And as Seddon as my witness, if any of you disobey me, I'll sling your carved asses outside these walls with a smile on my face. And I won't care a lick if you're missing arms, legs, eyes, ears, heads, kogs, *bells*, or whatever shite gurry's left. If you have no common sense, then I don't want you. You're of no worth to the house."

He paused and drew in breath, a sound like surf clawing back from some distant shore.

"Do you understand?" Goll finally asked.

"Aye that," Halm replied quietly, feeling both shamed yet oddly in the right. He scratched at his brow and didn't meet the Kree's gaze.

"Pig Knot?" Goll still seethed. "You answer me, or by Seddon's dying gasp, I'll skip you across the surface of the nearest lake."

"Aye that," he grumbled.

Goll waited for any other smart remarks, and when

none came, he deflated only a little. The house master was well and truly pissed, but the most dangerous part had passed.

"Shan," the Kree said curtly.

"Yes?" the healer replied, sounding terrified.

"See to this man's wounds. Do what you can for him."

"I will."

Goll's eyes burned into Halm's battered face. The Zhiberian thought the man was about to say something more, but Goll shook his head in loathing and marched out of the living quarters.

Shan stood in the hall, watching the Kree stalk away with passion enough to startle hellions from the blackest depths. His worn face gradually shed the bleached glow of fear.

"Is he gone?" Muluk asked quietly.

Shan nodded. "Aye that."

All heard the hairy Kree exhale with relief.

For a long while, no one said anything, just allowing the angry energy in Goll's wake to slowly dissipate. Other heads hesitantly poked out from behind their curtains, like worried animals, checking for casualties.

"Well," Pig Knot muttered in the aftermath. "That wasn't so bad."

29

Rain crashed down on the roof of Borl Grisholt's study, traversing not-so-secret passages inside and dripping into buckets lining his floor. The pitched *plunks* might have threatened to drive the old manager slightly mad if only one drop at a time had been falling, but luckily for Grisholt, water cascaded so heavily in places that the sound almost blended into one steady note. The roof needed repairs so badly that veritable *streams* poured into the waiting buckets, as if a collection of old men had stopped right above his head to loose stuttering rivulets of piss. The fact that his study usually got the worst of any rainstorm, despite what meager repairs his fighters attempted—Grisholt acridly noted gladiators weren't fit to do carpentry—left him no choice but to nominate a lad to empty the buckets when full.

In the old days, Grisholt would've had servants to do such for him.

Then again, in the old days, he would've had coin to

spend on proper carpenters.

That night, Grisholt sat, mulled, and drank wine before a single flickering candle. Black thoughts coursed through his head, as fluid and cold as rainwater sluicing through corroded and crumbling drains. The wine was a little gift to himself from the pot of gold he'd won on his last successful wager. Standing just inside the doorway, a burly pit fighter eyed the filling buckets, stooping to sop up any drops reaching the floor. Grisholt knew the punce didn't like the task, but neither did Grisholt, which was why *he* wasn't doing it. Thick-chested Brakuss stood in one dry corner, as still and brooding as a one-eyed ogre. With Brakuss about, the water boy would stay in line.

At least until Grisholt retired for the evening. And if the rain continued falling at that time, he'd order Marrok, his last true servant, to mind the buckets—which he would do unerringly. Not because he was Grisholt's sole remaining servant, his cook in fact, but because of Brakuss… and the beating the half-blind skull cracker would bestow upon Marrok's tender person if he strayed from his duty.

Wine—the one secret the Lords had bestowed unto man that made Grisholt believe in prayers. Wine helped him think. It enabled him to make crucial decisions. It also eased the aches of his tiring frame of fifty-six winters. He sat behind his large desk, sunken deep into his padded chair coated in fraying green. Ignoring the two buckets stationed to his right, he cupped a goblet of tarnished tin in his hands and gently swished its murky contents three times before every sip. He'd already downed two bottles of the grape and intended to down two more before the night was done.

If he was going to drown, he'd do so on his own terms.

HOUSE OF PAIN

A long, sonorous note of thunder rattled the sky, and Grisholt suddenly felt very small, for all he might do in life—all he might experience—was nothing compared to the power of the heavens, the oceans, and the earth. The thought of what it might be like to fly above the known world and simply observe it from afar freed Grisholt's mind from his skull, and he slipped into a vision of blue and green crusted with craggy lines of earth brown. The image became too great for him to maintain and dissolved into darkness… which wasn't entirely terrible to behold, either.

A soft rapping disturbed his dreaming, and a dark figure appeared in the doorway, motioning for Brakuss.

"You can tell me, you know," Grisholt grumbled. "Seeing as I do own the stable."

"Apologies, Master Grisholt," the figure spoke. "You have a messenger from the city."

"I do?" Grisholt's voice rose in pitch. "Send the lad in, then. Send him in. Must be something… grand, indeed. Eh, Brakuss?"

"Must be, Master Grisholt," the guard replied.

The shadow in the doorway retreated, and another, taller man stepped forth, gleaming in the meager light. Traveling canvas, draped over his head and shoulders, dripped water onto Grisholt's floors, nowhere near a bucket. The sight and sound of this unwelcome spattering plucked at the owner's nerves.

"Master Grisholt," the dripping traveller said, keeping his hood over his features.

Grisholt stroked his beard into presentable fashion and straightened in his chair. "Well met, though I must say anyone weathering tonight's storm has my respect. And my curiosity. Who are you?"

"My name isn't important."

Grisholt screwed up his lips at that. Names were very important in his mind, and he drew breath to order Brakuss to rattle this soaked stranger just enough to realize that.

"But the Sons have sent me to you," the stranger went on.

That brought the Grisholt back to the brink of sobriety. The Sons of Cholla. The old owner nodded with dawning realization, studying the visitor watering his study's threshold.

"There were no fights this day," Grisholt said guardedly.

"We're aware of that, but a bargain had been struck, and the Sons take their bargains quite seriously. Though you weren't in the city today, we took it upon ourselves to visit you tonight."

"Well..." Grisholt cleared his throat and checked on Brakuss and the pit fighter turned water boy, assuring himself he had the greater numbers. "I appreciate the gesture. I must admit, you picked poor weather to come here. The roads must be rivers by now."

"They aren't," the visitor said and reached under the folds of his dripping garb. "This... is for you."

An iron flask came into view, held up at arm's length like a spent torch.

Grisholt had learned long before not to grab things he didn't understand. "What is it?"

"It's victory for your gladiators."

"In an iron flask?"

The visitor didn't reply. Rain continued to fall in the room and outside the walls, filling the silence.

"Well, bring it here, then." Grisholt shrugged.

HOUSE OF PAIN

The visitor from the Sons took two steps and placed the mysterious metal bottle on the edge of the grand desk. The surface of the piece of furniture was utterly dry, which amazed Grisholt on such a night. The contours of the container rose up to end in a squat neck and a stopper that resembled a harsh crown. Metal bands grasped and sealed any seams in the container's heavy bulk. Grisholt studied it from the right for a moment before shifting his backside and inspecting it from the left, cocking his brow at the imposing vessel.

"What's in it?"

"As I've said," the Son of Cholla said. "Victory."

"I see. And just how am I supposed to, ah, *use* this victory?"

"Just before your pit fighter is to walk the White Tunnel, he must sip from the flask—just the barest sip—no more and certainly not a mouthful. We doubt any mortal man could survive any more than a taste. Your warrior will be given great strength and even greater rage. His fists will strike as mauls, his weapons as catapult shot. Pain will mean nothing to him, nor will he fall to ordinary blows, should his opponent be fortunate enough to land one."

Impressed, Grisholt focused on the iron flask with greater concentration.

"But some words of caution," the Son warned. "The fire contained in that will only work for a short time. Whoever drinks it must engage his foe quickly and end it decisively, else at the end, his very flesh and bones will weigh him down. The potion bestows great strength but burns itself out very quickly. And the same man mustn't drink from the flask again until two—perhaps three—days have passed. To do so earlier would mean his death."

Interesting. Grisholt reached out and caressed the container's hard curves, discovering them quite warm. "How much will this cost?"

"For you, Master Grisholt, nothing. I believe our position in this matter has been explained. The Sons see the games as a huge opportunity, but the scrupulous position of the Chamber and the honorable owners of houses have prevented us from, ah, actively participating. Simply revealing ourselves to them would invite visits from the Skarrs, which isn't good for business. You, however, approached us. And after much discussion, we are willing to forgo our fee this time."

"Most generous," Grisholt said warily, remembering Brakuss's retelling of his encounter with the Sons of Cholla.

"We do, however, require a list of your fighters," the Son informed him. "All of them. So that we may watch the boards and know when they are fighting. We will also require word of who will partake of the fire before they fight, so that we may make arrangements for wagers."

"One moment." Grisholt opened a drawer and produced a scroll, which he unrolled and held close to the candle's flame. He returned it with a frown, as it wasn't the document he wanted. The second scroll was a list of his current roster. He opened another drawer, brought forth a quill and a small inkwell, and drew lines through certain names. Once finished, he rolled the scroll, located a carrying case, and after slipping the document inside, handed it over.

"The names I've crossed out are the men already eliminated."

The Son made the scroll disappear underneath his still-dripping traveling garb.

"Well then," Grisholt announced, feeling the meeting concluded and needing to reacquaint himself with any bottle of wine. He wasn't inclined to share a drink with the stranger. "Thank you for this, and let's hope all goes in our favor in the Pit."

The Son didn't say anything for a heartbeat. Then he turned to leave, paused, and spoke.

"Pardon me, good Grisholt. There is one more thing I must impart upon you. We have high expectations. That flask has significant value to us, and it did not come into our possession easily or cheaply, nor do we give it up lightly. We expect victory from your warriors on the sands and plenty of it, as it means a sizeable return on our, ah, investment. If we do not…"

The Son's words ended in a hiss of rain not unlike a snake's warning.

"Have no worries, then," Grisholt finished, feeling a twinge of impatience. "You'll get your coin's worth."

The Son lingered, absorbing the reassurance with an unnerving stoicism, before continuing as if the old owner hadn't spoken at all. "If we do *not*, we'll regard the fault as our own—for failing to properly choose *who* we partnered with on this venture—and pursue measures to get back our investment."

Grisholt's face contorted in the candlelight. "What're you saying? Are you *threatening* me?"

In response, the Son pointedly inspected the doorway, the walls, and finally the study with dark interest.

"Are you saying you'll take my *house?*" Grisholt barked a laugh. "Try something like that, and you'll have a small war on your hands, *son*. Pay attention to when we fight. Make your wagers, and revel in your winnings—as I will—but don't attempt to frighten me. I don't frighten. I am quick to *anger*. And since you've soured this otherwise pleasant conversation, one of my own will see you to the door."

Grisholt pointed to the iron flask. "And thank you for this."

The man—a pit fighter—who'd escorted the Son to the study, stepped in behind the cowled traveler while the water boy moved to the front.

"Safe journey," Grisholt said coldly, "back to the city."

The Son of Cholla departed with his pair of escorts, without protest, and that made Grisholt unexpectedly nervous. He was dealing with criminals—he knew that—but desperate times called for equally desperate measures. He unquestionably had more to risk and to lose than Cholla's brood. If Grisholt chose to use the potion and was caught, the consequences would be devastating. The Chamber would cast him out from the games, leaving his name disgraced, and certainly end his family's legacy. The other owners would shun him, though he had to admit that didn't bother him as much as not being allowed to compete in the games ever again. His gladiators would desert him for houses and schools that would provide for them. Eventually, his debts would mount to an unmanageable level, and having no other source of income, he'd be forced to sell his property, possibly even being left completely homeless.

If that happened, Grisholt knew his life would be finished.

The iron flask stood on his desk, candlelight casting a malevolent hue over its curves.

Grisholt brightened with wickedness. If his warriors *won*, however…

That thought pulsed in his mind. There wasn't any

going back. The flask was right there, and the fighting season was nearing the halfway point.

Barros was the next gladiator who would fight—the next day, if the skies cleared.

"Brakuss," Grisholt said and reached for a wine bottle. "I believe our fortunes are about to change."

The rain stopped before dawn, and the sun rose with a humid heat that steamed the land. Grisholt dressed in the finest clothing remaining to him and slapped on generous amounts of perfumed water. Once ready, he and a handful of his minions left the safety of the walled villa and travelled in koches and wagons to Sunja's capital. Puddles and mud slicked and mired the road in places, slowing the procession's speed, but Grisholt was oblivious to it all. He mulled over dark schemes and pondered whether Barros should be the first lad to imbibe the Sons' potion. In the end, Grisholt decided that no question really existed. Since he was in league with the Sons of Cholla, he would have to find a balance between using it often enough to sate those sewer pricks and using it too often—enough to rouse the suspicions of the Chamber and the other houses. It would be a difficult task but one he believed possible. His koch rattled over a beaten washboard of a road, and while the sun blazed through the open shutters, a chill stole over Grisholt for the first time.

Without a few bottles of wine armoring him, the threat of the Sons seemed very dire indeed.

Brakuss closed the shutters of Grisholt's koch before it entered the city, for the old owner felt more comfortable traveling in privacy. The vehicle rolled through the capital's streets, engulfed by the shouts of merchants and the chatter of citizens. Grisholt didn't bother cracking open a shutter as sensing the peasant masses was enough for him.

The driver finally reined in the horses, stopping the koch. Brakuss knocked on the door and opened it a moment later. A hard-looking Caro hauled himself into the wooden confines.

"Caro," Grisholt purred. "A fine morning for the games."

His agent agreed with a nod, wrinkling his nose as if getting the drift of something overpowering.

"Something troubles you?"

Caro took a quick breath and shook his head. He composed himself, but his features remained stern with distaste.

"Hold on," Grisholt said, deciding not to dwell on him. He pulled out a small cloth sack from a hiding place and jingled it.

"Place this upon Barros's head, when the time comes."

Caro hefted the coin and eyed the owner. "Seems a little heavy."

"Heavy times." Grisholt smiled without a drop of humor. "Today is the day our fortunes turn for the better. Today, we become a house to be feared."

"You met with the Sons, didn't you?" Caro wasn't a supporter of the idea.

Grisholt feigned innocence. "Of course. A merchant of pain such as myself must consider all paths to victory on the sands."

Caro didn't like the notion, which showed on his face.

"You disapprove?"

"Master Grisholt," Caro said, pursing his lips. "Respectfully, yes, I do. But it's not my decision to make. If you've made a bargain with those hellions, then it's too late. Best to push forward and see what it brings us."

It wasn't the answer Grisholt wanted to hear, but he chose to focus on the positive parts. "Excellent. Then make sure you place all of that on Barros. *Our* man this time. I have a very good feeling. Now, anything to tell on that topper called Targus? The one friendly with the Zhiberian?"

"I made contact with the lad and warned him about the Zhiberian."

That simply tickled Grisholt. "Excellent, Caro… excellent. What did he have to say?"

Caro remembered how he wasn't certain, at the time, that Targus would even remember their conversation, but whispering a few fabricated evildoings of the Zhiberian had quickly sobered him.

"As you instructed. I told him not to trust the man, that most of his kills were men the Zhiberian had betrayed in the past seasons. To be wary about speaking with the fat brute."

"And he listened?"

"I would say yes," Caro admitted, remembering the slew of drunken oaths and the vows of finding and confronting the man. At the time, Caro thought another blood challenge was in the making. The Zhiberian would have a record of sorts before all was said and done.

"Excellent," Grisholt said.

Caro barely nodded and didn't immediately leave.

"Something else?" Grisholt asked.

"We've been watching the Zhiberian. I've received word from one of our spies that he actually participated in the Iron Games just a night ago."

Grisholt frowned with wary humor. "And?"

"He won, actually, though my man says it was a near

thing. The barrel-shaped ass suckler got bloodied but walked away."

"Wonderful. You had me worried there for a moment."

"A spy followed him out of the city, to the villa and training grounds of Clavellus. The entire House of Ten resides there now, it would seem."

"Old Clavellus," Grisholt remarked with a twinge of wonder. "Simply can't stay away. Curge will have his head. Regardless, you say the Zhiberian took damage?"

"Looked a mess, apparently."

"Can he fight?"

"We'll see."

That didn't sit well with Grisholt. Leave it to a Zhiberian to ruin his revenge. "Keep watch on him."

"I've already made arrangements."

"Good. Anything else?"

"Yes. He had someone with him at the games, perhaps in his forties: short man but blocky, powerful, dark hair going gray with heavy sideburns, no beard. We've seen him around the men of the new house. Very difficult to keep an eye on all of them. When there *were* extra eyes about, we quickly lost him in the alleys."

"A spy, you think?" Suspicion clouded Grisholt's face.

"Or an agent, yes," Caro offered.

"Even better. You've seen this man?"

"I have."

Grisholt's habit of stroking his beard got the better of him, and he pulled on it almost hard enough to produce milk. "The Ten will need a network eventually. I can see the old man having the connections to get something working this soon. How many spies they might have is a good question, but I think not many. They don't have the coin for it. Not this soon. Yes, this one lad might be it. No more than two or three. Do you know his name?"

"One lad was close enough to hear 'Borchus.'"

"Excellent." Grisholt nearly yanked the hair off his chin. "Excellent."

He took a moment to stare off into space, contemplating possibilities. Agents. Every established house employed them, and they in turn built webs of spies bent on scrubbing up any and every morsel of information pertaining to the season. It was an accepted practice. If one owned a house of gladiators, one needed a man—or even woman—to ferret out secrets that might lend an edge in the Pit. Spies were easily replaced, but agents not so. These people guarded their identities. To discover one could lead to orchestrated ruses leaking *false* information, just as deadly on the arena sands. It wasn't entirely unheard of to find old agents, their identities and reputations widely known to others in the profession, rotting in the sewers with half of their faces chewed away by vermin.

For one reason or another.

Granted, discovering corpses was rare, but it happened enough to know that certain houses held grudges.

And a house without an agent was both deaf and blind to the deciding undercurrents of the games.

Caro waited dutifully.

"Kill him," Grisholt said flatly.

"That might be difficult," Caro suggested. "I don't think we have anyone capable of doing the deed. Not so soon after Kurlin and his butchers."

"You could do it." Grisholt smirked.

"I could, but I'd rather stay in the shadows."

Grisholt recognized and appreciated the reasoning behind the thought. Dependable, proven agents should never be placed at risk. "Hm. Agreed. I'll have Brakuss arrange it. Perhaps I'll send him to the Sons after the day's fights. I doubt they'll mind a little extra business tossed their way. Especially if we win this day."

Caro nodded pensively.

"Something bothers you?" Grisholt asked, softening his tone to draw the poison out of his agent.

"No."

"You're certain?"

"I am."

"Any word on the punce Barros is fighting this day?"

"His name's Shoor. Fights under the House of Razi. Wears leather and favors a sword and shield. Hard-going lad. Likes to swing. Likes to push the pace, but no injuries to play upon. None that we heard about."

"Razi still third line?"

"He is."

"Razi, Razi…" Grisholt leaned back and sighed. "Today's not going to go well for you. Not at all. Any other matches of note?"

"The House of Gastillo has Prajus fighting this day. He's a near certain win over Malo from the School of Nexus."

"When does he fight?"

"Before Barros. Fourth match of the day."

That didn't sit well on Grisholt's hoary mind. He'd been keeping abreast of the one called Prajus. The man was as talented as he was vicious and as solid as coin in one's hand. Trouble was, *everyone* knew Prajus's worth, placing him as one of the pit dogs favored to win it all this season. Still, Grisholt anticipated making a very good profit that day.

If the potion from the Sons of Cholla did as promised.

"Off with you, then," Grisholt said and gestured

toward the door. Caro departed, and Grisholt sat in the koch's shade and ruminated on matters, specifically Brakuss. The one-eyed bodyguard didn't care who he killed—or hired to kill on his employer's behalf. Grisholt would send him off to the Sons with Borchus's description.

A short time later, the koch got moving.

The day was going to be a very important one for the Stable of Grisholt.

Outside the koch, Caro inhaled fresh air, free of the suffocating vice of lavender flooding the transport's interior.

Seddon above, the agent swore.

The old man bathed in the shite.

30

"Beautiful day for some blood spilling," Nexus chirped as he nestled his silk-covered ass into his seat. The sun-dried sands of the arena below oozed steam while humidity thickened the very air, which accounted for the wine merchant wearing a thin, sleeveless shirt of red. His silver hair had been pulled back and tied into a frayed ponytail.

Gastillo thought the style exceedingly out of place for some reason.

"Wouldn't you say so, Gastillo?"

Gastillo's golden mask rendered him impassive while underneath, he was anything but. Prajus fought one of Nexus's lads that day, and Gastillo had stressed upon his rebellious pit fighter the importance of *not* killing his opponent. During that warning, Prajus had only smiled in that infuriating fashion of his, leaving Gastillo wondering what the man might do. Gastillo did not want a war with Nexus. He needed good relations with the merchant to further his hope of leaving this gruesome existence behind, giving rise to a secret hope Prajus would lose.

"We needed the rain," Gastillo muttered, his own words sounding forced and empty.

"Yes, we did," Nexus remarked. "We did, indeed. Crops are scalding underneath this sun. Not good for farmers and harvesters who work the vines, but little I care about that. I worry about the grapes, however. Though I'm reassured that this year's crop continues to grow fat, which is all that concerns me. Other than this, of course."

"Your lads have been performing well," Gastillo stated, hoping the flattery wasn't overly sweet. He was very much aware of the wine merchants' gladiators. They had fought well this season—a combined sixty victories on the sands and only six losses. Nexus's record outshone that of his own men, which rankled Gastillo's pride just a little.

"They have, they have. I'm most pleased. I like this sport, good Gastillo. I believe this could have been my true passion, my true purpose, if I'd only learned of it earlier. Ah, if I were a younger man, I would've been down there myself, splitting skulls and flesh with the worst of them. I know I could have. How I envy you and your early beginnings. Ahhh," the merchant growled while brandishing a fist.

Once again, Gastillo had cause to be thankful for his mask. Listening to the merchant made his tongue curl in disdain and brought back memories of long days of training, endless drills, and frightening combats in which unspeakable things were done. Watching the games from a distance was all very exciting, but when it was *you* being swung at and having your face smashed from its skull, that was entirely different. Just hearing Nexus ramble about the life of a pit fighter as if it were *fun* offended Gastillo. He wondered what Curge might say if he were present.

"Still," Nexus continued, heedless of the other's rising temper, "it's a young man's game, and safer to watch from up here, eh?"

"It is," Gastillo replied. *You ignorant, shite-greased bastard.*

Then Curge entered the viewing box and plopped down beside the golden-faced owner. "Seddon damn this moist heat. I feel as if I'm being smothered in the sweat between Saimon's crack and balls this day. Already in need of a bath, and the day isn't even over. Gastillo. Nexus. See you both are up and eager to get at it, eh?"

"We were just wondering if you weren't going to show," Nexus said, not bothering to turn his head in the other's direction. "Weren't we, good Gastillo?"

Gastillo didn't bother replying. He disliked being included in such lies.

Even Curge ignored the question. "You lads gather anything new about the House of Free Trained?"

Gastillo smirked. Curge knew the real name, but he wouldn't acknowledge it—at least not yet.

"No afternoon pleasantries, Dark Curge?" Nexus asked.

"I already did that. Listen next time. You and your merchant friends might enjoy lathering each other's asses with such gurry, but here we cut to business as soon as our asses touch wood."

Nexus's normally pallid face reddened, and his black eyes flickered annoyance. "Ah yes, I constantly forget who I'm sharing this box with. You reminded me, Dark Curge."

"I never forgot." Curge huffed and glanced over his shoulder. He wiggled his fingers, and a servant brought a silver platter bearing a pitcher and goblets. Curge sighed impatiently and took the drink, draining half with one mighty gulp.

"This doesn't taste like piss. Good." He signaled for more.

"It probably came from one of my orchards," Nexus said.

"I just said it doesn't taste like piss." Curge scowled. "Why would I drink a second if the first tasted off? Really, Nexus."

"Brazen bastard," the wine merchant fired back, slowly shaking his nearly non-existent chin.

"What of the Free Trained? Have you learned anything?" Gastillo asked, seeking to divert the exchange of words.

"Oh, I found out where they're training," Curge seethed. "I found out."

"Clavellus, I believe he's called," Nexus said.

Curge regarded a smug Nexus, and Gastillo could feel the tension swell. But the brutish owner averted his gaze to the sands and the stands filling up with eager spectators. "That's him," he stated quietly. "The old bastard has push, I'll give him that. A bad mistake all 'round."

He paused and squeezed the goblet. "I tell you this for nothing. I'm not happy with Clavellus training these bastards. And I'm going to take measures that no one else will join that rabble."

"Measures?" Gastillo asked, not entirely certain he liked the sound of it.

"Measures," Curge repeated… and then informed them exactly what they were.

*

Below the stony floors and within the torch-lit hollows of general quarters, men teemed and shifted like swarming white-and-black beetles. The smell accosted Demasta's senses like flies on a cow kiss, but he forced himself to ignore it. Dark Curge had given him a task, and with four handpicked warriors from his master's household guard, Demasta would do as commanded. He and his men stood on the steps descending into the gloomy hell of the Free Trained. Hundreds crowded beneath the flickering of torches, preparing themselves for the day's butchering and probably wondering what condition they'd be in by the evening. Demasta's harsh blue eyes mirrored the unsightly mob, and he set his jaw, its shorn black beard making his face frightening.

The head guard of Curge's household thumbed the pommel of a broadsword at his waist and shook his head. He looked back and motioned one of his men to take a nearby torch from its sconce. The man did as told and handed it over.

Demasta waved it over his head, bellowing for attention. He got it as several faces lifted to see his muscular torso strapped with an X of leather.

"Free Trained!" he roared, his deep voice rebounding through the underworld. "You motherless hounds are fortunate this day. My master, Dark Curge of the House of Curge, is displeased that a handful of you have forgotten their place in the hierarchy of the Pit. Soon, fighters from the House of Ten will stain the sands above us. Let it be known that Dark Curge has taken offence with the maggots who fight under the banner of the House of Ten. He offers three times the amount of gold if you fight and execute one of these curs on the hallowed earth of the arena, before the world, as example to all to remember their place in the greater order."

The populace of pit fighters stood still, dirty faces

solemn, ears and eyes open. It pleased Demasta.

"*Kill* any from the House of Ten," he droned on. "Make a bloody spectacle of them, and Curge will reward you with gold... and perhaps even a favor."

Demasta smiled inwardly at that. Curge himself had instructed him to sweeten the hook with that very morsel. Free Trained who believed there might be "more" would venture into Saimon's hell and back.

Having said his piece, the burly guardsman handed the torch back to one of his henchmen and turned to exit.

The rumbling excitement he left behind informed him Curge's offer was being taken very seriously.

*

"You placed a *bounty* on their heads?" an astonished Nexus blurted. "You'll be thrown from the competition!"

Curge's bald head furrowed with annoyance. "No such thing will happen. The offer stands only if it happens in the arena. And there's no ruling against offering coin to motivate lads."

"Why are you telling us this?" Gastillo asked, but he suspected the answer.

"Because sooner or later, one of yours will fight these ripe bastards. And I'd rather you hear it from me than the streets."

That wasn't it at all, which Gastillo knew as well as he knew Curge's reputation.

The bald ogre *enjoyed* displaying the ruthless power he commanded as top house in the games, and the bounty on the House of Ten was a warning example—anger the House of Curge at your peril, for there will be consequences. Gastillo didn't care for such backhanded threats. Nexus, however, was nodding.

"I approve, you thick-necked punce," the wine merchant commented with a sly curl on his lips. "Never thought you were capable of such ruthlessness. Truth be known, I'm impressed."

Curge didn't even turn his head. "You *should* be worried," he stated and took another gulp of wine.

The fights occupied their attention then.

Two embarrassing matches featured Free Trained warriors, neither offering up a death or any dramatic excitement the crowds were hoping to witness. Onlookers cheered when each fight finished. The third fight featured a gladiator from the Stable of Slavol meeting a lone Free Trained warrior. The stable's pit fighter, called Punder, decimated his opponent in short time and left him alive but bleeding on the sands.

Then came the match Gastillo dreaded. He recalled the chilling smile hitched upon Prajus's youthful face, the emotionless shine of his blue eyes. "Don't kill him," Gastillo had ordered. "Don't risk reprisal from the School of Nexus. It would drain us."

But Prajus had only nodded.

Fear, pure and icy, slipped in around Gastillo's innards and clenched. Prajus was insolent enough to do exactly what Prajus *felt* needed doing. *Especially* if it defied Gastillo's wishes.

A feeling of uncertainty hung about every match, no matter how well trained a warrior might be, but in this instance, Gastillo felt only dread.

To his left, Nexus glanced over and winked at him.

It did very little to improve Gastillo's mood.

*

HOUSE OF PAIN

The portcullis lifted with a greased rumbling, and Prajus stepped into the sun, already feeling the heat underneath his gleaming vest of scale mail. Twisting, mewling throngs raved and shook fists at him over the arena walls. Like maggots they were, ready to drop and feast on the guts of whoever was handy. Seddon above, Prajus still loved them—loved their cheers, infusing him with power. Loved the women who would brazenly flaunt their bare breasts in his direction. Relished the rush of vitality just before the battle itself. He knew of no truer test, to face a fighter of equal worth and to best him in single combat. Prajus held a high opinion of himself, but the fact of the matter was… no one could best him in the Pit.

And he would prove it with yet another victory. Already, he had amassed four wins in the early part of the season, and he wasn't about to stop. Across the way, the portcullis opened, and the gladiator called Malo walked into daylight.

Poor bastard.

Malo protected himself with a vest of leather and its regular black adornments of spikes, greaves, and bracers. A black iron helm, similar to Prajus's own in fact, covered the man's head, complete with face cage. Malo carried an uninspired combination of a sword and a faceless shield into the arena—not at all like the iron dragon's head decorating Prajus's shield or the knee and elbow spikes Prajus had strapped to himself. Right now, he knew Malo was sizing him up in turn and loathing what he saw. For good reason.

Prajus projected the look of a beast, a killer unleashed upon a very small world, where only two men existed. A Seddon-damned *monster* of epic telling, and right at that very moment, he glared across the heat-shimmering sands, heedless of the introductions, and focused on Malo's person as if he were a bloody steak about to be devoured.

Don't kill him, Gastillo had ordered, smelling of fear as ripe and as fragrant as foul sweat. *Don't risk reprisal from the School of Nexus. It would drain us.*

Prajus knew Gastillo had had a career on the sands once, long ago. The fact that the owner had survived the season and become a champion of the games was the original reason why Prajus sought training from him. But as time under Gastillo's roof dragged on, Prajus and a few others sensed something many had not, something that became clearer with each passing day.

Gastillo had lost his hunger for the games.

That realization had amazed the young pit fighter, for who in his right mind could become jaded with all of *this?*

Malo lifted one arm when he heard his name.

Prajus took a step toward his opponent and hefted his own sword when he heard his.

And when the Orator's arm dropped, both men charged.

They clashed in the middle in a drizzle of sand and dust. Steel crashed off steel, the notes sparkling.

Then the fighters parted, and Malo jabbed at his opponent at arm's length, testing Prajus's defense. They circled, concentrating on each other, before Malo closed, slashed, and locked blades in a test of strength.

Then things went very wrong.

Prajus pressed his sword against his foe's blade but then whirled away, spinning and slamming his elbow spike into the side of Malo's helmet. Iron pierced iron, and Malo's head rattled within its metal shell. His knees buckled, and the fighter dropped, momentarily dazed.

Prajus kicked him square in the chest, splaying Malo

flat on his back.

Without hesitation, Prajus stepped in and stabbed the man through the guts, the tip of his sword puncturing Malo's leather vest with a dull *pop*. For a brief moment, Malo didn't do a thing, but then he curled up around the killing blade like a worm cut in half.

Prajus placed a boot against his fallen foe's hip and yanked the steel free. One of Malo's legs kicked out weakly, as if he dreamed of running, before he coiled around his killing wound and lay still.

The victorious gladiator held his arms up in a V to the adoring crowds.

*

The Nexus both Gastillo and Curge knew appeared.

"That useless punce! Useless topper! I'll leave his worthless carcass in the sun and let the dirt ticks lap up his blood. The cow kiss! The coin I'd invested in him to see that! That! What was *that!* It barely lasted the time it would take me to *piss*, by Seddon's rosy ass!"

"Your man showed good form," Curge said from the far side, clearly enjoying the rant.

"In your hole, you balding ass packer."

Curge quieted, the corners of his mouth hinting at evil amusement.

Gastillo silently cursed Prajus strutting around the dying pit fighter. The gladiator faced their viewing box and made a pompous show of bowing. The gesture infuriated Gastillo. Prajus made another spectacle of swaggering around the arena, soaking in the praise, before slipping inside the raised portcullis.

Prajus. The man would have to be disciplined, and the

thought made Gastillo's head ache dearly.

"Your man's a hellion," Nexus fumed nearby, breaking his worrisome thoughts.

"What's that?"

"Your man there." Nexus waved a hand. "Despite my losing, he accounted himself fairly. Why did the he-bitch have to kill my man is something I'd like answered."

"I have no idea," Gastillo admitted, the drool leaking from his mangled lips. He quickly dabbed at the troublesome fluid with a hand cloth. "You can be sure I'll be looking into the matter. It wasn't my intention for your fighter to be killed."

Nexus studied him for a moment before tossing his head back in derision. "Oddly enough, I believe you, you gold-plated kog."

"Should I expect a blood challenge?"

But Nexus wouldn't answer him.

31

Prajus.

It was a name Grisholt would remember. The gladiator had just hacked up one of Nexus's brood and exited the arena with a smile on his face. Roughly three weeks into the games, the more adept would start to rise above the pack, drawing attention to themselves with each quality victory, as Prajus had just done. Grisholt shook his head. The House of Gastillo had surely made a pleasant sum in wagers on the fight.

Someone knocked on the door of his private viewing chamber, making Grisholt turn around. Brakuss and another lad stood back from the armored form of Barros. Age, the stress of the arena, and constant training had branded crow's feet around his black eyes, and his brown hair gleamed with sweat. The gladiator was perhaps only twenty-eight.

"Are you ready?" Grisholt asked him.

"Ready, Master Grisholt," Barros replied, gripping his

pot helm under his arm all the tighter.

"You understand what this will do to you?"

Barros nodded and held out a hand sheathed in metal.

Grisholt produced the iron flask and studied its hard lines. He still hadn't opened the container, superstitious of some twisted, smoking hellion popping out of its thick neck and plucking out his eyes. The metal warmed his hands as he hefted it and marveled at its promise. He could still turn back, return the potion to the Sons and accept any penalty they might impose, but the thought put a ghost of a smile on his weathered features. The penalty would be his life, for there was no escaping those criminals, not after bargaining with them.

Grisholt glanced at Brakuss, then to Barros, and broke the seal on the flask. He plucked out the brass crown of a stopper and handed it to his chosen pit fighter.

"Just a sip, now. Just a sip."

Barros raised it to his lips with no fear at all, totally trusting of his owner. He tasted, shuddered at the taste, and swallowed with a growl.

"Well?" Grisholt asked.

"Tastes like bloody piss."

"Like piss?" a sour Brakuss asked out of turn.

"Like piss, with… with pulpy *chunks* in it."

"Never mind that." Grisholt flourished a hand. "How do you feel?"

"Sick."

Sick. Then it all became clear. Grisholt rolled his eyes and cursed the Sons for his unbelieving fortunes. For all he knew, the damn lot of them might have wagered *against* his man—a few days ago Grisholt would have done the very thing himself. And what better way to ensure victory than by poisoning his lad? With a word whispered amongst the lineups to the Domis, the Sons could potentially gain a sizeable sum of gold with Barros's loss. The more Grisholt mulled it over, the more the plot made sense, and the sicker *he* felt for being taken so.

"Well... do what you can, then," the owner blurted, suddenly feeling exhausted, bitter, and just a pinch of crestfallen.

Barros's face twisted and reddened, and for a moment Grisholt hoped the man wouldn't void his guts in the private chamber. That would just be a poetic gesture to seal this ill-conceived venture. But Barros did not, however, and he donned his helm, covering his face entirely. Sputtering like a cat choking on its own hair, the pit fighter took his shield and sword from a nearby warrior and walked unsteadily to the door. Grisholt watched him go, already mulling ways of revenging the Sons' treachery.

Then Barros stopped, coughed and gagged, and visibly shivered. His stomach grumbled with volcanic heat, loud enough for all to hear. He stood there, trembling, as if a great hook had him by the sternum.

Brakuss glanced at Grisholt, who held his breath at the involuntary action.

Barros grunted loudly, as if clearing his throat. Then he stomped a sandaled foot hard into the stone, the connection startling Grisholt.

"You all right?" someone asked.

But Barros didn't answer. Instead, he grunted once more, louder that time, and threw open the door with a force that made Grisholt jump. Barros rolled his shoulders as he stepped outside and charged the white tunnel, and every pounding step echoed along the stone.

An amazed Brakuss stepped outside and watched. "He's gone. He ran the whole way."

"He charged the whole way," Grisholt repeated in disbelief, as if in a nightmare suddenly becoming very, very good. He rushed to the arch opening onto the shimmering sands. His ill feelings vanished, replaced with bloody anticipation.

"Make them fear," Grisholt whispered in prayer, ogling the waiting crowds beyond the stone lip of the arena wall, savoring the lingering taint of blood from the last fight.

*

Lightning coursed through Barros's limbs and body, energizing him to a point where he felt every step he took left a stone shattered. He roared to take the edge off, like a kettle bleeding off steam, drawing the attention of the Skarrs. He screamed at them, causing several to flinch. Even the old gatekeeper shied away, recognizing the sheer mountain-pummelling might coursing through the pit fighter.

The potion was supposed to make Barros stronger—that he had understood before even taking it—but the orange core of snapping, crackling, flesh-melting *power* now pulsating within him rivaled the face of the very sun. He set his jaws and stretched them wide, hammered the walls with his fist, and left indentations in a mist of rubble. The tidal force racing through his person threatened to burn through his skin or burst it apart.

What pulsed within him wasn't just *strength*—it was so much world-splitting *more*.

Barros didn't wait for the portcullis to rise; he ran to the top of the stairs and helped it along with one arm. He burst into the Pit, nearly choking the hilt of his sword, and could not keep still while waiting for the Orator to finish his introductions. His shield felt frail beneath him, and he cast it aside with a contemptuous yell, bouncing the thing off the arena wall.

The sound gave the Orator pause. Several people also took greater note of the gladiator from the Stable of Grisholt.

Barros felt their eyes on him, but he didn't care. The potion bulged and stretched his veins with every aching, ramming pump of his heart. His eyesight sharpened. Barros bellowed back at the onlookers and clawed at his neck with his sword hand.

More people noticed his odd behavior, including his uneasy opponent from the House of Razi. Shoor peered uncertainly over his shield, toward the stone arch where his owner watched.

The Orator droned on while Barros stomped his feet, sending up tufts of hot grit. A painful push of blood surged through his frame, nearly exploding the straining cords of his neck. Barros panted, growled, and threw open his arms.

When the Orator finally shouted to begin, the gladiator did not simply charge, he *exploded* from his side of the arena with all the force of a ballista missile.

Barros thundered across the arena, screaming savagely and seizing his blade with both hands. The weapon whipped up over his head and came down with a howl that nearly ruptured Barros's throat. Shoor got his shield up to deflect the attack—but the blade split the iron band of the wooden barrier, split the leather bracer protecting his arm, and hewed through meat and bone before losing momentum in a snarl of metal and wood.

Shoor shrieked.

Barros's scream drowned him out. He kicked the

wounded man off his blade, sending him flat on his back. Before Shoor could recover, Barros leaped on the fallen warrior. He slashed open a bare thigh. Still squealing, Shoor gripped the sprouting wound with his hand, the pot helm making his voice pitched and frightening.

Barros gripped his opponent's helmet with one hand and plunged his sword down, impaling Shoor through the guts.

The stricken pit fighter doubled up like a dying insect, all breath leaving him.

Grunting, Barros ripped the blade free and hammered at his foe's helm in a violent flurry that horrified spectators. The gladiator battered Shoor's head as if it were harvested grain, and each strike of metal crunching into metal rang out with appalling clarity. When the iron wouldn't yield, Barros barked gibberish and chopped off an arm. Then the other arm. Then whatever was remaining. He wielded his sword two handed, sending arcs of bright scarlet into the humid air, drowning the heat shimmers.

An enraged Barros continued chopping, long after Shoor had stopped moving.

In a short time, the fury began to ebb. Barros slowed down, his limbs losing strength. His shoulders slumped. He staggered back a few steps, letting his bloodied blade hang from one hand. As if awakening from a dream, Barros regarded the speechless crowds, then the mutilated carcass at his feet.

The stunned onlookers, including a dumbstruck Orator, made not a sound.

*

HOUSE OF PAIN

From where he watched, a smile of evil delight curved the corners of Grisholt's mouth. He gripped the iron flask and eyed it with newfound interest.

Things had suddenly become very, *very* good.

32

The rumbling voices of thousands broke over the towering heights of brick archways and stout oak timbers, cascading down Vathian marble and Sunjan murals and rolling into the streets surrounding the Pit. At times, the air exploded with mighty blasts of jubilation, exclamations of sound announcing something grand had just transpired within that stony bowl of blood sport. Garl gazed in the direction of the arena at the end of the street and wondered, but usually he tried to ignore it and just listen to conversations... and mind the shadows.

He leaned against a thick slab of wood, which was also the rear wall of a water merchant's stall, balancing the fine act of appearing unconcerned yet listening for everything. Dirt coated his new clothes, and Garl inwardly wondered where he'd gotten the dust bath. He supposed it helped him blend in with the refuse besieging the streets.

He watched for any armed people who weren't Skarrs, either going to or leaving the arena, or anyone closing in on his personal space. Voices talking about pit fighters gave him pause. Old men who lounged at wooden tables discussing wagers and prospects regularly caught his attention. Passersby not even attending the games might very well know something about a particular gladiator. Once, a very long time ago, in the merchant's square, he'd learned how a group of fighters for the House of Vandu suffered from diarrhea, straight from a cook's mouth. Their opponents paid coin for that morsel of information.

However, Garl hadn't heard anything thus far about the House of Ten, nor any of its fighters.

In years past, Garl had had his favorite places to gather information—the streets and food-and-drink stalls surrounding the Pit, the taverns and alehouses after the day's matches; even lingering about the walls of the houses sometimes revealed valuable snippets that could be pieced together and used against an opponent or even sold for a few coins. Garl didn't like selling information as there was always the possibility that what he heard could be false, and then he'd be held responsible. There'd been instances where incorrect rumors had been released into the streets, just so the right ears would catch it at the most fitting time. It had happened in the past to people like Borchus. Sometimes the best bites contained poison, every bit as vicious and deadly as battling on the sands. Truths and lies.

Garl had once loved the challenge of the games, the bloody spectacle of the arena, but the loss of a leg by an axe and his resulting downfall had forever changed him. Now, the idea of individual combat for the amusement of thousands was madness, especially with a war raging somewhere to the west and north. He'd seen the games once as a boy, introduced to the season by his own departed mother and father. Why they had taken their only son to such revelry of violence, Garl would never know. Life was hard enough without having to watch men butcher each other. His time on the streets of Sunja had only strengthened that belief.

But this work meant another chance at life. Though he didn't care for the spectacle of the season, Garl didn't mind gathering information on the games, which meant coin in his hand and eventually a chance to leave Sunja, perhaps to start over. He'd have to leave. Borchus had seen to that the moment he convinced Garl to work for him once again. Once Garl decided it was time to get out, he would have to leave or perish. There weren't too many old spies about, but there were plenty of vengeful houses.

Something clattered behind him, and Garl flinched, froze, and caught a look of surprise from the gray-haired woman managing the stall he was leaning against, her sun-leathered face seeking the source of the noise. In a nearby alley, a young boy stooped to pick up a wooden crate from where it had fallen. Garl watched the youth stack the box on top of a pile of refuse, watched him hold out a steadying hand in case it fell over again, and waited until the youngster disappeared from sight.

Once he was gone, Garl tucked his crutches in his armpits, rose, and walked off at a casual pace for fear of the ruckus attracting undue attention. Though the very fibers of his mind screamed at him to bolt, he forced himself to not hurry, to at least *appear* at ease. He scanned both sides of the street, searching for any beggars who might recognize him, who might point a finger. He knew where they usually lurked, and he took care to avoid those areas. Still, with the game he played now, with the physical condition he was in, he had to be extra cautious of where he went and whom he might talk to, despite what Borchus

HOUSE OF PAIN

might have said about protecting his back. The agent was presently nowhere in sight, and Garl was a crippled man. Cripples were memorable. The paranoid part of his mind whispered they were *very* memorable, and one wrong move could attract unwanted attention.

Borchus—a ghost from his past if there ever was one. Garl mostly believed the story of why the man had fled the city so many years ago, but he wasn't certain if he entirely trusted the agent. Trust barely existed in the undercurrents of Sunja, where the homeless dwelt, where hellions preyed, where a scrap of food or drink could be in hand one moment and yanked away the next. The question of *why* Garl was doing this work again rose, and he scolded the inner voice with the answer, hoping to convince it for once and for all. It wasn't because he wanted to do it, it was because—after being beaten and left bleeding for so many times; after countless meals of scraps picked out of the dirt where others had thrown them; after being ignored by the populace, scowled at as a nuisance, or threatened with violence; and after years of simply surviving as opposed to living…

Borchus had offered him the opportunity to be a person with a purpose once again—even, Garl dared to think it, a person with *hope*.

His crutches dug into his armpits as he swung along a road, keeping close to one side, within the shadows cast by drooping eaves or extended tarps. In a short time, he circled back to the arena, sizing up its brooding magnificence with furtive peeks, and aimed for a row of food stalls set along the Gate of the Sea. He found a niche between a pair of booths and plopped down, easing his crutches off to one side. The gate was just to his right.

Moments passed, and eventually, a stream of people

exited, returning to their lives.

Garl waited and listened. Some people lingered around the booths, spending a few coins before heading home, presumably. Others stood and ate, dropping their crumbs onto the ground. Garl saw some bread crusts and remembered he had a small loaf back in the cellar with a small chunk of cheese, all waiting to be washed down with either water or the bottle of Sunjan Gold Borchus had purchased. Seeing the unwanted nibbles being tossed onto the ground made him anxious for some reason, and for several heartbeats, he couldn't reason why.

Then he realized he was staring right at it.

The scraps.

He had once *begged* for scraps.

Dread swelling in his chest, Garl got to his foot and crutches, heart now hammering in his chest. He struggled to maintain a casual air, but he desperately wanted to flee. He slipped out from behind the stalls and studied the clutter of bodies, deciding on the best path to take, trying to see everything at once.

His heart skipped several beats.

There, through the thinning crowds, appeared two beggars, reaching out with empty hands, pleading as citizens walked by.

Garl got moving, perhaps faster than he wanted, and wound his way back, away from the Gate of the Sea and the pair of vagrants. He wove through crowds and horse-drawn wagons, placing anything between him and those who might recognize him. The slabs of cut stone flashed by as he kept his head down, and he took only a few more hops before swinging himself down an alley. He turned several corners before placing his back against a white brick wall, peeking back the way he had traveled then looking ahead to the end of the alley.

Nothing.

No one.

Garl inhaled, his dark eyes wide and searching as he mentally navigated just where he was in relation to the safety of the cellar. In avoiding the beggars, he'd have to loop around and backtrack a bit—out of his way, but it was safer, and he knew the stone-fitted streets of Sunja.

His breath hitched in his throat as Strach walked past the alley's mouth.

Garl froze for a frenzied flutter of heartbeats. His bladder almost let go. He pressed against the wall and willed himself not to move, hoping he'd caught his whimpers and wishing he could just disappear. At best, he hoped to blend in with the city folks milling around him.

Strach!

The man resembled a tall poleaxe that had been crooked at the midway point—lanky but deceptively powerful with a vise-like grip, which Garl had personal knowledge of, having experienced those hands around his neck once before.

Men and women passed by Garl, not noticing how the man's eyes darted with fright or how the apple of his throat bobbed.

The tall thug known as Strach backed up to the mouth of the alley and stared down its winding length glutted with people, his predatory senses suddenly afire. Underneath a slicked mane of tin-gray hair, his sun-leathered face squinted with a question, and he lingered, his attention caught by something seen out of the corner of his eye. Citizens flowed past the splitting rock of his form, and he stood there, looking, smelling, *searching*.

In the end, he let it go. Sunja's Pit pulled him away.

Garl waited for moments more, breathing, his right hand trembling along the length of crutch he had prepared to swing if Strach returned and cornered him.

But the man didn't.

Eventually composing himself, Garl took a chance to look again and saw that the man had walked on. Images and stories of how Strach had terrorized beggars—besides Garl's own experiences—rattled all thought and got him moving. He swung out from his hiding place, merging with passersby, and concentrated on escaping.

Any district where Strach roamed was cursed for the one-legged spy.

Twisting his way back, Garl put space between him and the sighting and started to relax. Feeling he'd escaped a brutal beating and perhaps avoided the loss of a few particularly fleshy items of importance to him, he got his bearings and decided to continue on to a nearby alehouse, keeping amongst the flow of Sunja's citizens.

The evening sun had turned the sky orange when Garl finally sat on a bench under the open window of an alehouse. Smells of cooking pork and chicken wafted outside, making him realize he was hungry. Conversation came as a muddled din of noise, but Garl sat and eyed passersby while concentrating on picking out anything of interest: talk about women, some louder talk about the serving wenches, and talk about the day's fights.

Garl homed in on that one, tilting his head toward the window while separating the sounds from the street.

Fighters. The men talking were pit fighters.

Shouting drowned out the speakers, and Garl ground his jaw with frustration. Then the noise subsided, and he heard the same men once more.

Garl listened, frowning, and then his eyes bulged. The

men talked about the House of Ten and the decree of Curge. They prattled on for a short time, glad they weren't associated with the targeted house, and swore at that bunch of Free Trained who thought they could rise above anything else. The conversation went off into other areas, and Garl strained to hear more, but the knowledge he'd learned poked at him like a pointed stick, urging him to report back to Borchus.

Excited he'd learned something important and fearful of Strach lurking somewhere nearby, Garl stood and, with a quick inspection of the streets, started back to the cellar.

33

The day after the rains, the House of Ten's pit fighters limbered up with stretches under bright rays of morning light. Machlann shouted out instructions while Koba stalked the perimeter, searching for poor technique. From the balcony overlooking the grounds, Goll and Clavellus watched, their features barely discernible in shade, where the humidity still leeched away strength.

In front of the living quarters, at the other end of the training area, three men sat on mats, bundled up in swaths of bandages and crude splints. Gobs of healing salves smeared over their flesh kept away bothersome flies. They stared at the morning's exercise in reflective silence.

"So…" Halm finally said, feeling how the bandages tightened about his chin when he spoke. He tried very hard to not breathe through his broken nose. A part of him wished that Shan had given him more of whatever concoction had rendered him senseless for a day. The healer said it was for the best after he'd addressed the gaping bite in his arm. The ghastly wound had missed vital tendons, but a sizeable chunk of fat had been chomped out… so Shan only lathered in the foul-smelling ointments he so heavily favored. That morning, Halm had awoken with the others, drunk a vegetable broth for breakfast, and then left the common room for the thin comfort of the three mats waiting in the shade.

"This is what you've been doing?" the Zhiberian finished, his back resting against the outer wall of the living quarters.

"Aye that," Muluk answered, sitting to his left.

"Mm," Pig Knot grunted in the affirmative, seemingly deep in thought to the left of the Kree. His arms lay close by his sides as if they might somehow lengthen his legs. "This is it."

On the sands, Machlann droned on with instructions, and the gladiators followed.

"Could be worse," Halm supposed, but he couldn't think how—except perhaps being dead.

"You missed the fight yesterday," Muluk informed him. "That one there. Torello and the big one called Sapo. Almost came to blows."

"Over what?"

"The big one has no wind to speak of," Muluk confided. "And Torello couldn't resist making jokes of him. Sapo doesn't have a sense of humor. Not like Pig Knot."

Halm leaned forward just enough to catch Pig Knot's withering eye.

"What?" the Sunjan demanded.

"Nothing. Just taking a look. Not meaning anything by it," Halm answered.

Pig Knot put his attention back on the men, watching

how they moved about on strong legs.

"What's your take on these lads?" Halm settled back, feeling the aches of his many hurts. His hand felt the fresh layer of bandages covering the cuts where the stitches had burst. Shan hadn't been impressed with the breakage in the least.

"Well, that's a mouthful," Muluk admitted and rubbed his bush of black hair. "That Sapo one is damn angry about something. *Intense* is the word, and you didn't see it, but he and Machlann got into a tussle a few days back. That was something. That war goat is every bit as harsh as his voice and no slouch with the steel. He put that Sunjan on his ass in the sand and left him there with a warning."

"Did he now?" Halm asked, interested.

"Hard to believe, eh? Aye, he did, and I think in doing so, he damn near frightened the rest of them close to pissing. That Torello is a bit of a nuisance. The only time he isn't talking, it seems, is when he's out of breath. Kolo follows him around like he's unfit in the head or something."

"Not daisies, are they?"

Muluk shrugged and winced. Halm noted his friend's discomfort. Long bandages covered Muluk's shoulder and bound up his back. How he survived his battle with the murderous alehouse thieves would be talked about at tables in the years to come.

"No idea. Don't think so. Torello just might be the one that does the thinking for both of them, and for whatever reason, Kolo is content to listen. Not that it's a bad thing. The lad's pleasant enough."

"Hmm. What say you, Sunjan?" Halm asked, trying to pull Pig Knot into the conversation.

"About what?"

"The new lads."

"Whatever Muluk says is my mind as well."

"Trusting one, now, aren't you?"

"Right now, there's only two people I trust in this entire villa, and they're both beside me," Pig Knot muttered, not taking his eyes off the morning exercises.

"Not even Shan?" Muluk asked.

"All right, three then."

"Goll?" Halm inquired.

Pig Knot rolled his eyes. "Saimon can bleed that one. Untrustworthy dog blossom."

The curse silenced the pair, and they joined in watching. Their attention immediately went to the towering figure of the one called Brozz. The trainers directed the fighters to weighted swords and shields and paired them with wooden practice men. Machlann had them improve upon their two-strike combination and added a third, and the morning air soon clattered with every connection. Where the others still hacked, Brozz's weapon snaked in and out with a fluidity both Machlann and Koba noticed.

"He knows how to swing that," Halm observed.

"Look at the Perician on the end, then." Muluk nodded.

Halm did and beheld, for the first time, the wonder named Junger.

He was holding back—that much became clear to Halm right away. The Perician didn't just swing, he *flowed* without effort in his strikes, filling the space between Brozz's connections with two of his own. Junger reminded Halm of a set crossbow being loosed, only to be smoothly primed almost immediately. Where the others strained, reset, and freely sweated, Junger seemed at ease.

"Sweet Seddon," Halm breathed, impressed.

"He's a handful," Muluk agreed.

"Where did Goll find him?"

"Same place as the rest," Muluk replied. "In general quarters. A hole we all know it is, but something tells me there was at least one Free Trained shagger that could potentially put a house gladiator in the ground. Just look at him. You think with speed like that he'd lack power, but he's smashing that poor stick bastard. I dread to see what he might do to flesh and blood."

Halm couldn't help but be impressed. Junger's display almost made him forget his hurts. He'd been cut up so badly that Goll decided he should heal before ripping himself apart in training. In any case, he was glad to be on the side and merely watching rather than going through drills next to the blur of Junger.

After a short lunch, the training continued into the afternoon, with Clavellus directing Machlann and Koba to take the six men to the center of the sands.

"*Eee* now just watch," Machlann growled and hefted a wooden sword. He stood before Koba, who had taken up a sword and shield. The trainer showed how to thrust, high and low to the body. "Don't go for the head unless it's clear you can stab it, else go for the body. Thrust with the arm, snapping it out while straightening your arm, like so—" Machlann rapped the point of his weapon off Koba's shield. "Seek more power with the upward thrust while stepping into it. Wait until you are in close, then get your weight behind it and put a hand's length of steel into his guts. If he's at midrange, step forward and twist your shoulders for extra power, and make that punce wish he'd never heard your name. Like so."

Again the show.

"Ensure your feet are no wider than your shoulders. And if you lunge, don't over-extend, or by Saimon's pisspot, I'll brain you. Never lunge at your foe unless he's already half dead on his feet. Too many things can go wrong if you throw yourself at him like a spear. With any thrusting, know the length of your weapon, get within striking range, and stick it—straightening the arm, driving it up from your hip, or twist the shoulder. Stick it in, see what happens, and get out of there."

"Your missus teach you that, did she?" Torello asked, smirking with sweat rolling off his person. The quip was so well timed, the other five men—even the stoic Brozz—smiled at the joke.

Machlann scowled hard enough at the Sunjan to dissolve his delight at having amused his sword brothers.

"Torello, you might very well die sputtering on the sands tomorrow or the day after, but until then, you're mine, and I'm going to run you through Saimon's hell," Machlann growled, and proceeded to demonstrate thrusting three times, withdrawing after illustrating each separate attack.

"Now, line up and strike at Koba and make it count. And Torello, I swear by Seddon's rosy ass, if you even *grunt* the wrong way, Koba has my permission and full support in swinging *back*."

Unimpressed, the Sunjan glanced at his companions and concentrated on the task ahead.

They lined up, one after the other, and took their turns stabbing at Koba, which he dutifully turned aside.

"Good," Machlann cried out at times. "Kolo, more snap in the arm. Think on that next time you come around. *Eeee* Sapo, still wishing for that axe? Don't look at me with love in your eyes. Get away. Get away. In there, Brozz, get in there, you tall, sinister-looking punce. That's it. Hmm. Stop. *Stop!*"

Machlann held up a hand before Junger could set his feet and attack.

"Perician, you *strike* that shield, understand?" Machlann commanded. "Koba will stop it. But you don't hold anything back. Understand?"

A stoic Junger nodded and focused on an equally impassive Koba. And all attention intensified on the pair, just to see what would become of the command.

Machlann dropped his hand, and Junger *lunged*.

The wooden sword flashed forward like an unleashed ballista missile. It clapped Koba's shield and splintered upon impact, making everyone jump. Koba staggered back from the force of the blow, arms spiraling for balance, face a mix of disbelief and shock. All eyes went to Junger. The man had already recovered in a sorcerous display of speed, shattered sword still in hand, standing at ready guard with his expression muted and without a trace of haughtiness.

Koba inspected his shield and touched a crack in its surface. In the awed silence, Machlann studied the Perician's fragmented wooden shaft for a moment before turning and regarding an astonished Clavellus on his balcony.

A pensive Goll did not share the enthusiasm.

"Get yourself a new sword, lad," Machlann said quietly.

"You see that?" Clavellus asked, leaning back from the balcony's railing.

"Mm," Goll grunted, eyeing the splintered sword. Junger even bent down to gather up the shards while the other gladiators stood and watched in quiet wonder.

HOUSE OF PAIN

"That isn't the word I would use," Clavellus remarked with a chuckle and gently swished his mug around. "And that wasn't even a word. I'd use something else entirely."

"What would you use, then?"

Clavellus took a drink before answering and made a dismissive wave. "I'm not certain. The moment's gone. But I know it wouldn't be just a grunt. That's practically an insult to what we've just witnessed. I've trained warriors for over thirty-two years, Master Goll. Thirty-two. Feel that number for a moment. I've seen naturals, and I've seen men grow into their own. Seen some wondrous displays of skill-at-arms and some incidents that will never happen again. Smashing a shield and breaking a practice sword like that isn't something a person witnesses every day."

"Well, I suppose I'm not so easily impressed."

Clavellus held his tongue for a moment, his left hand quivering at his side until he made a fist. "No. I suppose not. Well, there's still a way to go, but if I were a man to place wagers, I'd place my coin on *that* one."

"Hmm."

This time, Clavellus directed his full attention to the sullen Kree. "Is there something wrong? Something I should know?"

"Not at all," Goll answered, his dark gaze lingering on the fighters as Machlann commanded them to resume attacking Koba, who had replaced his shield. "I just think you're making a fuss over one random occurrence. Nothing more."

The old trainer smiled, revealing teeth usually hidden under his thick beard. "Well then, Master Goll, let's see if that... *random* occurrence should happen a second time, shall we?"

I'm fine with that idea, Goll replied by way of screwing up his face.

Clavellus rubbed at his beard. "Machlann!"

"Aye, Master Clavellus?"

"When the Perician has his turn again, see if he can do the same once more."

"Aye that."

Clavellus regarded Goll with a mischievous twinkle in his eye. He dared guess that the Kree swordsman was attempting very hard to appear outwardly calm, though the tension in his posture was as obvious as any of the bandages on his arms or person.

"Do it again," Machlann said below.

Junger nodded, focused on Koba while the trainer stood behind his fresh shield and adjusted his own stance.

Then Junger's arm lashed out like a bolt of fire, cranking into the barrier and again knocking Koba off balance. The wooden sword did not break that time, but the Perician once again had split the shield in two. Koba composed himself and inspected the barrier, shaking his head and pointing to the sinewy breach. He then tossed the shield to the ground and fetched another.

"Again?" Junger inquired calmly.

"When your turn comes about, lad. No rush," Machlann answered, his natural growl subdued after the repeated display. Junger circled to the rear of the line while the others stepped up and tried to stagger the younger trainer off his feet. Despite the seriousness in their expressions and best efforts, none came close.

"Well?" Clavellus asked, interested in the Kree's response.

"I'm not impressed," Goll said, eyes narrowed and gazing to the ramparts of the far wall.

This perplexed the old trainer. "And why is that, Master Goll?"

The clatter of strikes resumed below. "You don't see it?"

"What is it I'm not seeing?"

Goll fixed him with a hard, unflinching look. "I expected better from you, Master Clavellus. Much better."

"What *is* it?"

Goll only just suppressed the displeasure in his voice. "He struck the shield only."

"He was told to do…"

Clavellus's beard hid his mouth dropping open. Dying Seddon above. The Kree might just be on to something. Goll believed, and rightly so, Junger *could* have struck Koba, as the drill had been intended, despite the trainer's best efforts to defend himself. But Junger didn't do that.

Machlann ordered him to strike the shield, and Junger, by Seddon above, did exactly as he was told… but he could've done *more*.

Clavellus studied the young pit fighter closer this time around. Machlann, Koba, they *all* had their suspicions, but now it was becoming abundantly clear.

Junger, the Perician, was only playing.

34

With the day's heat hammering on their sweltering forms, Machlann and Koba got the recruits on their feet and taught them close-quarter tactics for bringing down a man. Koba took the center of the sands and invited the black-bearded Vathian, Tumber, to dance with him. They crossed swords, and Koba demonstrated how a man could be knocked off balance by slapping Tumber's hand away and sending him into the sands.

Torello barked laughter and drew hard looks from the others.

To Goll's left, Clavellus shook his head. "Always one." He lifted his silver mug.

Goll remembered the leverage technique, having learned it from Machlann and Koba himself. Then a household guard followed the brick path marking the boundary of the sands, diverting his attention. One of Clavellus's gate keepers, he carried a scroll case.

"What's that you have there?" Clavellus called down to

the man.

"Message from the city."

"Really?" the trainer gave Goll an *imagine that* look that might have been three parts wine. "Toss it up here, then."

"I can bring it up."

"And have you track sand and dirt across my floors? My good lad, it's best my wife only trounces me this day and not you."

Clavellus motioned for Goll to catch the scroll, and the guard lobbed it into his hands.

"Who's it for?" Clavellus called down as Goll inspected the case.

"Master Goll, Master Clavellus."

"From Borchus, no doubt," the taskmaster muttered.

"I'm glad he remembered me," Goll said drily.

"Oh." Clavellus blinked, showing eyes practically red from the wine. "He remembered *you*. Have no doubts about that. That lad—well—let's just say there's little that escapes his attention."

"Or mine," Goll said, suddenly tight-lipped. But Clavellus didn't pay any heed as he'd gone back to watching the technique drill below. With a sigh, Goll opened the case and unrolled the message. His eyes became slits.

"What is it?" Clavellus asked after another sip of his drink.

Goll held out the scroll. The taskmaster regarded it and then Goll before taking the parchment, his beard moving as he read to himself. When he finished, he rubbed his mottled head with his shaking hand.

"Seems like the House of Curge doesn't want us to prosper at these games. At all." Goll frowned.

"This is because of me," Clavellus huffed sadly. "For

what happened years before. I'm sorry."

Machlann shouted at someone below, but Goll barely heard it. "No. This has nothing to do with you, so feel no blame, but we now have a problem. Curge has effectively turned the entire Pit against us with his bounty."

"The Free Trained," Clavellus corrected. "Just the Free Trained for now. Though, admittedly, it might very well extend to all houses. In their eyes, this is a hole of Free Trained warriors, a den of bare-assed dogs thinking they now have value. Daresay there isn't a house in Sunja too pleased about us competing in their games, and with the season almost half over. They can't protest it with the Chamber as that lot's already taken your gold, so they do what's left to them. Hunt our men in the arena. There're too many houses to fight, and we have only... six. Seven if the Zhiberian can still manage. The blood matches will entangle and ruin us... "

"I'm not worried about the blood matches," Goll said. "In truth, a man has to be ready to gut his opponent in the Pit. The blood matches only clear the intentions of both fighters."

"That's true," Clavellus reluctantly agreed. "But blood challenges take precedence over all other matches. And the house can directly assign whoever they think can kill the offending fighter. Or in this case, the chosen target. The way I see it, there's only one way to deal with this."

"Not compete?" Goll asked.

Clavellus wrinkled his nose as if he'd smelled something foul. "No, not that. They're probably *wishing* we won't compete. Probably think we're cowering right now. No. I think we should go the other way. Throw some of that fear back at them. The Free Trained are only individuals. While there are potential upsets, that one element has always been their weakness. There's no house behind them. The House of Ten will fight only Free Trained warriors on its first official day of competition, Free Trained brutes who'll be hunting for the seven heads we send onto the sands. I suggest we respond with our own message… and butcher whoever stands against us. Like it or not, the remainder of this season will be a chore in convincing doubters that the Ten belong in the games—that the house is a legitimate adversary."

Cries and grunts of exertion rose from the men training below. A pensive Goll barely nodded, deep in concentration. "I agree."

"Good."

"You can tell the men exactly that."

Clavellus nodded.

"But tell them nothing about the bounty."

That drew a look from the taskmaster. "What?"

"They don't need to know. Preparing to the best of their ability is all that's important to them now."

"They need to know."

"Why?" Goll challenged. "Tell our fighters they'll face Free Trained dogs that will likely attempt to kill them, so kill them in return. Our message that the House of Ten will fight all challengers is still conveyed to whoever is watching. Telling our lads that their foes are aiming to cut their hearts out is one thing, but if you say the entire *might* of the arena is out to kill them, that there's coin offered for our heads, well… that fear would cripple them. And… I'm not sure all would remain with us."

"You think they would desert?" Clavellus asked, sensing the answer even as he spoke it.

Goll nodded. "They joined because of a hurried speech and a promise. Training. Food and a bed. To just get out of the hell of general quarters. I'm not certain of who is serious, who is committed, and who is only biding his time until the season is over. But we need *someone* to send out on the sands, to attract more fighters for the seasons to follow. To make our presence felt and to show we care nothing about what comes forth from other houses. We have our name; now we must establish our will and our skill at arms—our reputation. If we tell our men about the price on their skulls, I'm not sure who will stay or flee. Perhaps none. Perhaps all. If it's even *half*, the embarrassment will become history. The House of Ten will crumble. Would you rather be known as the house that defied the Pit on their first day of competition or the one that didn't even peek around the corner? I know my choice. And I'd rather risk their lives first."

Clavellus carefully absorbed this. "So you wish to say nothing?"

"To our men? About this bounty?" Goll let it hang in the air before answering. "Aye that. Not a word."

"They'll find out. If not us, from others. On the first day."

Goll considered that. "By then, hopefully, we'll have built up their courage enough not to care."

That thought silenced Clavellus.

"Make the announcement," Goll instructed them. "Tell the lads they take to the sands in four days. Then let us talk of weapons, armor, and these men we'll be facing. And any other preparations to be made."

*

Torello and Sapo got paired up with each other, crossed wooden swords, and put their strength into it. With Koba watching in the background, the huge Sunjan slapped Torello's fist with his free hand and sent the man sputtering into the dirt.

He quickly sprang up. "What was that? What gurry was that? Are you trying to break my damn wrist?"

"That's the drill," Tumber hissed between taking turns with Brozz.

But Torello ignored that. "The practice isn't breaking *bones*, maggot shite. If you want to play hard, then by Seddon's crack, I'll play *hard!*"

Torello stepped into Sapo's personal space, red faced and fuming.

The larger Sunjan didn't appreciate the closeness, and with a contemptuous snarl, he shoved the smaller man back.

A suddenly stern Kolo disengaged Junger and strode toward the towering Sapo, intent on lending a hand if need be.

Sapo backed up a step, ready to take them both on.

And Machlann started screaming.

The rusty yelling of the old trainer caught Ananda by surprise, and she started at the sound, making Pig Knot think she was about to drop the pitcher of wine she carried.

"Best let me have that." He smiled as best he could manage under his bandages, his hands darting forward and grabbing her own. The soft skin of her tiny hands and wrists under his large, calloused paws made him hold on all the longer.

Ananda turned back to him and smiled with embarrassment. "Apologies, Master Pig Knot—the yelling startled me."

On the training grounds, Machlann had all the involved

men waddling like ducks from one end to the other.

"Lads," Pig Knot said soothingly, still holding onto her wrists. "That's what they do. One gets a little ripe at the other, and fists start flying. What can one do?"

Ananda smiled, and Pig Knot returned it. He gave her hands a quick rub and a pat and took the pitcher from her.

"Still, I'm grateful for it."

"Why's that?"

"Any opportunity to hold the hands of a pretty flower like yourself is one to take."

Ananda stared at him for a moment, unable to reply, and then she broke into an adorable smile and giggle before walking away.

Pig Knot watched her go, his eyes on her flimsy white robes, which just barely concealed her womanly figure underneath.

"Slick as greased pig shite," Muluk muttered next to him. "I'll warn her about you next time."

"You hardly know me," Pig Knot replied, nodding at Ananda when she abruptly looked back at him and smiled once more.

"I know you," Halm said on the other side of Muluk, "so *I'll* warn her."

"You're jealous you didn't act before I did. A cripple like myself has to do something for amusement."

"I can see you're amused," Halm remarked drily.

"I'm right and proper worried," Pig Knot countered. "The only honey pot worth looking at in this entire place is serving us, and you two'd rather watch a bunch of near-naked kogs, sweating and grunting over each other. You tell me what's right and what's wrong here."

"Slick as greased pig shite," Muluk muttered, looking onward.

HOUSE OF PAIN

Pig Knot returned to watching the training, catching the warning eye of a menacing Koba. He was in the middle of overseeing a drill, and the momentary distraction of what was happening with Ananda brought puzzled looks from the pit fighters waiting for instruction.

This time, a sly Pig Knot nodded and winked in the trainer's direction.

And Clavellus called for the attention of all of them.

35

The days leading up to the House of Ten's opening fights became punishing.

After Clavellus announced when they would be fighting, Machlann called the day's training finished and allowed them to collapse where they stood. The fighters wandered off toward the waiting baths and food, but as they left the grounds, Machlann warned them to rest well, for the next few days would be hell.

And he did not lie.

In the following days, Halm, Pig Knot, and Muluk sat on their mats and watched and mulled and commented. They witnessed—under the oftentimes painful tutelage of Machlann and the just-as-punishing eye of Koba— the men evolving. It came slowly and at times with a verbal lashing from the old trainer, but it was there, both fascinating and rousing to see.

They wore the armor they'd be wearing in battle on fight day. Brozz was the only one with armor that fit his huge size while Sapo had leather pieces stitched together for his large frame—only leather, as Goll informed them they hadn't the coin to afford better. The same went for their weapons, and Sapo was still denied an axe, much to his chagrin.

Slowly, the recruits gradually corrected their mistakes, learning new techniques and evolving into more effective warriors. Halm, Pig Knot, and Muluk observed the lads' shortness of breath ebbing, clumsy strokes becoming sharp, wasted movements being erased and becoming measured and fluid. Combinations went from single and two strokes to three and often four. Machlann's barking even seemed to lessen at times.

Junger was a wonder to behold, clearly much more than anyone might have suspected or could even believe. Brozz was no slouch himself, but where he and the others could only learn and improve, Junger shone. Excelled.

He even inspired.

"What do you think?" Muluk had asked his sitting companions one blistering afternoon, while the six recruits practiced.

"I think," Halm answered honestly, "that our Free Trained brothers will regret taking up steel against us."

The morning of the day before their first round of matches, the men of the House of Ten gathered themselves and their equipment almost solemnly and loaded everything into three wagons. Pig Knot and Muluk remained behind on Shan's orders, though they both plainly wished to accompany their sword brothers and take the sands. Halm waddled to the wagons and hefted himself into the rear with forced humor, only paying partial heed to the healer Shan.

They arrived at the great city near noon, and Goll directed the wagon drivers to deposit them at the house of Shan. The quarters for the large group of men lodging overnight were tight but bearable, despite the complaining looks from Shan's wife.

While the fighters rested from their journey at the house, Clavellus elected to stay indoors with the imposing Koba nearby, as well as the three once-Sujins Goll had hired. Goll and Machlann wandered to the Pit and descended to the lower levels. As they enjoyed recognized house status, Machlann showed him the way bypassing the hell known as general quarters and led him to their private viewing chamber, which looked out upon the arena from chest level.

Goll immediately went to the window, walking with a noticeable limp, and peered outside. The stands were filled, the day's fights half finished. Arena attendants set about raking the sands, covering up the bloody remnants of the previous fight. The day brightened considerably and threw a fearsome glare into the chamber.

"Master Machlann," a squinting Goll began quietly, watching the men go about their grooming. "Thank you for these last few days. I imagine it's trying on one's patience to work with such raw material."

Machlann cocked a questioning eyebrow at the house master. "At times."

"In all honesty, what do you think of their chances?"

"Our lads against Free Trained? Fair to average. With better odds for Brozz and Junger."

Goll accepted the trainer's opinion stoically, betraying nothing.

Sensing the short exchange finished, Machlann went

back into the corridor, leaving Goll to his thinking, but the trainer returned in short time.

"Any sign of Borchus?" Goll asked.

Machlann shook his head. "Here," he said, presenting a scroll.

"What's this?"

"The schedule for tomorrow's fights."

Goll's expression brightened a little as he took the scroll. It darkened upon reading.

"What?" Machlann asked.

"This has us fighting all on one day. Tomorrow."

Machlann's brow furrowed as he read what Goll showed him.

"The schedule's been altered."

"Can they do that?"

Just then, the door opened, and Borchus stepped through. The short man nodded and smiled at the scroll in their possession. "I gather you know the news already," the agent said.

"What's all this about?" Goll demanded.

Borchus shook his head. "I only noticed it yesterday. I inquired with the Madea, but he assures me there was nothing strange about it. Some fighters pulled out of their matches entirely, and he had to reschedule. Thought it grand that a new house fights all its opening matches in one day. Rather than exhaust a rider to bring you the news, I figured I'd save a few coins and inform you today upon your arrival."

"This smells of tampering," Machlann muttered.

"Certainly does," Borchus agreed. "But there's nothing I can do about it. The Madea's word is final. You're all here, and you have a day to rest before taking up arms. Nothing really changes."

Goll glanced over the schedule in his hand. "Halm's opponent is listed."

The Kree glanced toward the glare of archway.

"Someone called Targus."

*

"Targus?" Halm repeated, spitting out the name. "That can't be."

This perplexed Goll. "Why can't it be?"

Goll, Machlann, and Borchus had returned to Shan's crowded house to share the news of their matches happening the next day. The men, gathered on the ground floor and making the interior quite crowded, now quieted and watched the exchange between the pair of house masters.

"I know that man," Halm said, clearly confused.

"You know him?"

"Aye." The Zhiberian didn't sound so confident.

"Well, he's fighting you tomorrow. Perhaps you can talk to him then?"

That placed Halm on guard. "I'm not sure I care for your tone."

Goll's face darkened. His voice rose. "I'm not sure I care for where your mind is these days. Who is this Targus?"

"A Free Trained lad I drank with."

"You think of him as a friend?"

Halm shrugged awkwardly.

Goll nearly exploded. "Seddon above, I've just realized why it is you've never made a run of it in these games. You're too damn quick to *befriend* people. What gurry is that? This is *pit* fighting, you ugly bastard. Pit fighting!

Drink away whatever coin you have to your name if you want to sit and talk with other pit fighters. Have you ever thought perhaps one of them might have been thinking about fighting you all along? Perhaps attempting to shock you into making a mistake once the portcullis came up? This is blood sport, you stupid he-bitch. Blood sport. There are no friends in this, only competitors."

Goll regarded the listening house fighters. "What do you think will happen if only two of you get matched up in the champion's match? What will happen when the world is expecting to see blood spilled? I'll tell you what will happen. You'll *fight*. You'll fight to the last breath. There are no friends in this. There's only the next topper being put into the ground."

An uneasy silence filled the room then, and not one looked at another. All eyes remained on the house master.

"I befriended you," Halm said in a quiet voice.

"I'm not your friend," an angry Goll shot back. "When have I ever called you that? Never."

Halm shifted uncomfortably. "I won't fight the lad, then," he stated, changing the subject.

"Oh, you'll fight him," Goll warned. "You'll fight. And all of you will watch. You'll see the consequences of making friends during the games, and you'll learn from this one's mistake. You'll fight, Halm of Zhiberia, and you'll do so as if he were one of Curge's minions coming after your throat. For all you know, he is."

"He isn't." But Halm didn't look or sound confident.

Shaking his head with contempt, Goll waved a hand at them all. "Get upstairs. Eat. Rest. If you venture outside, stay close to the door. Tomorrow, you all fight. And I pray there are no other surprises between now and then."

With that, Goll glared at Halm one last time and

headed out the door to the side street beyond.

Halm said nothing, and eyes were on his back as he turned and climbed the steps to the cots on the second floor.

Machlann exchanged knowing looks with Clavellus, and the taskmaster cleared his throat.

"Off with you, lads. Clear the space for Shan's poor wife and be mindful of the property. Think on what Master Goll has said, for it's the truth. There's no room for the notion of friendship on the arena floor. There's every possibility of crossing blades within the confines of the Pit. Especially if you associate with those of other houses. These are the games. This is the profession, and that's the risk you all take. And you—you and your adversaries tomorrow are all merchants…"

He paused, considering his next words carefully.

"Of pain."

36

The dawn came too soon for Goll. He was anxious for the morning and barely slept a wink. With the amount of snoring amongst them all packed into the second floor, sleep was a commodity hard to obtain. When the sun came up, he lay on his cot filled with fresh hay and a single rough blanket and stared at the ceiling's dark timbers—lines crossing lines, all nailed together.

Thoughts ran through the Kree's head. Halm had avoided him for the rest of the previous night, which was fine in Goll's mind. The Zhiberian's casual attitude was getting on his nerves and would only be the death of him. And as he was a founder of the House of Ten, Goll could not allow it. The man was a walking wound even now and, by all rights, should have dropped out of competition long before.

But he was going to fight. And he was going to win.

He had to win.

Lines crossing lines, he reflected, noting how dark the

ceiling's shadows were in the quiet mornings, with the sun peeking up over the featureless morass of irregular angles and crooks of rooftops.

Some lines would be crossed that day.

As a house, they ate, though not as heartily as Goll would have liked. Conversation was nonexistent, and even the normally jovial Halm became withdrawn. He answered questions with grunts and nods, and the men left him alone to think.

That pleased Goll. Finally, the Zhiberian was taking things seriously.

He only hoped it would be enough.

When the time came, Goll and Halm and Clavellus led the procession through the streets of Sunja to the waiting arena. Clavellus had instructed them all to hold their heads high and to project danger, for they were exactly that.

Dangerous.

People bustled alongside, shouts sprinkled the air, and work carried on. The sun leached sweat from bare skin and clothed backs. Not many paid the pit fighters any heed, not with their worn-looking armor and weapons. These days, the public didn't find it uncommon to see large gropus of armed men walking the streets. The House of Ten marched through them all, focused on their final destination and the work to be done.

They arrived at the Pit in due time and bypassed the general quarters to find their private chambers.

The interior felt cramped in accommodating them all.

HOUSE OF PAIN

Goll mused that it would be tight only for a short time anyway as wounds from each conflict sent men to the infirmary. The Ten's fighters prepared themselves in silence, helping each other check their armor when needed. Koba edged his bulk through them to lend a hand where needed while Clavellus and Machlann leaned against the open archway, the stone lip pressing against their chests, and looked out onto the battlefield to be. Above, people slowly filled the stands. The heat of the day pressed down and steamed the lot.

Goll stopped beside the taskmaster and trainer and gazed pensively out at the ancient walls and freshly combed sands.

"Nervous?" Clavellus asked.

Goll's sun-browned face darkened. "Course I am."

"You should say something to the lads."

Machlann nodded once, supporting Clavellus's suggestion.

"Not certain what to say."

"If you like, I can," Clavellus offered.

Goll considered it and finally nodded, keeping his eyes on the arena beyond the archway.

With the house master's leave, the taskmaster gathered himself and faced the men preparing for their individual wars. He cleared his throat, gaining their attention. Torello was speaking to Kolo when Tumber slapped his shoulder, earning a black glare—which dissipated upon seeing Clavellus.

"Something to say, have you?" the Sunjan asked brazenly.

"I do," Clavellus said, taking a moment to compose his thoughts. "I won't bore you with my history, but some time ago, I thought I'd never come back to this place.

Thought my career was finished. Some time ago, I never would've considered ever selling my services or my trainers to hammering the cow kisses of the Free Trained into pit fighters of quality. I hated the Free Trained—looked upon them as a joke, a brazen insult to the real games, meat to be slaughtered by tried gladiators. But this one," he swung a hand at Goll, "convinced me otherwise."

"How much convincing did it cost?" Torello asked. "That's my question."

"Shaddup," Tumber fired with a dangerous glare.

"We all want to know," Torello defended himself.

"The man's talking."

When Torello simmered down, an amused Clavellus met his glare. "How much? More than you'll ever know, you noisy, complaining bastard. And every pot of gold passed through my hands and on to my wife."

That tickled the lot of them. Even Sapo smirked.

"In the short time we've had together, I've been watching you all, studying your strengths, your weaknesses—watched how Machlann and Koba hammered at you, shaking the rust free and revealing the iron underneath. The trainers have imparted unto you all they could in this short time together. Goll and I have discussed you at length, and during those conversations, during those long days, I recognized something that I haven't felt in a very long time. Pride. And an eagerness to see what you can do once unleashed. For whatever reasons you came to us, I'm glad you did. I'm glad you're here. And before you think I'm greasing you up, think on this—I didn't recommend any of you to be cast aside. Why not? Because I saw something on the training grounds. Free Trained you once were, but Free Trained you are no longer. Though we've only just begun with your schooling, and though the beginning of this house is ripe for our adversaries' scorn, right now, before my old eyes, you are *gladiators*. You are shaped the same as any other claiming to belong to a house of note. You are *destroyers* of anyone with the bells to face you upon those sands. Those sands are *yours*. Defend them from all, and woe unto the poor bastard standing across from you, for this day, the House of Ten unchains her sons upon unsuspecting opponents, upon an unknowing, unsuspecting audience. When it's your time, you show them it was no mistake you came here this day. You show them your spirit."

Clavellus paused and met each set of eyes, captivating them all, inspiring, and even earning a nod of approval from Junger near the back.

"You *show* them you belong."

Silence, as each man absorbed the taskmaster's words.

"Today, you fight Free Trained," Goll resumed, finding his voice while gazing out the archway. "They'll try to drag you back to their level. Don't allow them. They'll try to kill you for leaving their folds, for thinking yourselves better. Kill them first. This day, there are no survivors—only deaths, only messages, only promises… to those who are watching you, *judging* you. You show them."

Goll turned on a heel and regarded his fighters. Halm looked at the floor.

"The House of Ten is *not* to be taken lightly."

A fist rapped on the door, startling the spellbound men.

Koba answered it and nodded at an arena attendant outside. Words were spoken. The big trainer regarded those within the room then.

"Time," he said.

Tumber exhaled and walked to the door. His leather

cuirass, studded with knobs of brass, creaked softly as he moved. A small, square buckler edged with spikes adorned his left arm and appeared more like a strange saw, while he favored a broadsword in his right hand. The weapon was huge, long, and heavy looking—a chunk of edged steel with the sole purpose of hewing flesh and bone. Bracers and greaves of plain design had been strapped onto his muscular limbs, and he paused at the door, the iron face of his helm studying it for one dire instant.

"Tumber," Goll called.

The helm flicked toward the house master.

"No matter who faces you this day," the Kree declared grimly. "You kill him."

"Right and proper," Torello said from where he stood.

"Right and proper," Goll echoed, noticing how increasingly uncomfortable Halm appeared.

Tumber touched his encased forehead with the flat of his blade and exited the room.

*

Like three forgotten kings, Nexus, Gastillo, and Dark Curge sat and stewed in their viewing box and waited expectantly for the first fight of the day. Clouds moved in and blocked the sun and shrouded the entire spectacle of the Pit in a comforting shade—ideal weather for blood sport.

Curge's eyes lingered upon one end of the arena with enough intensity to melt its very foundation. His spies had revealed the archway where the House of Ten dwelt. *House of Ten,* he thought scornfully. Clavellus's defiant presence galled him to the point of strangling someone. The old bastard didn't heed Dark Curge's warning. He didn't stay away. Even had the bells to march through the city as if on parade, for everyone—including Curge's spies—to see. Bright Seddon above, Curge vowed to make the aged taskmaster pay, win or lose on the sands that day. He hated relying on Free Trained to do his bidding, but the calmness in his guts suggested all would work itself out nicely. Even, if Seddon heard his prayers, the bastard Zhiberian whose very existence continued to rot his craw.

"So tell me," Gastillo spoke up. "How did you arrange for all of the House of Ten to fight on one day?"

Nexus smirked with knowledge. "That, good Gastillo, is information I cannot reveal. But I'll tell you this, there are not many beyond my range of influence."

Or your shite flinging, Curge thought but kept it to himself.

"Old Clavellus is down there somewhere," Nexus damn near purred. "That must tickle you the wrong way, Curge."

"You once told me Clavellus trained your men," Curge replied without facing the wine merchant.

"Bah. I'll tell you anything to get your nose out of my affairs," Nexus admitted, leaning back in his chair and holding out a goblet to be filled.

"I only wish." Curge ignored the owner sitting an arm's length to his right. "I only hope the Free Trained embarrass the entire lot of them."

He had wanted the chair at the far side of the box, away from the punce Nexus, but to his horror, the wine shagger plopped down next to him. Though there was a sizeable gap between the chairs, Curge didn't want Nexus anywhere near him, for fear of tossing the merchant's pampered ass over the wall.

"I'm sure that sizeable bounty you offered will bring

out the teeth in the dogs. What do you say, Gastillo?"

The manager on the far end took his time answering. "I believe… we'll be witness to a statement this day. From one end or the other."

Curge rolled his eyes. Trust Gastillo to speak his mind yet say nothing at all.

The Orator took to his stage and began his introductions.

"Ah," Nexus said with interest. "Let the hammer fall, eh Curge?"

That time, the ogre-like owner unleashed a glare of such magnitude upon the silver-haired wine merchant that concern clouded Nexus's face. He quickly hid his ill ease behind a lengthy sip from his goblet.

The roar of the crowds brought Curge's attention back to the Pit.

*

Tumber gazed across the arena at his opponent. The pit fighter was a Sunjan called Bubruk, and Borchus didn't know much about him beyond his record of two victories and the weapons he used. Tumber could tell the man was confident just by his lack of armor. Only leather bracers, brass greaves, and a helmet with a face cage protected him while his upper legs and powerful-looking chest, already shiny with sweat, lay bare for all to see. A foul-looking blade with a distinct downward curve in its length filled his right hand while his left hand flexed a club with a single war spike. Tumber sighed. The lad seemed right eager to get started.

Right on the Orator's shout of *begin!* Bubruk strode toward him.

Raising his own chosen tools, Tumber ventured forth to meet his opponent.

They met in the center while applause showered over both. No words were spoken, for Tumber knew what he had to do.

He slashed with his sword, seizing the initiative and driving Bubruk to his right, where Tumber spun and lashed out with his fanged buckler.

Except Bubruk ducked.

And lunged forward, chopping with the curved sword and connecting with Tumber's knee. The Ten warrior buckled and dropped to the sands, throwing up his buckler to protect his head.

Exactly as Bubruk wanted.

The war club whistled down with frightful force and punctured the thin buckler and the limb attached to it. The tip of a bloody spike exploded from Tumber's forearm, setting it afire, gripping the warrior in a paralyzing vice of pain and astonishment.

Bubruk yanked back, digging in his heels, and dragged his foe off balance.

Tumber held onto his sword and flailed, splitting only a breeze, before he landed hard on his side and looked up…

*

From the arched window of the Ten's chamber, Goll felt his stomach knot up in dread right from the first exchange, and then it only became worse when Bubruk's wicked blade fell and half chopped Tumber's head from his neck in a juicy burst of scarlet. Like a wicked spider playing with a meal struggling in its web, Bubruk yanked Tumber's impaled arm again, stretching him out before hacking into his body. The crowds rose, cheering the victor on, and Bubruk responded by striking twice more before Goll lowered his eyes. He did not turn his head. Not with the remainder of his men in the room. Nor did Clavellus or Machlann speak. They stood beside him and watched the gory finish on the arena floor.

"What's happening?" Torello muttered anxiously somewhere behind. "What's the cheering about?"

"Did he win?" Halm asked.

"Sounds like someone did."

"Tumber killed him that fast?"

Goll exhaled and failed to shed the thousands of chains he suddenly felt heaped upon his shoulders. The days of practice had been short but intense, and to lose that time and effort poured into one man was disappointing. Gone. All gone. Never to be recovered. But even worse than the loss of life was the damage done to the house's name.

To have a gladiator killed by a Free Trained.

The hateful irony wasn't lost upon Goll.

The cheers from outside rose up like a blanketing curtain, and the Kree felt his aches and pains anew.

"No," he stated with a heavy voice, "Tumber's dead."

Those three quiet words stilled the questioning voices at his back while the crowds outside continued to lavish praise on the victor. Clavellus gripped the brick sill and shook his head in disbelief while a stoic Machlann stared on, his huge moustache as unmoving as the rest of him.

"Koba," Clavellus spoke discreetly, without falter, "see to it that they hold onto Tumber's body before… they burn him. With your approval," he aimed at Goll.

The Kree nodded, and the hulking trainer departed.

"Nothing's ever certain on the sands," the taskmaster stated, disappointment dragging down the whole of his face. He rubbed at his bearded chin.

Goll didn't need to be told what he already knew. He turned around and found the brooding face of Sapo. That one look projected everything Goll needed. Sapo nodded in understanding of what was before him.

The message delivered, Goll faced the arch once more and eventually heard the rap upon the chamber door.

*

When Bubruk smashed Tumber through the arm and hooked him off his feet, a slick smile stretched across Curge's face like juice tracing the folds of fat jowls. When the Free Trained viciously executed the house warrior on the sands, the smile became wider. The victory pleased him immensely, but by no means were the day's fights over. Six more of the House of Ten's he-bitches were scheduled to bleed on the arena floor. One of which was the Zhiberian. His death would be the pinnacle of the house's gutting.

"One," Curge growled.

"In better spirits now, I see?" Nexus asked slyly, gently swishing his goblet about.

"Much better, good Nexus."

37

Piecemeal leather armor covered Sapo, and he felt as light as a feather on a breeze. It wasn't a good feeling. He didn't like being near naked on the sands. It made him feel vulnerable. He'd taken plate armor from the Pit's quartermaster before, for his earlier matches, but since he represented the House of Ten, he was told not to do such. *Gurry,* he fumed. The armor was there and waiting, but because the house couldn't afford its own, he had to make do with what they did have. He certainly didn't like the sword and shield Machlann insisted upon him using, preferring the weight and devastation he could inflict with his axe. Still, his new masters felt they knew best, and even though it went against the Hill's instinct, he was willing to try to take out his frustrations on his opponent.

When Sapo's foe stepped into the light, his jaw dropped.

They called him Tevos, and Borchus had been able to discover a few items of note about him. The Free Trained warrior was Sunjan, agile on his feet, and quick to jump to the attack. Like Sapo, the man had donned an open-face helmet and a leather vest and had strapped on greaves and bracers. Tevos had amassed three victories in the Pit, and while most would have been impressed with the record, Sapo was not. He didn't know whom the punce had fought. None of those men had been him. In fact, none of the information Borchus had revealed had impressed Sapo.

But Tevos stole Sapo's attention the instant he appeared in the arena, leaving the big man shaking his head in stunned, indignant disbelief.

There, across the sands, Tevos brandished a battle axe.

A battle axe.

A double-bladed weapon that gleamed in the daylight, instilling fear.

That this whelp had the strength to even lift such a ferocious tool of war blackened Sapo's thoughts.

Sapo gazed down at the smaller man with the most frightening face he could summon. The sword he held in his right hand felt far too light; the few practice swings he took made him think he was whipping a branch instead of a real weapon. *Like that axe.* Compared to all others, he was the only *man* in the Pit while all others only pretended, and Seddon above, *he wanted that axe!*

The Orator bellowed introductions, and something in his voice reminded Sapo of Machlann's frayed drone, which had grated on his nerves for the last week. That furry little white mouse *shite* of a man needled him incessantly ever since besting him on the training grounds. That defeat smoldered in Sapo's mind like fire gone underground. The House of Ten wasn't a real house in his mind. It was more a means to getting out of the hole of general quarters until the conclusion of the games. One day, when everything was over, regardless of whether he was eliminated from the competition or not, he would find Machlann's sleeping quarters and wring the old bastard's scrawny neck until flesh and bone broke beneath his fingers. And the whole while, Sapo would stare into the man's eyes as the light faded from them, as his rattle of a voice died with a wheeze.

That was the gift Sapo intended to give himself. Perhaps even after this season.

But first, he'd kill this little cow kiss with the axe. Tevos was a brazen sort. As Sapo made a show of loosening up his limbs, Tevos actually had the nerve to mirror him. The Hill wasn't the only one to have noticed. Some of the people in the crowds laughed and shouted out.

"Gut that big bastard, Tevos, lad!"

"He's trying to outshine you!"

"What's this gurry, then?"

What *was* this gurry? Sapo wondered. Anger swelled within and fueled his arms. He roared, an unchecked bestial blast, interrupting the Orator, who shot a warning glare. Sapo stomped his sandaled feet into the sands, shook out his arms with even greater flourish, and became infuriated even more when Tevos *again* imitated him like some ridiculing monkey.

Begin! came the command, and Sapo charged across the Pit's expanse at his smaller foe. Tevos let him cross the floor, tensing up in anticipation of the clash to come.

Sapo closed in and brought his sword down in a heavy-handed cut, but Tevos darted out of harm's way while the crowd *oooh*ed. Tevos twisted around, and Sapo deflected his foe's answering cut with a well-timed swing of his shield. Tevos chopped twice more as if prodding for attention, catching only wood and iron and earning a rotten look from Sapo.

"Good!" Tevos shouted, nodding earnestly. "Good! Come on! Come on! Curge'll pay more for your head with this showing."

Sapo drew up for a moment, his fury momentarily abated. "What are you on about?"

"Your *head*, you mountainous pile of shite! The price on it! On *all* of you unfit bastards!"

Sapo's face contorted into angry confusion.

A bounty?

A bounty on *his* head?

And this mouse had the nerve to try to take it? *With an axe no less?*

Sapo's temper soared. He screamed and threw down his sword, wasting no further time with the hated thing. His hand shot out in raw fury, faster than Tevos or anyone watching expected, and clamped around the smaller man's neck. Fingers dug into flesh like spikes, crushing vertebrae, bringing blood. Tevos gurgled in shock and fear. His face purpled, nearly exploding, while his eyes bulged. He attempted to hack at Sapo's legs, but the big man grabbed the shaft of the battle axe and yanked it from his clutches with no more effort than stripping well-cooked meat off a bone.

Sapo shoved Tevos backward. The Free Trained warrior landed on his rump in a cloud of dust, a hand over his ruined neck. Blood seeped through his fingers.

Sapos hefted his true weapon of choice. The axe felt heavenly in his grasp, and he took a moment to twirl its killing doubled-bladed length before himself, gauging the weight, admiring the edges, the design. He wondered how he could have ever thrown aside such a godlike weapon for something so mundane as a sword. Holding it, relishing how natural it swung, Sapo knew he'd made a grave mistake.

But one that was correctable.

The crowds urged Sapo to fight, and taking a heartbeat to acknowledge them, Sapo turned upon Tevos's twitching form and sank the axe square into the fallen man's chest. Leather split. Blood spouted. Sapo wrenched the axe free of ribs and rained destruction down upon the smaller man.

He chopped Tevos apart.

Each impact of the axe summoned a collective gasp from the crowds. They recognized power when they saw it.

Sapo blasted the air with another fearsome cry and went insane.

Until his arms became slick with blood.

Victorious, Sapo scuffed a wave of sand over the carcass at his feet. He shook his new axe at the crowds and at the elite viewing box where the king would've been seated.

The crowds answered with a chorus of applause and derisive groans.

Sapo didn't hear any of it, for he scanned the baseline of the arena, where the sands met stone, searching the archways.

Until he located the faces he recognized.

Raw, undiluted anger still pumping through his veins, Sapo marched over to where a stunned Goll, Clavellus, and Machlann watched. He stopped five paces away and roared hatred at the three men, making himself heard above the tidal force of the crowds.

"You pack of dog blossoms! You know what that shite licker said to me before I smashed his head in? There's a *price* on my head! Curge put a price on it. On *all* of our heads! The House of Curge, no less! Bloody rotting *gurry*!"

A disturbed Machlann glanced at Goll and Clavellus, but the pair showed no surprise at all.

And that infuriated Sapo all the more.

"I'm leaving the House of Ten!" he yelled at them, froth spraying the air. "Done! I'm done with you and you and especially *you!*"

He finished by jabbing a meaty finger at Machlann. Koba loomed over the heads of the three masters, his brow cocked in an angry question, his snake-like scar rippling up along the left side of his face.

"I'm done!" Sapo raged and waved his bloody axe as if dispelling bad magic.

Then he backed up, glared at the shouting crowds, and marched toward the raised portcullis.

Still volcanic, Sapo stomped down the steps and stormed past an old gatekeeper shying away from Sunjan's heat. Skarrs, normally as impassive as statues, felt for the hilts of their weapons as the beast of a man raged past them. Sapo paused at the tunnel intersection, and instead of returning to the House of Ten's private room, he considered the other direction, toward general quarters, and stomped off toward it, where lamp and torchlight illuminated brick.

Sapo's form filled the tunnel mouth, and as he beheld the shadowy inhabitants of the cavernous underworld beneath the Pit, their heads lifted like snakes and rats.

"You know who I am?" he shouted, captivating hundreds of faces. "You!"

Sapo nearly lunged at a nearby gladiator preparing for his own match. The armored man backed away, raising his bared sword.

"What do you know about a price on my head?" Sapo demanded, ignoring the weapon while cheers from the above world warped and echoed through the tunnel. Even the Madea and his protective wall of Skarrs directed their attention to the Sunjan.

"You're House of Ten?"

"I am." Sapo nearly blew the man's head off with the force of his reply.

"Then there's a bounty on your head," the pit fighter said, his face shaded behind a face cage. "Put there by the House of Curge. Three times the coin for anyone cutting you down in the arena. Maybe more."

"What's more?"

The pit fighter hesitated. "I don't know. He never said."

"Who?"

"Brute of a man. All I know."

"What he says is true," spoke a man pausing in his donning of a vest of chainmail.

"Aye that," said another. "House of Ten. Kill them on the sands, only the sands, mind you, but Dark Curge would show you favors."

That leeched the fight out of Sapo. His shoulders sagged, and his frame suddenly felt very tired. Curge had placed a bounty on his head? His *dead* head! Lords and Seddon above, did that battered punce Goll know? Did any of them know? Then he thought of Tumber and how he died. *Three times the gold...*

Three times that could have been *his*.

Sapo shook his head, simmering over the ugly revelation. He had sworn no allegiance to the house and certainly felt none. Three times the coin for a House of Ten scalp—and the favor of Dark Curge, whatever *that* might entail, but it felt substantial and certainly much more than the dismal package offered by Goll and his drunkard taskmaster and gurry trainers and ill-fitting rags of leather. Again he cursed his impulse to join when Goll stood there calling for recruits, but at the time, anything had seemed better than the bowels of the Pit.

Sapo felt his back when he straightened and faced the pit fighters slinking about the shadows.

"I renounce the House of Ten," he shouted at them. "I'm done with them and, from this time on, fight as my own man!"

That sank into the masses, rendering them uncertain.

Sapo strode over to the Madea's station, confronting the worried attention of the arena official. The Skarrs bunched around him and made ready to pull steel.

"I killed a man out there this day," Sapo declared. "Pay me my winnings."

The Madea met the giant's eyes and, unblinking, drew a deep steadying breath.

"Your name's Sapo?"

"It is."

"You say you're with the House of Ten?"

"No longer."

"So you say you're no longer with the House of Ten."

"I said that, yes."

The corners of the Madea's mouth curled into a smug smile. "Unfortunate. I can't give you the winnings belonging to a house. That wouldn't be right."

Sapo's expression darkened impossibly. "What?" he asked in a frighteningly reserved tone of voice.

The thin figure of the Madea did not buckle under that murderous scowl. "House owners collect their winnings from another official. I only pay out funds owing Free

Trained. The reason for the Skarr presence about this area. Just in case."

The Madea left the rest unsaid.

Sapo looked ready to kill.

"If you wish to be paid, I'd suggest talking with the owner of your once house," the arena official stated simply and stood there, mildly curious as to the reaction of this monster of a man. The Skarrs to the left and right of the Madea gripped weapon hilts, their helms cold and indifferent. Sapo caught the movement, and even though he was ready to fight anyone, he wasn't ready to take on a pack of Sunja's city guard.

Fuming, Sapo stalked back into the white tunnel and stopped, unsure of where to go from there. The urge to barge into the chamber of the House of Ten and demand his gold made his chest ache. There were too many, and Koba would certainly be a challenge, but the temptation of cursing the old trainer Machlann into the dirt also appealed to Sapo's sense of reprisal for all the days under his gnarled thumb.

"Excuse me," a voice said from behind. "Undecided, are you?"

Sapo spun around to face a small boy of a man with worn but smooth skin.

"What did you say to me?"

The little man smiled, and it shone in the white tunnel. "Follow me out of this place, and I just might be able to help you. You might even be able to collect your coin. In the end."

Sapo's brow crunched up in puzzlement at the speaker, who backed into the crowd of fighters. Sapo considered the lonely length of whitewashed, fitted brick before flicking his eyes back toward the little man disappearing amongst torsos and limbs.

Huffing impatience and poisoned with frustration, Sapo took one last withering look in the direction of the House of Ten and made his decision. With a face ready to spit lightning and bark thunder, the Sunjan walked into the parting mass of pit fighters, axe swinging, following the little man.

Bezange paused at the steps leading out of the Pit's gloom, just to check to see if he was being followed.

He wasn't disappointed.

38

If the death of Tumber had left the remaining House of Ten fighters in a sober state, then Sapo's savagery had rattled their nerves entirely. As Goll watched him storm through the raised portcullis and leave the arena, he knew he'd have to turn around eventually and face the others.

"What did he say?" Kolo asked in wonder.

"He said there's a price on our heads," Torello answered.

"Dark Curge placed a bounty on us?" Halm asked aloud.

Goll caught the resigned eye of Clavellus and saw Machlann's moustache quiver as he turned around to face the men.

"He said," Goll stated clearly, "Dark Curge has placed a bounty on your heads. I can only believe that it's only in the Pit, in each of your matches. I don't think it applies outside of the arena."

The slack expressions of bewildered dismay on the

faces of Torello and Kolo troubled Goll. Brozz appeared as emotionless as stone, as did Junger, who looked at his feet with a cool detachment. Halm, however, eyed him with suspicion, and Goll knew there would be another confrontation in his future.

"I had no idea this would happen." Goll chose his words very carefully, looking from face to face. "None. I never would have thought there would be such… hostility toward the House of Ten. But, despite Sapo's outburst, I have no reason to doubt what he said is true. Thus, if you wish, if you feel this has gotten out of hand, I'll harbor no ill will toward you if you decide to leave the House of Ten."

"And what will you do?" Torello asked.

"Oh, I'll fight on," Goll said right away. "I made my choice long ago."

The cheering of the crowds intensified. Outside, another fight clanged and grunted to its visceral conclusion.

"Where's Sapo?" Halm asked, his question causing the others to ponder that very thing. The man should have returned by that time.

"He won't be coming back," Clavellus stated dourly. "Not after what he said out there. He's gone."

Goll could see Torello weighing the same decision while Kolo waited.

"This is the House of Curge," Clavellus reminded them. "If he's behind this bounty, you can be sure he'll rouse the entire Free Trained roster and any gladiator willing to lift a blade to his cause. If I were you, I'd head back the way we came in and leave this season's games. Leave Sunja, even, and never look back."

Another wave of cheers flooded the chamber. Once it

settled, Brozz, standing in his battle attire and wearing his intimidating necklace of crow heads, caught Goll's attention.

"I'm staying," he said in a quiet, weary tone, drawing the attention of the men.

"You're staying?" Torello blurted. "After this? Are you unfit?"

But Brozz didn't waver, nor did he repeat himself.

"I'm staying as well," Junger announced. "No reason to leave."

Torello shook his head in dismay and settled on the swordsman. "You heard what they said? There's a price on your head, placed there by none other than the ruling house of the games?"

"Means nothing to me." Junger shrugged. "Not the first time someone's wanted me dead."

The Perician met Goll's unflinching gaze and held it. The impassive Kree found it unsettling and, despite his usual stubborn streak, broke away first and looked at the others. "Make your choices."

Torello rolled his eyes and shrugged with exasperation. "I'll stay."

That surprised them all.

"I'll stay as well, then," Kolo added, not really surprising anyone—where Torello walked, Kolo followed. "Nowhere else to go, really."

Torello regarded the Zhiberian. "What about you, then?"

For the whole time, Halm had claimed a section of the wall and leaned against it, listening and ruminating on serious thoughts. The question brought him back to the world, and he straightened while warily eyeing Goll. "There's no question to ask. I'm staying. I have my own questions to ask… of a man called Targus."

The statement fell upon the whole room, a room filled with men realizing with just a twinge of pride that no one had decided to leave.

"Then that's settled," Goll declared without a trace of emotion. "I'm glad to see you all still with us."

Torello smirked. "Was with you this morning. Now I'm just mad."

Perhaps because of the relief at no one having renounced the house upon learning about the bounty, Clavellus chuckled at the pit fighter. Even Machlann allowed one part of his thick moustache to hook upward just a little to the right, showing grim amusement.

"Stay that way, then," Goll said and returned to gazing out the archway.

A knock caught the house's attention. "Junger!" cried a voice.

The Perician nodded, utterly unconcerned that he was fighting next, and gripped the hilt of his blade, the weapon in its scabbard belted to his waist. A cheap leather vest covered his torso, and an open helm protected his head, but he wore no other protective adornment. No shield hung off his arm. Junger appeared as naked as a newborn and just as oblivious.

"Masters Goll, Clavellus, Machlann, Koba," he said coolly, dipping his head at each in turn. "And Master Halm."

"Junger," Goll said, bringing the warrior to attention, "kill the man. Make an example of him. Show them all the House of Ten isn't to be trifled with."

Junger's eyes almost appeared troubled at the command, and he looked at the floor. "I understand," he finally said and walked to the door. There to open it stood the towering menace of Brozz, the necklace of dead crow heads prominent on his chest. The Sarlander held out a fist to the Perician. The gesture seemed to raise Junger's spirits, and he pressed his own against it.

Then he left.

The masters looked out the archway,

"I don't know about you," Machlann muttered, his moustache barely moving, "but I'm looking forward to this…"

*

Junger walked through the white tunnel as if strolling through a garden rampant with full blooms. The lines of the fitted stone passed beneath his feet, yet he was keenly aware of each Skarr as he passed, feeling their inspection and discerning their curious thoughts. Junger detected no threat, but he didn't relax entirely. He'd learned long ago never to do such a thing, not even while sleeping.

The steps leading up to the grim portcullis lay at his sandaled toes, and he waited for the gatekeeper's signal.

"You look familiar to me," a gravelly old voice said.

Junger didn't look up, but he nodded and smiled nonetheless.

Above, at the end of the stairs, the gate cranked open.

"Well, off with you, then," the gatekeeper said.

Squinting at the cloudy sky, Junger climbed up the steps, toward the light. The temperature remained high but not as hot as his previous fights.

Regardless, when he stood on the sands, he again pulled off his vest of leather, revealing the brown shading of his skin. The act captivated the audience and triggered the memories of more than just a few. Even the Orator paused to witness the act. Junger smiled to himself. The armor fell from his fingers, and he stretched his arms and shoulders as if he were anywhere but in the Pit. He didn't bother looking, but he sensed the undisguised shock emanating from Goll and others. If he were close enough, he could probably have heard them cursing.

Have no fear, he thought to them, and a faint yet wholly confident smile flickered across his tanned features.

Across the sands, a bear of a man stood watching with sword and dagger in his hands. A coat of fine ringmail protected his torso and upper limbs. His horned helmet leaned to one side in puzzlement, but in the end, the warrior remembered himself and assumed his fighting stance. The smiling grillwork of the visor appeared eager to get to business.

Junger undid the scabbard from his belt but made no move to unsheathe the blade.

The Orator finished his introductions, and the Perician brought his padded weapon before him, gripping it two-handed. Some first-time onlookers leered and mocked, but most held their tongues, wondering if they would see a spectacle of arms from this one. They'd heard the whispers from those nearby, who'd seen this strange man fight before, and like a whining child being covered by a blanket, the arena hushed.

His opponent's name was Bvar, a pit fighter hailing from nearby Marrn. Borchus had informed him the man had four victories to his name already. Junger had listened to the other minor details, but it was really Bvar's record that interested him the most. The warrior would be his best challenge yet in the Pit.

His awareness extended nearly five paces out, an unseen wall of alertness surrounding him, a veritable fortress of danger sensing. Anyone breaching that invisible mental barrier would be known to him. Anyone venturing within his personal space would be dealt with.

"Kill the man." Goll's command spoke in his head. *"Make an example of him. The House of Ten isn't to be trifled with."*

Bvar came closer, edging toward Junger as if the very earth might give away underneath. The Perician frowned. He would satisfy one of Goll's wishes, and that would be all.

Truthfully, no more would be needed.

On some grandiose yet silent note, Junger extended the scabbarded blade toward his opponent, pointing at his foe's head. A low rumble of cheers as warm as the recent rainstorm flowed from the spectators. Junger circled to his right while a pursuing Bvar swatted at the covered weapon in annoyance.

"Draw your sword." Bvar's metallic voice grated with chagrin. "Pull it, damn you."

Junger did not.

Instead, he tilted his head, gauging the distance, taking aim at Bvar's person.

"Draw your *steel*, damn you!"

Junger kept circling just out of reach, completely focused.

And Bvar attacked.

He charged in, horned helm lowered. He stabbed and slashed with his blades, stabbed and slashed again, repeating a deadly combination while grunting with every effort. Junger, however, sidestepped and jumped back, parried and leaned away. Metal clattered. Bvar split the air with an overhand chop, and Junger skipped away from harm while maintaining his guard. Bvar whirled around, slashing his dagger across the empty space where the Perician's head had been just an instant before.

Bvar caught himself from spinning off balance, stomped in the sand, and studied the other man over his weapons. The audience approved the flurry of action and voiced their enjoyment.

The pit fighter from Marrn shook with growing anger. "Draw yo—"

Junger's sword blurred ahead and slapped the horned helm left, right, and left once again before *gonging* Bvar's helm with a monstrous over-the-shoulder chop that seemed to travel the breadth of the world before it smashed down. And when it connected, the very earth leapt.

A stunned Bvar crashed hard to his knees and attempted to rise as if awakening from a prayer far too quickly.

Junger did not want the man to rise and so cracked the pit fighter's head across the skull once again.

Bvar toppled and was still.

The Perician's foot hooked the warrior's sword and sent it flying. Junger drove a knee into his downed opponent's chest and unsheathed a hand's worth of sharp edge before placing it to Bvar's stubbly throat.

Amid cries for his life, clarity returned to the fallen pit fighter's eyes—and then terror. *"Hold!* Hold, I beg you, *hold!"* He released his dagger and held both hands over his head.

Poised like a dangerous bird of terrible appetite, Junger considered the gesture for a moment before snapping the length of exposed steel back into its scabbard. He stood and stepped away from the defeated man at his feet.

The crowds stood with him. Cheers cascaded as hard as

a sun-warmed waterfall, and Junger regarded the thousands applauding him before walking back toward his slowly rising portcullis.

*

Above, in the private viewing box of the three owners, Gastillo marvelled at the nearly sorcerous display of swordsmanship he'd just witnessed upon the sands.

"Who *is* that half-naked pisser?" Nexus choked out, staring with wide eyes and wondering if he possessed anyone of equal quality in his school.

Curge concealed his surprise much better than the others, but then his chin dipped, his brow furrowed, and his eyes took on a murderous, contemplative shade of black.

*

In the private chamber of the House of Ten, a short chuckle burst from Clavellus's lips. Machlann straightened and blinked, the only bit of emotion he'd allow himself to show.

"What was that?" the taskmaster chortled and stroked his beard with genuine delight. "What was *that?* Machlann?"

"Unknown," the trainer growled, the word glazed with wonder.

"Unknown," Clavellus repeated in whole agreement.

"What happened?" Torello wanted to know.

"What happened was…" and Clavellus glanced from Machlann to the unimpressed expression of Goll, though he failed to recognize anything wrong. "Several people just became very much aware of the House of Ten. Very much aware. Wouldn't you say so, Machlann?"

"Aye that. I'd say so."

An enthusiastic Clavellus lifted his shaking hand and gripped Goll's shoulder. "I hope you had Borchus place coin on that lad."

"I did," Goll replied, tight lipped. The Kree took a breath and faced the others, singling out Torello. "There's another fight, and then… you're next."

39

Torello listened to the Orator yelling the introductions in a straining voice badly in need of wine or beer—something to wet those burning vocal cords. As the old man tortured his throat, Torello tightened his grip around his sword, hefting his round shield. His open-faced helm cooked his head like a tough roast, leaching considerable juice from his skull, the sweat flowing down the sides of his face and the dastardly stubble on his chin and neck. *Heat.* Dying Seddon. Made a man want to die just to escape it. Surely Saimon's hell wasn't as hot. His stomach knotted and threatened to void, but that didn't bother Torello. He was standing on the world's biggest shite trough, and if his bowels demanded it, well, he suspected the crowds would no longer complain about cow kisses in the road.

The thought made him smile just a little.

Torello stood in the flesh-baking wrath of the sun and regarded the man across the way.

Cron of Sunja wore a vest of toughened leather.

HOUSE OF PAIN

Bracers protected his forearms while greaves covered his legs from the knees down. He carried a sword-and-shield combination, and one look informed Torello that the punce was feeling the heat as well. *What do you know about heat?* Torello chided, his eyes becoming slits. *You're not the one with a gurry price on his head.* Placed there by Curge of all people, not that Torello cared. He had a natural dislike for men and women in places of power, believing them all corrupted. That belief enhanced his usual scornful tongue and got him into trouble. And as much as he might complain about it, secretly, he was quite satisfied having joined the House of Ten. No other would have taken him on so lightly. Not the Ten, however, and he still wondered at times how he'd removed himself from the hell of general quarters to his own little cot—above the floor, even, with a curtain to pull across the way at night. Then there were the meals and the baths! The baths alone were worth whatever punishment he endured at the hands of the trainers—Machlann in particular was a right and proper old bastard that extracted the best and the worst from the Sunjan. Though he openly complained at every turn, to the very brink of being slapped upside the skull, Torello very much wanted to win this fight. He very much wanted to impress his trainers, Machlann in particular.

To show they weren't wrong in taking him into their ranks.

To show he had learned a few things in the short time under their teachings.

And to prove to himself he was the equal of any other... if not better.

For all his miserable, wretched, beating-the-weak life—and for a few coins, a meal, or a drink—he'd dispensed violence for someone: innkeepers, merchants, anyone harboring a grudge or looking to retrieve coin owed, deplorable men who likened themselves to kings and ordered the cruelest punishments for commoners late with payments. Torello had broken the fingers and wrists of husbands and fathers, even wives and mothers for that matter, while children bawled and pleaded—haunting cries that still woke him from nightmares. He had done that for four years, alongside Kolo, his friend since childhood, an orphan like himself, left to survive off Sunja's scraps. Only this year had he decided to not hurt innocents anymore… at least, not on another man's command.

Torello felt sick because of that, fully expecting to die horribly because of what he'd done in the past.

Fighting in the Pit, however, was different.

It was for him and for him alone.

An evil smirk slunk across his sweaty features. *Equal to any of them… except Junger. That one was unfit.*

It took Cron of Sunja moving toward him to break Torello of his thoughts. He crouched into his guard and lifted his shield, peering over the edge at his countryman. A tingling uncertainty rushed up Torello's spine like a cold stream of water.

He was determined to show them all.

Cron rushed in, swinging for the hills with mighty expulsions of breath as if he were heaving boulders into the air. He slashed for Torello's head and missed, slashed for a shoulder and got parried by a shield, stabbed for a gut and had his blade knocked aside.

"That all?" Torello grinned evilly over the edge of his shield. "You stain of maggot shite."

It obviously was not all, for Cron waved his sword and split the very air right underneath the nose of Torello, who jerked his head back a blink before the edge could open a second mouth. That sudden flat slash heralded a veritable storm of steel flying from the other man, each blow powered by an animalistic grunt. He stabbed, slashed, hammered, and hacked at his moving opponent.

And Torello moved.

Remembering the lessons from Koba and Machlann, he backed up and sidestepped, parried with sword and shield, or got out of the way entirely. But Torello wasn't the sort to just allow each miss or near miss to go by without saying a few words.

"What gurry was that? Are you sick? Unfit, lad, unfit. Come on then, try again. There you go! Come on, try once more, you ugly punce. See how easy I turned that aside? Who'd you expect to meet out here? More, he-bitch, try again! Aha!"

Free Trained, he thought all the while. *I was once like him.*

Then Cron apparently had enough of the dance. He swung for Torello's head, blade whistling from his shoulder with the full strength of his arm and hips behind it, looking to give a deadly haircut.

Torello ducked, however, and struck—slashing his sword at Cron's bare thigh, cutting up underneath the meat in one bloody flash and slicing open a fleshy flap, straight to the red bone. Torello spun away from Cron, dragging his sword free of a thigh frothing from a lipless mouth. Cron's face paled, and he collapsed to his knees, sending up a small cloud of dust that clung to the flowing brilliance of that terrible, terrible wound. He dropped his sword, threw off his shield, and clutched at his thigh, shifting the chunk of meat and causing even more blood to spill forth.

Torello saw it all.

And as Cron bent over at the hips as if in prayer,

Torello moved and punched his sword through the back of the man's neck. Another spectacle of blood, but the crowds screamed for more, even as Torello put his foot to the dead man's back and yanked his sword free.

"Ten!" Torello raised his arms and screamed. "House of Ten!"

He circled the corpse at his feet, screaming back at the crowds, even exchanging curses with a select few.

Then, his entire frame seemed to ooze a sheen of sweat all at once, soaking the padding underneath his leather. The battle rush drained away, and Torello felt almost ripe and ready to drop dead himself. His breath quickened, vision blurring. His heart thundered in his chest and ears. He saw a portcullis rise, and he walked toward it, feeling the ground beneath his feet suddenly shift and elongate into a journey measuring days. The roar of the spectators became a garbled rush of underwater sound.

But through force of will, he did not fall.

He made it into the tunnel and leaned heavily against the wall. There he stayed, shaking, hearing the portcullis drop behind him, and waving off the gatekeeper's questions at the bottom of the stairs. Torello wouldn't have talked to the crusty old shagger even if he were feeling normal.

Shoulders heaving, Torello pulled his helm off, felt better for doing so, and continued summoning deep calming breaths into his lungs. He bent over and blinked, watching glistening beads of sweat fall away from him. After a few moments, he felt strong enough to walk.

"Dying Seddon," Torello breathed.

The first time that's *ever happened.* He'd have to talk to Shan about it and see what the healer had to say.

Keeping the wall nearby, Torello straightened and

carefully returned to the viewing chamber of his house.

40

Kolo wasn't so fortunate in his fight.

He was paired against a Sunjan called Cota, a smaller man that strode into the arena flashing a set of short swords and a grinning visor adorned with tusks. Upon the Orator's command, they lunged at each other, and Cota darted nimbly away while Kolo dropped his sword. In that briefest contact, so fast the eye couldn't follow, Cota nearly slashed Kolo's arm off right at the elbow. Kolo stood in agony, all thoughts of defense gone. He lifted his right arm up while his forearm dangled and wept scarlet, the weight of the barely attached limb pulling down on the raw joint. The sight of the wound caused even Goll to wince.

Cota wasn't a cruel man, and once he saw and heard Kolo's cries, he hacked into the side of his opponent's neck—twice—hard, killing strokes that drove Kolo to the ground.

Then Cota stabbed him through the back.

HOUSE OF PAIN

The audience loved the butchery, and the raucous sound erupted from the Pit like a ripe volcano.

"Well?" Torello asked from a bench, resting against the wall and appearing as if he could sleep for a week.

A stern Machlann turned away from the window. He looked into Torello's eyes, gave a curt shake of his head, and broke the stare first.

Torello bent over until his chest touched his knees and then held his face. Halm reached over and gripped the Sunjan's shoulder.

"Unfortunate," Clavellus muttered. "I liked that lad."

Goll didn't know the man long enough to know if he liked him or whether Kolo was good or bad. He seemed close enough to Torello, perhaps the only friend that one had. Goll hoped it wouldn't affect his morale going forward in the tournament. Thus far, the House of Ten wasn't faring nearly as well as he'd hoped—two dead and one deserter leaving in a fit of rage.

Not the start Goll wanted.

"Brozz," he called without looking back. "It's time."

No sooner were the words spoken than the knock came at the door.

The tall Sarlander stood to his full height like Death itself lording over a field of recent dead. Black eyes twinkled within the hollows of his helmet, and the long, flowing moustache hiding his lower lip only added to the gloomy air pulsing from the warrior. Unlike the others, he retained his own leather vest, which was just as well, as there hadn't been anything else ready to fit his size. The five dried-out heads dangled around his neck, black beaks fixed in tiny screams. Crowhead gripped his shortsword and hand axe and left the room without a word.

*

Brozz defeated and killed his opponent in short time, muting the crowds. Unlike the finessed Junger, the man called Crowhead was brutally efficient in his fight, weathering a few probing strikes until lashing out with maximum force and putting his foe down. Some of the audience members even cheered for the dark man, and he returned to the house viewing chamber like a haunted shadow seeking its crypt. He entered the room to the quiet nods and approving looks from the trainers. Brozz took his helm off and dropped it on the stone floor, fragrant and shiny with perspiration. He drew a heavy arm across his brow and accepted a cloth from one of the hired guards.

"A fine performance." Clavellus beamed at him. "A solid display of skill. You can be sure you caught the eye of many this day, good Brozz."

"Even frightened a few," the taskmaster muttered low enough for the trainers to hear.

Goll didn't waste words on the Sarlander. He focused on Halm.

"You know what you have to do."

Halm reluctantly nodded. "Aye that."

"Then… go do it."

*

The gatekeeper said something to Halm, but the Zhiberian registered it as a voice coming from somewhere off a foggy shoreline. *Targus.* He shrugged. He absentmindedly slapped the leather sleeve protecting his sword arm and inspected the rest of himself. His bare gut hung out like a swollen water bladder, stitched and bandaged and barely holding itself together. One sharp move too much in one direction, and Halm figured he'd just burst apart at the seams. That put a faint smile on his face. If that happened, it'd be interesting to see how much saywort and thread young Shan had in his pocket.

The smile didn't last as deep thoughts overcame him again.

"Hope you perish out there, Zhiberian," the gatekeeper said vengefully. Halm took to the stairs, toward the opening portcullis. He didn't bother replying to the old man.

Outside, the sunlight made the sweat on his frame sizzle. His conical helm started to slow cook his skull. The day was the kind on which, if wisdom prevailed, people would stay in the shade. Halm wished he was on a grassy hillside somewhere with a few bottles of firewater beside him.

Targus was already on the other side of the arena, war braid flung over one shoulder. Ill-kept leather armor covered the lad, the same ill-fitting garb he had worn the day Halm first set eyes on him. A round shield decorated the Sunjan's arm while his shortsword was already out and ready.

Eager, Halm thought pensively and hefted the square shield on his left arm.

The Orator shouted to begin, startling the Zhiberian. It seemed as if he'd only just stepped into the sun, but somehow, he'd missed the introductions.

"Ho there, good Targus," he yelled out, forcing cheerfulness into his voice.

Targus started walking toward him, briskly, to the rumbling approval of the spectators.

Halm drew forth his Mademian sword, just in case. The temptation to call out again struck him, but he squashed it. Targus had heard him the first time.

As the young warrior came closer, Halm could see the expression only partially protected by an open helm.

"Targus." Halm nodded, speaking the word over his raised shield. "Surprised to see you here."

Targus face pinched as if insulted. "Afraid, are you?"

"Why would I be afraid?"

"You haven't bought me with gold to stay away from this fight."

Despite the oppressive heat beating down upon his frame, Halm's innards crystallized as if sunk in a winter sea.

"What?" he got out, practically breathless, circling to his left.

"You heard me. I saw you a few days ago. In the rain." Targus shook his head with disdain and leaned closer so the crowds would not pick up on the conversation. "You paid a Free Trained fighter to stay away from the games, and he took the coin but vowed to see you dead next season. I've heard stories about your nature, Zhiberian, but Saimon paddle my ass for believing otherwise."

Halm's ears burned with the poisonous revelation.

"You heard what?"

Targus shook his head. "Not so brave now, are you? Now that I know how you do things. No one would dare fight you, and the Madea actually made a public announcement asking for fighters. This was after Curge announced his bounty for any of your house fighters. 'Well,' I thought, 'I wager I can do better than any.'"

All color drained from the Zhiberian's face, and Targus smiled evilly when he saw it.

"I'll make it easy for you, Zhiberian," Pit Knot's haunting twin said. "You pay me double Curge's price. He was tripling a winning purse for killing any of the Ten. You give me your word, and we'll settle up outside the arena. Just you and I. And you'll never see or hear of me again. Until next season, of course."

Targus's smile turned into a gloating grin, as if he knew Halm had no choice.

Far from it.

"No," Halm of Zhiberia said. "I won't do that."

Targus's expression shifted to one of sly surprise. "Think you can fight your way out of this? Think you can defeat me? Take the easy way out. Your kind usually does."

"Who else knows of this?"

"Is that what's bothering you?"

The crowds began booing now, as what promised to be a good match was quickly slipping into gurry.

"Who else?" Halm demanded.

"No one else knows," Targus said, shaking his head. "Just you and me. And whoever else you've bribed, of course. Which makes me wonder. Why did you kill the other men? They wouldn't go along with your plans?"

"This—" Halm began, his voice buried in a slide of jeers from the stands. He kept circling, "This doesn't have to be to the death, Targus. Listen to—"

"Agree to pay, or it will be."

To make his point, Targus feinted a quick jab that made Halm flinch in retreat. His reaction caused a sneer to split Targus's face.

Halm regarded this youthful version of Pig Knot and realized, with a sinking heart, it wasn't Pig Knot at all. Not even close.

"Well?"

Halm attacked, Mademian blade coming over the shoulder and down, but Targus was already moving. He slashed as he evaded, slicing the protective leather sleeve of Halm's swordarm and the flesh underneath. A ribbon of scarlet snaked through the air. The crowds erupted in cheers at the sudden flurry of blows. Halm spun until he faced the younger foe.

Targus charged forward. He stabbed for fingers, slashed for knees, and made an unexpected swing at Halm's chin with the edge of his shield. Halm parried, parried again, and jerked his head back from the iron saucer flashing across his face.

Before something burned across his ribs.

Crafty Targus had used the shield to cover the real threat, the one splitting the hairy flesh above Halm's existing bandages, right along the lower ribs—one more long, pink mouth spitting blood into the sand.

"Pay!" Targus shouted.

Some in the audience even took up the cry. "Pay! Pay!"

Halm grimaced, his right side lighting up as if something had bitten into it and was refusing to let go. Then Targus made to jab again, jerking his arm back but simultaneously punching out with the shield edge once again. The quick movements befuddled Halm, and he averted his head to the side at the last instant. The shield rocked the side of his head instead of his unprotected jaw, making him stagger backward.

"You unfit pisser," Halm hissed and squared his feet.

That wiped all pleasantries from Targus's face.

The Sunjan came forward with a yell, throwing himself against the larger man. Steel flashed and became streaks of light, metal crinkled against metal. Targus loosed a surprisingly swift combination of thrusts and stabs while closing, meant to back the Zhiberian up on his feet. But Halm refused to be moved and stuck one leg behind him, propping himself in place, and absorbed everything with his shield. A livid Targus fixed on that barrier and hacked into it with uncompromising power. The first strike landed, and the iron band across the top rim bent, forcing Halm's arm down. The second one shattered the strip, dropping the arm further. Targus's face morphed into wicked glee.

The third blow came down as fast and as frightening as an aimed thunderbolt, splitting the wood to the second iron band reinforcing the middle, no more than a finger above Halm's forearm.

Targus yanked the weapon back, and Halm went with it, punching his Mademian sword though the leather vest of his opponent, through his chest, and four fingers out the other side, pitching a slow-rising tent in doing so. Halm stood practically chest to chest with the Sunjan and glared into his face. Blood spurted rhythmically onto Halm's chest. Targus shivered, blood flecking his paling lips, eyes already bleached with shock. His arms dropped, and his mouth worked at forming words that had no sound. He convulsed twice and became too heavy for the Zhiberian to bear.

He let his sword go, and Targus tumbled over onto his side, gasping like a fish. It didn't move for long.

Halm inspected his ruined shield and shrugged it off his arm, letting it fall to the ground. He reached for the blade in the dead man's chest after all movement had ceased, and the sand drank deep of blood. Halm struggled with freeing his weapon from the man's ribs but yanked it free eventually, pulling the corpse up from the gruesome mud forming about its torso. The Zhiberian felt his wounds and discovered he wasn't feeling so bad about killing the young man.

But the fight had also changed him.

Goll might have a point after all.

Perhaps it was best to be on one's own.

Only then did the cheers of the crowd and the rattling of chains of the rising portcullis reach his senses.

Not sparing another look at the body at his feet, Halm grimaced at the burn of his newest cuts and made a weary march off the field.

He slumped against the wall as he descended, dripping blood and sweat with every step.

"You're bleeding on my stairs," the gatekeeper shrieked.

"Apologies," Halm grunted as he walked by, ignoring the opportunity to engage the old man. He bled every step to the house viewing chamber as well, but the last few paces, shadows detached themselves from the doorway and surrounded him. Voices spoke soothing words of comfort and congratulations while hands took away his sword and clapped him on the back.

Halm smiled weakly and looked upon the faces of his friends—no, his *companions*, he corrected himself, feeling a writhing knot of feelings within his breast. Goll came into view and allowed a stoic nod before turning back to the archway. Halm ignored him.

He didn't care about the approval of the Kree anymore.

He wondered if he ever had.

41

With his hands on his hips, Sapo stood in the middle of a dark room with a wall covered in a display of weapons drizzled with dust. Shortswords, daggers, and maces hung from nails, their intimidating edges and points still sharp, still deadly. Face cages and dented helms of fearsome design stared back at him. Sapo didn't like the helmets, for the empty eye sockets seemed to follow him wherever he stood in the room. Armaments adorned the wall, enough to outfit a dozen or more gladiators. Part of him wondered if there was a room full of body armor as well, but he didn't chance looking for it. The walled compound the little man had led him to reeked of wealth and power, and Sapo was mindful enough of where he was in the city to know that the owner was of considerable import. He just didn't know who it was.

Curtains parted at one end, and the little man with the youthful face walked through, meeting his eyes.

Then came Dark Curge.

Sapo froze and stared at the legendary once-gladiator.

Dark Curge sized him up from head to toe with intense scrutiny. Not many men could look Sapo in the eye, but Curge could. And despite his age and missing left hand, a vibration of pure dread ripped through Sapo's back.

"Master Curge," the little man announced and then dipped his fair features toward the pit fighter. "Sapo of Sunja."

"Sapo of Sunja," Curge rumbled and scratched at a bare belly not quite as grand or scarred as the Zhiberian's. "I believe you won your fight this day."

"I did, Master Curge." Unlike Clavellus or Machlann, Sapo did not hesitate showing due respect. The very air crackled around this arena legend, demanding he be addressed by title.

Curge grunted and glanced at the smaller man. "Bezange here is very much aware of the undercurrents of the arena. He's a quick thinker. A very quick thinker. Faster than me, in fact, and he's smart enough not to boast about it, else I break open his head. He saw potential in you today, as I did, but for different reasons and acted accordingly. Quickly, even."

Sapo held his breath.

"I'm not one for extended pleasantries, you understand, so I'll get to the point," Curge growled from underneath a cocked brow. The shadows of the room transformed his expression into an unpleasant grimace.

"You were one of the first pit fighters to go with the House of Ten, yes?"

"I was, Master Curge."

"And you trained with them for over a week?"

"Aye that."

"And given the display on the sands today, I suspect

you aren't particularly fond of your former house?"

"No, Master Curge."

"Well, then. I think we can strike a bargain—if you're agreeable, of course. I'm looking for information on that very house, the warriors they have remaining, and anything of note you might think is helpful to me. In return, I have need of a gladiator or two on my roster this day." Curge fixed an eye on the big man. "Would you care to fill one of those positions?"

Sapo's jaw dropped.

And without hesitation, he blurted his answer.

*

They approached the towering white shell of the Gladiatorial Chamber with the grim cadence of invaders about to offer terms to the besieged. Heavy plate armor rattled as the procession walked through the streets. Six Axemen, King Juhn's personal guards selected for their enormous size, surrounded a polished koch pulled by a team of four horses.

The driver kept the animals at a slow trot, not wanting to hear any warning from the six warriors protecting the vehicle. The sun hung halfway down its evening slope, knotting the left side of the driver's face into a squint. He regarded the Axemen and figured a man in that heat, wearing *that* heavy armor, would be quick to lash out at anything if the feeling took hold.

Inside sat Lord Schull, appointed messenger for King Juhn. His metal-gray hair had only just started to thin, his skin and eyes pallid with age. He peered out at the streets and the indifferent Sunjans going about their business, wishing he could go about his own life with such ignorant bliss of the world beyond the city walls. Schull disliked having to lower himself to such duties, even though it was his king's wish for him to visit the Chamber for the betterment of the throne and the country. His fingers fluttered at each citizen as if weaving wicked spellcraft.

A metallic-gray giant of a man clattered just outside his opened window, weighed down with enough steel and iron to appear inhuman. The Axeman's conical helm studied the streets ahead for threats, though Schull wondered who exactly might threaten him. The warrior held one of the legendary poleaxes to his shoulder. No weapon was as feared as that monstrous man-chopper, and the strength it took to wield the thing—to simply *carry* it—was enough to cure any dissenter of seditious thoughts.

Only six Axemen had been afforded him. Schull had requested a dozen—not for fear of his life but reflective of his status, his importance, the palpable aura of prominence heralded by an escort of Axemen. And frankly, his person *demanded* pageantry. Schull held himself in the highest of regards, and being allotted only half the force befitting his station soured his mood considerably. The koch, while impressive in the eyes of peasants, had only one driver and no other servants attending to his needs. The interior felt cramped and the cushions uncomfortable. The small decorative cabinet contained only a single bottle of wine and a pair of silver goblets. A *single* bottle. Schull simmered with black thoughts and shook his head over such a slight. He deserved more than this—much more. Such hardships, he told himself, would have to be endured this trip. Schull intended not to touch a drop, to refrain from even cracking the lining of the bottle, just for spite.

The koch eased to a gentle stop. An Axeman stepped up and opened the door for Schull, who grimaced in the furious heat of the sun. Then he looked at the five-story building that was the Chamber's home. A row of six white marble columns, their bases too wide to embrace, rose up from street level to a brooding overhang, granting protection from the weather when needed. Scenes depicting small battling figures and ferocious animals decorated their marble bases. A pair of great oak doors, fashioned to fit an archway, lay just beyond. Six Skarrs stood on either side of the entryway, their backs against a wall cut with a scattering of windows fixed with wooden shutters. The dozen warriors guarding the entrance carried sword, shield, and spear. Their visors remained fixed ahead, watching Schull and his escort of Axemen as he stepped down from the koch and approached.

The Skarrs nearest the doors hauled them open for Schull, and with a scowl on his lined face, he entered the Chamber hall with four of the king's guardians at his heels. Attendants flitted about inside, and their gasps upon recognizing his person pleased him. Some froze in place, the shock of seeing Schull setting their minds a-fluttering. More doors opened for him as he marched ahead, ignoring the inspiring ambiance of the entry foyer, and entered the Chamber itself. Schull frowned at the cream-colored marble floor. The workmanship seemed shoddy, the shade unquestionably off. Vathian, he suspected. Never liked the country or the people. He regarded the raised semicircular bench of red wood, which passed as "grand" here, where the nine Chamber members presided. Schull scowled. Squalor. He was literally bathing in squalor. One of his own latrines had more polish than this hole.

The Chamber members, usually weary and bored looking to most visitors, stood and appeared noticeably on edge with Schull's appearance, as expected. The king's man stepped out from his armored escort and regarded each of them in turn, conveying his disdain with eyes as frosty as shaved ice. He didn't care in the least for how these glorified merchants of pain dressed themselves with white and gold, a cheap attempt at elevating themselves above their station. They squirmed under his inspection, clearing their throats, very much aware of how they appeared to one above them. Schull sneered at the waist-high table where commoners stopped and addressed the Chamber and instead positioned himself in front of the furniture, in full contempt for their self-inflated sense of courtly decorum.

The place wasn't a royal court. It wasn't even a *court*.

In Schull's eyes, the Chamber was nothing more than a cheap room filled with old men and lost dreams and missing more than a few body parts.

Schull kept his hands at his sides, a pose he felt was just as intimidating as if he placed his fists on his hips. Not one of the Chamber men made a peep, still standing, too startled to lay eyes on one imbued with the King's power. At least, Schull mulled, these dogs recognized importance. He allowed the silence to stretch on, enjoying their growing unease.

When his own patience started to thin, he lifted a finger.

"King Juhn addresses you with his appointed voice, his noble emissary and noted son of Sunja, the honorable Lord Schull," one of the Axemen declared in a voice that boomed in the stillness.

The nine members bowed unevenly, noticeably unaccustomed to having to do so. *Dog blossoms,* Schull fumed. After the sloppy display of reverence, they sat.

"Lord Schull did not allow you to sit," the same

HOUSE OF PAIN

Axeman informed them, and all nine jumped to their feet—or at least, they jumped as well as old men might.

Shaking his head, Schull let them sweat for a few moments longer, hoping a few of them had to clench their bowels. Only when he nodded did they finally sit.

"Who is… Odant?" Schull finally asked, curling his lips as if sampling sour wine.

An elderly brute missing an ear and feigning importance got to his feet. He cleared his throat. "I am Odant, Lord Schull."

"I'm not one to mince words in any company short of our majestic ruler himself, so I'll be brief. To the point. King Juhn wants the season lengthened."

Odant blinked at this as if digesting something ill-fitting. The others appeared no better, some even incredulous.

"With the greatest respect—" Odant began.

Schull cut him off with a dismissive wave. "I've been granted permission to be privy to the king's mind and to those of his commanding officers, and through this frail frame, he addresses you. You are hereby commanded under penalty of death that the information I'm about to disclose not leave these walls. If it does, you can be sure his Majesty's executioner will harvest exactly nine heads. Are we understood?"

The Chamber members nodded so fast it was almost comical.

"Very well. The war, such as it is, is not progressing favorably for us. The citizens of Sunja must not give in to fear of defeat, thus, it's the king's wish to amuse them. It diverts their attention away from the Nordish front. The most logical way is to lengthen the games since they're already in progress. Do not worry about the finances for such an extended period of time, for as always, the king will continue to fund the Pit's expenses from his own treasury. All monetary awards will remain the same, and each and every victory shall be paid in full."

The sound of Odant clearing his throat made Schull's own tongue curl in his head.

"You wish to say something?" he inquired with a withering glare.

"Lord Schull." The Chamber member lurched. "The games can't be extended."

"What did you say?" Schull interrupted.

Odant appeared to be struck with pain. "What I meant to say was… it will be most difficult to do such since the season is practically half over."

"Lengthen. It." Schull stated imperiously before smiling coldly enough to impart frostbite.

"There are problems." Another member rose to his feet, a balding sort who had perhaps consumed an ocean of beer at one sitting.

"Problems aren't a concern of mine," Schull countered with forced pleasantness.

"The tournament is elimination style. One loss, and your season is over."

"And there's the problem of an ever-shrinking pool of fighters to draw from once a man is defeated," Odant added. "There are only a handful of established houses and schools producing gladiators for the games. Even with the addition of the Free Trained—"

Schull lifted a hand, invoking silence across the room.

"I gave you my ear, and you pissed nonsense in it. I'm well aware of your… games. Your problems aren't problems at all, merely thoughtless excuses. All who have lost, who have been eliminated to this point, will be allowed to fight again if they are physically capable. Instead of one loss, make it so that the sum of a man's inflicted wounds will prevent him from continuing in the season. Essentially, allow them to fight until they drop. The top gladiators, presumably the undefeated or those with the fewest losses, will fight on to the champion's match."

Skeptical silence greeted this.

"What about the number of fighters? There are ten to fifteen matches in one day. Even with the Free Trained, to extend the games past another month will—"

"You. Weren't. Listening," Schull snipped, stretching his mouth to its contemptuous fullest. "I just said allow defeated fighters back into the tournament. Even if they amass a losing record, let them fight if they still wish. If they can pull steel, let them into the arena. And your blood matches. The rulings on those fits of vengeance are to be limited. No more of this nonsense about just anyone demanding a blood match over the slightest insult. Especially amongst the Free Trained. Bring those dogs to heel. If a House loses a fighter, allow them their chance at retribution, but only if one of their own is killed."

The expression on Odant's face spoke of his spirit nearly broken. This pleased Schull. He sought to instill dread into these old husks. He wanted them to know the king was very much aware of their games.

"King Juhn, in his infinite wisdom, wishes the games to be extended; thus, they *will* be extended. I've instructed you how to proceed; now see it done. If you do not, I'll return. And let me be very, very clear upon this matter—I don't *wish* to return here. If I do, heads will bounce off this slab of piss-stained rock you seem to think is marble. Your greatest concern is having enough men to feed the games? King Juhn offers this since he has already considered such.

His Eminence will scour the city's dungeons for prisoners capable of wielding a blade. He'll allow you to arm these he-bitches—to the teeth if you wish or with sticks if it amuses you—for the sole purpose of having them fight in the games. To hew at whoever you place in front of them."

Odant cleared his throat once again.

Schull mentally vowed if he heard that goat-milk-curdling noise again he'd have an Axeman strike the old bastard's head from his shoulders.

"We're to have... *criminals*... fight in our tournament?" the Chamber member asked almost petulantly.

"You are." Schull nodded with false sympathy, inwardly delighting at the old he-bitch's drooping expression. "The king has, in fact, already combed the dungeons for conscripts and pressed those most capable into service, as his remaining Klaws require fighting men. But several hundred were kept back for whatever reasons—deserters, murderers, thieves. Essentially, the passed-over shite of the lot. Perhaps they would've caused more trouble than their worth on a Sujin line. It's my understanding there are even Nordish captives shackled in chains somewhere. Prisoners taken in battle. These you may use and churn up in whatever fashion takes your fancy. But make the experience... dramatic if at all possible. Uplifting. Anything to take minds off what's happening on the front. Anything to instill a rousing pride in the watching populace. The king wishes to see sport. *Theater* if you can manage it. But *no* outright executions. If he wanted to hear the chop and bounce of the executioner's axe, he would've sentenced the prisoners to death long ago. Do you understand?"

Odant already looked thoughtful. "Yes, Lord Schull,"

he replied on the Chamber's behalf, as the topper should.

"Excellent," Schull announced, grateful that he would be away shortly. He wouldn't give them the opportunity for any further questions. "Then I leave you to your thoughts and the task ahead. With the King's blessings."

With hurried impatience, Schull turned and left the chamber, relieved that an unpleasant task had been completed. Cracking open that single bottle of grape lodged in his koch's cabinet suddenly appealed to him. It would do until he found a more palatable quantity, served by women with wide hips and inviting smiles.

The Axemen followed, frightening reapers on his heels.

In his wake, the Chamber came alive with an outbreak of voices.

42

Nordish Front

Arrus dawdled until a Sujin shoved him hard from behind, the spear slamming him broadway across his back. The Nordish man tripped in his ankle chains and stumbled to the ground, bringing another prisoner down with him. He rolled onto his side, dead leaves coating his bare, bruised skin, and cowered there while angry voices barked nonsense overhead. The Sujin, chainmail shirt and plates of iron strapped to his torso, loomed overhead with a spear poised at Arrus's half-opened eye.

Another soldier yelled, and the one about to puncture Arrus's head balked. His eyes blinked behind his visor, and he shouted a reply full of venom, but the man withdrew from striking a killing blow. Instead of gouging a length of spear into Arrus's eye, the soldier delivered a hard boot to the Jackal's left kidney, the kick powerful enough to rob the Nordish of his breath.

"Get him up, Noll," a harsh voice commanded in the native tongue. *Dogslaw*.

"I think he's done."

"You think everyone's done. Get him up."

Hands pulled on Arrus and got him to his feet. Four powerful-looking Sujins, three with spears and one with a shortsword, stood ready to kill if necessary. The soldiers herding the Nordish prisoners to the southeast weren't concerned in the least about executing a few men along the way just to prove a point or to ease their burden.

Or simply for amusement.

Ankle chains connected two lines of captured Jackals, totaling thirteen. They had numbered close to twenty before they started marching, but killings along the way had reduced the number. The Sujins didn't feed the Nordish regularly. When the thought struck the soldiers, they tossed scraps of bread crusts amongst the prisoners or emptied a pot of gruel over some rocks—prompting the starving men to lower themselves and lick it off those hard plates. In two weeks, Arrus had gone from lean to practically emaciated. His cheeks hollowed, his eyes darkened, rashes exploded upon his skin, and he panted heavily all the time—much like the rest. The Sujins did give them water—two cups per man, taken from the water barrels hauled along in horse-drawn wagons.

One in the morning and one in the evening.

Arrus's gullet was clawed by a thirst so wicked that he could have drunk piss.

"Get up, damn you," Lokan urged. Dirt and sun darkened his own gaunt features, drawing attention to an ugly scar running across his upper lip and cheeks.

"I'm done." Arrus grimaced. "I'm going to piss blood this night."

But Lokan leaned in. "Get to your feet, Jackal, or I'll stomp on your skull."

That made Arrus study the Jackal in a careful light, and he didn't like what he saw. He didn't know Lokan in the least, but right now, Arrus knew he was very close to dying.

Grunting, he did as told, noting that Lokan obviously disliked the pained effort.

The Sujin who had kicked Arrus barked an order, and the line got moving along a pitted road hemmed in by a thinning forest. Arrus had no choice but to shuffle along, straining to keep up with the others. Sujins clanked alongside them, grunting and conversing in that piggish tongue of theirs, chuckling at times.

Arrus wanted to kill them all.

"In time," Lokan muttered behind him. "We'll have our day."

"I don't think so," Arrus whispered back, eyeing the soldiers fearfully.

Lokan didn't respond.

They marched in silence, naked except for stained loincloths, through a crippling bellows of an afternoon, and a loss of sweat made Arrus tremble with weakness. Two wagons led them along while a third brought up the rear. At one point, a Sujin halted the other line of chained Nordish men and drove his spear through a captive's midsection in a burst of gore. That killing delayed the line until the Sujins could detach the corpse. The prisoners were surrounded with bared steel and forced to sit while two soldiers directed the Nordish men nearest to the dead man. The death was unfortunate, but Arrus was grateful for being able to sit and rest, if only for a short time. All the while, he stared at the body, ogling it while shivering.

"Thinking about taking a bite?" Lokan asked nearby.

The very thought made Arrus shake his head with revulsion. "Haven't gone that far yet."

"I have."

A visor-wearing Sujin stepped between the two prisoners selected to haul the dead man. The man grunted a few syllables to another, and a soldier with a battle axe came along and made quick work chopping through the legs of the corpse. Once the body was freed, the prisoners extracted the ankle bits and tossed them into the underbrush.

"*Skolla*," Noll grumped and eyed Lokan with distaste. "Have you lost your head?"

"No." He smiled evilly and licked his lips. "Not at all." He stared at the place where the feet had been discarded then at the corpse being dragged to the side of the road.

Arrus did not like the gleam in the man's eyes.

"If you go that far, you'll find my length of chain around your neck," said a nearby man called Heelslik—another Jackal, once tall and sinewy with muscle. Now, his shaggy head appeared as if it had been beaten once too often, his eyes like black marble.

Lokan bowed his head, convincing Arrus that not all was well with the Nordish man.

"Curlord's heavens, I hope we don't move soon," Arrus heard himself say.

"They might march us straight into the grave," Lokan said quietly. "Or kill us as an afterthought, like that poor curnos they just made shorter there."

"I've heard stories," Dogslaw said, leaning in close enough for Arrus to catch a whiff of the man's rancid breath, "where the Sujin just took a few prisoners at a time and just walked them around behind wagons—like these—

until they dropped from exhaustion and died on the spot."

"That's possible," Noll agreed. "Feels like that now."

A group of armored Sujins began talking loudly at one end of the second lead wagon. Other soldiers resting in the rear came to attention, listening in on the conversation.

"What a curnos language," Dogslaw muttered and clawed at the loose earth, blackening his already filthy hands. "They have more in common with sows. Any time, I expect them to root at the dirt."

"Some words almost sound the same as ours," Noll noted, "but different meanings. Maddening."

"I'll kill them all," Lokan seethed, setting his jaw and drawing attention from the three others. "Every last Sunjan. Every last one."

Arrus met the eyes of Noll and Dogslaw. Neither put his thoughts into words. In the background, the shouting dropped off and became more civil—at least for men speaking a pig language.

"You control yourself, Lokan," Dogslaw whispered. "Until the time is ripe."

"When?" Lokan's voice grated just a little too loudly, drawing the attention of at least two Sujins carrying spears. Arrus felt his innards constrict.

"I don't know when," Dogslaw answered, "but it's coming. I promise."

Lokan abruptly leered at the visors looking in his direction, a horrid grin with receding gums. Arrus didn't understand the language, but their postures told everyone the Sujins were not impressed with Lokan's behavior. Then the Nordish man did a truly disturbing thing. He clawed up a portion of dirt and ate it, jamming it into his mouth and chewing with relish. Specks dropped from his lips.

HOUSE OF PAIN

A glaring Dogslaw swatted him across the head for that, and Lokan spat most of the filth out.

One of the officers barked an order, and the Nordish men were prodded to their feet. It took longer to do so after each rest, and Arrus felt his entire body groan from the effort. *Not much longer,* he suspected. At least they left them their boots. If they had to walk barefoot along this pebbly road, he suspected he would've been killed a week earlier.

"Hold *firm*, Jackals," Dogslaw grunted to those close enough to hear. "This journey's coming to an end. One way or another."

The wagons got moving.

They marched again at length, leaving the dead Jackal on the side of the road. Arrus didn't know how far they had gotten before he heard the calling of crows.

By evening, they'd left the sparse shade offered by the overhead tree limbs. A golden ocean stretched out before them, swaying ever so slightly under a sky bloated with purple clouds and a bleeding horizon. The Sujins said nothing as they marched along, but the eyes of the Nordish men widened. None of them had ever been this deep inside enemy territory. They'd heard of the flatlands and the wheat fields of Sunja but had only distantly wondered if one day they'd ever actually see them.

The Sujins herded them along, and the Jackals walked, enraptured with this undiscovered country.

As the sky darkened overhead, the wagons halted for the night. Chains were attached to wheels, and the twelve survivors were surrounded by a square where each point was a watchful Sujin. Arrus didn't think they needed the guards. No one had the strength to do anything. A pair of Sujins rationed out cups of water to the Nordish prisoners and surprised them all with chunks of bread and strips of salted beef. The food startled the Jackals, but thoughts of final meals vanished with the first bite.

If they were going to die, at least it would be with full bellies.

After eating, they collapsed like old men, on beds of long grass. Gnats or other multi-legged pests took to and crawled upon their bare flesh. Arrus swatted at his limbs, quickly grew weary, and resigned to stare at the stars peeking out from the Curlord's heavens.

"Beautiful," he whispered.

"The Sunjans have stars just like us," Noll muttered sleepily. Lokan and the others already slept. Dogslaw even snored.

"What will become of us, Noll?" Arrus asked. "Speak plainly. Please."

Noll exhaled softly. "Oh, we'll all die. No doubt. Our war was done the moment they took us prisoner back around those hills."

"Thank you," Arrus said.

"Arrus."

"Yes?"

"Your brother was a good man."

The stars twinkled in a wisp of milky gauze, millions brilliant.

"Thank you, Noll."

"You'll be seeing him shortly, I expect."

Arrus frowned at that.

He supposed the older man was right on that point.

In the morning, the Sujins fed them well once again, much to the dismay of the Nordish prisoners.

"This is it," Heelslik muttered while he gulped down his portion of bread and salt beef. "They're fattening us for a killing."

"For something," Noll agreed.

"They won't let us get too strong," Dogslaw muttered. "For fear of attacking."

Arrus didn't care. After two decent meals, he felt ready to roll over and die. He almost felt like a man again. *Starvation.* Once, the word had meant nothing to him, but now, having experienced it, he didn't think there was anything crueler.

"At least Lokan isn't eating dirt anymore," Heelslik said.

Lokan heard his name and looked about, a frightening wildness haunting the depths of his eyes.

"You still with us, Lokan?" Dogslaw asked with some concern.

"Still, Jackal," Lokan said, looking to the southwest. He smacked his lips loudly and then commented. "Something is out there."

Puzzled, they all gazed off in that direction but could see nothing.

A short time later, the Sujins marched the prisoners toward the shifting horizon, while crickets scratched with the breeze.

By evening, they all saw it.

It rose up on a monstrous plateau like the stony crown of the Nordish Curlord himself.

Sunja.

As the sky darkened, a deep glow seeped into the heavens above the capital, and Arrus realized the light came from lamps and torches. The city was a fat, sprawling thing collared with grandiose stone walls and high, menacing battlements. A road ran from side to side, rising up from the fields and traversing the side of the mountain, ending in a black mouth.

"They've kept us alive…" Dogslaw gasped and winced, "for this?"

"Have no doubt," Noll muttered. "We'll all perish in there. And not like men."

His words disturbed Arrus, however, seeing the heart of his enemy filled him with awe and loathing. He so dearly wished he could have been part of the Ikull when they finally arrived to tear it all down. He dearly wished his brother was still alive. But most of all, he wearily acknowledged, he was grateful to finally see the journey's end. He'd had enough of damn walking to do him a lifetime.

"Sunja," he whispered, enraptured by the glow of the enormous city.

His companions looked on as well but did not speak.

"What will happen to us there?" Arrus asked and felt his nerves come loose. He swallowed and wiped at his eyes before anyone could see, but he need not have feared. No one heard his question.

The city mesmerized the Nordish men as they walked through a prairie as high as their hips. Bright fireflies wrote invisible messages in the air as they traveled over the plains, rendering the scene even more magical.

What will happen? Arrus asked the heavens and heard only the creaking of the wagons, the scuffle of worn feet, and the guttural language of the nearby Sujins brandishing weapons.

What?

About the Author

Keith C. Blackmore is the author of the Mountain Man, 131 Days, and Breeds series, among other horror, heroic fantasy, and crime novels. He lives on the island of Newfoundland in Canada. Visit his website at www.keithcblackmore.com.

DISCOVER
STORIES UNBOUND

PodiumAudio.com

www.ingramcontent.com/pod-product-compliance
Ingram Content Group UK Ltd.
Pitfield, Milton Keynes, MK11 3LW, UK
UKHW041301180426
11947UKWH00009B/594